ADVENTURERS
WANTED

BOOK FOUR

ADVENTURERS
⊸WANTED⊶

SANDS
OF NEZZA

M. L. FORMAN

SHADOW
MOUNTAIN

First printing in hardbound 2013.
First printing in paperbound 2014.

Visit us at ShadowMountain.com

Library of Congress Cataloging-in-Publication Data

Forman, Mark, 1964– author
  The sands of Nezza / M. L. Forman.
      pages cm.—(Adventurers wanted, book 4)
  Summary: When Alexander Taylor, wizard and warrior, is summoned to the land of Nezza in order to save a friend in need, he finds a country where war is a part of daily life, where adventurers are imprisoned by the Brotherhood, and where all magic is believed to be black.
  ISBN 978-1-60907-329-9 (hardbound : alk. paper)
  ISBN 978-1-60907-936-9 (paperbound)
  1. Fantasy fiction, American. [1. Friendship—Fiction 2. Wizards—Fiction.
  3. Adventure and adventurers—Fiction. 4. Magic—Fiction. 5. Freedom—Fiction.] I. Title.
  PZ7.F7653San 2013
  [Fic]—dc23   2012048126

Printed in the United States of America
R. R. Donnelley, Harrisonburg, VA

10 9 8 7 6 5 4 3 2 1

To Scott—brother, friend, and mentor.
Thanks for always pushing.

CONTENTS

ACKNOWLEDGMENTS

There are so many people who help out and work on a new book that it's difficult to thank them all. I'm sure I don't know them all or even what they all do, but I do know that their work is important to making this book come alive. So for all of you hardworking people who remain behind the scenes of not only my books but so many others as well, thank you for all that you do. You know who you are.

Special thanks to Chris Schoebinger, the mystery man behind Shadow Mountain. To those of us who know him, though, his hard work is not a mystery. He has helped me so much, and I want to thank him for pointing out the problems that were still in the book even though I thought it was done. Thanks, Chris—you are the man.

Many, many thanks to my editor, Lisa Mangum. Lisa is the brains, the one who makes it all look good and who fixes my writing so that you all can read it without stopping to say, "What?" I know Lisa loves her work as an editor, but I sometimes wonder if I don't test her resolve and make her work a love/hate relationship.

Thanks to Brandon Dorman, the illustrator. Brandon gives

the story a face, and he always seems to know exactly what face the story should have.

Thanks also to Richard Erickson, the art director at Shadow Mountain. I still haven't met Richard face-to-face, but I am grateful for all the work he puts into making everything look just right.

And finally a big thank-you to you, the readers. I couldn't do this without you, and I hope that the stories I tell will always make you happy. You are the biggest reason that these stories are told.

CHAPTER ONE

AN UNEXPECTED MESSAGE

The sun shone brightly on the grasslands of Alusia, and the wind rushed through Alex's hair. The openness of the country and the speed of his horse, Dar Losh, were made for each other. He loosened the reins so the horse could run freely. He wasn't worried about where they would go or how they would get back. There was no need to worry because Alusia was now his home. Alex laughed as the wind whistled past him, pulling at his hair and clothes.

Alexander Taylor looked like any other seventeen-year-old boy. The truth was, however, that he was different from not only the other boys his age but from almost everyone else as well. Alex was an adventurer. Not just any adventurer, either. He was an adventurer and a wizard, and perhaps something more.

It had been little more than a year ago when he'd first seen the magic sign in the window of Mr. Clutter's old bookshop. A year in the home he had always known, but nearly five years in the distant lands that most people in his world would never see. Time was different depending on which side of the adventure shop door he was on, and though this difference in time had been difficult for him to understand at first, now he hardly even thought about it.

His new adventurer friends had told him that no matter how long he was on his adventure, he would always be able to return home at almost the exact moment he'd left. At the time, Alex thought they must be mad, but he soon learned the truth of their words and did, indeed, return home from his first adventure at the same moment—and at the same age—as when he'd left. Alex knew that was a good thing, because he didn't have to explain how he'd aged more than a year in less than a second. But somebody did notice he'd been on an adventure—somebody he would never have expected.

Alex's stepfather, Mr. Roberts, knew instantly about Alex's adventure when he saw the leather bag that Alex was carrying over his shoulder. It was a magic bag that Alex had bought at the beginning of his first adventure, a bag that allowed him to carry a great many things in a small and easy-to-conceal place. Alex was shocked to find out that Mr. Roberts knew all about magic bags and adventures. Mr. Roberts, however, had once been an adventurer as well, and told Alex that he had suspected that Alex might find his way into an adventure of his own someday.

Alex's mind was pulled back to Alusia as he reined in his horse on a hilltop. The sun had started to sink in the west, and Alex took a moment to look across the landscape. At first he saw only the open grasslands with a few groves of oak trees dotted here and there between the hills, but then Alex's vision seemed to shift. Darkness filled the world around him, and he could see things moving in that darkness.

Shadowy armies marched toward unknown battles. Massive unknown creatures of evil stalked the land, destroying everything in their paths. Burning forests, ruined villages, and broken cities appeared before his eyes as death and destruction flowed like water into the known lands.

The darkness lifted slowly from his vision, and the grasslands of Alusia returned, but Alex felt that what he had seen was a true vision. Darkness, evil, and war were moving into the known lands, and, as a wizard, it was his duty to stop them.

Rubbing his eyes, Alex spoke a few quiet words to his horse. It was time for him to return to his new home. He had to prepare for what he knew was coming, even if he had no idea when it would come.

Dar Losh raced the winds that blew across the Alusian hills until Alex reined him in. He looked down at his house with its tall tower and the flowing stream next to it. This was home, and even though he missed his stepfather and stepbrother, he did not want to go back to the life he had lived before.

"Go, my friend," Alex said to Dar Losh after he had removed his saddle and bridle. "Go and run free. I will call you when I need you."

The beautiful palomino whinnied in reply and then nuzzled Alex's shoulder before heading back into the open grassland. Seeing the pale golden horse run made Alex feel hopeful, and he watched until the horse was out of sight.

Closing the front door behind him, Alex heard a sudden, familiar honking noise. He turned to find a strange bowling-pin-shaped creature standing on a single birdlike leg, waiting for him on the table. The creature was a bottle-necked geeb, a messenger that traveled between the magical lands.

"Do you have a message for me?" Alex asked. He hadn't been expecting anything.

"Ding," the geeb answered, its head taking the shape of a small bell.

"May I have it, please?"

"Ding," the geeb answered again, producing a piece of paper from the large mouth in the middle of its body.

Taking the paper from the geeb, Alex noticed that it was worn and dirty. The edges were uneven, as if it had been torn or ripped from a larger page. Just holding the message in his hand, Alex could tell something was wrong.

His thoughts returned to the dark images he had seen out on the Alusian plains. Monsters, war, destruction, and who knew what other dark things were already in the known lands. The grubby bit of paper the geeb had brought made him feel cold inside.

"Have you been paid?" Alex asked the geeb. He turned the message over in his hand, delaying the moment when he would have to unfold it.

"Honk," the geeb responded, its head taking the shape of a small bicycle horn.

"Hang on a minute, then," said Alex, taking a seat behind the long wooden table that he often used as a desk. He turned the paper over once more. Trying to ignore his worries, Alex unfolded the paper and began to read.

Alex,

> *Need your help. Come as soon as you can to the city of Karmus, in the land of Nezza. Come on foot. Don't let anyone know what you are.*

> *Skeld*

Alex read the note, looked at the geeb, and then read the note again. It seemed strange, and, for a minute, Alex wondered if his friend Skeld was playing some kind of joke on him. But the urgent tone to the note didn't sound like one of Skeld's jokes, and that worried him. Alex noticed that the note was written with what looked like charcoal, which was not something Skeld would do. His friend must really be in some kind of trouble. Skeld was a good fighter and could take care of himself, so if he was asking for help, something had to be very wrong.

"Can you take a message back to my friend Skeld?" Alex asked the geeb.

"Honk."

The answer surprised and worried Alex even more than the message did. He had never had a geeb refuse to take a message to anyone.

"Is Skeld still alive?" asked Alex, more to himself than the geeb.

"Ding."

"Is it too dangerous for you to take a message back?"

"Ding."

"Very well. Here is your payment for delivering the message."

Alex took a small diamond from the table and tossed it toward the geeb. The geeb bounced up, catching the stone in midair, and then dropped onto the tabletop. With another ding and a small popping noise, the geeb vanished.

Alex looked at the message again. "'Don't let anyone know what you are,'" he read out loud, wondering what Skeld meant. It was a warning, but Alex wasn't sure what his friend was trying to say. On previous journeys, letting people know he was an adventurer hadn't mattered; in fact, it had been helpful. Perhaps Skeld meant he should not let people know he was a wizard. But that didn't make any sense either, as wizards were generally welcome and respected in all of the known lands.

Alex let his thoughts roll around his mind as he read the message a third time. Skeld wanted him to come on foot, which seemed almost as odd as not telling people he was an adventurer and a wizard. Nothing in the note made any sense, and after several minutes of thinking, Alex decided that there was only one thing he could do. He would go to Nezza, on foot, as Skeld had asked.

Alex folded the note from Skeld and slipped it into his pocket. He wondered if he should tell his teacher and fellow wizard Whalen Vankin where he was going. Whalen always seemed to know what to do and when to do it. Alex knew, however, that Whalen was on an adventure of his own, and he didn't want to wait for an answer that might take days to arrive. Skeld's message sounded desperate, and Alex wanted to get to his friend as fast he could. He would simply have to send Whalen a message when he reached Nezza and let him know what was happening.

As Alex locked the front door of his house with a magical spell, he knew there wasn't time to reach the great arch by horse. There was only one way he could quickly reach the magical portal that would take him to the land of Nezza: he would have to change his shape into something fast, something that could reach the arch before night grew old.

Stepping away from his home, Alex changed himself into the shape of an eagle and rose into the evening sky. There was a strong breeze blowing from the south, and, in his eagle shape, Alex soon had the wind under his wings, rising higher into the sky. He sped north, following the main road that led to the great arch, his mind racing with unanswerable questions.

Alex arrived at the great arch before dawn. He dropped down and returned to his own shape in front of it. Whalen had taught him how to use the arch to move between lands directly, and, for a moment, he thought he would go straight to Nezza. Whalen had also taught him the importance of gaining knowledge, and Alex knew that rushing off to Nezza without finding out what might be happening there would be both dangerous and foolish. No, first he would stop at the adventure shop of Mr. Cornelius Clutter. Mr. Clutter organized adventures after all, and if Skeld was on an adventure and in trouble, Mr. Clutter might know why.

Alex worked the magic that opened the arch in seconds, then changed and took flight as an eagle once more. As fast as his wings would carry him, Alex sped to the village of Telous. He flew past Telous just as the first rays of sunlight were reaching across the land, but instead of landing in the town itself, he flew to a large green field outside of Telous. He transformed back to his own shape on the soft grass, taking a moment to get his bearings and shake off the freedom of flight.

Raising his staff, Alex knocked three times on the empty space in front of him, then stepped back. A silver line appeared out of thin air exactly where Alex had knocked and quickly took the shape of a door. As he watched, the door swung toward him, and he could see Mr. Clutter's office on the opposite side.

"Oh my," cried Mr. Clutter as Alex stepped through the doorway. "How did you manage to open the back door?"

"I need to get to Nezza as soon as possible," said Alex, ignoring Mr. Clutter's question. "I've received a note from a friend of mine who is in trouble there."

"No doubt, no doubt," said Mr. Clutter, nodding. "Lots of troubles in Nezza these days, I don't mind telling you."

"What kind of trouble?"

"Well, Nezza has never been a great place for adventures, as you may know," Mr. Clutter said. "Too many wars have made it a hard place for adventures to happen, if you follow me."

"I know there are several small kingdoms in Nezza," said Alex. "Are they at war often?"

Mr. Clutter nodded. "It seems that at least two or more kingdoms are always at war. It would be a grand place for adventures, if only there was a single true king in Nezza once more. Or if the kingdoms could reach an agreement about the land rule, things might improve. As things are, well . . ."

"And you say there is more trouble in Nezza than normal?"

"Things have become worse over the past few months,"

Mr. Clutter answered. "There's talk that some of the kingdoms have outlawed magic and adventurers altogether."

"Why would they do that?" Alex asked, finally understanding why Skeld had told him to conceal his identity.

"I don't know," said Mr. Clutter. "I would guess that some of the kings don't like the idea of adventurers helping their rivals, or of having magic used against them."

"Be that as it may, I need to get to Nezza as soon as possible," said Alex. "My friend Skeld sent me a note, asking for my help."

"Skeld?" Mr. Clutter asked. "Skeld from Norsland?"

"Yes."

"Ah, yes," said Mr. Clutter thoughtfully. "He joined an adventure to Nezza a month or six weeks ago."

"Can you tell me anything about his adventure?" Alex asked hopefully.

"No details," said Mr. Clutter, the smile fading from his face. "I was only partly involved with setting it up, so I can't say much about it. Even if I knew all the details, you know I'm not allowed to tell anyone, not even a wizard. I can say that he went with five other adventurers, all with excellent records."

"Five others," Alex repeated. "Do I know any of them besides Skeld?"

"I don't believe you do," said Mr. Clutter. "I wish I could tell you more, but the rules of the adventure shop . . ." He cleared his throat, and his hopeful tone returned. "You might be able to find a few people in Telous who have been to Nezza recently."

"Perhaps," Alex agreed. "But I don't have time to search for someone who might know something. Skeld could be in real trouble, and I don't have time to waste."

"Yes, of course," Mr. Clutter agreed. "I suppose you don't even have time for a spot of tea."

"Not today, thank you," said Alex.

"You know," said Mr. Clutter, "I might be able to help you in another way." He moved to one side of his office. "Let me see. Yes, his name begins with a *J*, I'm sure of that."

"Whose name?" Alex questioned.

"What's that?" Mr. Clutter asked as he opened a huge drawer full of files. "Oh, he's a retired adventurer that I know. As I recall, he moved to Nezza when he stopped going on adventures, and if he's still there, he might be a great help to you. Now let me see . . . Jacob? Joshua? No, it wasn't a common name."

Alex didn't want to wait while Mr. Clutter sorted through the seemingly endless files. He was about to say something when Mr. Clutter triumphantly pulled a file from the drawer.

"Josephus!" Mr. Clutter shouted. "Josephus Sebastian Savage. I knew he was in here."

"Josephus?" Alex questioned.

"Well, everyone calls him Joe," said Mr. Clutter. "Can't say that I blame him. Now, let me see, my notes say he was living on a small farm a day or two from the great arch. South of the main road into Nezza, on the east end of some hills."

"And you think he'll still be there?" Alex asked.

"I would think so. Oh, now that's odd," said Mr. Clutter.

"What?"

"There's a note here that says he's become something of a

hermit," Mr. Clutter answered. "Strange—I remember him being a friendly, outgoing sort of fellow."

Alex thought the land of Nezza didn't seem like the kind of place an adventurer would retire to, considering all the wars and other troubles there. Mr. Clutter could be wrong about Joe, and Alex didn't want to waste time searching for someone who might not even be there. Still, if there was a retired adventurer in Nezza, he could tell Alex everything he might need or want to know.

"I'm sorry I don't have more information," said Mr. Clutter. "I've written to him a few times, but it's difficult to find geebs that are willing to go to Nezza. Then again, Savage was quite serious when he told me he was retiring. The last letter I did manage to send was returned unopened."

"I see," said Alex. "So he might not be too happy if I turn up asking questions."

"Oh, I'm sure if you are able to find him that he'll help you in any way that he can. You're a wizard after all, and not many people are foolish enough to be rude to a wizard."

"I don't care about that, just so long as he can answer my questions," said Alex.

"Now, I know you're in a rush, so I won't keep you any longer," said Mr. Clutter as he moved to the back wall of his office. "I'll just open the door for you, and you can be on your way."

"You have been both kind and helpful," said Alex. "You have my thanks."

"No thanks needed," said Mr. Clutter. He knocked three times on the stone wall, and the hidden doorway opened.

"When you get back from Nezza, I'll find a proper adventure for you to go on."

Alex nodded and stepped through the door into the green fields outside the village of Telous. The door closed, and the silver outline vanished with a small pop.

As eager as Alex was to head directly to Nezza, he knew from his previous adventures that he would need some supplies before he left. Instead of changing shape and flying back to the great arch, Alex started walking toward the village, his mind spinning with thoughts.

Savage might be helpful—if he really was in Nezza, and if Alex could find him. Alex didn't have time to waste searching for him; Skeld was in trouble. Alex figured he wouldn't be noticed by the people of Nezza, at least not until he reached the city of Karmus. If he flew most of the way to Karmus as an eagle, he would only need to blend in once he reached the city.

"I can find my own answers as I travel," Alex said to himself, but he wondered how much trouble finding those answers might be.

As Alex walked into the streets of Telous, he mentally made a list of the items he'd need for his adventure. He would have to buy food and maybe some more water bags. He'd also need some new clothes, including some good walking boots.

His shopping trip went better—and faster—than Alex had expected. The shopkeepers were all keen on helping him, and he suspected it might have something to do with his recently becoming a true wizard. He purchased a large supply of food and several dozen water bags, and he even picked up a few items at the apothecary's shop.

While eating the midday meal at the Golden Swan, Alex considered his plans. He was worried that he didn't know enough about Nezza or what was going on there, but he reminded himself that his biggest problem was finding and helping Skeld and his company of adventurers.

It won't be as easy as you think, Alex's sixth sense said in the back of his mind.

CHAPTER TWO
THE ROAD IS CLOSED

Alex paid for his meal and left the Golden Swan. He collected his supplies from the shopkeepers and made sure he wasn't forgetting anything. His plan was to change into an eagle as soon as possible, then fly to the great arch. After passing through the arch, he would camp for the night, and then tomorrow he could take eagle form again and look for the eastern end of the hills that Mr. Clutter had told him about. If he could find Savage quickly, he would get as much information from him as he could before moving on; if not, he would have to find his own answers as he traveled.

As he walked down the road, Alex's thoughts returned to Skeld and the company of adventurers he was with. Skeld had said they were in the city of Karmus, and Alex wondered how long it would take for him to make his way there, and how much longer it would take to find the group after that. He'd studied the map of Nezza and knew that Karmus was a fair distance from the great arch. He couldn't hope to reach the city quickly on foot, but he didn't plan to walk. He would transform himself for most of the journey, and, if things went well, he would get there in a few days.

Only change yourself at need and never for very long, Whalen's voice echoed in Alex's head.

Whalen had given him good advice on the subject of changing his shape. The transformation was not difficult, but it could be dangerous.

"You will find that you enjoy taking another shape," Whalen had said. "There is great freedom in the shape of a bird, rest in the shape of a tree, strength in the shape of the bear. But be careful—the longer you remain in a shape that is not your own, the more you risk forgetting who and what you are. If you forget yourself, you may remain changed for the rest of your days."

Then there was the dragon form. On his last adventure, Alex had met Salinor, the oldest living dragon, who had told Alex he could change into a dragon at will without any risk of losing himself. Alex was in fact part dragon, and while taking the form of a dragon might allow him to reach Karmus faster, it was a shape that terrified most people. It might be one of his natural forms, but Alex thought it best not to become a dragon unless he really needed to.

After walking about a mile along the main road, Alex moved into a small grove of nearby trees. He looked to make sure he was alone before once more taking the shape of the eagle. He moved upward, soaring in the afternoon sun. He enjoyed this shape and had spent quite a bit of time in it. Now he focused his mind on the task at hand and sped off to the south, where the great arch waited.

Long before he had grown tired of flying, Alex was circling downward. The arch was only a few hundred feet below him, and he could see the spring where he'd filled his water bags on other adventures.

Landing and taking his own shape, Alex splashed some cold water from the spring on his face. It took a few seconds before the sense of freedom from being an eagle left him.

Retrieving the empty water bags from his magic bag, Alex filled them at the spring. When he was done, he looked at up at the sun, trying to judge how much daylight was left. He had traveled from Telous to the arch in less than an hour, a trip that would have normally taken half a day. It was just after noon, and he thought he could walk through the arch and still have plenty of daylight left to find a camping spot for the night.

Alex paused for a moment before walking toward the arch. He wondered if he should arm himself with his sword as he had done on his previous adventures. He knew there was trouble in Nezza; it would be foolish for him to walk into it unarmed.

Best to be prepared, the voice of his dwarf friend Thrang echoed in the back of his mind. *Never know what you might meet on the other side of the arch.*

It was good advice, but if the lords of Nezza didn't like adventurers, then the less he looked like an adventurer, the better. If he carried his wizard's staff, however, he might be able to pass as a simple traveler. After some more thought, he left his magical sword in the bag but withdrew the dagger that he'd had since his first adventure.

Taking a final look around the spring, Alex started along the road. He was nervous about going into a new land alone, but he didn't have a choice. He knew that if he had been in trouble and had sent a message to Skeld asking for help, Skeld would have come as quickly as he could. Alex also remembered a promise that he'd made on his last adventure—a promise to always help his friends when they needed him.

"I just hope it's nothing too serious," Alex said to himself.

Walking wasn't as much fun as flying, but Alex focused on his surroundings, watching as he moved forward and looking for the change in landscape that would let him know he was in Nezza. The change between lands was barely noticeable, though as Alex passed beneath the great arch, he felt a small tingle of magical power pass through him.

The ground ahead of him suddenly had a few gently sloping hills, and Alex climbed one so he could look west into the land of Nezza and still remain hidden. He looked at everything, especially at the road that led west. The land was green and covered with small groves of trees separated by open grassy areas. A short distance from the hill there was a camp that was full of what looked like soldiers.

Clearly, the soldiers were there to stop anyone coming into or leaving Nezza, but what would they do with the people they caught?

Alex didn't want to deal with soldiers, at least not yet, so he moved down the hill to the south, away from the road. Without warning, Alex found himself lying flat on his back. It felt as if he had walked into a solid wall, his own momentum bouncing him backward into the dirt.

Alex scrambled to his feet. He couldn't see anything that looked out of place, but something was blocking his path. After a few careful steps forward, he encountered the invisible wall again. Reaching out, he put his right hand on the surface of the barrier; it felt both cold and damp. He pulled his hand away and looked at it, but it was clean and dry. Alex pushed against the barrier, and it seemed to stretch as if it were made of rubber. It was magic, of course. That would explain the surge of power he'd felt when he'd passed through the arch.

Alex felt along the edges of the barrier with his magic and realized it wasn't just a wall. It was more like a three-sided box, the walls forcing him toward the road and the back of the box blocking him from reaching the great arch. It appeared that he had no choice in the direction he would travel.

Alex thought about using his magic to open a hole in the barrier, but he decided against it. Using magic might alert the soldiers guarding the road. Removing the barrier completely wasn't an option either, because whoever had created it would know the moment the spell was broken.

Alex wondered who could have created this barrier. There weren't any wizards in Nezza as far as he knew, but that didn't mean there weren't other magical people. His first thoughts were about the Gezbeth, the group of magical people he and Whalen had talked about at the end of his last adventure. The Gezbeth had caused a lot of trouble in other known lands. They could have done this, but why?

Someone with strong magic had created this barrier, but Alex didn't know if the barrier was meant to keep people in Nezza or to keep outsiders away. It was clear, however, that traveling in Nezza was going to be more dangerous and difficult than Alex had thought it would be.

Alex moved back down the hill, pausing to work a little

magic of his own when he reached the road. He wanted to avoid the soldiers ahead of him if he could, and a simple invisibility spell would solve his problem. He made his way forward, being careful not to make any noise as he went. The invisible walls were soon behind him, and he turned south, away from the main road.

As the sun slipped below the horizon, Alex started looking for a spot to spend the night. After a little searching, he found a small hollow surrounded on three sides by trees, with the fourth side opening to the south. He collected wood for a fire but didn't bother setting up his tent. The air was warm, and he guessed it was late spring or early summer here in Nezza. He was worried he had not moved far enough away from the arch and the camp of soldiers, but that couldn't be helped.

After cooking a small dinner, Alex wrapped a blanket around his shoulders and sat staring into the fire. He usually enjoyed sitting next to the fire on his adventures, but this one was different. He was alone, and he wished he had someone to talk to. Before, he and his companions had laughed and told stories around the campfire, but there were no stories to tell or hear tonight. Tonight, only his own troubled thoughts would keep him company.

Alex was almost asleep when he heard the sound of horses moving in the darkness beyond the light of his fire. He thought about putting out the fire with a word, but that would be pointless. Whoever was out there already knew where he was. He closed his eyes and listened, trying to estimate how many people and horses there were. The horses stopped moving, and Alex could feel someone watching him.

Could they be bandits, preparing to attack a lone traveler in these wild lands? Alex stood up and leaned on his staff. He gazed into the darkness. There was no sound for a long time, and then a voice called out, "Hello the camp. Are you friend or foe to Lord Bray?"

"I am neither," Alex called back. "I do not know Lord Bray, but I have no quarrel with him."

There was silence again, and then the voice called out, "Stand still and do not run. If you try to flee, we will regard you as an enemy."

Alex waited. Slowly, three horses approached, shadowy figures appearing at the edge of the firelight. They looked like the soldiers he had seen along the main road earlier that day. If their master, Lord Bray, was the one trying to block the road, they might be able to tell him all kinds of interesting things.

"Warm yourselves," said Alex in a kindly tone as the riders approached and stopped their horses. "You look as if you've ridden far."

"Far enough," said a grim-faced man who was obviously in charge. "But we'll not share your fire—not until we know where things stand."

"As you wish," said Alex, taking his seat. He laid his staff across his knees and watched the three men.

"You say you do not know Lord Bray, yet you travel his lands," the grim-faced man said.

"I travel many lands," said Alex offhandedly. "I did not know that these wild lands had a master."

"Lord Bray rules the lands from the Silver River to the magic arch," the man declared.

"I've never seen a magic arch so well protected," said Alex.

"We guard our lands and keep the evils from other lands from entering ours," said the man.

"I did not know the land needed protection," said Alex.

"Then you know little of this land," the man answered, looking surprised. "Much evil has already come into our lands from the outside—or at least that's what we are told."

"Come, sit down and let us speak of this," said Alex, waving his hand.

All three men climbed off their horses and moved forward to sit by the small fire. They looked tired, as if they were about to fall asleep.

Alex mumbled a few words, casting a spell to relax the men in front of him. The magic would not force the men to tell the truth, but it would make them comfortable enough that they would speak freely.

"Tell me what evils you fear," said Alex. "Tell me why so many men have been sent to watch the magic arch."

"Lord Bray has commanded us to watch the arch and stop any travelers who enter our land," the man replied in a monotone voice, completely under Alex's spell. "He tells us that there are dangers beyond the arch and that we must prevent those dangers from entering our lands. He says that all the wars of Nezza have been fought because of evil from beyond the arch."

"But you do not believe what he says?" Alex prompted.

"There is enough evil in Nezza. We need not look outside this land to find what troubles us," the man answered. "Bray is weak and only repeats what Lord Lazar of Karmus tells him."

"Tell me about Lazar of Karmus."

The man's expression changed to one of contempt. "Lazar claims to be king of Nezza, but his claim is false, and the people know it. He is an evil man who only wants power and riches for himself. He has killed many people to gain his power, and some say he has even killed members of his own family to keep the power he has. With his nephew Prince Rallian missing, perhaps those stories are true."

"Bray does as Lazar commands?" Alex questioned.

"Bray fears Lazar and does all that Lazar commands him to do. It is said that Lazar knows dark magic and has used it to control Bray and others. There are many stories told of Lazar and what he can do, though I have never seen him do more than bully those who serve him."

"Tell me about Prince Rallian," said Alex.

"He is, or was, a good man," the soldier answered. Sadness replaced the contempt on his face. "Many of the noble houses of Nezza recognized his claim to the kingship, though he never made the claim himself. He has recently come of age, and if he was not missing, he would become the lord of Karmus, removing Lazar from power."

"The people would have accepted Rallian as their king," Alex said, more to himself than to the soldier.

"Most of the people would accept Rallian," the man answered, sounding determined. "But he has vanished from this land, and Lazar remains in power."

"What reason has Lazar given for Rallian's disappearance?" Alex questioned.

"Lazar claims the prince has gone on a quest, but he won't say anything more."

"Do many people believe that story?"

"The servants of the prince have all vanished as well, so there is nobody to ask if the story is true."

"I see," Alex said, filing the information away in his mind. "Now, tell me about travelers who come from outside Nezza. What does Bray command you to do with them?"

"If they surrender themselves to us, we take them before Bray," the man answered. "Then Bray sends them to Lazar. What Lazar does with them we do not know, but no travelers have ever returned from Karmus."

Alex pondered the soldier's words, looking deep into the fire as he thought. Was Lazar a dark wizard trying to take control of Nezza? Was he simply an evil king who bullied people into doing what he wanted? What had really happened to Prince Rallian? Did any of this have anything to do with Skeld and his fellow adventurers? He was here to help Skeld and his company, not to change things in Nezza, but something in the back of his head told him he needed to know as much about this land and its people as he could.

"Have you caught many travelers from outside of Nezza?" Alex asked.

"A group of adventurers about a month ago," the man answered. "They surrendered to our men and were taken."

"How long would it take them to reach Karmus after your men caught them?" Alex asked. He hoped that Skeld and his company had not been in Karmus for long.

"Three, maybe four weeks to reach Karmus on foot. All prisoners must walk to Karmus—that is the order of Lord Lazar."

Alex considered this information. If it had taken three or four weeks for Skeld and his company to reach Karmus, then they couldn't have been there long. What would Lazar do to them when they got there, and how soon would he do it? He forced his worries out of his mind and returned his attention to the men sitting around the fire.

"Have other people from Nezza gone missing?" Alex questioned. "People that Lazar might fear, for whatever reason?"

The soldier nodded. "The young lords of the inner kingdoms. They were close to Rallian—one was his cousin. We know they went on a quest of their own, as a group, but what that quests was, we do not know. Some say they traveled north, following the path of the last king. If Lazar has done something to them, we know nothing about it."

"Sleep," said Alex softly. "Sleep and forget all that you have seen and spoken."

Alex watched as the three men closed their eyes and fell into a deep, enchanted sleep. He knew they would wake up when the sun rose and would not remember anything from this night.

Alex needed to move fast. If Lazar was in fact a dark wizard, there was no way of knowing what he might do to Skeld and the rest of his company. And if Lazar was a dark wizard, Alex's duty as a true wizard demanded that he face him and try to break his power. While Alex wasn't afraid to face a dark wizard, there were dangers that he would need to consider.

Alex unsaddled all three horses and then pulled his own saddle from his magic bag and placed it on the strongest horse. He tied the other two horses to a nearby tree. He would ride west, staying south of the main road into Nezza. If he was lucky, he would find the retired adventurer Mr. Clutter had told him about and learn more about what was happening in Nezza from him.

Alex mounted his borrowed horse and spoke a few soft words of encouragement to the animal before turning south and trotting into the darkness. Once he determined that he was far enough away from the arch that he would not meet any more soldiers, he turned east and urged the horse into a gallop.

As the eastern sky began to lighten, Alex could see the dark shapes of hills in front of him. He had paused to scan the land ahead of him, making sure that there were no soldiers he needed to avoid, when he felt something out of place. It felt like someone or something was watching him. He looked back along the path he had followed but saw nothing. He moved forward, his senses alert and his magic ready, just in case.

The sun was just up when Alex stopped his borrowed horse at the edge of a clearing. A fine-looking house stood on the south side of the clearing with a barn and a chicken coop close by. Alex hoped this was the house of the retired adventurer, Joe Savage, and not just some lonely farm. Dismounting, he removed his saddle from the horse and rubbed its forehead gently.

"Return to your master," Alex said softly, patting the horse's neck. "My thanks to you for making a long journey short."

The horse whinnied, then turned and walked back to the east.

Alex yawned. He'd been awake for a long time, and a few

hours of sleep would be helpful. He looked at the house for a long time. Once again he felt like he was being watched, and once again he was unable to find a reason for the feeling. He grew more and more uneasy. There were no lights to be seen and no smoke from the chimney. There were no animals in the barn or the coop. The front door of the house hung at a strange angle, as if it had been knocked in with a great deal of force.

Something bad had happened here, Alex was sure of it. A chill ran through him that had nothing to do with the temperature.

CHAPTER THREE

THE HERMIT

Alex stood in the shadow of a large tree, watching the farm for several minutes. Nothing moved. He guessed that whoever had lived here had either been taken away or had run away when the trouble came. Whatever had happened, it looked like Alex's one hope for learning more about Nezza was gone.

After several more minutes of watching and seeing nothing, he decided to take a closer look. He might find something that could help him, but Alex's hopes weren't high.

Carefully Alex moved forward, looking at the ground and watching for tracks that had been left behind. He'd learned something about tracking on his previous adventures, and what he saw now troubled him. It looked like a dozen horses, possibly more, had visited the house. The tracks were at least a week old, but the story they told was clear. Soldiers had come, stayed for a short time, and then left.

"It looks like they took everything they could carry with them," Alex mumbled as he moved toward the house.

A dirty boot print on the broken door meant that the soldiers had not come peacefully. They were looking for someone or something and hadn't waited for the door to be opened. That was bad. Alex knew that no adventurer would go quietly if soldiers turned up and kicked in the door. There would be a fight, even if it was a short one.

Pausing outside the door, Alex sniffed the air, but all he could smell was dust and old wood. Carefully he pushed the door out of his way and stepped into the house. There wasn't much to see. Chairs had been knocked over and left on the floor, and a fine layer of dust covered everything.

Moving farther into the house Alex froze in his tracks and raised his staff. He'd thought for a moment he'd seen someone else in the house, but when his eyes adjusted to the dim light, he realized it was just his reflection. A huge mirror, the bottom of which had been shattered, covered the wall to his left. Taking a deep breath, he moved forward.

There were no signs of a fight. It looked, at least to Alex, like nobody had been home when the soldiers broke in. Perhaps Joe the adventurer had been away at the time. If so, Alex might still be able to find him, except he didn't have any idea where to look.

He finished his inspection of the house and started back toward the front door. As his eyes came to rest on a large cast-iron frying pan hanging on the wall next to the fireplace, he stopped. The pan normally wouldn't have interested him, but there was a strange design in the shape of a flower carved on the back. Alex had seen that flower before.

"The order of Malgor, here?" Alex reached out and touched the design with his right hand, allowing a bit of his own magic to enter the iron. The flower design glowed white at his touch, and then started to move randomly on the pan's surface. It only took a few seconds for the moving lines to reform, and Alex immediately recognized the new designs for what they were.

The letters were elvin, but the words didn't make any sense. Alex stared at the pan for a few minutes, and then he realized that the letters were written backward. There was a message here, but it had to be read in a mirror.

Taking the pan from the wall, Alex returned to the first room he'd entered. He held up the pan to the broken mirror. The elvin letters seemed to double in number and grow smaller at the same time. Not sure how long the message would last, Alex read and tried to memorize it as fast as he could.

If you've found this message, then trouble has come. Behind the massive oak at the southwest corner of the yard there is a trail. Follow it to the meadow with three massive stones at the center. Wait there.

Savage

The message was clear enough, but Alex wondered why had it been so carefully hidden. Perhaps Savage had been expecting trouble and had created this message before the soldiers arrived. The design on the pan was clearly for the order of Malgor, and if Savage was working for them, then the message had to be for them. Members of the order might come looking for Savage if they didn't hear from him for a long time. Anyone from the order would recognize the symbol, just as Alex had. They would also know how to read the message and where to look for Savage.

Alex made sure that the message returned to its original design and then left the frying pan on the wall. He knew where to look for Savage now, or at least where to go so that Savage could find him. He left the house and crossed the farmyard, being careful not to leave any tracks, and made his way to the trail behind the oak tree. It wasn't much of a trail, at least not at first, but Alex managed to follow it into the hills.

It was almost midday before Alex found the clearing with three massive stones. He was hungry and tired, and he really wanted to find a safe spot to sleep. He needed to talk to Savage, however, so instead of looking for a place to hide and sleep, he sat down next to the stones. Alex took an apple and some cheese out of his magic bag for a quick meal, and then he used his magic to let his body rest. His mind was alert for any sound and his eyes remained open, but he rested just the same.

A few hours later, Alex heard a sound that was out of place; even if he couldn't see anything, he knew someone was close. His muscles tensed. Slowly, as if waking from a nap, Alex got to his feet and stretched. Turning in a circle, he worked the stiffness out of his muscles, and his eyes came to rest on a shadow that didn't look quite right.

"Better trained than most," a slow, deep voice commented as the shadow moved. "Other agents I've worked with wouldn't have noticed me at all."

The man who emerged from the trees was at least a head taller than Alex. His clothes were old and tattered, his face was dirty, and his dark, graying hair was cut short and stuck out at strange angles from his head. This had to be the retired adventurer Joe Savage.

Savage moved into the clearing and stopped to take a good look at Alex. "You're not from Nezza, that's clear enough. Didn't the order tell you anything about traveling in this land?"

"I'm not—" Alex started.

"Not that the order pays any attention to what I say. I've been telling them for the past six months about the troubles here, and you're the first sign I've had that anyone is reading my reports at all. I'm actually surprised you got here so fast. I guess my last report about soldiers invading my house got someone's attention."

"It might have," said Alex. "But I—"

"Still, I would think they'd have told you not to dress like that," Savage continued as though Alex hadn't spoken. "You stand out like a diamond on a pile of sand. Did they tell you anything about what's going on here? Did they let you read any of my reports? How you've managed to get this far into Nezza is what I'd like to know. Soldiers prowling the roads and stopping everyone they see. Yet you walk in looking like the prince of the paupers and find your way to my door."

"I'm not from the order," said Alex before Savage could go on.

"Not from the order?"

"If you mean the order of Malgor, I wasn't sent by them."

"Of course I mean the order of Malgor, what else would I mean? If you weren't sent by them, how did you find me? Who sent you? How did you even know I was in Nezza?"

Savage looked nervous. Clearly he'd been expecting someone else, and he wasn't sure what to make of Alex. His body had shifted from relaxed to a ready-for-action stance.

"A mutual friend told me you were here," said Alex. "He also told me that you prefer to go by the name of Joe."

"Joe," Savage repeated in a thoughtful tone. He paused for a moment, and then went on. "Has to be Clutter you're talking about."

Alex nodded.

"That old so-and-so," said Savage. "If I've told him once I've told him a dozen times. I am not interested in going on any new adventures. Just because he's sent you here to get me doesn't change that."

"That's not—" Alex started but was cut off again.

"I don't care what the adventure is, do you hear me?" said Savage. "I don't care who's in trouble, or what reward has been offered to get them out of trouble. You can tell Clutter that I'm not interested, do you hear me?"

"Yes, I—"

"Right, so you can just turn around and get yourself out of Nezza as fast as you can," Savage continued. "Not a safe place these days, as you might have gathered on your journey here."

"I am Alexander Taylor, adventurer and—" Alex started once more.

"I don't want to know who you are," said Savage. "I can see you're an adventurer plainly enough—that magic bag stands out like a sore thumb. Whatever else you might be doesn't matter to me. Take my advice and get out of Nezza."

"—and wizard," Alex finished. "I'm not here to get you to join a new adventure. I'm not here to get you to do anything at all."

"Then why are you here?"

"I'm here to ask for your help," said Alex.

"So you *are* here to get me to do something," said Savage with a slight laugh.

"Well, yes, that's true," said Alex. "I need your help. I need to know anything and everything about Nezza you can tell me."

"Why?" Savage asked.

"Why? Why what?"

"Why do you need to know what's going on in Nezza?" Savage asked. "Why are you here at all?"

"I can explain—" Alex started.

"Not here," Savage interrupted.

"Is there danger?" Alex looked around, his hand tightening around his wizard's staff.

"We're standing in the middle of an open meadow," said Savage. "You already know that there are soldiers all over the place, watching the roads and stopping everyone they see. They may not have found this meadow yet, but that doesn't mean they won't find it soon. We should move someplace where we can talk without worrying about being interrupted."

Without another word Savage started back toward the trees. Alex followed, unsure if he was making the right decision. Savage seemed to have a lot to say, at least on some subjects, but he hadn't said anything useful yet.

Savage led Alex deeper into the hills. He didn't seem to be following a path, or at least Alex couldn't see anything that looked like a path as he hurried to keep up. The sun was going down before Savage finally stopped. He looked around quickly and then dropped to his knees and started crawling under a tangled tree. Not sure what Savage was doing or where he was going, Alex followed.

After a few minutes of crawling, Alex found himself in an open space. The tree he'd crawled under was behind him, and massive stones formed three walls in front of him. Savage was already sitting against the back stone wall, his eyes resting on Alex.

"So, explain," said Savage.

Alex looked around the enclosed space. "An easy spot to get trapped in," he said to Savage.

"Not as easy as you might think," Savage replied. "You'll notice the stone I'm leaning against, here at the back, is a bit smaller than the others. If a quick escape is needed, we can easily climb over it. So, explain why you are here, and what you need to know."

"Right," said Alex, sitting down and leaning against one of the stones. "I am here because a friend of mine sent for me, asking for my help."

"An adventurer friend, no doubt," said Savage.

"Yes, he is an adventurer," Alex answered. "He and a company of adventurers came to Nezza a few weeks ago. They have been taken prisoner and are either in Karmus or on their way there. I've come to rescue them."

"And get them all out of Nezza, I hope," Savage said.

"I don't know about that," said Alex. "I don't know what their quest is. If it is something simple, then perhaps I can help them finish it quickly before we leave Nezza."

"Just get them out," said Savage. "Things have gone from

bad to worse here. Better to abandon the adventure and live than to stay here and die."

"You might be right," said Alex. "But until I find them and free them, I need to blend in, if you know what I mean."

"Oh, I know what you mean. You'll need to dirty up a bit if you want to blend in with the people of Nezza," said Savage.

"Dirty up?"

"There are only three kinds of people in this land," said Savage with a sigh. "Lords, who dress far more richly than you ever could and who never go anywhere without at least a dozen soldiers around them. Then there are the soldiers, who are always in uniform and always in groups of three or four."

"And the last group?"

"Peasants," said Savage. "The common people, who are all poor and worn out. Your clothes are too new, your boots are too shiny, and you don't look worn down by years of struggling just to get enough to eat."

"I do have some older clothes that I can wear," Alex said. "And some old boots as well."

"Nothing with too much color in it," said Savage. "Most of the common people here wear gray or brown clothes. Only the lords can afford to wear clothes with bright colors in them."

"I understand," said Alex.

"Also, keep your head bowed as much as you can," said Savage. "Remember, peasants are the bottom of the heap here. They don't ask questions. They don't stand up to soldiers or look them in the face. Peasants do what they're told and only speak when spoken to."

"Not a pleasant life," Alex said in a thoughtful tone.

"No, it's not," Savage agreed. "It's not so bad in some of the kingdoms where the lords aren't so greedy and hungry for power. I think Karmus is probably the worst place in all of Nezza, and Lazar is the worst lord in this land."

"I've heard something of Lazar," said Alex.

"Nothing good, I'm sure," said Savage.

"No, nothing good. I did manage to talk with a few soldiers when I first arrived here—and don't worry, they don't remember talking to me," Alex added quickly after seeing the concern on Savage's face. "They seemed to think that Lazar might have magic of his own."

"Lazar—magic?" Savage laughed. "I'd bet my boots have more magic in them than Lazar has. He's nothing but a greedy bully." Savage paused. "But there is the old man . . ."

"What old man?"

"Magnus," said Savage. "Not sure what name you wizardly types would give him—enchanter, magician, dark wizard, whatever. I've never seen him do anything really impressive, but he's got his own magic, I'm sure of that."

"More than you might guess," said Alex.

"How's that?" Savage questioned.

"Unless there are other magical people in this land, I suspect Magnus has worked some fairly impressive magic at the great arch."

"Not many magical people in Nezza at all," said Savage. "Magic is feared by almost everyone in this land, and all the old stories say that wizards are evil. I'd have to agree that Magnus is the source of any magic you've run into. What has he done?"

"There's an invisible barrier in front of the great arch," said

Alex. "It forces anyone entering this land to follow the main road, where the soldiers of Lord Bray are waiting."

"If this magic helps Bray, then it helps Lazar as well," said Savage. "How did you manage to get around the barrier?"

"I didn't," said Alex. "I did, however, use my own magic so that the soldiers couldn't see me. It was after I'd slipped away from the main road that I managed to talk to a few of Bray's soldiers and get what little information I could."

"Little enough, I'm sure," said Savage. "Soldiers may know something of their lord and his business, and maybe something of what's going on in the land as well, but mostly they think about where their next meal is coming from and if they'll be sleeping in the rain or not."

"The soldiers did mention a prince named Rallian," said Alex, fishing for more information.

"A common enough subject these days," said Savage. "He is, or rather he should have been, the lord of Karmus. He was just coming of age, and all at once he goes missing. No doubt his dear uncle Lazar has something to do with his sudden disappearance."

"Do you think the prince is dead?" Alex asked. "The soldiers I spoke to said they had been told he was on a quest."

"Hard to say," Savage answered in a slow, thoughtful tone. "I think Lazar would be happy to get rid of any threat to his power, but . . ."

"But?"

"Rallian is from the line of the true king," said Savage. "Killing people doesn't bother Lazar, but killing a real prince is different. There are stories about what happens when royal blood is spilled. I'm sure Lazar would think twice before taking any chances."

"I suppose he would," said Alex. "I only asked because I was curious. The soldier I spoke with seemed sad that Rallian was gone, and that seemed odd to me."

"Not so odd," Savage replied. "The people of Nezza have been looking for a true king for a long time. They don't talk about it much, but everyone seems to remember the good old days when there was one king in Nezza. Rallian was believed to be the best chance for the land to have one true king again, and now that he's gone missing . . ."

"The hopes of the people begin to fade," Alex finished for him.

"Yes," said Savage. "I suspect the hope will return when another prince is found, but who knows when that will be?"

"That might be a long time," said Alex. "I understand that seven young lords have also vanished."

"Not exactly," said Savage. "They haven't been seen for some time, but nobody is really looking for them. If you ask me, the lords of the inner kingdoms know where their kinsmen are, and they don't want to talk about it."

"You've been a great help to me," said Alex. "I think, with a change of clothes, I can do what I came here to do."

"Perhaps, if rescuing your friend and his company is all you want to do. I saw the look in your eye when I told you about Magnus," said Savage. "I know enough about wizards to know that you have some code or rule of wizardry that says you have to make him answer for any evil he has done with his magic. Is that not true?"

"There are rules, but I don't have to go looking for trouble," said Alex, avoiding the question.

"When it comes to Magnus, you may not go looking for trouble, but I think you'll find it just the same," Savage said.

"What do you mean?" Alex asked.

"Since I've been in Nezza, I've taken the time to listen to the old stories and find out a bit of the history of the land. I've learned some interesting things about Magnus."

"What have you learned?"

"Magnus is just the name he uses now," said Savage. "Twenty years ago, he was called Simeon, and he had another name before that. I can't prove it, but I think Magnus has been here in Nezza for at least two hundred years—maybe longer."

"So what is he doing here?" Alex asked. "Why would he stay in Nezza for so long?"

"I can't say why, but I know what he's been doing. He's been stirring up old hatreds between the lords and keeping the kingdoms of Nezza from working together," said Savage. "The stories about Simeon all talk about how war and trouble followed him. He used to travel the land, never staying in one place for long. Wherever he went, something bad followed. Sometimes it was war, sometimes the crops failed, sometimes there would be a drought or a flood."

"So what has changed since he became Magnus?" Alex questioned.

"Ah, that is the question," said Savage. "He's stopped traveling around Nezza—or at least nobody's seen him travel. He keeps himself close to Karmus, and he pretends to serve Lazar."

"Pretends to serve?"

"Lazar is a bully and a fool. I think it likely that Lazar serves Magnus, and not the other way around."

"But why?" said Alex.

"I can't say," Savage answered. "You know how you can look at some people and just sort of know what they are like? Well, I know that Magnus is no good."

"It sounds like he's the cause of the trouble here in Nezza," Alex commented.

"Let me give you some advice about dealing with Magnus: he is a planner. What I mean is that if you face him, for whatever reason, he will have at least three plans."

"Three plans?" Alex asked.

"One to defeat you," Savage continued. "A second one for his own escape, and a third one that you never thought about."

"That will make it hard for me to defeat the third plan," said Alex with a slight smile.

"Laugh if you will, but I'm serious," said Savage. "I know enough about Magnus to know he probably already has a plan to avoid running into any wizard who might come to Nezza, and a second plan to deal with them if he does meet them."

"I'm sure you're right," said Alex. "But the fact remains, I don't have to go looking for trouble, so I might not have to worry about his plans at all."

"Worry about them anyway," Savage warned. "He might have a plan to use you in some way and turn your sudden appearance here to his advantage."

"You have a devious mind," said Alex. "But no one knows I'm in Nezza except for you and Mr. Clutter, so I can't see how Magnus could plan to use me."

"Just because you can't see it doesn't mean it won't happen."

"I'll keep that in mind," said Alex.

"Good. Now, I don't suppose you have anything worth eating in that magic bag of yours? My own bag isn't as well stocked as I would like, and with the current situation in Nezza, it might be some time before I can restock it," said Savage.

"I'm sure I have plenty for the two of us to eat," Alex said with a laugh. "And I can probably help restock your bag as well."

Alex conjured up a fire to cook on and started taking things out of his magic bag. Savage actually did the cooking, and Alex was glad that he did. Savage was an excellent cook, and they were soon eating and talking about the different small kingdoms of Nezza.

They had just finished their meal when Savage suddenly stopped talking and held up his hand. Alex remained quiet as well. With a wave of his hand, Alex put out the fire. He listened to the darkness that had fallen around them. He could hear something moving on the hillside. It sounded like something big, and it wasn't worried about making noise.

Chapter Four
Stoics

Alex and Savage crawled back under the low hanging tree, stopping at the edge of its shadow to look down the hillside. The sound of something moving was growing louder; it was getting closer to them. The moon had just risen, and its light cast long shadows between the trees. Alex and Savage waited in silence, and then Savage pointed at something in the darkness.

Alex had seen the movement as well, but he couldn't make out what it was. The creature continued forward until it was only twenty yards away from Alex and Savage's hiding spot, and then it stopped. The night grew silent, and time seemed to stand still.

"What is it?" Savage whispered.

"No idea," Alex whispered back.

For several minutes nothing happened. Alex was trying to figure out what the creature was, but it was impossible to guess in the darkness. The creature remained silent, as still as stone. After what seemed like a long time, Savage spoke once more.

"Do something."

"Like what?" Alex questioned.

"You're the wizard. Do something, you know, magical," said Savage, holding up his hands and wiggling his fingers.

Alex rolled his eyes at Savage and then turned to look at the creature in the darkness. He didn't like the idea of facing an unknown creature. It might be something friendly; it might not even know that he and Savage were hidden under the tree. Unfortunately, Alex didn't think this creature was friendly, and he was sure it knew exactly where he and Savage were.

After a few more minutes went by, Alex crawled out from under the tree branches and got to his feet. Lifting his staff, he caused the end of it to ignite with a brilliant white light.

"I am Alexander Taylor, wizard and friend of the council of wizards. What is your business here?"

There was no reply. The creature stood still for a moment, and then it seemed to bend forward slightly, like it was bowing. Alex tried to get a better look at it in the light of his staff, but his light did more to show him to the creature than it did to show the creature to him.

The creature suddenly moved, charging forward at Alex.

Jumping to his left, Alex caught his foot on a dead branch and half stumbled, half rolled out of the way. He was back on his feet as an ear-splitting crack filled the air. It was the sound of stone striking stone, and it sounded as if at least one of the stones had broken.

Alex looked over at Savage. He had managed to get out of the way as well, though he appeared to be tangled in a nearby bush. Not waiting for the creature to make another charge, Alex sent a ball of flame crashing into it. The fireball exploded on impact, filling the narrow rocky space with light.

His fireball didn't harm the creature, at least not as far as Alex could see, but the light was useful. The creature appeared to be made of stone that had been carefully carved into the figure of a giant man.

The creature bowed again, and Alex knew it was about to charge. He cast a binding spell to hold the creature in place and was stunned when he felt his magic slide off the stone creature like water. He changed his magic to a tangling spell, hoping to keep his attacker in the narrow space between the giant stones and to give himself time to think.

His tangling spell had taken the form of a mass of heavy vines wrapping around the creature's body and pulling it back into the gap. The spell was working, but only just. The creature was incredibly strong, and Alex had to add more power to his spell to keep the monster from breaking free.

As strong as the earth, a voice said in the back of Alex's mind.

The voice was Alex's O'Gash, what most people would call his wizard's sixth sense. He had heard the voice many times in the past, and it had always helped him when he needed it most.

"Oh," Alex said out loud, suddenly realizing what the creature was.

It was an earthen stoic, a creature summoned by magic and given a human form. Stoics were hard to create, even for a wizard, and harder to destroy. The creature wouldn't get tired, it couldn't be reasoned with, and it had only one task to complete before it would be free. Alex knew he had to force the stoic out of the shape it had been given in order to destroy it, but how? As he desperately tried to find an answer, his O'Gash spoke once more.

Heat can crack the hardest stone; water can wear it down. If heat and water work together, what will happen? said the voice.

"Heat and water," Alex said out loud. He began searching for a stream or a well that he could use against the earthen stoic.

There wasn't a stream on the hillside, but there was a great deal of water just the same. Pouring more magic into his tangling spell, Alex added another spell as well. He poured dragon fire into the narrow gap between the rocks; the deadly, almost liquid fire was one of a dragon's most deadly weapons. The stoic vanished in the flames, but Alex knew that it wasn't dead yet.

"Do you think making it hotter is a good idea?" Savage asked from behind Alex.

There wasn't time to explain what he was about to do, so his answer was a short one. "Find some cover."

Sending his magic out in every direction, Alex worked as fast as he could. Trees creaked and groaned as his magic touched them, and the plants at his feet withered and crumbled to dust. When he thought his magic had gathered enough water, Alex pushed his magic into the body of the stoic. His mouth went dry as he let the magic go, diving to the ground and throwing his arms over his head for protection.

The night was silent for a moment, and then a whistling hiss filled the air. The sound of escaping steam lasted only a second before an explosion ripped the silent night apart. The ground shook under Alex, and he could hear bits of stone flying through the air. After a few seconds, he looked up. The dragon fire had gone out, and the narrow gap between stones where his enemy had been was empty.

Alex got to his feet and leaned on his staff, trying to draw in enough air to fill his lungs. He felt like he'd run for miles, and his dry throat made every breath painful.

Savage walked up beside him, holding out a water bag. "I'm glad you said to take cover, but the noise will let everything for miles around know where we are."

"You think there are more creatures like this one out there?" Alex asked after taking a long drink.

"I don't even know what this one was," Savage answered.

"A stoic," said Alex.

"Not easy to create something like that I'd guess," said Savage in a thoughtful tone. "It'd take some time and know-how to do something like that."

"Weeks, maybe months, of work and planning," said Alex, nodding. "Why?"

"I'm just wondering why it showed up here—tonight," said Savage.

"I don't understand," said Alex.

"Was this creature sent here to destroy you—or me?"

"A good question," said Alex, taking another long drink. "I don't think we should stay here to find the answer though. Is there a stream or a pond close by?"

"There's a stream about two miles southwest of here. Why?" Savage asked.

"Because I don't think I can work that same magic twice in

one night," said Alex. "I'd like to have some water close by, in case another earthen stoic shows up."

Savage nodded and started walking. Alex followed close behind, not wanting to get lost in the darkness. His legs felt weak, and he knew it was because of the magic he had used. Magic had a price after all, but Alex thought that weak legs and being dead tired were a small price to pay for escaping the stoic.

They walked for almost a mile before Alex had to stop. The magic he'd used to destroy the stoic had taken more out of him than he'd thought, and all he wanted to do was to rest.

"Wait," said Alex, reaching out to touch Savage's shoulder. "I need a few minutes to catch my breath."

"This isn't the best spot to be sitting and resting," said Savage.

Alex looked at the hillside they were standing on. There were no trees and only a few small bushes. He suddenly felt very exposed.

"We should find better cover. But I'd like to rest and perhaps talk for a few minutes before going on," said Alex.

Savage nodded and headed down the hill. Alex followed slowly, each step a little harder to take than the last. He paused after only going about fifty yards, focusing his mind and using the elf magic he had learned to help him rest. Alex's body relaxed, his muscles loosened, and he continued on more quickly. The elf magic would let his mind and body rest, almost like he was sleeping, but he could continue to move and talk just the same.

It wasn't long before Savage stopped and sat down on a

fallen log. They were surrounded by pine trees, and Alex found a comfortable spot at the roots of one of them. He leaned back against the tree and closed his eyes.

"What did you want to talk about?" Savage questioned.

"The order of Malgor," said Alex. "I want to know why you were surprised when you thought they had sent me here."

"Let's just say the order isn't what it used to be," Savage answered.

"They aren't able to get things done the way they used to?"

"I'm not sure they get anything done at all these days."

"Why do you think that is?" Alex asked.

"I don't have to think—I know," Savage answered in a fierce tone. "There are too many lazy people in the order, making decisions about what is and isn't important. Not enough information is getting to the top levels of the order anymore. Nobody checks up on things because it's easier to say there isn't a problem than it is to find out what the problem really is."

"Don't you send your reports to a central location?"

"I used to, but they changed things a few years back, just after I started working for them," said Savage. "There were rumors that someone with evil intentions was interfering with the order, maybe even trying to kill the leaders of the order, so the order became more secretive."

"I can understand the concern," said Alex. "I'm sure the order has made a lot of enemies over the years."

"Not as many as you might think," said Savage. "The order has never played favorites, so today's enemy might be tomorrow's friend, if you follow me."

"Yes, I understand. The order passes information to the

people who need it, even if those same people have been a problem in the past."

"Exactly, so I don't see the reason for their fear," Savage continued. "Whatever their reasons, all the reports have to pass through levels. At each level, a person or a group of people decides what is important enough to pass on and what isn't."

"That's the problem?" Alex asked.

"No, the problem is that I don't know who's reading my reports and what they are passing on," said Savage. "If I say that it looks like all of Nezza may soon be at war, someone higher up might decide that Nezza has been at war for years. They might think that war in Nezza is normal, but they've never been here and they don't know what it's really like. But they pass on the message that everything is normal in Nezza, and nobody higher up knows that there is a problem."

"Yes, I see," said Alex. "But couldn't you send a message to someone higher up and tell them what's going on?"

"That's where the new security becomes a problem," said Savage. "I don't know anyone higher up than my contact."

"What?" Alex asked in disbelief.

Savage shrugged. "Oh, I know a few other agents, but looking at it as a sensible man, I have to wonder if I'm even working for the order of Malgor. I have no way of knowing for certain. I know my contact has a pendant with the symbol of the order on it, but that's all. I have to trust that I'm working for the order and hope that I'm doing some good."

"I'm sure you are," said Alex. "I wish there was something I could do to help the situation."

"Maybe you can."

"How?"

"Talk to your wizard friends," said Savage. "I'm sure some of them must know members of the order, members who are higher up in the chain of command than I am. Maybe they can point out the current problems and get things changed."

"I'll do what I can," said Alex.

After a few more minutes, they continued on. The campsite Savage had mentioned would be a good place for a longer rest, and Alex was still a little worried that another earthen stoic might turn up. Having a larger source of water nearby would be useful if one did, but he'd used a lot of magic already today. There were limits to every wizard's powers.

When they came to the campsite, Alex liked it at once. The mountain stream fell noisily over a nine- or ten-foot waterfall, filling a deep, wide pool before continuing down the hillside. Alex walked to the stream's edge and stuck his head into the falling water. Shaking the water out of his eyes, he turned back to look at Savage. The cold water had refreshed him, but the look on Savage's face turned his bones cold.

Turning back to the stream, Alex saw a creature in the shape of a man standing in the center of the pool, seemingly floating on top of the water. The moonlight reflected off the water stoic's body. Its skin seemed to flow like a fountain in the middle of the stream.

Alex didn't need his O'Gash to tell him how to deal with this stoic; the answer was obvious. He could turn the stoic into ice and shatter it with a blast of lightning. He lifted his staff and spread his feet, then sent a freezing spell into the creature's liquid body. Ice formed over the surface of the monster, but before Alex could work any other magic, the ice seemed to melt and fall away. The fluid nature of the stoic's body was drawing warmer water up from the stream, and the ice Alex had created was only on the outer surface of the creature.

Knowing that his magic was almost used up, Alex reached out for the power of the dragon, a power that had saved him more than once in the past. He knew his dragon powers would restore his magic and make him stronger, but when he reached for it, he found nothing. The power of the dragon simply wasn't there. Nothing answered his call.

Panic filled Alex's mind and heart. The power of the dragon had never failed him before. It was always there; it was part of him. He turned, looking for Savage. He wanted to yell for him to run, but Savage was gone.

Before Alex could start running, a stream of water hit him like a fire hose, sending him tumbling across the ground. He tried to get back on his feet but slipped on the wet ground and fell into a muddy puddle.

A second blast of water rolled him out of the puddle and across the ground. Alex managed to get to his knees and look at the stoic. He knew he couldn't stop this creature with the little magic he had left. He gritted his teeth and staggered to his feet. If he was going to die, he would die standing, and he would put up as much of a fight as he could. Maybe he could slow the stoic down, giving Savage more time to escape—maybe.

Alex took a step forward, lifting his staff. There was no way out of this fight. He didn't have any hope of winning, but he would fight just the same. He took a second step, and the stoic lifted one of its arms, preparing to hit him with another blast of water. Alex started to take a third step but froze in place as the power of the dragon flooded into him. He let loose the magic without thinking, knowing what he wanted it to do. Snow and mist filled the air as he took another step forward. His clothes were stiff with frost, and Alex was surprised by how powerful his spell had been.

The water stoic was a blue-and-silver statue at the center of the frozen stream. There was no sound of falling water; the waterfall had turned into a solid wall of ice. The power of the dragon filled his mind, and Alex lifted his staff as a growl of rage escaped him. He, a dragon, had been attacked for no good reason, and now his attacker would pay for its foolishness.

Alex hesitated as something unexpected caught his eye. Savage appeared from behind the stoic, moving like a skater over the smooth ice. The former adventurer held a massive two-handed sword over his head. The sword glowed deep red, as if it had just come out of the forge. With amazing speed, Savage slammed his glowing sword into the frozen stoic, filling the air with steam and a loud hissing noise. The magical creature exploded into thousands of little pieces, and Savage glided to the stream's bank.

Alex was going to say something about his friend's good timing, but he didn't. Savage's eyes were glowing like the dying embers of a fire, and as they came to rest on Alex, he lifted his sword once more. Alex could see the hunger in those eyes, and he knew what he needed to do.

Alex's staff hit the ground with a loud thud, like a massive stone being dropped from a great height. He felt his magic form around him, crackling like ten thousand electrical sparks, all of them jumping from place to place and forming a globe of raw energy. A few magical sparks jumped from the globe to Savage, and Alex gladly let them go.

"Josephus Sebastian Savage. I am not your enemy. Put away your sword until it is needed once more," Alex commanded.

Savage hesitated, looked at the sword in his hands, and then slowly lowered the blade. Once the sword was back in its scabbard, Savage looked at Alex. His eyes were still glowing embers, but the hunger was gone. He turned away, then spoke in a low, gravelly voice.

"Rest now, if you can, wizard. Your questions can wait until daylight."

Savage walked away, and Alex let him go. He had many questions, but not all of them were about the sword Savage carried.

The power of the dragon hadn't been there when he'd called for it, and he didn't know why. Was there some dark power that had kept his dragon magic from coming to him? Only Whalen knew that he could take dragon form, and he was sure that Whalen would never tell anyone. What force could stop the power of the dragon?

You've only yourself to blame, Alex's O'Gash whispered.

"Myself?" Alex asked. "How? Why would I do this to myself?"

Alex waited in the darkness for an answer. Finally, when the eastern sky was changing from black to dark blue, his O'Gash whispered once more.

All talents and abilities must be used or they will fade.

Alex thought about that for a long time, and he knew that

it was right. He had only used the power of the dragon when he'd been forced to use it. He hadn't worked with it, hadn't tried to discover what it could do, hadn't even thought about it in his everyday life. He knew that would have to change. He would have to accept this power and make it part of everything he did. The idea worried him because the power of the dragon would change him, and he didn't know how.

Alex was sitting in the sun and writing a letter to Whalen when Savage returned to the stream. Alex didn't look up, and Savage didn't say anything until Alex had finished his letter and, after two tries, summoned a geeb to take it away.

After another moment, Alex said, "Your sword? Is it a demon blade?"

"Yes, it is," Savage answered. "It is a weapon from myth and legends. A weapon not meant for this world. It found me on my last adventure."

"It is the reason you stopped going on adventures," said Alex. It was not a question.

"The blade has a hunger for battle and for blood. As you saw last night, it doesn't always care about who is friend and who is foe."

"Which is why I have given you a small part of my magic," said Alex.

"Is that what I felt last night? But how can you give me part of your magic? Why would you . . ." Savage fell silent.

"It is said that such weapons change the person who wields

them, and not always for the better. You are a good man, you have kept this blade safe, and you have not allowed its hunger to overcome you. The magic I have given you will help you control the sword's hunger. It will make it easier for you to remember who your friends are, and it will help keep the sword from making you do something you would regret."

"A great kindness," said Savage, bowing slightly. "Though I think it best not to test your magic. I will continue as I have been and only use the weapon in times of greatest need."

"Yes, your timing was very good last night," said Alex.

"Hardly," Savage replied. "If I had waited a few moments longer, you would have defeated the monster. I only used the sword because I thought you had used up your power and had nothing left but the will to fight."

"That is true," said Alex.

"But you froze the entire stream, you—"

"Magic can be strange," said Alex, not explaining how or why he'd regained his power so quickly. "We need to consider the question you asked last night: Who were the stoics after, and why?"

"We should also consider who created them," said Savage.

"I think Magnus must have created them, but I don't know when he would have done it or why," said Alex.

"You don't think they were sent after you?" Savage questioned.

"Creating a stoic takes planning and work. Until two days ago, I didn't even know I would be in Nezza. I can't see why they would be after me," said Alex.

"And to send two such creatures after one man does seem a bit foolish," said Savage.

"I agree," said Alex. "I do have some ideas about why the stoics turned up here."

"And?" Savage asked.

"I think they might have been sent to come after anyone who entered Nezza through the invisible barrier. I've been thinking about that barrier, and I don't think just anyone could get through it. I only managed to enter Nezza because of my magic, and so perhaps the stoics were sent to destroy anyone magical enough to get through the barrier."

"I can see that," said Savage. "If Magnus is behind this, I'm sure he would not want anyone with magic running around loose in Nezza."

"Still, as you said, two stoics is a lot of power to send after any one person, unless . . ."

"Unless what?"

"How many people know about your demon blade?" Alex asked.

"Only a few," said Savage. "Just the adventurers that were with me when I found it—or when it found me—but they've all been sworn to secrecy about the blade."

"Did you tell anyone else? Did you maybe mention it in one of your reports to the order of Malgor?" Alex asked.

"Yes, I mentioned it to the order," Savage admitted after some thought. "When I first came here—what is it, ten? fifteen years ago?—I told the order I had the blade. I expected them to say something about it. At the very least I thought they would tell me never to use it, but . . ."

"You never heard anything about it," said Alex, nodding.

"Never. It's possible the information about the sword may not have been passed on, or at least not passed on to trustworthy members of the order."

"You think there are traitors in the order?"

"Perhaps," said Savage. "Or perhaps only misguided people who don't know where their reports are going. I think it is also possible that not everyone in the order keeps their secrets as well as they should."

"And if Magnus heard about your demon blade?" Alex questioned.

"If he believed it was true, and if he knew I was in Nezza, he would want me out of the way," said Savage.

"Or he would want to tempt you. He might want to force you to use the demon blade so that it would change you into something he could use later," said Alex.

"Yes, that is possible," Savage answered in a thoughtful tone.

"Evil seems to be more organized in all the known lands these days," said Alex. "I wonder if Magnus has someone passing him information from outside Nezza."

"Possible, but I have doubts," said Savage. "You've seen a little of what Nezza is like. You said yourself that a barrier has been created to keep outsiders from entering this land. Why would Magnus be working with someone outside of Nezza?"

"Because I think he is part of a group that the council of wizards is calling the 'Gezbeth.'"

CHAPTER FIVE

THE DUNGEONS OF KARMUS

Two days later, Alex arrived in Karmus. He'd felt the need to hurry, so he'd flown most of the way. He had explained the idea of the Gezbeth to Savage and given him enough supplies to get by before leaving. In return, Savage had repeated his earlier advice: if Alex managed get Skeld and the other adventurers out of Karmus, then the best thing to do would be to get out of Nezza entirely.

"If you can't get out of Nezza, then go north," Savage said. "The lords of the north are not as afraid of outsiders, or of magic."

Alex appreciated Savage's advice, but he wasn't sure what he would do once he'd rescued Skeld and his company. The rescue would be difficult enough. Deciding what to do after that would have to wait.

Karmus was an impressive city. It was divided almost in half by the River Pol, and in the middle of the river was an island that rose up like a small mountain and overlooked the city. On the island there were tall buildings that looked like they had once been grand houses and palaces, but now they were uncared for and unused. A high stone wall encircled the

entire island, and while it might have once been richly deco-
rated, now it looked more like a prison wall.

Alex spent the morning near the riverbank, studying the
island fortress. Few people were allowed onto the island unless
they had some official business with one of Lazar's ministers.
He was certain that Skeld and his companions were somewhere
on the island.

As the day wore on, Alex walked away from the river and
found a little-used alleyway behind some empty buildings. He
moved a few old boxes and boards that were there, making a
hidden spot where he could not be seen even if someone did
happen to wander into the alley. Once his hiding place was finished, he stepped into it and transformed into a small swallow.

In less than a minute, Alex was flying over the island.
There were more soldiers than he'd expected to find, possibly
more than in the rest of the city. He continued to search the
island. It didn't take him long to find the entrance to the dungeon, and when he did, he wasn't happy.

The dungeons of Karmus was a solid stone building with
few windows. A square tower sat on top of the main building.
A quick inspection revealed that there were only two narrow
doors to the entrance of the dungeon. One door, at the front
of the building, was open, but it was guarded by more than a
dozen men. The second door was at the back of the building
and closed; four armed men stood close by. Alex guessed there
would be more men inside the building, and more still in the
dungeon.

Alex wasn't sure how he would get into the dungeon, but
then he saw a way. Around the outside of the building were

several oddly shaped pits, and when Alex flew closer, he saw that they were windows. The windows were half underground and had heavy iron bars over them, but no glass. Alex guessed they were designed to let sunlight and fresh air into the first level of the dungeon.

Having found a way to get into the dungeon without being seen, Alex returned to his hidden place in the alley and took his human form again. As the sun began to set, Alex made his way to one of the many taverns that lined the main road leading to the island fortress. Getting into the dungeon wouldn't do him any good if he couldn't find Skeld and the other adventurers. He hoped he could learn something more about the dungeon from the locals.

Alex entered a tavern and his heart sank. The main room was filled with soldiers, and there were only a few people who were not wearing uniforms of some kind. Skirting around the crowds, he made his way to a shadowed table at the back of the room. For several minutes no one paid any attention to him, but eventually one of the servers made his way to the table and asked what Alex would like.

Alex ordered a drink and waited, listening to the men around him talk. He soon learned that all of these men, and many more as well, were guards for the island fortress. The information surprised him, because he knew that the inner kingdoms of Nezza had been at war for years. It seemed odd that so many men would be called away from war to protect a fortress that was already surrounded by a river and a wall.

After listening for some time, Alex knew he would need to talk to one of the soldiers if he wanted to learn anything useful.

The problem was that the soldiers were drinking in groups, and to get anyone alone seemed almost impossible. Just then, Alex saw a soldier enter the tavern. The man looked like an officer, and the other soldiers didn't seem to be too friendly toward him.

Focusing his attention on the officer, Alex moved his hand slightly under the table. Instantly, the man turned and looked directly at Alex. Without speaking, and seeming not to notice anything else in the room, the man walked over and took a seat at Alex's table.

"You are young to be in a place like this alone," the man said.

"Not too young," said Alex in a casual tone.

"You are new here. I have not seen you in the city before."

"I am," was Alex's only answer as he moved his hand slightly again.

"Strangers seldom come to Karmus. It was once a happy city, and people came from all over Nezza to visit and conduct their business, but times are not what they were."

"Have there been other strangers here recently?" Alex questioned.

"Not in the tavern," the man answered, laughing grimly.

"No, not in the tavern—in Karmus."

"They are in the fortress," the man said. "In the dungeons under the fortress to be exact."

"Are they well?" Alex asked in concern.

"They're alive, or at least they were a week ago when they went into that hole."

"Can I see them?"

"Not unless you're in the dungeon with them. Trust me, you don't want to be there."

"I must find a way to see them," said Alex in a matter-of-fact tone.

"No one enters the dungeons except the black guard and the prisoners."

"There must be a way."

"Only for the black guard, and perhaps mice," came the reply. "Though I doubt even mice would go down there. It is an evil place."

"And how would a mouse get to that place?" Alex asked thoughtfully.

"The pipes under the fortress, I suppose. There are all kinds of pipes under there."

"What part of the dungeon are the strangers in?" Alex persisted.

"I've no idea," the officer said. "But if I know Magnus, he's put them in the darkest hole the place has."

Alex noticed that a few of the other soldiers were looking in his direction. He needed to end his talk soon or risk drawing unwanted attention to himself.

"What of Rallian?" Alex asked. "Does he live? Is he in the dungeons as well?"

"Rallian?" said the man, a look of sorrow on his face. "Rallian is lost to us, and Lazar has forbidden any talk of the prince."

Alex thought about everything he had learned for a moment, and then he waved his hand again. "Forget," he said softly.

The officer blinked several times, then rose and bowed slightly to Alex before heading toward the main bar.

Alex sat for a few minutes longer, and then he made his way to the door. Skeld and his companions had only been in the dungeon for a week, but that was already too long. He had to get into the dungeon and find them—and fast. There was also the small piece of information about Rallian. Alex wasn't sure why he had asked about the prince, but the soldier's answer was interesting. If Rallian had really died, as the rumor said, why would Lazar forbid all talk about him? Alex shook his head. He was here to help Skeld and his company of adventurers, not to change the way things were in Nezza.

As the tavern door closed behind him, Alex moved down the street and into the shadows. He didn't want any of the soldiers in the tavern to follow him, and a few of them looked like they might. After walking for several minutes and making several turns, he slowed his pace. Finding Skeld and the others was the first problem he had to solve, and he didn't want to spend all night solving it.

As he returned to his hidden spot in the alley, Alex decided that he would have to put Skeld and his company inside his magic bag. If they were all in his bag, he would only have himself to worry about. He would need to make some changes inside his bag before attempting the rescue, however, as he had some dangerous things in his bag.

Alex stepped behind the old boards and stopped to listen. Everything was quiet, but he still waited a few minutes to make sure he was alone. Taking his magic bag in hand, he spoke softly into the top of it. The strange but familiar falling sensation swept over him, and soon Alex was moving around the main room of his bag.

Working his way through the different rooms inside his bag, Alex gathered up the books and letters he'd left lying about. He also moved his magical items into either his treasure room or his library. After one more quick check of the other rooms, he magically sealed his treasure room and library so no one but himself could enter them. Then he set out some food and water so Skeld and his friends would have something to eat once he had found them. With a simple command, he was back in the dark alley, his bag still slung around his neck. It was nearly midnight, and time for action. If all went well, Skeld's band of adventurers would be free by morning.

Flying back to the island fortress and finding one of the half-buried windows was harder than Alex thought. The eyes of a swallow were not made to see in the dark of night, but Alex managed to fly through one of the windows and flutter down to the floor. A pale, flickering glow came from under the door, giving him enough light to see that the room was empty and he was alone. Returning to his own form, he moved to the door. There was no way to know what was waiting outside this room, so, working a little more magic, Alex became invisible.

The heavy wooden door wasn't locked, and Alex pulled it open just enough to look into the hallway. Torches hung on the stone wall opposite the door, one about every twenty feet. There was no sign of guards. As fast as he could, Alex opened the door, stepped into the hallway, and closed the door once more.

I'm in. Now what? Alex thought.

Alex had no idea how large the dungeon was or where in the dungeon the adventurers might be. He didn't want to wander aimlessly, but it seemed unlikely that there would be a map with the cells the adventurers were in marked on it. The well-lit hallway gave him an idea. If the hallways had light, then there must be guards who needed that light. If he could find a guard, or even two or three guards together, he could get the information he needed from them.

He started down the hallway, his ears straining to hear any sound. The dungeon seemed to be deserted, which didn't make any sense. Why have so much light if there was no one to see it?

The sound of doors banging open echoed down the hallway, forcing Alex to freeze in his tracks. The sound was followed by the more dangerous sound of marching feet.

Alex's heart sped up. The hallway turned left about fifty yards in front of him, and that was the direction where all the noise was coming from. For a moment he thought about going back the way he had come—maybe even hiding in the room he had first entered—but his curiosity got the better of him. He ran toward the turn, stopped short, and looked around the bend.

The hallway was longer than the one he'd just come down, and at the far end of it were dozens of soldiers. As Alex watched, groups of soldiers broke away, turning down other hallways. As the soldiers moved forward, Alex saw that six men would turn into each new hallway they came to. He also saw that some of the men were replacing the torches along the walls.

Alex did a quick count and he knew that there would be

six soldiers turning into the hallway where he stood. He moved back the way he had come, thinking as hard as he could. He could magically put six men to sleep at one time, but how long would he have to talk with them? Would they be expected to meet up with the other soldiers once they'd replaced the torches? If he used magic on these men, he would have to do it fast and hope they could answer his questions quickly.

Moving to the fourth torch from the bend in the hallway, Alex magically put it out. Looking behind him, he put out the next torch as well. Even though he was invisible, the darkness made him feel safer and less exposed.

The marching feet came around the corner and started toward him, not slowing despite the shadowy space in front of them.

As one of the men reached out to take the dead torch from the wall, Alex used his magic. The soldiers all froze in place, their eyes open but unseeing. Alex hesitated a second, watching to make sure his magic had worked as he'd planned. Satisfied, he moved a few steps closer to the men.

"The adventurers that are held here, where are they?"

"Fifth level, in the pit," came the mumbled reply of six voices.

"How do I get there from here?"

"Center stairs to the second level, east stairs to the third, south stairs to the fourth, and west stairs to the fifth," the men all answered. "From the bottom of the stairs, go north until you come to the stairs that lead to the pit."

The directions were clear enough, but Alex wondered how these men knew what direction they were going underground.

Not wanting to slow this group down, he didn't ask. He moved around the company and then broke his spell with a whisper.

"Forget, and carry on with your task."

The soldiers moved as a unit, marching along the hallway. Alex watched them for a few minutes, but they didn't look back or slow their pace. Turning, he hurried down the empty hallway, looking for the center stairs.

The center stairway was easy enough to find. His biggest problem was dodging the groups of soldiers who were either replacing torches or marching back to the guardrooms. Alex might be invisible, but he was still solid, and to avoid bumping into the soldiers, he had to press himself flat against several walls before he reached the stairs. Moving to the second level of the dungeon, Alex found that it was as well lit as the first. Fortunately there were no guards changing torches on this level, and he was able to find the east stairs without any trouble.

After the second level, Alex found himself in darkness. The only lights he saw came from the guardrooms located at the top and bottom of the stairway. He quietly slipped passed the rooms and moved to the next set of stairs.

He made it to the fifth level with ease, but once there he found that, unlike the other levels where the hallways were all straight and level, the floor here was not so even, and the walls seemed to curve slightly as he moved along them in the darkness.

Finally, afraid that he might miss the final stairway, or worse, fall down in the darkness, Alex conjured up a small weir light. Sickly gray-green slime covered the walls and floor, and the sound of dripping water echoed in the darkness. He continued forward, ready to put out his magical light if he saw or heard anything that might be trouble.

"How much longer are we posted down here?" a muffled voice questioned.

Alex instantly put out his weir light. A slight glimmer came from a door to his left; that was where the muffled voice had come from as well.

"Same as always—ten days on the bottom," a second voice answered.

"How long have we been down here now?" the first voice asked. "Hard to keep track of days when there's no sign of sun or moon."

"It's only been five days and you know it," said the second voice. "Now come on, it's time to relieve the others."

Two men stepped into the hallway, each of them carrying a lamp. Alex carefully watched every move they made.

"Seems foolish to me," said the first man. "Nobody gets out of the pit, you know that."

"Maybe not, but orders are orders. If we don't follow them, we'll find ourselves in the pit," said the second man.

"Maybe something worse than that, what with the mood Magnus has been in," said the first man, pulling the door shut.

The two guards moved off in the direction Alex had been going without saying anything more. Alex waited for a moment and then followed them.

After walking for a few minutes, the two guards started down a worn stairway. Alex glided along in the darkness behind them, unseen and silent. The stairway went down and down, with an occasional hallway leading away from it.

Finally, they reached the bottom of the stairs, and there was only one way for the men to go. It was cold down here, and Alex could hear a small, steady stream of water running near his feet. There was a nasty smell in the air, and sounds echoed strangely in the darkness. The passageway sloped downward, and here and there Alex could see small metal grates that allowed some of the water to drain away.

After what felt like a very long time, a light came into view ahead of them. Two more guards were standing in front of an iron door, each of them holding a lamp.

"Are the prisoners quiet tonight?" asked one of the men Alex had been following.

"A few whimpers," one of the men guarding the door answered. "They can't last much longer."

"Very well," said the first man. "In the name of Lazar, we relieve you."

"In the name of Lazar," said the second man.

The men who had been guarding the iron door stepped aside to allow the new guards to take their places. Alex held his breath and tried to push himself into the wall as the guards walked past him and vanished into the darkness of the passageway. After waiting a few minutes to make sure the other guards were gone, Alex focused his thoughts on the two men in front of him.

"Sleep," Alex whispered with a wave of his hand.

As soon as he had spoken, the two men at the door slumped to the floor. Alex smiled and moved forward. The iron door was locked with two heavy bolts, but there was no keyhole at all. Alex extinguished the lamps the guards had been holding before trying to open the bolts, just in case there were more guards behind the door. The bolts moved with only a slight scraping of metal on metal, and, with a small push, the iron door swung open.

Alex felt a spark of magic as the door opened. He instantly brought up his staff, ready to defend himself, but nothing happened. He waited for a second, listening. No alarms echoed through the passageways; no sound of running feet filled the air. Alex suspected that Magnus knew that this door had been opened, but how fast could he do anything about it?

Everything in front of Alex was dark, but the smell was almost unbearable. Alex listened for a moment. He could hear people moving around, but he couldn't see anything. He took a step forward, holding out his hand in front of him so he wouldn't run into anything. He stopped when he heard some faint whispers to his left.

"My friend will come," said a dry voice. "I know he will."

"He may come, but will it be in time?" questioned a second voice.

"He will come as soon as he can," said the first voice. "If not in time to save us, at least in time to avenge our deaths."

"Little comfort in that," said a third voice.

"Take comfort where you can," said the first voice.

"Skeld?" Alex whispered.

"Alex?"

Alex broke his spell of invisibility and turned toward the voices. It sounded like he had found Skeld and his companions only just in time. Conjuring a weir light that seemed incredibly bright after the total darkness, he had to blink several times before he could really see anything.

"Thank goodness I've found you," said Alex, shocked by how thin and pale Skeld looked.

"I knew you'd come," said Skeld happily, struggling to get to his feet. "I knew you would find us."

"How long have you been in this hole?" asked Alex, moving to the door of the cell that held Skeld and his companions.

"Longer than I care to remember," answered Skeld, coughing as he met Alex at the cell door.

Taking a moment to examine the lock, Alex whispered a few magic words, then hit the door with his staff. With a loud crack, the lock broke away, and the cell door swung open. Alex caught Skeld as he fell forward with the door.

"I should introduce you to my companions," said Skeld, pulling away from Alex and turning back to his fellow prisoners.

"There will be time for introductions later," said Alex. "I've got to get you all out of here."

"How did you get in?" Skeld asked.

"Magic, of course," answered Alex. "And that's how we're getting out as well."

"But—" Skeld began.

"No time," said Alex, cutting him off. "Where are your bags and weapons?"

"Taken," said Skeld. "We were forced to put them in an iron lockbox after we were captured. If we'd had our bags, we could have escaped before ever reaching this cursed city. The lockbox was brought here as well, but I don't know where it is now."

"I'll see if I can find it, but no promises," said Alex. "I'm going to put you all inside my bag for the time being. There's plenty of food and water there, and there's a fire burning to keep you warm. If I can find your things I'll call you out again so you can collect them."

"It would be better if we made our own way out of this dungeon," said one of Skeld's companions. "The rules of honor—"

"None of you looks like you could make your own way out of this pit without help," Alex cut in. "And as for the rules of honor, well, I'm invoking my wizard's privilege to waive them. There will be no loss of honor to any of you for accepting the safety of my bag."

"Wizard's privilege—and some common sense," said Skeld with a weak grin.

"There is a dark wizard here," said one of the other adventurers. "You should be careful of him as you search."

"I will be," said Alex. "Now, everybody up. I think you'll find my bag more comfortable than this pit." He looked around. "Wait. I was told there were six of you. I count only five."

"There were six of us," said Skeld, a look of anger on his face. "The men of Nezza have no honor. They shoot first and ask for a peaceful surrender after."

One of the other adventurers touched Skeld's arm and he fell silent.

Without waiting for further discussion, Alex held out his

magic bag and gave the command for it to put all five prisoners inside it. There was the sound of rushing air, and Alex was suddenly alone in the dungeon. He moved back to the iron door, then put out his weir light.

The guards were still asleep. Alex rebolted the iron door and relit the guard's lamps. Then he worked his magic and became invisible once more. He thought it would be best to wake the guards before leaving. If someone found them asleep, it might raise questions and suspicions. Awake, the guards might remain where they were for hours. Plus, then they might be able to tell him where to look for the adventurer's magic bags.

"Wake," Alex commanded.

The two guards stirred, then struggled sluggishly back to their feet. They looked confused and worried.

"The iron box that holds the adventurers' possessions—where is it?"

"Nothing came with the adventurers," one of the guards answered.

"If there was something of great value, where would the wizard keep it?" Alex tried again.

"Things of value to the wizard would be in his private rooms at the top of the tower," the guard answered.

"Forget," Alex said.

The worried looks on the guard's faces vanished, and they stood at attention on either side of the door. Turning away, Alex headed back up the passageway as fast and as quietly as he could. The guard's answer was not what he had hoped for. He wasn't ready to face Magnus, and recovering the stolen magic bags might mean that he'd have to. As he started up the stairway, he considered leaving the magic bags where they were for now.

Alex was almost to the stairs that would lead him up to the fourth level of the dungeon when he stopped short. The sound of moving men echoed through the dungeon, and torchlight filled the hallway in front of him.

"What's all this?" a voice asked in the darkness.

"Orders," came the answer.

Alex moved closer. He wanted to hear what orders had been given.

"The dungeons are to be searched from top to bottom. Every room is to be inspected without exception," said a man who looked like an officer.

"We haven't got enough men to do that," another man answered. "There are rooms down here that nobody's ever seen, and passageways that end in bottomless pits."

"More men will be coming," the officer answered. "For now, all of you are to stand guard in front of the stairs. Nothing is to get past you to the fourth level. Understood?"

The guards nodded and spread out across the stairway.

Alex's only escape had just been blocked off.

CHAPTER SIX

THE ESCAPE

As he retreated from the torchlight, Alex let his right hand brush against the wall. His mind felt empty, unable to think or plan. When his hand found an open space in the darkness, he turned into another hallway. After walking another hundred yards, he stopped and closed his eyes.

What is Magnus doing right now? Alex asked himself.

The answer came to him, and it was as if Alex could almost see what Magnus was thinking. He knew that Alex was in the dungeons somewhere, and he knew that he'd found the adventurers. With guards at all the stairways, and more searching the dungeon from top to bottom, there was little chance for Alex to escape. Alex thought he could magic his way past most of the guards, but sooner or later someone would notice, and then Magnus would know exactly where he was.

Conjuring a weir light to guide him, Alex broke the spell that made him invisible. If Magnus could track Alex by his magic use, then Alex couldn't stay invisible forever.

He has a plan; he must, Alex thought, remembering what Savage had told him.

Magnus had known that Alex was in Nezza for at least four days. He might have been planning for something like this for years, but what was his plan? Alex couldn't guess, but one thing became clear in his mind. Whatever Magnus had planned, he would need to be close by to make his plan work. Magnus would want to be in the dungeons when Alex was found.

"If I wasn't stuck in the bottom of the dungeon, now would be the perfect time to enter Magnus's rooms and find the missing magic bags," Alex said.

Then you need to find a way out of the dungeon, his O'Gash answered.

The soldier in the tavern had mentioned the pipes under the dungeon, but Alex didn't think there was much hope there. He was so far underground that any pipes leading to the river would be flooding the dungeon with water. Still, if he could find the pipes, he might be able to use them to move into one of the higher levels of the dungeon.

Alex continued to walk, keeping his eyes open for any sign of pipes along the walls or drains in the floor. He shivered in the cold, damp air, and he pushed his right hand into his pocket to get it warm. If he'd known he'd be trapped in the dungeon, he would have worn warmer clothes.

After what felt like a long time, Alex was forced to stop at the edge of a large open pit. The floor appeared again about twenty feet beyond the pit, but everything ahead of him was in darkness. He sent his weir light down into the pit but soon called it back. The pit was deep, and he didn't want to think about what might be at the bottom of it.

Wake up! Alex's O'Gash screamed inside his head. *Magnus's magic is dulling your wits already.*

Alex hadn't felt any magic, but he knew it was there just the same. Magnus had done something to put him into a trance-like state. If he didn't shake himself out of it now, it might be too late.

"What options do I have?" said Alex.

Go back the way he had come? No good—too many soldiers. Staying where he was only meant that the soldiers would eventually find him. He could move forward, but to where? The passageway might continue on the far side of this pit, but there was no way for him to know where it would lead. He could wonder aimlessly for days and still be stuck in this dungeon.

Someone built the passageway, so it must go somewhere, said his O'Gash.

Forward was his only real choice, but he didn't like it. He sent his weir light across the empty space, changing into a swallow to follow it. Alex instantly returned to his own form on the far side of the pit and increased the brightness of his weir light. There was little chance of anyone seeing the light, and the glow made him feel more awake.

Worried that Magnus's magic would dull his mind if he didn't stay focused, Alex started off at a quick pace. He felt more awake and was even curious about why this passageway had been made so far under the city. He continued to watch for pipes or anything else that might help him, but he saw nothing.

The tunnel started to bend and twist as he followed it, and

in places it seemed to be moving in an upward direction. The possibility that the tunnel might lead to the surface encouraged Alex, and he hurried forward. The bends became regular corners, turning sharply every hundred feet or so. When the floor became steeper, he knew that the passage was leading toward the surface and he had to slow his pace.

A short set of stairs appeared out of the darkness. The stairs went down into what looked like a massive room. Alex took the first two steps down and then froze in his tracks. His eyes went wide as he looked into the room, and his whole body felt cold. There was a huge pile in the middle of the room and crawling over and around that pile were thousands and thousands of rats.

Go back, go back, go back, a weak-sounding voice at the bottom of Alex's brain squealed.

Why? They're only rats, said a stronger voice at the top of his brain.

Evil, disgusting, nasty rats, the weak voice answered. *They are watching every move I make. They are watching for their chance to attack.*

Alex looked around the room, and thousands of little eyes reflected his weir light, shining back at him. The rats were watching, but that was all they were doing.

They see the light and are afraid of it, the stronger voice in his head said. *If I enter the room, they will run away from the light.*

They will attack and drag me down with their numbers, the weak voice answered.

Alex tried to swallow, but his throat was too dry. He ran his tongue over his lips and it felt like a piece of sandpaper. Cold sweat ran down his back, and his whole body shivered.

I've seen rats before, and I'm not afraid of them. I don't have time for this, the stronger voice said. *I can see a path on the far side of the room. I need to hurry, so stop complaining and get moving.*

Alex tried to move but he couldn't. His muscles were tight, ready to break into a run, but they would not obey his commands. A strange, squishy, splatting noise pulled his eyes to the rat-covered pile at the center of the room. He looked up and saw a faint light coming from the ceiling. There were holes in the ceiling. The light seemed to flicker, and then shadows fell onto the pile below.

I must be under the kitchens, said the strong voice. *They are dropping their garbage into this room to get rid of it. That's why all these rats are here. I'm close to the surface now.*

They are breeding the rats to destroy anyone who tries to escape the dungeons, said the weak voice. *If I go too close, they will swarm over me. Rats will eat anything they can get their paws on—dead or alive.*

No. This is Magnus's magic, Alex's O'Gash said. *It has slowed your mind and magnified your fear.*

I'm not afraid of rats. I just don't like them, said the strong voice in Alex's mind. *The rats won't do anything if I move forward. They are too busy with their trash pile to care.*

Something terrible will happen if I go in there! the weak voice shrieked.

Alex tried to move forward, but it was almost impossible. His right foot slid a few inches across the ground and stopped.

His left leg didn't move at all. Magic or not, the fear in his brain was holding him in place.

I feel happy, I feel sad, I feel angry, I feel afraid. Fear is just another feeling. It can only hurt me if I let it, Alex's strong voice reasoned.

It is real, the weak voice whined. *I . . . I can't . . .*

Alex dragged his left foot across the step, and he moved forward. A second effort pulled his right foot to the floor of the room. He closed his eyes, not out of fear but in concentration. He had to move forward in order to break the spell of fear that held him back. Again and again his feet shuffled forward, and with each painfully slow step, the weak voice at the bottom of his brain howled for him to run.

After what seemed like forever, Alex opened his eyes and found that he was only a few steps away from the far side of the room. The tunnel he had been following was in front of him, and he almost jumped into it. He paused to look back into the room. The rats were still swarming the trash pile, unconcerned with Alex and the battle he had just won.

Alex followed the tunnel, changing directions and climbing one last steep section using his hands and feet. He was breathing hard and sweating, but he'd found what he was looking for. In front of him the tunnel wall dropped down, leaving a much smaller opening. Pale light shined through the opening, and he could smell fresh air. He put out his weir light and stood still for a moment, catching his breath. When he felt like he could move quietly, Alex dropped to his knees and crawled through the opening.

Alex looked up at the night sky. Only ten or twelve feet

above him was an iron grate that covered the stone box he'd crawled into. With no time to waste, Alex became a swallow, fluttering up and through the iron bars.

Landing, he found himself in what looked like a forgotten garden. Roses grew across stone paths and clung to small stone statues. A quick glance told him that he was in the center of some large building. He flew up into the open air and got a better look at the city around him.

To Alex's surprise, he was still on the island in the middle of the river. The building he'd just left looked like it might have been a palace once, but it was shabby and run-down now. The entrance to the dungeon, and the tower where he hoped to find the magic bags of the adventurers, was close by. He flew to the top level of the tower only to find that the windows on the top level had all been bricked shut, but that seemed like a small problem now that he was out of the dungeon.

Dropping down one level, Alex found a barred window that he could slip through. He landed in a dusty storage room full of books and scrolls and returned to his own form once more.

The door was unlocked, and Alex pulled it open just far enough so he could see the hallway outside. There were no sounds, and the dimly lit hall appeared to be empty. Alex pulled the door shut behind him and moved toward the near end of the hall, looking for a stairway that would lead him to Magnus's rooms.

At first Alex moved with caution, thinking that Magnus would have guards posted. Finding no one to block his way, though, he realized that all the guards must be in the dungeons below, searching for him. How long had it been since the search had started? The moon had been setting in the west, so it had to be four or five hours since he'd first entered the dungeons. How long would it take to search the entire dungeon?

It doesn't matter. I need to hurry, Alex thought.

Finding the stairs he was looking for, Alex started to climb as quietly as he could. He didn't know for certain that Magnus would be in the dungeon; that was only a guess. He let his thoughts and magic move outward, searching for any signs of magic or any kind of trap that Magnus might have left on the stairway. There was nothing, and there was no magic around the locked door at the top of the stairway either.

With a twist of his hand and a little magic, Alex opened the door to Magnus's private rooms. Everything was dark except for a strange ball of pale green light to Alex's left. Closing and locking the door, Alex moved toward the ball of light. At the center of the ball was an iron lockbox sitting on a polished table.

The ball of light completely enclosed the box, and bending down, Alex could see the bottom of the ball extend underneath the table. The spell was obviously meant to keep the box safe. He needed to get the box out of the ball of light, but breaking the spell would alert Magnus to Alex's whereabouts, and that would mean trouble.

Leaning his staff against the wall, Alex magically lit several candles around the room. He put his hands under the edge of the table and lifted. The table and the box together were heavier than he thought they would be. He checked his grip and lifted the table a little higher. The ball of green light stayed where it was, and so did the lockbox. Grunting with the effort, Alex lifted the table even higher. The box scraped on the table and moved a few inches, but the ball of light didn't move at all.

Alex took a deep breath and jerked the heavy table even higher. The box suddenly slipped, scraping the tabletop and crashing to the floor. Alex almost dropped the table, his eyes darting to the door as his heart raced with fear.

Magnus's spell remained where it was, and there were no sounds of anyone racing up the stairs to see what all the noise was about. Alex took a few deep breaths and reached for his magic bag. He would take the box with him and open it when he was someplace safer.

Having placed the lockbox safe inside his magic bag, Alex was about to put out the candles when something else caught his eye. Next to the table was a large desk, and sitting on that desk was a dark crystal ball that Alex recognized as a scrying orb. He knew they were like an oracle's crystal, only not as powerful or as clear to see things in. Next to the orb was a folded letter. Alex wondered who would be sending letters to Magnus.

Alex moved behind the desk and picked up the letter. Unfolding the page, he held it up so he could read it in the candlelight.

Magnus,

We have been informed that your foolish lord has imprisoned a company of adventurers. You are to dispose of these adventurers as quickly as possible. You are to remove all trace of them and to dispose of or transfer

any soldier who knows that they have been brought to
Karmus.

In the name of the Brotherhood,
Gaylan

Alex read the letter twice. The fact that it was signed "In the name of the Brotherhood" made a chill run down his spine. This was not one person giving an order to execute Skeld and his friends, but a person giving orders for a larger group of people—the Brotherhood.

Here, in Alex's hand, was the first real proof that the Gezbeth, or "the Brotherhood" as they called themselves, existed. His emotions rose and then fell just as fast. He could prove that the Gezbeth was a real threat, but to whom? What was Magnus doing for them here in Nezza? Why did the Brotherhood care about a handful of adventurers?

"I can puzzle this out later," Alex said to himself, slipping the letter into his pocket. He would have to tell Whalen about this as soon as possible

Alex held out his magic bag and moved the scrying orb from the desktop to his own treasure room. It was a useful tool to have, and he didn't want to leave it here for Magnus to use. With a wave of his hand, the candles all went out. He moved back to the door guided by the green glow of Magnus's spell, but before he could leave the room, he heard the sound of heavy boots rushing up the stairs.

Moving to stand so he would be behind the door when it opened, Alex waited. The boots stopped, and Alex heard a scraping sound as a key turned in the lock. The door swung open, and Alex saw a guard holding a torch. The guard was alone, but Alex didn't wait to find out why he was there. With all his strength, he kicked the door shut, slamming it into the guard's face.

There was a lot of noise from beyond the door as the guard tumbled down the stairs. Alex pulled the door open and hurried after his enemy. He found the man at the bottom of the steps, unconscious and bleeding from a broken nose but alive. He left the guard where he'd landed and hurried toward the nearest door. It was time to get out of Karmus, and any window he could squeeze through as a bird would be good enough.

The door was locked, but Alex's magic had it open in a flash. He spun into the room and had the door shut and locked again before realizing he was not alone. A pale-faced young man jumped to his feet as soon as Alex entered. He was dirty, his clothes were worn, and it looked like he hadn't had a good meal for weeks.

"Who are you?" the prisoner questioned, his voice shaking slightly. "What do you want with me?"

"Who are you? And why are you being held here?" Alex asked in reply.

"I am Rallian, prince of Karmus. I'll ask again, who are you and what do you want with me?"

"I am Alexander Taylor, adventurer and wizard. I wasn't looking for you, but now that I've found you, I think you should come with me."

"I've heard tales of adventurers and wizards, and they all seem too big to be believed. If you're trying to escape the tower, don't bother. There are too many of the black guards for you to slip past them all. You might as well go back to the cell you were in."

"I don't plan on slipping past the black guards," Alex said. "I am leaving this tower and the city of Karmus. If you would like to have your freedom once more, you are welcome to join me. If you'd prefer to stay here under Magnus's care . . ."

"If there is any chance of freedom, then I'm with you."

"Then we should be on our way," said Alex.

Alex moved toward the window at the same time that Rallian moved toward the door. The moon had gone down, and the sun would be rising in less than an hour. It had been a long night for Alex, but there was no time to rest.

"This way, I think," said Alex, pointing at the window.

"It's more than fifty feet to the roof of the dungeon below," said Rallian. "Unless you have a great deal of rope hidden on your person or can sprout feathers and fly away, I think the stairs are a safer bet."

"Sprouting feathers and flying away is exactly what we are going to do. Now, quickly, we must leave this place."

"You're a madman if you believe you can fly," said Rallian, taking a step back from Alex.

"Not mad," said Alex, waving his staff in Rallian's direction. "A wizard, as I said."

Rallian's reply was the croak of a raven. Before the prince could make another sound, Alex changed himself into a raven as well and flew to the bars in the window. He squeezed himself through, then, turning to look at the prince, he used more magic. The spell was like a magical rope that would bind them together, forcing the prince to stay close and follow where Alex led.

"Come fly with me," said Alex in his raven's voice. "The hour of your freedom has arrived."

Unsure of his wings and confused by his sudden transformation, Rallian managed to fly up to the window and squeeze through the bars as well. He teetered on the window ledge.

"Spread your wings," said Alex. "You'll get the hang of it."

Alex spread his own wings and took flight. He circled and turned back toward the tower, waiting for Rallian to follow. Rallian hesitated, squawked once, and finally spread his wings and glided away from the window. Alex worried that Rallian would either simply glide until he ran into a building or fell to the ground. After a few seconds, however, Rallian flapped his wings out of instinct. Slowly the prince climbed into the dark sky to fly at Alex's side.

"Into the west we go, young prince, and the future of Nezza goes with us," said Alex.

He was surprised by his own words. He hadn't actually planned to go west, and he had no idea what the future of Nezza might be. What he did know troubled him. His quest to rescue Skeld and his company from the dungeons of Karmus had become something new. He wasn't sure why things had changed, but everything was different now. Perhaps it was finding Magnus, a dark wizard, in Nezza. Maybe it was the note from the Brotherhood that he'd found. Whatever the reason, Alex was now on a bigger quest, and the fate of all of Nezza hung in the balance.

Chapter Seven

Many Meetings

Alex might have enjoyed his flight into the west if he hadn't had so many things to be worried about. This new quest had chosen him, and he was sure that Magnus would fight to the death to win. Even if he didn't have Magnus and the Brotherhood to think about, there was Skeld and his companions. They hadn't looked good when he'd found them, and they would need time to regain their strength. He needed to find a safe place for them. Once they were well enough to travel, what would they do?

Alex's spent most of the flight thinking about the letter he had found. A group calling themselves the Brotherhood wanted the adventurers to disappear and all trace of them removed. But why? Why would the Brotherhood care about a few adventurers? And what would the Brotherhood do once Magnus told them the adventurers had escaped?

Will he tell them? Alex's O'Gash questioned.

Alex could see the bloodred dunes of the western desert growing larger and larger as the day went on. They were a long way from Karmus, and he felt that now there was time to find answers to his questions. He pushed his worries to the back of his mind and started looking for a place to land.

Circling a small valley, Alex made sure there was nobody nearby before descending. His raven eyes could see every detail of the land below him. He landed near a spring on the south side of the valley. The spot was less than a mile from the red desert sands, and the closest village was more than thirty miles away.

As soon as he landed, Alex returned to his normal form. He stretched and looked around for Rallian. The prince had landed on the far side of the spring, his bird head tilting to watch everything Alex did. Alex smiled and, lifting his staff, he returned the prince to his natural form. Rallian stumbled backward, his eyes wide with amazement and fear.

"Splash some water on your face," said Alex. "It will help to clear your mind after our flight."

"That . . . that was incredible," said Rallian. "I never thought that those old stories of magic and wizards . . ."

"Not all magic is evil and not all wizards are dark," said Alex. "I'm not here to harm you, but to help you. And, as you've seen, magic can be a useful tool."

"Yes," said Rallian. "I just don't . . ."

"I understand," said Alex. "You don't need to try to explain what you're feeling. For now, I think a good wash and a change of clothes would be best. I have some clean clothes that I think will fit you. Once you are presentable, there are some people I need to talk to."

"I don't understand," said Rallian. "Where do you keep

spare clothes? What people? We are miles from anything and anyone."

"I told you that I am an adventurer," said Alex. "Do the stories of Nezza say nothing about adventurers and their magic bags?"

"Yes, of course, but . . ."

"The people I need to talk to are inside my magic bag," Alex explained. "They are also adventurers, and they were thrown into the dungeons of Karmus by your uncle and Magnus. Rescuing them from the dungeons is the reason I came to Nezza, but now I feel that I have other work to do in this land."

"Yes, my uncle and Magnus wouldn't hesitate to throw adventurers into the dungeons. They've put a lot of people in the dungeons in the past few years."

"Including you," said Alex. "Now, rest and get cleaned up. If all goes well, you'll meet the adventurers shortly. Though when I call them out of my bag, I think it might be best if you don't say anything, at least not at first."

"I will do as you wish," said Rallian. "You saved me from the dungeons of Karmus, from my uncle, and from his creature, Magnus. I am in your debt, and so I am your servant."

"You are not my servant, young prince, but I hope that we will be friends," said Alex.

As Rallian washed his face with the spring water, Alex took a towel and a set of his own clothes out of his magic bag. The prince was smaller than Alex, but the clothes would be a close fit, and they were better than what he was wearing. When the prince was ready, Alex led him away from the spring to a mostly level spot near some trees. He explained to the prince that he would vanish for a short time and then reappear with five adventurers.

"Remember, don't say anything until after the adventurers introduce themselves and I've asked a few questions," said Alex.

"I will remain silent," said Rallian.

Alex nodded and then spoke softly into the top of his magic bag. Instantly, he was standing in the main room of his bag. He looked around at the faces of the adventurers he had rescued. They didn't look as sickly as he'd thought, but they were all still thin and pale.

"Alex," said Skeld, rushing forward and wrapping his arms around his friend in a bear hug. "I knew you'd come. I knew I could count on you."

"I only wish I had come sooner," said Alex. "If I'd known how desperate your condition was, I would have tried to move faster."

"You came faster than I thought possible, even for a wizard," said Skeld, wiping tears of happiness from his eyes. "Now, let me introduce you to the rest of my companions."

"Perhaps the introductions should take place outside," a tall blond man standing behind Skeld interrupted. He was obviously the leader of the adventure. "That is, if we are past any danger."

Alex nodded. "We are many miles from Karmus, and we are safe enough, at least for the time being."

"Yes, of course," said Skeld, nodding to the blond man. "It

would be best if we left your bag's protection, Alex. Then we can meet on more honorable terms."

"As you wish," said Alex. "If you all are ready?"

There was general agreement from the five adventurers, and Alex waved his hand. It wasn't the normal way to exit a bag, but he didn't want to reveal his passwords in front of strangers. There was a rushing sound of wind, and then they were all standing in the bright sunlight of Nezza.

"Your powers continue to grow," said Skeld.

"My understanding of things has grown," Alex said.

Skeld's glance darted to Rallian, who stood behind Alex.

Alex smiled. "Introductions and a few questions first, and then explanations."

"As you wish," said Skeld. "Allow me to introduce you to Virgil, our leader. He comes from Norsland and is Lilly's cousin."

"We are in your debt, Master Taylor," said Virgil, stepping forward and bowing deeply. "Skeld has told us much about you, and I, for one, am happy that his stories were true."

"My pleasure," said Alex, returning Virgil's bow. Alex could see pride in his face, but also a great deal of kindness. He felt that he could trust Virgil. "I know Skeld well, so I am also happy that the stories he told were true."

Virgil and Skeld both laughed, and Alex thought how similar the two men seemed to be.

"If you will permit me, Skeld," said Virgil, "it is my duty to make the introductions."

Skeld nodded and stepped back.

"Master Taylor," Virgil began, "it is my great pleasure to

introduce my company to you. Thanks to you, we are still a company, and very much in your debt."

"Please," said Alex, looking at the adventurers. "Call me Alex."

Virgil nodded, then turned toward the company. "You know Skeld. This is Cameron Dixx, from West Ard—we call him Cam. Dain Goldstone, a most excellent dwarf from Neska. And last but not least, Thomas Aquil from Barkia. He is our youngest member, and this is only his second adventure."

"A very great honor," said Thomas, bowing so low that he lost his balance and stumbled forward.

"Easy, Tom," said Virgil, catching Tom before he fell. "You need rest and healing before making such deep bows. As you know, Master Taylor, we had another member to our company—a dwarf named Thorson Ironshoes from Moorland. He was killed when we were taken prisoner, and I mention him out of respect."

"It is my great pleasure to meet you all," said Alex. "I am pleased I was able to help you in your time of need."

"Your service has been great," said Virgil. "We are all in your debt, as I have said, and will happily repay you in any way that we can."

"We can talk about that later," Alex said. "Right now I have a question or two to ask, and then I think you should all rest."

"We will freely answer any questions you might have," said Virgil. "We will hold nothing back."

"Then tell me, what brought you to Nezza? What quest are you on in this land?" Alex asked.

"Our adventure was to be a simple one, though it now appears that it will end in failure. We were asked to discover the fate of Prince Rallian of Karmus and then to take that news to the people paying for our quest."

"You were only to discover his fate?" Alex questioned.

"No, I'm sorry, let me explain," Virgil answered. "If the prince was alive, and if we could find him, we were to take him with us to the north. If Rallian was alive but no longer in Nezza, or if Rallian was dead, we were to take word back to the people paying for our quest."

"And who are these people?"

"The lords of the north. Our primary contact in Nezza is Lord Talbot, but we have not yet met him," Virgil answered.

Rallian let out a slight gasp when Talbot's name was mentioned.

Alex turned to look at Rallian, a question in his eyes. Rallian nodded, and Alex gestured for the prince to stand next to him. He turned to the other adventurers.

"If you will allow me, I would like to introduce you all to Prince Rallian of Karmus," said Alex, bowing to the prince. "I was fortunate enough to find him in the tower above the dungeons, and he agreed to come with me."

"Prince Rallian," said Virgil, dropping to one knee and bowing.

The other adventurers knelt as well, lowering their heads as a sign of respect.

Rallian hesitated for a few seconds and then spoke. "Rise most, noble adventurers. Rise, so that we may speak as equals."

Virgil and the others stood up, but nobody said anything.

Rallian seemed at a loss, and the adventurers remained silent, waiting for the prince to speak first. Alex saw the problem and broke the silence himself.

"We have a great many things to talk about, but I think we should all get some rest before making plans. I know that Prince Rallian was up early this morning, and it doesn't look like the rest of you managed to sleep while you were in my bag."

"We were waiting, hoping you would find our magic bags," said Virgil.

"Yes, your bags," said Alex. "I was able to collect them before leaving Karmus."

Alex whispered into the top of his magic bag, and the lock-box appeared on the ground in front of him. He magically un-locked the box and opened it so the adventurers could reclaim their bags.

"I will carry Thorson's bag and return it to his heir," said Virgil, taking the final bag out of the box.

"A noble task," said Dain. "I hope you will also carry news that his death has been avenged."

Virgil nodded in agreement.

Alex studied the adventurers as they took blankets and other items out of their magic bags. He was trying to decide what they would do now that the goal of their quest had been found. He suspected they would want to take Rallian north to Lord Talbot, but then what?

"Prince Rallian, I have some blankets you can use," said Alex.

"I'm not tired, and I have a lot to think about," said Rallian.

"You should at least try to rest," said Alex. "There will be time for thinking, and talking, later."

Rallian took the blankets and found a spot a little apart from the adventurers to lay them out. Virgil and his company had taken their weapons out of their magic bags but were now spreading their blankets out to get some rest. Alex spread his own blankets out and sat down on them, but he wasn't think-ing about sleep, at least not yet.

The adventurers were all soon asleep, but Rallian remained sitting up, a look of deep thought on his face. Alex used his magic, and after several minutes, Rallian laid back, closed his eyes, and was soon fast asleep. With everyone asleep, Alex reached for his magic bag and took out the scrying orb he'd taken from Magnus's rooms. He was sure he could use it, and he wanted to know what Magnus was up to.

Concentrating on the dark crystal in front of him, Alex focused his mind on the dark room at the top of the tower. He remembered everything he could about that room, and slowly the crystal came to life. The world around him faded away, and Alex found his mind floating above the desk where he'd found the orb.

"What have you found?" an old man with long gray hair asked. He was sitting behind the desk, and Alex knew at once that this was Magnus.

"My men have found nothing in the dungeons," answered a second, younger man.

"Of course they've found nothing in the dungeons," Magnus snapped. "The wizard managed to slip past your men, and nobody noticed anything. The wizard then got into the tower, into my own rooms. He has taken the lockbox, and more importantly, he has taken the prince as well."

"I . . ." the younger man started and stopped.

"How did he know where to find the lockbox? How did he know the prince was here, in the tower?" Magnus shouted.

"Magic?" the younger man offered.

"Of course he used magic, fool. He's a wizard, but that doesn't answer my questions. Even with his magic, he shouldn't have found Rallian so easily. No matter what magic he used, I would think at least one of your worthless guards would have noticed something."

"I . . . I don't know. Nothing has been reported, and I'm sure all of the men were alert and watching as you ordered."

"Someone has talked," said Magnus. "One of your men has obviously betrayed us."

"Sir, I don't think that—"

"You don't think! You don't need to think. I'll do the thinking here, Captain. You do as I say. Now, how many of your men knew about the lockbox? And how many of those men also knew where Rallian was being held?"

"A fair number knew about the box. It wasn't, well, we didn't really keep it a secret."

"And?"

"Very few of the guards know anything about the prince. No more than a dozen know which room he was being held in."

"Then question those men," Magnus ordered. "At least one of them is a traitor, and I want to know who it is. Find the traitor, Captain. Find him today or there will be a new captain of the black guards by morning."

"As you command," the captain answered.

Alex blinked as the vision faded. He picked up the scrying orb, put it carefully into the box, closed and relocked the box, and then returned it to his magic bag. He thought about what he'd just seen and smiled. Magnus thought there was a traitor close to him, and he was afraid. Magnus's worries and fears had to be a good thing, but Alex wasn't sure if they would be of any real help.

Pushing his own troubled thoughts to the back of his mind, Alex stretched out on his blankets. A few hours of rest would do him good.

That evening, Alex woke to the smell of cooking food. He sat up and looked around. The other adventurers were all up and moving around, stretching their muscles and working the kinks out of their bodies. Rallian was sitting on the far side of the fire, the look of deep thought still on his face. Alex rolled off his blankets and walked to the campfire.

"We thought it best to let you sleep," said Skeld as Alex sat down on a large rock.

"A kind thought," said Alex. "I'm glad I woke up in time to eat."

"Wait until you taste it before being glad," Cam said with a laugh.

"If you want to take over the cooking duties, you're welcome to," Dain answered, stirring a pot on the fire.

"No, he's not," said Virgil. "I don't want to trust my health to Cam's abilities as a cook."

The adventurers all laughed, and Alex laughed with them. Rallian, however, did not look happy. Alex could tell he was frustrated and unhappy that the adventurers seemed unconcerned and relaxed. He thought he should say something, but Virgil spoke first.

"We should talk about our future," said Virgil.

"Our future, and the future of Nezza," said Alex.

"Whatever else the future holds, I see a lot of walking in the days ahead," said Skeld.

"We can't rush off in just any direction. Not the way things are now," said Dain, starting to dish food onto plates.

"And I think there is more to consider than our simple quest to find Rallian," said Virgil, his eyes fixed on Alex. "You've rescued us from the dungeons and found the goal of our adventure in one day. My company will need to decide how to repay you."

Alex waved away his words. "Things in Nezza are in turmoil right now. If we are not careful, we might walk into a war—or worse. I don't think we need to decide on a course of action tonight. In fact, I think it would be better to decide what we should do and where we should go tomorrow."

"But there is so much to do," Rallian objected. "We must make plans and hurry north to Lord Talbot's castle. Talbot is my father's cousin, a kinsman to me. I should have known he would send help."

"We can decide that in the morning," said Alex in a kind but firm tone. "You have all been through a great deal, and you still need time to heal. It will be easier to decide what to do once everyone is well rested and we've had time to think about our options."

"We need to move now, before my uncle and Magnus can react to our escape," said Rallian. "My uncle will send men in every direction trying to find us, and Magnus has ways of discovering things that I can't explain."

"There will be time in the morning," Alex repeated. "I'm sorry, Rallian, but we can't just run off and hope for the best. We need to be smart. We need to think things through and make the best plans we can. I don't think we should make any decisions about our future until after the midday meal tomorrow."

"As you wish," said Virgil, nodding.

"But . . ." Rallian started and stopped, looking helplessly at Alex.

"I understand your desire to press forward, but I've learned that you often make more progress if you move a little slower and make sure of your path first," said Alex.

Rallian nodded and turned his attention to his plate of food. Alex could see that Rallian wasn't happy, but there was nothing he could do about that. There was more to think about that just going north to Talbot's kingdom. The prince would understand how much more there was to think about soon enough.

Alex had a lot on his mind when he returned to his blankets later that night. Rallian was eager to go north, and it was likely that he would want to return to Karmus as well and expose his uncle as a traitor. Neither idea seemed good to Alex, at least not right now, but he didn't have any better ideas of his own.

Alex thought about Magnus and what his plans might be. He knew he had to face Magnus before he could leave Nezza—face him and defeat him. If he won the battle with Magnus, everything in Nezza might change for the better. If he lost, Nezza would fall into darkness, and everyone living in this land would suffer.

Nezza was in trouble, but Magnus was only one large piece of the problem. The Brotherhood was another piece. What would they do when they learned about Alex? Every kingdom of Nezza seemed ready and willing to go to war over the smallest spark. Nezza needed a true king once more. Everything he had learned, even his own feelings, told Alex that Rallian was the best choice to be king. If Alex really wanted to help the people of Nezza, he would have to help Rallian become the king of Nezza. The trouble was, he wasn't sure if Rallian wanted to be king. Rallian had never made a claim on the kingdom after all. With all these thoughts bouncing around in his mind, Alex let himself drift off to sleep.

As he slept, Alex's dreams took him west, deeper into the red sands of the desert. He moved over the sand in a great rush, as if looking for something he'd lost and could not find. In his dream, he came to a dried-up riverbed and followed it deeper into the desert.

Soon, Alex found himself standing in the middle of a large oasis that was surrounded by many buildings. He looked around, wondering why anyone would build such splendid buildings in the middle of a desert. His eyes came to rest on a massive pyramid at the center of the oasis, and, just before he woke, a name came into his mind.

Chapter Eight
The Empty River

Alex woke long before any of the others. His thoughts were still troubled, but he had a few ideas that might prove useful, including the name that had come to him in his dreams.

Alex was adding wood to the fire when Virgil woke up. He looked better than he had the day before, well rested and with a bit of color in his face. Virgil put away his blankets and walked to the fire. After several minutes of silence, he finally spoke.

"We need to plan," he said. "Of course you must do what you think is best. I hope that you will travel with us, but I would guess that you have plans of your own."

"I have a few plans, but nothing is settled yet," said Alex. "Perhaps we will be able to travel together. Before we make any decisions, I need to speak with Rallian—alone."

"Yes, of course," said Virgil, looking into the fire.

"After breakfast I will ask Rallian to walk with me," said Alex in a casual tone. "I'm sure we won't return until it is time for the midday meal. Then we can discuss what needs to be done."

"You are wise for one so young," said Virgil, looking at Alex.

"I am young," said Alex, "but I have already seen more than many older men. As for wise, we will have to see about that."

Virgil smiled and nodded his understanding. The two of them sat quietly by the fire for several more minutes before anyone else woke up.

"I feel strong enough to battle a troll," said Skeld, as he stretched and walked to the fire.

"But not a three-legged troll," said Alex, remembering his first adventure.

"No, not a three-legged one," said Skeld, laughing. "I'll leave those to you, as you are so good at dealing with them."

"Don't talk nonsense," said Dain, rolling out of his blankets and joining the group by the fire. "Only a madman would willingly fight a three-legged troll."

"Well, I wasn't really willing," said Alex.

"What's that?" Dain asked, stunned. "You fought a three-legged troll?"

"Not by choice. That, however, is a story for another time."

Dain let the matter drop, busying himself with preparing breakfast, but he continued to glance at Alex from time to time as if hoping for the story to be told. Alex was not in the mood to tell stories, and he simply waited by the fire for their breakfast to be ready.

Rallian was the last to wake, and he only began to stir when the sausages and eggs were nearly done. He sat up quickly, looking around in confusion. He looked surprised to be there and a bit lost as well.

"Forgive me," said Rallian, getting to his feet. "I thought that you were all a dream and that I would wake up in the dungeon tower of Karmus once more."

"You don't need to worry about that," said Dain as he bit into a sausage. "We're all real enough, and the breakfast is too. Come and have some before young Tom here eats it all."

Tom couldn't reply because his mouth was too full, but he tried anyway. Tom coughed and spit bits of food, and the rest of the company laughed.

"I don't know much about cooking here in Nezza, so I hope it's to your liking," Dain said, bowing and handing a plate to Rallian.

There was little talk as they ate. Rallian was a bit with-drawn, visibly nervous to be among so many strangers. Alex was thoughtful, considering the plan he had formed in the night. The others seemed to be thinking as well, and even Skeld was unusually quiet.

"Will you walk with me?" Alex asked Rallian, handing his empty plate back to Dain. "We should talk, and I think Virgil and his company would appreciate the chance to talk in private."

"Yes, of course," said Rallian, quickly handing his own plate back to Dain and thanking him.

Alex led Rallian away from the others, moving west toward a high spot that looked out over the desert. He did not speak as they walked, though he noticed that Rallian kept looking at him nervously. When they reached the high spot, Alex stopped and looked out across the red sands.

"The oracle Tempe lives out there somewhere," said Alex, turning his gaze from the desert to Rallian.

"I have heard stories," said Rallian, his own gaze dropping to the ground.

"It would be good to speak with the oracle if we can," Alex said. "Oracles can see many things that men—and even wizards—cannot."

"I have heard that it is dangerous to seek the oracle," said Rallian. "There are many dangers in the desert, and few of my people go there willingly."

"The only danger in visiting an oracle is finding out about yourself," said Alex, turning west. "Oracles see possibilities, and right now it would be good to know what the possibilities are."

"I will go where you lead," said Rallian in a resolute tone.

"So your desire to go north to Lord Talbot as fast as possible has cooled," said Alex.

"The excitement of being free from imprisonment clouded my judgment," said Rallian. "Lord Talbot sent Virgil and the others to find me; I am in his debt. I must go north to thank him for his kindness, but for now I will follow where you lead."

"But I do not lead," said Alex. "I came to Nezza to help my friend Skeld. Virgil is the leader of this group of adventurers, and they came to rescue you."

"Still, I will do as you say," said Rallian, his voice firm.

"You saved me from my uncle and from Magnus. I am your servant and will obey your wishes."

"You are not my servant, Rallian," said Alex. "You owe service to your people, not to me."

"But I must repay my debt to you," Rallian said. "What kind of prince would I be if I did not repay your kindness?"

"A poor one," Alex admitted. "Still, you can best repay me by helping your people. They have suffered much under the rule of your uncle and his servant Magnus."

"Yes, Lazar has never cared about the people. He thinks the people owe him respect and loyalty because he is born of high blood."

"Respect and loyalty must be earned," said Alex. "But I see that you know that already. In my short time here, I have heard stories about you, and I think you would make a good ruler of this land, but it is not my place to say who should rule."

"If not yours, then whose?" Rallian asked, turning to look directly at Alex for the first time.

"Only you can decide if you will be king of Nezza," answered Alex, holding Rallian's gaze. "Only you can decide if the risk is worth the prize."

"Some of the lords of the outer kingdoms have urged me to claim the kingdom," said Rallian. "I have hesitated only because I doubt my own ability to rule."

"All men have doubts," said Alex. "Perhaps you are better suited to be king because of your doubts."

Alex gave Rallian several minutes to think about his words. He watched the prince; he knew how hard it was to overcome self-doubt. In the end, Rallian smiled and nodded to Alex.

Alex returned the smile, then began to explain the plan he had come up with during the night.

———•◦•———

"Telling stories, Skeld?" Alex asked as he and Rallian walked back into the camp a few hours later.

"He was pressed into it," said Virgil, getting to his feet and bowing to Alex.

"Our friends wanted to know more about you," said Skeld. "You don't need to worry; I've left out the best parts."

"Then I fear your storytelling has been long and boring." Alex laughed.

"Long, but not boring," said Virgil. "I appreciate the time and the privacy you granted us, Master Taylor. We have discussed the matter at length, and there is one matter that remains unsettled between us. You have given aid to our company when it was most needed. We are in your debt and would offer you payment for your kindness."

"As you wish," said Alex, bowing to Virgil. "Such payment is customary between adventurers, Rallian. You don't need to look so concerned."

Rallian nodded and took a seat beside the fire.

"Master Taylor," Virgil began, "as leader of this company, I offer you one half of all rewards we may receive for this adventure. Further, though we have not found any treasure yet, I will add one half of any secondary treasure we might gather on this adventure. Lastly, we have decided that each member of this company will make an additional payment to you. These payments will be a private matter between you and each of us. Are these terms acceptable to you?"

"You are most generous," said Alex, bowing to Virgil and the rest of the company. "Perhaps too generous. I cannot accept. Instead, I will ask one quarter of any rewards your company receives for Rallian's rescue, and only an equal share in any secondary treasure gathered. As for any additional payments, I will discuss them with each of you as time permits. Are my terms acceptable to you?"

"Now you are too generous," said Virgil. "You have saved our lives and rescued the prince. Surely, one half of our promised reward is a small thing compared to what we owe you."

Alex looked around at the company. "Very well. I see your minds are made up on this point. I will accept one half of all rewards. But I will insist on only an equal share in any secondary treasure—no more. Anything more, I will discuss with each of you as time allows."

"Agreed," said Virgil, looking relieved.

"I told you he would try to get out of it," Skeld said to Virgil.

Alex hadn't really expected to make any money on this adventure because he hadn't signed an adventurer's bargain or agreed to follow Virgil as the company's leader. He was only here because Skeld had needed his help. Now he was deeply involved in a new adventure—an adventure that none of his new friends were aware of.

"Prince Rallian," Virgil said, turning to face the prince. "We were hired by Lord Talbot to search for you. He and some of the other lords of the north wanted to know if you were still alive. I believe our duty now is to take you to Lord Talbot."

"I see," said Rallian thoughtfully. "And if I choose not to go north to Lord Talbot at this time?"

"We will not force you to travel with us," said Virgil, his eyes moving from the prince to Alex and back again. "We only ask that you accompany us. If you wish to go elsewhere, we will do what we can to assist you."

"Master Taylor has advised me to seek Tempe the oracle," said Rallian. "I think his advice is good. As he will also be traveling in that direction, I would ask that you and your company join us in our visit to the oracle. Once that is done, I will be in a better position to decide my future."

"Master Taylor is wise," said Virgil. "We will travel with you to the oracle. If, after your visit, you wish to go north to Lord Talbot, we will be happy to accompany you there. If you wish to go some other way, then we will do all that we can for you."

"You are most kind," said Rallian, bowing.

With their plans made, Dain began cooking their midday meal. Alex took a seat beside Skeld, intending to ask him what stories he'd been telling. He didn't get a chance because the rest of the group started asking him questions about his first adventure as soon as he sat down. As it turned out, Skeld had told the majority of the story but had left out a great many details. Alex found himself retelling the story almost from the beginning.

When it was almost time for their evening meal, Alex had only gotten as far as the bandit attack that he and his friends had faced in Vargland. He was starting to lose his voice and said he would have to finish the story another time. Normally, it wouldn't have taken so long to tell the story, but everybody kept interrupting and asking him questions.

"You have met elves, then?" Rallian questioned, a look of wonder on his face. "They are real and live in other lands?"

"Yes," said Alex. "Are there no elves in Nezza?"

"We only have stories of them," said Rallian. "But like many things here, they are stories for children. They say the elves live in the mountains of the far north and in the far west, beyond the desert. I've always hoped the stories were true, but I've never heard of anyone seeing an elf in Nezza."

"Elves are hard to see unless they wish to be seen," Dain said. "With all the wars in Nezza, I am not surprised that no one has seen an elf for many a long year."

"There is little magic of any kind in Nezza," said Alex.

"True enough," said Skeld. "It took us more than a week to summon the geeb we sent to you."

"And he would not return when I asked him to," said Alex.

They all fell silent for a time, waiting for Dain to finish cooking their meal.

"You look troubled, Alex," Virgil said once Dain began handing out plates of food.

"I am," Alex admitted. "There is little information about Tempe, and I'm not sure how we should start looking for her."

"I can help you with that," said Virgil. "I once knew an adventurer who claimed to have met Tempe. He said there was a river flowing into the desert, and if a person followed the river, he would find Tempe."

"Did he say how far into the desert the river flowed?" Alex questioned, remembering his dream from the night before.

"He did not, but as long as there is a river to follow, we should be fine," said Virgil.

"True, but rivers that flow into deserts do not always flow out again. With all the trouble Lazar and Magnus have been making, the river may no longer flow into the desert at all."

"But the riverbed would still be there," said Virgil. "That at least would be a guide."

"Perhaps," Alex agreed. "I just wish we had more information."

Alex could see that his own troubled thoughts were now bouncing around Virgil's mind. The *Adventurer's Handbook* didn't say much about Tempe and nothing at all about a river running into the desert. In fact, the book advised people looking for Tempe to take plenty of water with them. It was possible that the adventurer Virgil knew had never even been to Nezza, so looking for a river flowing into the desert might be a complete waste of time. Still, Alex had dreamed about the river, and Tempe's name had come to him before he woke.

The next morning, Alex was the first one awake again. He wandered away from the group and stood looking west. He was taking a chance going into the desert, but he thought the rewards would be worth any risks.

"Where do we start our search?" Virgil asked over breakfast.

"There is a wide valley leading into the desert a few miles

north of here," Alex said, remembering the landscape he had flown over as a raven. "It is as good a place as any to start looking."

"And if there is no river?" Virgil asked.

"Then we will find another way," Alex said with confidence. "I'm sure we'll find a way into the red lands. Whether Tempe will speak to us when we get there, I cannot say."

"You mean she might refuse?" Rallian asked, looking from Alex to Virgil.

"Oracles speak only to those they wish to speak to," said Alex. "But I believe she will speak to us."

"Then let us begin our search," said Virgil, sounding bolder than he looked. "If Alex thinks the oracle will speak to us, I believe that she will."

Once everyone had finished eating and packing, Alex led the group north toward the valley. Virgil and Rallian walked on either side of him.

The valley Alex had seen was actually farther away than he'd thought. By the time they reached the edge of the valley, it was well past midday. Virgil and the rest of his company were nearly worn out, and Dain set about fixing them a hurried meal.

Alex wanted to press on as soon as possible, but he knew he should let his friends rest. He walked toward the edge of the valley alone. It was as if something was calling to him from the desert—a strange voice that he could only feel and not hear. He stood at the edge of the valley and saw what looked like a dried-up riverbed cutting through the red lands.

Something strange caught his eye, and he blinked to make

sure he was seeing clearly. Places along the riverbed were shining in the sun. It looked like there might be some water in the dry riverbed after all, but only in spots. As he watched, the shiny spots seemed to move from place to place.

At the end of the hour, Alex got the others on their feet and pressed forward. He had great hopes that the river he had seen shining in the sun would lead them to the oracle.

The ground between the edge of the valley and the river was crisscrossed with dry gullies and covered with large broken stones. Between the difficult terrain and the weakness of Alex's companions, it was nearly dark before they reached the banks of the river.

"The river is dry," said Cam, his voice dry and raspy.

"Mostly dry anyway," Skeld added as he walked toward a small pool of water. "It can't have been dry for long though, this water is still fresh."

Alex followed Skeld to the pool and examined it. He didn't think it was the same one he'd seen from the hills above the valley. He had seen movement, and, as far as he knew, puddles did not move.

"Strange," Rallian commented as he looked up and down the river. "These pools are fresh, but the rest of the river is dry. I would say the pools were from the rain, but rain is scarce in western Nezza this time of year."

"If it was rain, the rest of the riverbed would not be so dry," said Dain.

"Something's not right here," Alex said as he looked around.

"You sense something?" Virgil asked.

"I do," said Alex.

Alex didn't know how to explain what he was thinking and feeling to his companions, so he chose not to speak at all. He stood watching the dry river as Dain cooked their evening meal and the others made camp. Alex felt like he was waiting for something, but he didn't know what it could be.

After the meal, Alex returned to watching the river, trying to understand what he was feeling. Something was going to happen, he was sure of it. There was magic at work here, but he couldn't put his finger on what it was or why it was here.

"You should rest," Rallian said to Alex as the rest of the company were rolling into their blankets. "You have done more than any of us. Surely you need rest more than we do."

"I am fine," said Alex. "But I've forgotten—I'm carrying your blankets."

"The others have provided," said Rallian with a slight bow. "You are distracted, and they have been most kind."

"Then rest, my friend," said Alex without looking away from the riverbed. "Our journey may be a long one, and you will need all of your strength."

The empty river filled Alex's mind. For a moment, he thought he must have been falling asleep, because he thought he saw water flowing in the river. He blinked and saw only the dry sand.

"Please," said Rallian at last, "you need to rest. Without you, I don't think any of us will see our homes again."

"A sad thought," said Alex, turning away from the river for the first time all evening.

"Perhaps so," Rallian agreed. "But I will feel better if I know you are resting with the rest of us."

"As you wish," said Alex, bowing to Rallian and rejoining the company. "Perhaps sleep will help me find what I am looking for."

Rallian seemed to relax as Alex rolled himself into a blanket.

Alex, however, did not go to sleep. He lay awake for a long time, thinking about his plan to find the oracle. Then he thought about what was happening in Nezza. He also thought about what Magnus might be up to and tried to imagine what he would do if he were Magnus.

Alex jumped up when the noise came. He looked around, trying to determine where the noise was coming from and what it was. Everyone else was sitting up as well, anxious and alert. Alex realized he was hearing the sound of moving water—and it was coming from the river. He ran back to the edge of the river, stopping before he fell into the water.

"But . . . it was dry," said Tom, walking up behind Alex.

"Full enough now," said Dain.

"There is more water here than there should be," said Rallian. "The western rivers are always low this time of year."

"Where would so much water come from?" Skeld asked.

"There is both more and less water here than there should be," said Alex.

"More *and* less?" Virgil questioned. "How is that possible?"

It was a moonless night. Alex conjured several balls of bright white light so they could see the river better. The river looked almost ready to flood. For several minutes, they all stood watching the water rush by, unsure of what to do next.

Finally, Alex sent his weir lights dashing back and forth across the river, then upstream and down again. He wanted to know how much water was really in the river. This was old magic, and he didn't think Magnus had anything to do with it.

As suddenly as the noise of rushing water had started, it stopped. There was no sound at all and no water in the river beside them. Once again Alex sent his weir lights dashing about, but the riverbed looked as dry as it had when they'd first arrived.

"This cannot be," said Rallian.

"Some evil magic," said Cam. "Magnus has done something to the water so it only flows in spots."

"Magic, yes, but I don't think Magnus has anything to do with this," said Alex, calling the weir lights back to him. "Now I understand the shining I saw before. The river flows in some places, and the water reflects the sunlight. But the magic is like nothing I've ever seen before."

"Why would anyone try to dry up a river?" Skeld asked.

"Perhaps to keep people from following it," Virgil answered before Alex could. "If someone thought this river led to the oracle, they might want to discourage people from following it. It would be difficult to guard the entire river, so Lazar had Magnus dry it up."

"This is not a matter to take lightly," said Rallian. "Dark magic is at work here. We should leave this place as soon as possible."

"Calm yourself," said Alex. "We have nothing to fear. This is old magic, very old. This is not the work of Magnus."

"Perhaps not, but I would be happier if the river were either all dry or all wet," Rallian answered.

"I think all wet would be best," said Alex.

The rest of the company laughed slightly at Alex's words but stopped when Alex stretched out his staff toward the river. He spoke softly, his mind focused on the river in front of him. He paused, calling up the power of the dragon to help him break this spell. After a moment, he struck the dry riverbed with the foot of his staff and commanded, "Flow free" in a loud voice.

There was a gurgling sound where Alex had struck the sand, and water appeared. Alex pushed his magic outward, knowing that it would have to move along the entire length of the river.

Suddenly a warning from his O'Gash shouted in his mind: *Wait! There is something more behind this!*

It was too late. Alex's body tightened like a wire, every muscle pulling into knots and holding him in place. His muscles were so tight he couldn't even make a sound. The water spread out across the sand, filling the empty riverbed. Alex remained motionless. For a moment, the waters of the river stood perfectly still, and then they started to move. The cramps that had seized him relaxed as soon as the water moved. He staggered slightly, catching himself with his staff before he fell. The sound of the river hid the gasp that escaped Alex, but not the cry of pain that came from Rallian.

"Prince Rallian?" said Virgil.

"I'm all right, just . . . just give me a second," Rallian answered. He was on his knees, trying to get back to his feet.

Virgil and Skeld stood on either side of the prince, helping him to stand.

"What happened?" Alex asked. His own body felt weak.

"I . . . I'm not sure," said Rallian. "For a moment, when the water started to flow, well . . ."

"You cried out in pain and collapsed," said Skeld when Rallian didn't continue.

"A few moments of pain," said Rallian. "It felt as if every muscle in my body was about to tear itself apart. I'm fine now, I think."

"Aye, we'll all be sore and stiff before morning," said Dain. "Especially if you're not used to all this walking. Cramps can often take you with no warning at all."

"Yes, that must be it," said Rallian.

Alex wasn't so sure. There was some connection between the magic he had just broken and Rallian. He understood why he had felt the pain—he was the one breaking the magic—but why had Rallian also felt pain?

"Your magic is powerful," said Cam in an awed voice, looking at the river.

"It was a strange spell—not what I expected," said Alex, his eyes still on Rallian.

"Freeing the river from its curse and letting it flow freely again is a noble deed," said Skeld.

"When the desert river flows, and the eastern wind blows," Rallian recited softly.

"What was that?" Alex asked.

"Nothing," said Rallian. "Just an old story that has no meaning."

"There is always meaning in old stories, even if we have forgotten them," said Alex, more to himself than to anyone else.

"I think we should all try to get some sleep," said Virgil. "Tomorrow we enter the red lands of Nezza, and we will need all our strength."

CHAPTER NINE
THE RED LANDS

The next morning, Alex woke to the sounds of Dain cooking. While breaking the spell on the river had not been difficult, it had taken a great deal of power. Alex moved slowly as he rolled out of his blankets, worried that the cramps from the night before would return. There had been some other magic at work, something tied to the curse on the river, something very old. His O'Gash had tried to warn him, but the warning had come too late.

The smell of cooking bacon reached Alex's nose, making his stomach rumble. He pulled his boots on with care, testing his body as he moved. The other magic had been set loose when he'd set the river free. It had caused him pain, and it had also hurt Rallian. There was some link between that magic and Rallian, he was sure of that, but now he could find no trace of that magic.

"So we've found the river that flows into the desert," said Virgil. "Now we must see how far into the desert it flows."

"Perhaps not," said Alex, moving toward the campfire. "Tempe may not live at the end of the river but somewhere along its banks."

"I hope it is not too far," Cam commented. "Even with a river close by, the desert is a hard place to travel."

"A little sun will do you good," said Skeld. "Our time in captivity has left you as white as a lily."

"Speaking of lilies," said Alex. "How is it that your wife, Lilly, let you go on this adventure? You haven't been married long enough for her to grow tired of you already."

"I told you, Virgil is Lilly's cousin," said Skeld. "He's the one who talked her into letting me come along."

"And I am glad that I did," said Virgil. "If Skeld had not called on you for assistance, we would still be guests in Lazar's dungeon."

"And I would be bored at home," said Alex.

"Better to be bored at home than in the dungeons of Karmus," Dain observed, handing Alex a plate full of food.

"He wasn't in the dungeons for long, was he," said Tom.

"And neither were we, once Master Taylor arrived," Cam added.

"Please," Alex said. "I am happy I could help. I am pleased you are all recovering from your imprisonment, but please, call me Alex."

"Don't be too hard on them," said Skeld with a smile. "Few adventurers ever get to travel with a wizard."

"And fewer still call them by their first names," Virgil added, putting his blankets back into his magic bag. "I suppose we should make a start as soon as everyone is finished eating."

"The red lands of Nezza," said Cam thoughtfully. "I have heard stories about these lands, even in my far-off home."

"Then you have heard more than most," said Dain.

"I know a few stories," said Rallian, a nervous note in his voice.

"Stories to fear?" Skeld asked.

"I would guess that Rallian's stories are less than accurate," said Alex. "It seems that most stories in Nezza have been told to keep people from knowing the truth."

"I'll not deny that," Rallian admitted. "Our stories say that all wizards are evil and all magic is black, but I can see that those stories are not true."

"Well, whatever stories there are, we will have time to hear them as we travel," said Virgil.

Once they all had finished breakfast, Virgil led the group along the riverbank and into the red lands. Alex walked beside Rallian, watching the young prince. He could see how nervous Rallian was and admired him for moving forward without complaining. He thought Rallian would make a good king, but it was not up to him to decide who would be the king of Nezza.

They walked all day, stopping now and then to rest. Cam told them some of the stories he'd heard about the red lands as they walked. The best ones were about the fabulous wealth hidden in the western desert, hidden treasures that were protected by some kind of monster.

"Our stories speak of the different monsters that live in the desert," Rallian commented after Cam finished his story.

"I wonder if any of them are true," Tom said, excited. "It would be good to collect some treasure while we're here."

"What good is treasure if you don't get home to spend it?" said Dain, his eyes scanning the desert.

"Always looking at the bright side." Skeld laughed, giving Dain a friendly push.

When the sun started to sink in front of them, they found a sheltered spot near the river to camp for the night. The land they had been walking through was a desert, but it was not the sandy wasteland that Alex had expected. There were many trees growing along the river, and their green leaves stood out brightly against the red rocks that covered most of the ground.

"Not much of a path," Dain observed as he cooked their evening meal. "You would think the path to an oracle would be in better condition."

"I've seen no sign of a real path all day," said Tom. "Perhaps this is not the river we should be following."

"Tempe may be well known, but not because a lot of people speak with her," said Alex. "She is known for the things she has done."

"What things?" Rallian asked.

"She once named the ruler of the three lands," Virgil replied when Alex remained silent. "Most people who have spoken to her do not talk about the experience. Perhaps she is best known for what people don't say."

"Mystery is always a friend of oracles," said Dain.

"What kind of things will Tempe tell us?" Rallian asked.

"What an oracle says to a person is for that person alone," Cam answered.

Rallian frowned and then began to ask more questions. Alex smiled as he remembered the first time he had spoken to an oracle. He had spoken to Iownan, the Oracle of the White Tower in Vargland, one of the best known oracles in all the known lands. He hoped that Tempe would be as kind as Iownan had been.

The next morning, they continued to follow the river into the desert. The sand dunes now came down to the river's edge on its far side. The sand near the water was bloodred, and it looked as if the desert was trying to get a drink from the river.

"How long do you think we have before Lazar comes looking for us?" Virgil questioned as he walked beside Alex.

"I'm sure he is already looking for us," said Alex. "I suspect he will look east first, thinking we will try to get to the arch and escape from Nezza."

"East first, but then what?" Virgil questioned. "He knows this river leads to the oracle. He might send men to prevent our going this way."

"Then he has already failed," said Alex. "I doubt that Lazar will send too many soldiers this way in any case. We are outside of his kingdom here and sending soldiers here will cause trouble."

Their second day in the desert ended, and the rocky valley walls had almost disappeared. The sand dunes were set well back from the water's edge, kept away by large rocks. It looked as if the river had washed the sand away, leaving only a wide path of bare rock that the company could walk on. There were no longer any trees along the river, only a few small bushes.

"No wood for a fire," Cam commented, sitting on a nearby rock.

"It will get cold tonight," Skeld added. "The desert may be hot in the daytime, but the nights will be cold."

"We should have brought some wood with us," said Tom grumpily.

"Why didn't you say so before we left the wood behind?" Cam asked, also sounding grumpy.

"A cold dinner, then," said Dain.

"Not at all," said Alex. "What good is a wizard if he can't provide a cooking fire from time to time?"

Alex moved to where Dain was taking food out of his bag. He found a low spot between two large rocks and conjured up a bright yellow fire. Dain looked skeptical, as if a magical fire could not possibly cook their food. Alex laughed at the dwarf's suspicious look and sat down next to the fire.

"A useful bit of magic," said Dain, still eyeing the fire.

"Hot meals are always better than cold ones." Skeld laughed, winking at Alex.

Alex let the fire continue to burn long after their meal was cooked. Even when everyone began rolling themselves into their blankets, Alex continued to sit by the fire. He moved his hand slightly, and the flames became smaller. He didn't feel tired, and his mind was still puzzling over what had really happened when he'd broken the curse on the river. The other magic had always been there, waiting for someone to break the curse, but why?

"You should rest," Rallian said, looking over the fire at Alex.

"You worry too much," said Alex.

Rallian didn't reply but lay down and closed his eyes.

Alex knew that Rallian was still unsure of wizards and magic, but he couldn't do anything to change that. After thinking things over once more and finding no answers, Alex pulled out his own blankets and rolled into them. Skeld was right: it was going to be a cold night.

Alex let his magical fire go out, and as its light vanished, the night sky came alive. Alex didn't think he had ever seen so many stars. He lay awake, looking up at the sky and taking note of where the brightest stars shined. It would be good to know the night sky of Nezza in case they had to travel at night. With Lazar hunting them, there was a good chance of that happening.

When Alex finally fell asleep, he dreamed about the desert around him. The sand was soft and warm, not hot and scratchy like real sand would be. He moved through the sand effortlessly, gliding gently over the dunes and sometimes diving into them like they were water. It was a wonderful feeling, and at first Alex didn't realize what shape he had taken in his dream. When he came to the river in his dream, he saw his reflection in the water. He was a giant snake, brightly colored with bands of red, yellow, and black around his huge body.

Alex looked across the desert of his dreams. Dark clouds filled the sky of Nezza, and in the distance, he could see flashes of light. Even being so far away from the lightning he could still feel it, like a thousand tiny sparks running through him. His massive snake body twitched nervously, and unexpected fear flooded into him. Danger was moving toward him, and he wasn't sure that the deep sand of the desert would be enough to protect him from the storm.

Virgil's voice broke into Alex's dream. "He's gone! Wandered off or lured away."

"Who's gone?" Alex asked, rubbing his eyes and getting to his feet.

"Rallian," answered Virgil. "Gone in the night from the looks of it. His tracks lead into the desert."

Alex looked to where Rallian had been sleeping. The blankets were still there, but Rallian was not. Without saying anything, Alex ran toward the red sand dunes. He could hear Virgil and the others following him, but his mind was focused on Rallian and the storm in his dreams. Tracks led up the dunes, and Alex charged toward them as fear gripped his heart.

The dune was difficult to climb; the sand shifted under his feet, making him slide back down the dune and pulling him away from his goal. Gasping for air as he reached the top of the dune, Alex's eyes automatically followed the tracks Rallian had left in the desert sand.

Not far from the bottom of the dune, Rallian stood as if he'd been turned into a statue. In front of Rallian was a huge snake, its head raised slightly off the sand. It almost looked like the snake was talking to Rallian, but Alex could see that Rallian was too terrified to speak or even to run away.

"Hold!" Alex yelled, rushing down the dune, his staff held out in front of him.

Alex was concentrating on the snake, but Virgil and the others must have thought he was yelling at them because they stopped at the top of the dune and did not follow.

Half running, half sliding through the sand, Alex prepared to freeze the giant snake if it moved to attack Rallian. The snake turned its head to look at Alex, and at that moment, Alex stumbled in the sand. He tried to get his feet under him but discovered that there was nothing there. The sand dune had been hollowed out, and as Alex fell into the empty space, he realized it was a trap.

Desperately, Alex tried to move forward, away from the dune. Sand was all around him, falling into the empty space with him, and he knew that if he didn't do something fast, he would be buried alive. A jarring pain hit him, and his legs folded as he hit solid ground. Instantly he pushed off with all the strength he had, leaping free of the trap. He landed face-down in the sand and immediately tried to roll away from the dune.

When he opened his eyes, all Alex could see was dusty sunlight. He tried to get up but found that he was buried up to his waist in sand.

Rallian was still standing where he had been, but the snake had vanished. Twisting as far to one side as he could, Alex saw that Virgil and the other adventurers were still standing at the top of the dune with stunned looks on their faces.

"Rallian," Alex called. "Come and help me."

Rallian turned toward him slowly—he looked confused and lost—and then he moved a few yards toward Alex.

"Rallian, I need your help," Alex said, working on digging himself out of the sand. It was nearly impossible for Alex to move the sand and free himself because every time he pushed some of the sand away, more of it slid down the slope to cover him.

"What . . . what happened?" Rallian asked as he dropped to his knees and started pushing sand away from Alex.

"It was the serpent," said Alex.

"What serpent?"

"I'll explain later. Help me get out of this sand."

Rallian worked fast, and together they managed to clear away most of the sand. Then Alex felt something that turned his blood cold. A vibration traveled through the sand, a vibration that told him something was moving nearby. Twisting to look back at the dune, Alex could see the sand was moving above him, and more sand was sliding down the side of the dune toward him.

Virgil, Skeld, and Dain ran down the side of the dune toward Alex and Rallian while Cam and Tom remained at the crest of the dune, scanning the desert. When the dune shook again, the three would-be rescuers stopped in their tracks. Alex realized what was coming. He managed to pull his staff free of the sand and let loose a bolt of lightning that struck the dune about halfway between himself and Virgil.

The sand glowed white-orange where the lightning bolt struck, and Alex gritted his teeth as the electric charge danced through the sand and his buried legs. The giant snake under the sand must have felt the shock as well, because it almost jumped out of the dune. Its body slithered between Cam and Tom, sending them tumbling down the far side of the dune. At the same time, a wave of loose sand came crashing down on Virgil, Skeld, and Dain, sending them tumbling head over heels down the dune.

"Get your company together on this side of the dune," Alex yelled at Virgil.

Rallian was digging near one of Alex's legs while Alex scanned the dunes for any sign of the serpent. Virgil managed to get back to his feet and was yelling for Tom and Cam. He got his feet under him and started back up the dune. Skeld followed Virgil, and Dain ran to help Rallian free Alex. The serpent had vanished again, but Alex was sure it hadn't gone far.

It took less than a minute for Dain and Rallian to pull Alex free of the sand, but it felt longer to Alex. He saw that Virgil was almost at the top of the dune, but he froze when a bone-chilling scream filled the air. Tom came flying over the top of the dune as if he'd been tossed by a giant. He almost knocked Virgil down as he landed and rolled through the sand. The serpent appeared right behind Tom, and, to Alex's horror, Cam was clamped in the serpent's jaws.

"Cam!" Virgil yelled, rushing forward to attack the snake.

Virgil's attack was pointless. The serpent dove back into the dune, vanishing from sight and taking Cam with it. For a second, Alex was dumbstruck, unsure of what to do or how to do it. Virgil appeared to be lost in rage and confusion as well. It was Skeld who took control.

"Virgil, to me," Skeld yelled, dragging Tom to his feet.

The three adventurers stumbled down the sandy slope, and Alex, Dain, and Rallian met them a few yards from the base of the dune. Alex held his staff up, ready for another attack. He sent his magic out, searching for the serpent and Cam, even though he knew there was nothing at all he could do for Cam.

"A difficult creature to get hold of," said Virgil.

"Are you sure you want to get ahold of it?" Alex asked.

"We could retreat to the river," said Skeld. "This serpent cannot hide so well in the stones near the river."

"Could we get back over this dune without being attacked?" Virgil asked.

"I don't understand how we got here," said Rallian. "Why are we in the desert at all?"

"The serpent enchanted you," Alex answered. "It used magic to lure you out into the sand, knowing that the rest of us would follow."

"A magical enemy, then," said Virgil. "How do you suggest we deal with this, Alex?"

"We force the serpent out of its hiding place," Alex answered. He made a gesture, and a small cloud appeared over the company, a cloud that looked like a hand. Closing his eyes for a moment, Alex finished his first bit of magic, then lifted his staff.

"You might want to cover your eyes," he said.

Alex let his magic loose. A massive bolt of lightning shot from the head of his staff, striking the sand behind the company. Another lightning bolt flew to the left side of the company, and a third to the right side. Alex continued to blast the desert with lightning, and after seven or eight bolts had struck, he felt a vibration under his feet. He let another bolt loose, this time directly in the middle of the company.

"Careful with those," Skeld shouted.

"Be happy you have your boots on," Alex shouted back, shuffling his own bare feet in the sand.

The giant snake exploded out of the sand in front of them, forcing them to close their eyes and put their hands up to keep the sand out of their faces. Then the serpent raced for a dune that was fifty yards away and dove into the sand like it was water.

Alex pushed out his right hand, and the cloud he'd created slammed like a meteor into the sand where the serpent had vanished.

Alex closed his eyes in concentration as his magic raced after the snake. He probed the air in front of him with his right hand as though looking for something, and then he closed his hand into a fist. Slowly Alex drew his hand back, and, when his hand reached his chest, the sand in front of the company grew into a mound. Rallian and the adventurers all moved behind Alex, their eyes looking from the growing mound to Alex and back again. Finally, the sand slipped away and the massive serpent appeared, its head held in Alex's ghostly fist.

"By the ancients!" said Virgil.

"I've never . . ." Skeld started.

"Speak," Alex commanded the snake. "Speak if you have anything to say."

"I speak only to curse you," hissed the snake in a language that Alex not only recognized but could understand. He had heard this language twice before, both times from the mouths of dragons.

"You would curse me for defending myself and my friends? Your curses have no power, and if they are all you have, then I will silence you forever."

"Perhaps, but you will pay for my destruction," the serpent answered. "My masters will crush you, wizard. Your power is nothing compared to the power of the . . ."

"The power of what?" Alex asked.

"The power of my master," said the snake.

"First you say masters, and now you say master," said Alex. "I think your rage has betrayed you. You were going to say the power of the Brotherhood, weren't you?"

"I know nothing of a Brotherhood," hissed the snake. "Kill me if you will—I cannot stop you."

Alex twisted his closed fist, forcing the serpent to look directly at him. "First you must show me all that you have done."

"Never!" screamed the serpent.

"Never?" Alex repeated. "Then I will ask you one question. If you answer true, I will kill you quickly. Lie to me and you will suffer a slow and painful death."

"What is your question?"

"The young lords of Nezza—the seven who have vanished—were they sent to you?"

"Yes, they were given to me," the snake answered. "If you are looking for a king to rule this land, your plans have failed. There will be no true king in Nezza now, wizard."

"Rallian still lives," said Alex. "Why did you not kill him when you had the chance?"

The serpent did not answer, and Alex didn't expect it to. Closing his eyes, Alex clenched his fist as tightly as he could. He could hear the serpent thrashing in the sand in front of him, trying to break free of his magic. A loud cracking snap filled the air as the serpent's neck broke in the grip of Alex's cloudlike hand. Alex opened his fist, wiped his hand on his pants, and then waved away the magical cloud he had created. He turned away from the dead serpent and started back toward the river.

Later, as Alex and his friends ate their breakfast by the river, Rallian told them how the serpent had called him into the desert. To Rallian it had all seemed like a dream, at least until he had woken up face-to-face with the giant snake. Nobody said anything about what Alex had done to the snake, which Alex was grateful for.

"Two members of my company dead, and our adventure not yet near its end," said Virgil, glancing at Alex. "I must have been a fool to accept this adventure."

"It was my plan that brought you into the desert," said Alex. "I should have thought things through more carefully."

"Stop that, both of you," Dain interrupted. "You'll forgive me if I'm out of place, Virgil, Master Taylor, but it's no good you two blaming yourselves for what's happened. Adventures are dangerous at the best of times, and from what I've seen of Nezza, these are not the best of times."

"Dain's right," said Skeld. "We all know the risks. We don't talk about it, we try not to even think about it, but we all know what might happen."

Virgil and Alex exchanged a glance and then nodded. Alex knew his friends were right. Adventures were dangerous, people got killed, and there was nothing he could do about it.

Alex was troubled, however, because Virgil and the others looked to him for answers, and he wasn't even part of their company. He didn't want to be in charge, and he didn't want to offend Virgil by acting like he was in charge. What he really wanted was to be part of the company, but that was not possible.

There was something else Alex knew, something he didn't feel ready to share with his friends. Their quest to find Rallian and take him north had become something more important. They were fighting for the future of Nezza, even if they didn't know it. He would have to explain things to them soon, but for now he didn't have the words.

"Another day in the sun and sand, then," said Skeld as they started off after their meal.

"And how many more days before we find what we are looking for?" Tom questioned.

No one offered a reply to Tom's question. None of them knew how long it would take to find Tempe, and it was no use guessing.

Alex walked behind the company as they traveled. He wasn't sure what he wanted or even what he should do. All he knew was that he felt alone, even though he wasn't.

CHAPTER TEN
TEMPE

For two more days, the company followed the river into the desert, and to Alex each day seemed a little longer than the one before. At night he sometimes wondered why and how he had been chosen to save Nezza from evil and to find a true king for the land. Surely there were other wizards who could do a better job. Wizards with more knowledge, more experience—wizards who actually looked like wizards.

Alex knew he was young to be a wizard, and he was painfully aware that he looked even younger than he really was. How could he possibly convince all the kingdoms of Nezza to follow one true king?

Alex had come to find Skeld and help him, and that was done. Virgil and his company had come to find Rallian, and that was done. Alex knew there was more he still had to do, but he didn't know how he could do it. He traveled forward looking for answers, talking little and laughing less as the days passed.

Skeld tried to cheer Alex up, but Alex would only smile at his friend's jokes before returning to his own thoughts. Alex was grateful for Skeld's efforts, but there were too many dark thoughts in his mind for him to remain happy for long.

On the morning of their fifth day in the desert, the company was sitting around the fire that Alex had conjured, eating their breakfast, when a large raven landed on Alex's shoulder. Alex was as surprised by the sudden appearance of the bird as everyone else, and was even more surprised when the raven spoke to him.

"Greetings, young wizard and dragon lord," said the raven in a croaking voice. "Greetings from Tempe, the Oracle of the Red Lands."

"My greetings to Tempe," said Alex, shaking off his surprise.

"Tempe has sent me to answer any questions you might have," the raven continued, "and to say that though you will reach her house by midday, she will greet you this evening."

"Alex," said Skeld suddenly, his eyes wide with wonder. "Can you understand this bird?"

Alex looked around at the others and noticed the amazed—even stunned—looks on their faces. He didn't understand their looks, as the raven seemed to be speaking the common language clearly enough despite being a bird.

"Of course I do," said Alex. "Can't you understand him? He's speaking plainly enough."

"They can't understand me," the raven croaked. "They don't know how to listen properly, so they hear only a raven's rough caws."

Alex turned his attention back to the raven. "What do you mean they don't listen properly?"

"Their minds are tangled with unimportant things. Too busy to listen."

"I see," said Alex. "Tell me, most noble bird, what questions can you answer?"

"Almost any that you have," the raven answered, hopping up and down a few times on Alex's shoulder.

"Well then," said Alex, "why is it that Tempe will not greet us until this evening?"

"She will greet *you* when evening comes," said the raven, cocking its head at Alex. "The others will not be greeted until tomorrow."

"Why is that?" Alex asked.

"The others are not wizards and would not have come this way without you, so she will not greet them until tomorrow."

"I see," said Alex again. "What is your name? How should I address you?"

"I am Stonebill," answered the raven, flapping his wings slightly. "And you are Master Alexander Taylor, wizard, elf friend, dragon slayer, dragon lord, and many other things as well."

"You seem to know a great deal about me, Stonebill," Alex remarked.

"Tempe told me some," said Stonebill, tilting his head. "I can see most of it for myself."

"Then you see more than most," said Alex.

"I do," said Stonebill.

"Alex," Skeld said in a nervous tone, "what does the raven say? How is it that you can speak the language of the bird?"

Alex turned to Skeld, confused. "I'm not. I'm speaking the common tongue."

Skeld shook his head and looked nervous. "Your voice . . . it croaks like the raven's."

"Magic is strange at times," Stonebill said to Alex. "There are few who can talk to birds, and there are many stories and legends about such a gift. Your friends have probably heard stories that ravens are ill omens, but those are only stories."

Alex nodded. "Allow me to explain things to my friends, then you and I will have a long talk as we walk to Tempe's house."

Stonebill did not reply but fluttered down to land on Alex's knee.

Alex explained to his friends that the raven had come from Tempe, and that they would reach her house by midday. That much was easy for the company to understand, but they did not understand why she wouldn't greet them until the next morning, or how Alex could talk with the raven.

"Does the oracle not wish to speak with us?" Tom asked.

"Oracles do as they please," said Dain. "It is not our place to question Tempe."

"But why send a raven and not a geeb?" said Virgil, looking at Stonebill.

"I'm sure it's all right," said Alex in a reassuring tone. "Stonebill said that ravens are not bad omens, so you can stop worrying about that."

"Ravens are respected in Norsland," said Skeld. "Many people offer them shiny objects and other such things that they like as gifts. They hope the ravens will bring luck to their homes."

"They are feared in Barkia," said Tom nervously. "It is said they can cast spells and bring evil on people."

"I don't know about that," said Alex. "I am sure that Stonebill is not here to bring evil on us."

"Ravens are rare and noble creatures," said Rallian suddenly. "There is a raven on the royal seal of Nezza, and there is a story that the first king of Nezza had a raven he could talk to."

"Perhaps he did," said Alex. "We should be on our way. We can discuss ravens and the stories about them when we reach Tempe's house."

The others agreed, but only Skeld, Virgil, and Rallian seemed pleased by the raven's presence. Tom and Dain both continued to look at the bird nervously. Personally, Alex was happy that Stonebill had come. He spent his time talking with the raven as they marched forward.

"Around the next bend we will see Tempe's house," Stonebill said to Alex a few hours later. "It is a fine house."

Alex told the others what Stonebill had said, and they all walked a little faster, wanting to see the house of the oracle. Around the next bend, they came to a high waterfall with steps cut into the red stone beside it. The steps led down to a lush green oasis.

"An unexpected find in these harsh lands," said Virgil, reaching the top of the steps and looking down toward the oasis.

"Not at all what I expected," said Dain, admiring the stonework of the steps and path.

Alex looked down the steps as well, remembering the dream he'd had. Several fine-looking buildings were visible from where they stood, but the most impressive building was the massive red pyramid that stood at the center of the oasis.

As they moved down the steps, Alex felt a familiar tingling in his hands and feet. He smiled, remembering the first time he'd felt it. Back then, he had been on his first adventure and hadn't known anything at all about oracles. It seemed a long time ago, and he now knew a great deal about oracles and their powers.

"The large house to the right has been made ready for you and your friends," said Stonebill in Alex's ear. "There will be food waiting, as well as baths and beds and anything else you might need."

"Tempe is most kind," said Alex.

Alex directed the others to the large house, and as Stonebill had said, everything they could need or want was waiting for them. Alex was a little surprised to not see servants in the house, but Stonebill told him that Tempe's servants were seldom seen. Alex nodded and continued to question the raven about Tempe and her household.

By the time Alex and his companions had finished bathing and eating, the sun was sinking. Stonebill had given Alex directions to a fountain near the pyramid and told him Tempe would meet him there. Then Stonebill flew out the window and vanished into the shadows.

"You should all remain here," said Alex to the rest of the company as he prepared to leave for his meeting with Tempe.

"Is there danger?" Virgil asked.

"No," replied Alex. "Tempe has prepared this house for us, so I think it best that everyone remain close to it."

"As you wish," answered Virgil with a bow.

Alex left, suddenly realizing that while telling the others to remain at the house had been the right thing to say, Virgil should have said it. In fact, Alex felt sure that Virgil *would* have said it, if he hadn't spoken so quickly. Now he worried he had taken away from Virgil's honor.

"You are greatly troubled for one so young," said a soft, kind voice.

Alex looked up in surprise, not realizing that while worrying about speaking out of turn he had already reached the fountain. Tempe was standing beside the fountain. She wasn't at all what Alex had expected. She was short and plump, with a round, happy face and pure white hair. He stopped to look at her for a moment, and then, remembering his manners, he bowed.

"You're not what I expected either," said Tempe, her smile widening as she spoke. "I look so little like your friend Iownan, and even less like your other friend, Katrina."

Tempe laughed as she finished speaking. It was a warm, good-natured laugh, and Alex felt himself relax.

"I know enough to not judge oracles by their looks," said Alex with another bow.

"There's no need to be so formal," said Tempe, waving off Alex's bow. "I may be an oracle, but you are a wizard and a dragon lord. If we can't speak plainly to each other, then to whom can we speak?"

"There is wisdom in what you say, but plain speech can be a dangerous thing."

"You also show wisdom, but I think there is little danger for the two of us," said Tempe. "Come now, let us sit by the fountain and discuss deeper matters."

"Deeper matters?"

"You hide your thoughts well. Some you even hide from yourself," said Tempe, moving to the side of the fountain and sitting down. "Yet in your heart you know these hidden thoughts, even if you doubt them."

"Yes," said Alex, nodding. "I have thought about many things these last few days, and many of those thoughts I've tried to hide."

"I will dig them out for you," said Tempe, motioning for Alex to sit down.

"A simple enough task for an oracle."

"A wizard's mind is no simple thing," said Tempe, her smile fading and her tone serious. "I will try to help you, but in the end, only you know your own mind."

"Help is always welcome," answered Alex, sitting on the edge of the fountain.

"Then I will ask, why do you think you are here?"

"I came with my friend Rallian to seek you out."

"No, not here in the desert—here in Nezza," said Tempe, looking into Alex's eyes.

"I came to help my friend Skeld. He and his companions were in trouble, and I came to help them."

"That is done. Why do you remain?"

"I . . . There is more for me to do here in Nezza. This

land is in danger of falling into darkness. The land needs a true king, and I must confront Magnus of Karmus and try to destroy him."

"Good, you see the bigger picture," Tempe said softly. "Unblock your mind. Share your thoughts and feelings with me."

Alex focused his thoughts, then slowly let his troubles melt from his mind. For a long time there was silence, and then Tempe spoke again.

"You should not doubt your feelings. They are often correct and should be followed."

"But it is not my place to choose the king of Nezza."

"You are a wizard, and in most places that is enough. You are also a dragon lord, and that should be more than enough."

"A young wizard with little experience," said Alex. "How can I choose a king when I know so little about this land?"

"The land of Nezza has chosen him," Tempe said matter-of-factly. "If this land has also chosen you to help the king rise to power, then I think it has chosen wisely."

"Perhaps," Alex allowed. "But, wizard or not, I am still young."

"Age does not matter. You are a wizard and so must do those things that only a wizard can do."

"It will be difficult, even dangerous, for my friends."

"They have paid a high price already, and that price may grow larger still. Everything of worth is difficult. Your friends know why they are here. They have already chosen this danger for themselves."

Alex listened to the water falling in the fountain, pondering what he should do next. Tempe did not interrupt his thoughts, but let him sit in silence.

"I know little of Nezza and its people," Alex said at last, "but I would not force a king on them, even if they need one."

"Then we agree that the prince should be king," said Tempe, understanding what Alex was trying to say.

"Yes. But with things in Nezza as they are, I cannot see how Rallian will win the crown."

"If he can win the crown, it will still be difficult to hold, at least at first," Tempe added. "There will be those who claim to accept him, thinking to betray him later."

"Will you tell him that he is to be king?"

"I will tell him he *can be* king," Tempe answered with a smile. "*Will be* is very definite, and I have not grown so old that I would say something like that."

"Then what path should I take? How should I lead him?"

"Lord Talbot is a good man," said Tempe. "He is honored by all the lords of the outer kingdoms and feared by most of the inner ones. If he will accept Rallian as the true king, the path to the crown will be smoother."

"Then I will take the prince to Lord Talbot," said Alex. "That will make Virgil and his company happy."

"A company that you wish to be a part of?"

"There is a bond between adventurers. I am not a member of this company, and I miss the bond. I feel like an outsider, an outsider that they all look to for answers."

"Get to know them. They all respect you, but they fear you as well. Even your friend Skeld is a little afraid of you."

"Perhaps a little fear is a good thing." Alex laughed.

"Not fear, but perhaps wonder."

"Wonder, then," agreed Alex.

"Now, I must ask you about the curse that fell on you and Rallian when you set the river free," said Tempe. "Have you discovered what it is? Do you understand the price you've paid?"

"The curse that was on the river was not Magnus's doing," said Alex.

"No, it was not," said Tempe. "But you did not answer my questions."

"I had a moment of great pain, as did the prince," Alex answered slowly. "I can find no other trace of the magic, or what it was meant to do."

"The river was cursed many years ago, when the last true king of Nezza left this land. Your pain was part of the pain this land has endured. You felt it because you broke the curse. Rallian felt it because he is of the royal line. The true kings of Nezza are connected to the land. As the king prospers, so does the land. If the land is in pain, the true king will feel it."

"Why was the river cursed?" Alex asked. "Did the magic do something more than just cause pain to Rallian and myself?"

"The river was cursed because I failed," Tempe answered. "The last true king of Nezza came to me, seeking counsel. I warned him about what would happen if he left this land in search of a dream that could never be. He would not listen to my advice, and the river was cursed—broken, just as the kingdom was broken. Now you have removed the curse, and by doing so you have released another magic into this land, a magic that is a danger to all who live here."

"How so?"

"The magic is a spell of remembrance," said Tempe. "The spell that you set free moves across Nezza even now, reminding the people of the past. They will recall old injuries, old hatreds. This magic will make men seek revenge on old enemies, and it will drive all the kingdoms to war."

"But the kingdoms are all at war now," said Alex.

"Not open war," Tempe answered. "They may not work together, and they may attack each other from time to time, but it has been many years since all of the kingdoms of Nezza were openly at war with each other."

"Then I have been a great fool," said Alex. "I have brought a great evil into the land of Nezza."

"Perhaps," Tempe answered. "But this magic will also make the people of this land remember what it was like when there was a true king. They will desire to have a true king again. That is the chance you need to make things right, a way for this great evil to be turned to greater good."

"How?"

"Such unrest will make it easier for Rallian to raise an army. He will surely need an army if he is to win his crown."

"A dangerous game, the making of kings," Alex observed.

"Yes, a dangerous and costly game. A game that we must win," said Tempe.

Alex sat in silence for a time, thinking about the task in front of him. He thought about the army Rallian would need to build and the battles that would have to be fought. He had to help Rallian become the king of Nezza, and at the same time prevent all of Nezza from being destroyed by war.

"One more answer before we part," Tempe said. "The

question you have not asked about Magnus: What are his plans? Is he connected to the Gezbeth, the monster that you and the other wizards hunt?"

"You know about the Gezbeth?" Alex asked in surprise.

"Yes," Tempe answered. "The council of wizards has informed me of their thoughts regarding this greater evil. I believe that this Brotherhood you've discovered is the evil, but you should consider something. In all the years of war, no one kingdom has ever taken control of Nezza. The evil has never taken control of Nezza. It seems that this Gezbeth wants the wars of Nezza to go on and on."

"Yes, I see what you mean," said Alex.

"Magnus has been a part of all this," Tempe went on. "He has worked for years to keep the kingdoms from growing close. He is also responsible for the young lords of the inner kingdoms finding their deaths in the desert sands. Yet the serpent did Rallian no harm."

"Magnus has a plan," said Alex. "I don't know what it is, but I'm sure he has a plan."

"His plans are dark to me as well," said Tempe. "I see no order in what he does, but I fear that you, Rallian, and the adventurers you travel with are now at the center of his plans."

"What can I do?" Alex asked. "How can I protect Rallian and the others?"

"Do what you feel is right," Tempe answered. "That is all anyone can do."

"And the Gezbeth?" Alex asked.

"I believe that the council is wrong in its thoughts," said Tempe. "This idea of the Gezbeth does not hold. Evil does not trust or willingly share power. If many evils in different lands are working together, they do so out of fear or with the hope of gaining greater power. Yet there will be only one master, one that all the others fear and obey. He will not share his true goals with the lesser evils that he uses."

"I agree," said Alex. "But we must fight the lesser evils that we can see. If there is only one head, it is well hidden. We have to destroy the smaller evils and hope to find the head, or perhaps force the head to reveal itself to us."

"We are in agreement, then. Tomorrow I will speak with you again," said Tempe as she got to her feet. "Then you should be on your way. Time has become your enemy, at least for now."

Alex left the fountain behind, but he did not return to the house where his friends were. He walked along the path and stood next to the pool at the bottom of the waterfall. Tempe had given him a lot to think about. For a long time he stood there, and when the stars began to fade, he turned and walked back to his friends.

⋅•⋅

The next morning, the company awoke to find breakfast waiting for them by the fountain. There was little talk as they ate, and Alex could see that his companions were nervous about meeting the oracle. Stonebill arrived while they were eating. The raven stood on the table, talking to Alex and looking around at the others as they ate. When they finished, Stonebill told Alex that Tempe was waiting for them by the pyramid.

"Strange for the oracle to speak with you last night," Skeld said as they walked along the path. "Wizards are normally the last to speak to an oracle."

"Oracles keep their own counsel," said Dain nervously.

"Tempe said she would speak with me again today," said Alex. "*After* she has spoken with all of you."

They reached the open ground in front of the massive pyramid and found Tempe standing at the bottom of a stone stairway. The stairs led part way up the pyramid to a large opening. Tempe smiled as they approached, and bowed slightly to Alex.

"Welcome, dragon lord," said Tempe. "Welcome, Prince Rallian of Karmus, and welcome, noble adventurers. Welcome to the pyramid of the red lands. It has been a long time since any have come this far into the desert."

"We thank you for your greeting and your kindness," said Virgil, bowing to Tempe.

The rest of them bowed when Virgil bowed, and Alex could see how much this pleased Tempe. She looked at all their faces, pausing for a moment on Rallian. Virgil and the others began to shuffle their feet a little, nervous at the long silence.

"Walk with me, Virgil of Norsland," said Tempe at last, holding out her hand.

Virgil stepped forward, taking Tempe's hand and bowing once more. Tempe led him up the side of the pyramid, turning back once they reached the entrance.

"Stonebill will let each of you know when it is your time," she called.

With these final words, Tempe and Virgil disappeared

inside the pyramid. Alex and the others stood watching for a moment before finding a place to sit down to wait.

"She greeted you as dragon lord," Skeld said. "Is it true? Have you become a dragon lord?"

"On my last adventure," said Alex.

"How? Where? You must tell us this story," said Skeld.

"Another time," said Alex. "For now, you should each consider what you will ask the oracle."

"I've never been to such a well-known oracle before," said Tom, his tone both nervous and excited.

"How were you chosen as an adventurer?" Alex asked, glad to steer the conversation away from his becoming a dragon lord.

"An old witch who lived near my home told me," said Tom, embarrassed. "She is a healer, and a finder."

"And something of an oracle, I would guess," said Alex.

"I believe so. She has named other adventurers," said Tom.

"There is no need for shame," said Dain. "Few adventurers are chosen by great oracles. I believe most of us were told by wise women or witches, or perhaps old magicians."

"What is this choosing?" Rallian asked.

"Adventurers do not choose themselves," Alex explained. "Not just anyone can be an adventurer; it is something different and special, so they must be chosen by oracles or by other magical means."

"Do you think I could be an adventurer?" asked Rallian, a hopeful tone in his voice.

"I think you could be," said Alex. "But I also think you are chosen for some other task. We should wait and see what the oracle has to say."

Rallian seemed a bit dejected, but he quickly shook it off. He asked the others how they had been chosen.

"A stone mage," said Dain, looking proud. "That's not to say he was a wizard. A stone mage has power over rocks and earth. They are much honored in the dwarf realms."

They went around the group, each one telling how they had been chosen and joking with each other as they went. In the end, Rallian looked at Alex.

"And how were you chosen?" Rallian asked.

"I was chosen without knowing it," said Alex. "I saw a sign in a window and asked about it. I knew nothing about adventures or magic or oracles, but suddenly I was on an adventure."

"Stop that," said Tom suddenly, and they all looked around at him.

Stonebill was pecking at Tom's shoe and squawking at him. Tom was trying to get up and pull his shoe away from the raven at the same time, and he wasn't able to manage either.

"He says it is your turn," said Alex.

Tom stood up nervously and tried to smile at the rest of them. He climbed the stone steps and soon disappeared inside the pyramid.

"Where is Virgil?" Rallian asked, sounding as nervous as Tom had looked.

"It is customary not to rejoin your company until all have spoken to the oracle," Skeld answered. "We will see him this afternoon."

There was little talking while they each waited for their own turn to speak with the oracle. Rallian asked a few more questions, but the answers always seemed too short to satisfy him.

Soon, only Alex and Rallian were left waiting. Alex watched Rallian, and it was obvious that Rallian was extremely nervous.

"You have nothing to fear," said Alex, trying to calm the prince.

"Nothing and everything," said Rallian without looking at Alex.

"It is pointless to worry," Alex said. "What will come will come, and when it comes we must face it."

"I feel a great weight settling on me," said Rallian, his tone sad and troubled.

"Truth can be a burden."

"Perhaps a burden that I cannot carry," said Rallian with a deep sigh.

"You will not have to carry it all at once, and not completely alone. At least not at first," said Alex.

Rallian stared at the ground in front of him. He looked pale and afraid, and Alex wished there was something more he could say. After several minutes of silence, Stonebill told Alex it was time for Rallian to speak to the oracle. Alex nodded and put his hand on Rallian's shoulder.

"The oracle is ready for you," Alex said softly.

"Then I must go, though I fear I go to my doom," said Rallian.

Alex watched as Rallian slowly stood and made his way forward. It clearly took all the willpower and determination Rallian had to climb the steps and enter the pyramid.

"He is brave," Stonebill commented to Alex once Rallian

was gone. "He knows nothing of oracles but the lies he's been told since he was a child, and still he goes."

"He trusts," said Alex. "It is difficult for him to let go of what he thought he knew, but he trusts what I and the others have told him. I can understand his fear."

After fifteen or twenty minutes of silence, Stonebill told Alex that it was his time. Alex nodded and climbed the steps. Stonebill remained on his shoulder, and Alex was glad to have the company.

Alex followed the passage into the pyramid, which soon opened into a large, well-lit chamber. A bright beam of sunlight shone down from the top of the room, falling on a single silver chair where Tempe was seated.

"Last and greatest," said Tempe as Alex approached.

"A humble servant," said Alex.

"Humble, but no servant."

"Did Rallian accept what you told him?"

"Reluctantly. He fears what becoming king will cost him."

"And will it cost as much as he thinks?"

"Far less, I hope," said Tempe. "Now, what can I tell you that you do not already know?"

"You answered most of my questions last night," said Alex.

"There is a question you have forgotten," said Tempe. "It is a question you have waited a long time to answer."

"What question is that?"

"What is the ring?" Tempe said with a smile.

"Yes, the ring I won on my first adventure," said Alex, a light coming on in his head. "Iownan said that she could not tell me what it was but that I should keep it safe and never wear it."

"Show me this ring," said Tempe, leaning forward in her chair.

Alex took the ring out of his shirt pocket, where he'd put it days before. He'd known that he wouldn't be carrying his magic bag when he talked to the oracle but had forgotten about the ring with everything else that was going on. The ring was pure gold with a large black stone set in it. He had always thought it was beautiful, but he had never discovered anything special or magical about it. Tempe examined the ring for a moment then leaned back in her chair.

"This is the great ring of the kings of Nezza," she said, a look of wonder on her face. "All the true kings of Nezza have worn it. I am surprised that you carry it, and I wonder how it came to be in distant Vargland, where you found it."

"Then this ring belongs to Rallian. I should give it to him before he makes his claim as king," said Alex.

"No, not yet," said Tempe, her eyes fixed on the ring in Alex's hand. "Rallian must first decide if he will make such a claim. If you give him the ring now, it will force him to make his claim. Wait. You will know when the time is right to return it to him."

"You do not wish the kingdom to be forced on Rallian," said Alex. "You think it would be best if he chooses to be king."

"Yes," answered Tempe. "Keep the ring safe for him, or for another, if Rallian chooses not to be king of Nezza."

"Is there another?"

"There is always another," said Tempe with a smile. "Many

may make a claim to be king, and if Rallian chooses not to make a claim, then you may want to look for another before you leave this land."

Alex returned the golden ring to his pocket. He would keep the ring and wait for the right time to return it to Rallian, or to whoever turned out to be the true king of Nezza. He knew he could not force Rallian to be king, though he felt in his heart that Rallian would make a very good king.

"Have I added more worries to your young mind?" Tempe asked in a kindly voice.

"Not worries," said Alex. "Though there always seems to be more to think about. Always something that is unexpected."

"Yes, that is the way of life," said Tempe. "Whenever we think we have it all mapped out, life changes, and the map no longer has any value."

"Even for an oracle?" Alex questioned with a smile.

"Yes," said Tempe. "Even for an oracle."

Alex and Tempe talked about other things for a time. When he finally left, the sun was setting. He stood for several minutes, watching as the sun sank below the red dunes, and then slowly walked back to the house where his friends would be waiting.

CHAPTER ELEVEN
THE FLIGHT NORTH

———◦┼◦———

When Alex returned to his friends, he put away his concerns about the Gezbeth and the Brotherhood. He would keep his eyes open, but mostly he would focus on this land and the work he had to do. He would also remember the ring he carried and look for a time to return it to the rightful king of Nezza.

"You have been a long time with our host," said Virgil as Alex entered the house.

"We had many things to discuss," said Alex. "You all seem to be in better spirits than you were this morning."

"I daresay many cares have been lifted," said Virgil.

"And new ones given," Rallian added.

Rallian looked happier than he had been, but Alex suspected he was still worried about where Tempe's words would lead him. Alex gave him an understanding nod and a smile before turning his attention to the food that was laid out for them. He felt more like part of the group now. It was as if Tempe's words had lifted a weight from him, or at least lightened the load he had to carry.

"We should leave at first light," said Virgil, looking at Alex for his opinion.

"A wise plan," said Alex. "You will be going north, then?"

"Yes. Rallian has agreed to travel to Lord Talbot's kingdom with us," Virgil answered. "We would be honored if you would travel with us as well. Perhaps we can repay some of the kindness you've shown us."

"I believe that my path lies north as well, and we would be safer traveling together," said Alex.

"Will you come with me to Lord Talbot?" Rallian asked, a hopeful look on his face.

"I will if you wish," said Alex, bowing slightly to Rallian.

"She told you," Rallian said to Alex in a low voice.

"Tempe did not tell me what she said to you, as that would break the trust. She helped me understand what I already knew, and what I already believed to be true."

"Are wizards also oracles, then?" Rallian asked, looking puzzled.

"Wizards see many things others do not," Alex answered. "I am a young wizard, and I don't always understand what I see."

Rallian seemed to accept this answer and turned his attention back to their meal. Virgil began discussing their plans to go north as they ate, and he sounded confident. Personally, Alex worried about what Magnus and the Brotherhood might be doing. Soldiers could make things difficult, especially if there were a lot of them, but Alex didn't think Lazar would risk sending too many men into the nearby kingdoms.

"Lazar will have spies looking for us, even if he won't send soldiers," Virgil said.

"As soon as we are seen near a town or village, word will be on its way to Lazar," said Skeld.

"If we blunder into any group of soldiers, whether they are Lazar's or not, things could get ugly," said Dain, scowling.

"Not if Master Taylor is with us," said Tom, glancing at Alex.

Alex smiled at Tom but did not reply.

"If we are careful, we can avoid any soldiers, and most, if not all, of the spies," said Skeld.

"It will be dangerous, no doubt," said Virgil, holding up his hand for the others to remain silent. "We will travel north and face what dangers there are as we go."

With Virgil's final words, the discussion was over, and the conversation slowly turned to happier topics and stories of past adventures and dangers. Alex listened to their stories, interested in finding out more about his companions. Rallian sat apart from the others, and Alex could tell he was thinking about what his future held and not really listening to the stories at all.

The next morning they ate breakfast, which again had appeared without any sign of Tempe's servants. Stonebill flew into the house about halfway through the meal. He fluttered down on Alex's shoulder and told him that Tempe wanted to say good-bye to them all by the fountain. Alex told his companions, and the news seemed to cheer them all.

"A send-off from the oracle is a good omen," said Dain, finishing his bacon quickly.

"A sad parting," Skeld noted. "We have come far and fast to find the oracle, and already we must leave."

"We have an adventure to continue," Virgil said. "We have been a long time getting things done."

"And we would have been longer . . . " Tom started and stopped, glancing at Alex.

Alex could see that Tom was both impressed by him and afraid of him. There was something about Tom that caught his attention, but he couldn't quite put his finger on what it was. His thoughts were interrupted by a small pop and a loud ding.

"A geeb!" said Virgil in surprise.

"A what?" Rallian asked, looking in wonder at the strange creature that had suddenly appeared on the table.

"A bottle-necked geeb," said Virgil. "They are magical creatures used to carry messages."

"I've never seen anything like it," said Rallian.

"I'll explain about geebs as we travel," Alex said to Rallian. Rallian nodded, but his eyes didn't leave the geeb.

"Do you have a message for us?" Virgil asked the geeb.

"Honk," the geeb answered, its head taking the shape of a small horn.

"Do you have a message for me?" Alex asked, pushing his plate away.

"Ding," the geeb answered, its head now taking the shape of a bell.

"May I have it please?" Alex asked.

"Ding, ding, ding," the geeb replied.

"I sent a message to my friend, Whalen Vankin, before I found you," Alex told the others as he accepted the message from the geeb. "I had heard there might be dark magic in Nezza and wondered if Whalen knew anything about it."

"You know Whalen Vankin?" Tom asked, amazed.

"Who is Whalen Vankin?" Rallian asked at almost the same moment.

"Whalen Vankin is possibly the greatest wizard alive," Alex said to Rallian, and then, looking at Tom, he added, "Whalen is my teacher. He's the one who asked me to take my staff."

Alex opened the message the geeb had given him, far too interested in what Whalen might have to say than in answering any more questions.

> *Alex,*
>
> *Something must be going on in Nezza, because I've never had such a hard time finding a geeb to deliver a message.*
>
> *I haven't heard of any dark wizards in Nezza, but so little news comes from there that it is difficult for me to say what's happening there. Be careful in your travels, and try not to let yourself be known. I don't think you'll run into anything you can't handle, but if you need me, I will come.*
>
> *Keep me informed, if you can find any geebs that will deliver a message.*
>
> *Yours in fellowship,*
> *Whalen*

"Well, it seems even Whalen has had trouble sending geebs to Nezza," said Alex, handing the note to Virgil. He turned to the geeb. "Have you been paid?"

"Honk," the geeb answered.

"Can you take a reply back to Whalen Vankin?" Alex asked.

"Ding."

"Here you are, then," said Alex, tossing a small emerald toward the geeb.

The geeb bounced off the table and caught the emerald as it fell through the air, leaving several coins on the table in exchange.

Alex quickly took out his writing things and started his message. He wanted to let Whalen know how things were going and also to pass along the clue he had discovered about the Brotherhood and a person of interest named Gaylan. To make things quicker, Alex magically duplicated the letter he had found in Magnus's room and attached it to his own short note.

"Please take this message to Whalen Vankin," said Alex, handing the envelope to the geeb. "If you require more payment, you can return, or Whalen will provide it."

"Ding," the geeb replied, and then it vanished.

"Amazing," said Rallian, looking at the space where the geeb had been.

"Useful creatures," said Alex, collecting the coins the geeb had left for him. "Now I think we should go say good-bye to Tempe. We have kept her waiting long enough."

With Alex's comment, they all filed out of the house and headed for the fountain where Tempe was waiting.

"And so it is good-bye already," said Tempe. "Though perhaps some of you will return one day."

"We would all hope to return," said Virgil, bowing to Tempe.

"Travel quickly if you can," said Tempe, looking from Virgil to Rallian. "Time may be on your side, if you move quickly enough."

"You have our thanks," said Virgil.

"A word, if I may, Master Taylor," said Tempe.

Alex stepped forward, and Tempe led him to the other side of the fountain.

"I have a favor to ask," she said, a worried look in her eyes.

"How may I be of service?" Alex questioned.

"Well, it's Stonebill," said Tempe. "He wants to travel with you and see a bit of the world. I told him I'd ask you if he might come along."

"A welcome addition," said Alex. "Can you spare him?"

"For as long as he wishes to be gone. And he is useful," Tempe added quickly. "He knows a bit of magic and can speak to most of the animals of Nezza."

"Talents that may come in handy," Alex said thoughtfully.

"I'll warn you now, though," said Tempe, looking concerned. "He may become quite attached to you and beg you to take him with you when you leave Nezza."

"And you think I should not?" Alex asked, puzzled.

"I think you should do what your heart tells you," said Tempe, her smile returning. "I just don't want you to think you have to take him."

"He is welcome to come now, and when I leave Nezza, we will see," said Alex.

"Very well, then, he will catch up with you along the river," said Tempe.

With Alex's agreement to take the raven, Tempe said her

final good-bye to the company. Alex and the others bowed to Tempe and did not rise until she had left. Once she was gone, they turned around and started back toward the river and their adventure.

It was midday when Stonebill caught up to Alex and the others as they marched beside the river. He seemed happy to be there and thanked Alex for taking him along. It seemed to Alex that Rallian was almost as happy that Stonebill would be traveling with them as Stonebill was.

"Ravens are a symbol of the king," said Rallian. "It is a good sign to have so noble a bird with us."

Stonebill, who understood the common language, was pleased to be called a noble bird. So pleased, in fact, that he asked Alex to thank the prince for him and to ask him if he might ride on the prince's shoulder. This request made Rallian happy, and Alex smiled at them both as they walked along the red stone path.

They made better time coming out of the desert than they had going into it. Their speed was improved mostly because Virgil and the others were almost completely healed from their stay in the dungeons of Karmus. But they also wanted to hurry in case Lazar had sent guards to the river in an effort to prevent them from leaving the desert.

Days later, when they were nearing the valley where they'd first entered the desert, Alex sent Stonebill ahead to search for any soldiers that might be there. He suspected that someone would be watching the river and he wanted to know for sure.

"I will find them if they are there," said Stonebill.

"And be careful," Alex added, watching as the raven took flight.

Alex and his companions continued to follow the river, but at a slightly slower pace, stopping several times to talk and plan. They needed to know what was ahead of them and be prepared to face whatever it might be.

As the sun was setting they made camp, but Stonebill did not return. Alex was worried but decided that the raven knew his business and would return as soon as he could.

Virgil suggested that they keep watch that night, and they all agreed that it would be a good idea. Virgil refused to allow Alex or Rallian to draw a watch, insisting that it was his company's duty. Alex accepted Virgil's decision, but Rallian seemed unhappy about it. He wanted to do his share, and his desire to do his part impressed Alex.

As the others were climbing under their blankets, Alex remained by the fire. He didn't feel tired, and his worries about Stonebill lingered at the back of his mind. Dain, who had drawn the first watch, sat beside Alex in silence, and together they watched the flames of the fire die to glowing embers.

The flutter of wings startled Alex from his thoughts as Stonebill landed on his knee. The fire was almost out, and Dain had been replaced by Tom.

"What word?" Alex asked Stonebill.

"A dozen men are camped on the north side of the river, just at the edge of the desert," reported Stonebill. "They seem unhappy with their post and are not watchful."

"Any others?"

"A second group, maybe twenty men, is riding east along

the river," answered Stonebill. "They are miles away from the desert and should not trouble us in crossing the river."

"The men at the edge of the desert—do they have horses?" Alex asked, considering the landscape and how far they had to travel.

"They do," said Stonebill. "The horses are tied a short distance from the camp but are not guarded."

Alex remained silent for several minutes, thinking about what to do. He could see Tom's sleepy face in the dim glow of the dying fire.

"Are you too tired for another flight?" Alex asked Stonebill, who was still perched on his knee.

"Not tired at all," said Stonebill.

"Then I think you and I should see about getting us some transportation," said Alex.

"And the others?" Stonebill asked.

"Let them sleep for now," said Alex. "Skeld drew the second to last watch. When his watch is near its end, he can wake the others."

"If the word gets passed to him," said Stonebill, cocking his head and looking at Tom, who was almost asleep by the fire.

Alex quickly explained to Tom what he wanted the rest of the company to do, and Tom, in spite of his sleepiness, nodded as Alex stood to leave.

"Remember," Alex said softly as he walked away. He was sure Tom would try to remember everything, but the simple spell would make sure that he did.

Moving along the river was difficult in the darkness, but

Alex only walked a short distance. He paused beside the river to clear his mind and then changed himself into a raven. It wasn't long before he could see the too-large campfire of the soldiers, and he flew toward it. Gliding down in the darkness a short distance away from the camp, Alex returned once more to his true form.

"They are fools," Stonebill said, fluttering back to Alex's shoulder. "They build up the fire and talk too loudly."

"That is good for us," said Alex. "Are they all still awake, or only a few of them?"

"Three are awake. The rest are sleeping upstream from the fire."

"Can you get to their horses unnoticed?" Alex asked.

"Easily, why?"

"Go to the horses and tell them I am coming," Alex instructed. "If they are willing to go with us, I promise they will be well cared for."

"I think they will go with us," said Stonebill. "These soldiers do not care for their horses as they should, and I don't think the horses have any love for them."

"Very well," said Alex. "I'll be along as soon as I put the soldiers into an enchanted sleep."

"I will wait with the horses," said Stonebill, and he disappeared into the darkness.

Alex crept forward in the darkness, making his way toward the camp. He had only moved fifty or sixty yards along the riverbank when the sound of voices reached his ears.

"How long we gonna be here anyway?" said one voice.

"'Til the captain sends word," a second voice replied.

"A waste of time," said a third man. "Our real enemy is to the east."

"That's true enough," the first man answered. "With the river flowing again, I'd say old Magnus is up to somethin'."

"That's old woman's talk," the second man retorted. "Ain't no such thing as magic, not in this land in any case."

"The river's running again, ain't it?" a third voice said. "Lot of stories about this broken river. Might be some truth in some of them stories."

"If you ask me, old Magnus is behind it all," said the first man, a nervous tone to his voice. "Him and Lazar are up to something, and we'd do more good in the east than we'll ever do here."

Alex moved closer to the fire, and just as the second man started to speak once more, he put a sleeping spell on all three of them. He stepped into the firelight, checking to make sure that all the guards were fast asleep. With that done, he cast a second spell to make sure none of the soldiers would wake until well after the sun came up.

"That didn't take long," said Stonebill as Alex approached the spot where the horses were tied up.

"The magic was simple enough to work," said Alex. "What about the horses? Are they willing to go with us?"

"They are happy for the change," answered Stonebill.

Alex nodded and started saddling the horse nearest to him. He would ride this horse and lead the others to his friends. He felt bad about leaving the soldiers with no horses, but he didn't want word of missing horses to get to Magnus for as long as possible. With luck, he and his companions would be well north of the river before any news reached Magnus at all.

Alex swung into his saddle and turned to ride east along the river, leading eleven horses behind him. He rode for a mile or two and found a spot near the river where the bank was low. He climbed off the horse and looked at the sky. The others wouldn't be here for several hours, even if they moved as quickly as they could. He let the horses wander freely and graze on the short grass while he found a comfortable place to sit down.

"Should I go and make sure they are coming?" Stonebill asked when it was getting close to the end of Skeld's watch.

"There is time," said Alex, lying back and looking up at the stars.

"But if the message wasn't passed on," Stonebill pressed.

"It was," said Alex, stretching out. "But if you are worried, you can go check."

Stonebill didn't reply, but after several minutes of silence, he flew off into the darkness. Alex knew that Tom would pass the word on, and he also knew that Skeld would not wait until the end of his watch to get everyone moving. Skeld's efficiency was a good thing. The sooner they all got here, the sooner they would be riding north toward Lord Talbot.

Stonebill returned just ahead of the rest of the company. He reported that he had first checked that Virgil and the others were on their way, and then he had flown east to check on the other group of soldiers he had seen.

"They are miles away," reported Stonebill, sounding tired.

"You should rest," said Alex, getting to his feet. "We will need your eyes along the road."

Stonebill perched on Alex's saddle and folded his wings. Alex walked down to the river, looking into the darkness, trying to see his friends. He could hear them moving along the riverbank, but the stars were not bright enough for him to see much. To help the others find him, he conjured up several small weir lights and sent them floating across the water.

"Such lights might be spotted," said Virgil in a worried tone as Alex helped him out of the river.

"The soldiers near the desert are asleep," said Alex. "The others are miles away."

"Once again we are in your debt," said Virgil, looking at the horses and saddles that Alex had brought with him.

"We must travel as fast as we can, and this seemed the best way," said Alex. "I would have woken you, but I didn't see any point in waking you up just so you could wait."

"Wise and kind," said Skeld, patting Alex's shoulder.

The horses were saddled in no time, and the company was ready to go. Alex led the six extra horses behind him and rode at the back of the company with Tom at his side. Virgil led the company into the darkness, moving with caution as they climbed out of the valley and into the open lands beyond.

By the time they stopped for breakfast, they were at least ten miles away from the river. As the others ate their meal, Stonebill flew ahead, looking for more soldiers or anything else that might slow their travel. When Stonebill returned, saying there was nothing to be seen for miles, they rode on.

So they went north and east, stopping only for meals and to

rest at night. Stonebill kept them well informed of anything or anyone along their path, so they managed to avoid being seen without any trouble. The land changed little as they traveled. It was mostly open, with only small clusters of trees to break up the rolling grasslands. It was a pleasant ride, and if Alex hadn't been worried about their situation and what Magnus might be up to, he would have enjoyed it a great deal more.

CHAPTER TWELVE
THOMAS THE HEALER

After they had ridden north and east for almost three weeks, the landscape began to change. Rolling hills grew into tall mountains to the north, and the open, grass-covered fields changed to dark pine forests. As they rode toward the forests, Rallian was happier than Alex had ever seen him.

"Lord Talbot's lands begin on the other side of these mountains," said Rallian. "Lazar would not dare send his soldiers there. At least not until he was ready for open war."

"But Lazar's soldiers may guard the paths over the mountains," said Virgil. "What we need is a way across the mountains that Lazar does not know about."

"If he has any brains at all, he will know about every path there is," Dain said, spitting on the ground.

"There is an old path that he may not know," said Rallian, a look of deep thought on his face. "My father told me about it when I was young. He once pointed out the peaks that the path led through."

"If your father knew, Lazar would know as well, wouldn't he?" Virgil asked.

"Lazar has never traveled much," said Rallian. "My father told me that my uncle always preferred to stay in Karmus, close to the seat of power."

"But your father did not believe that Karmus was the seat of power," said Alex.

"My father was wise. He knew that a king's power came from the people he ruled," said Rallian, a touch of pride in his voice. "He knew that no true king would make slaves of his own people or put unneeded taxes on them for his own gain."

"You have learned well from your father," said Alex. "If you can remember where the path is, we may be able to slip into Talbot's kingdom without Lazar knowing about it."

"East," said Rallian, looking toward the mountains. "The path should run along that large round mountain to our east, though finding the beginning of the path may be a problem."

"We will find it if it is there," said Virgil, bowing to Rallian.

They rode east, staying just outside of the pine forests as they went. They had to move slower because the ground was more uneven and many small streams flowed out of the mountains. Rallian rode in front beside Virgil, which pleased Alex. He thought it was a good sign that Rallian was learning to take command, and a better sign that he knew when to let Virgil make decisions. Stonebill continued his habit of flying ahead of the company to see what he could, and it was on one of his flights that he discovered the path Rallian had spoken of.

"The path begins inside the trees," Stonebill told Alex. "There is no one guarding the beginning of the path, and I saw no one along it as far as the round mountain."

Alex told the others what Stonebill had seen, and Rallian

was obviously pleased that his memory had served him so well. With Stonebill's information and guidance, it didn't take them long to find the path.

"We should rest here," said Virgil, looking from Rallian to Alex. "The climb over the mountains will be a hard one, and both horses and men need rest."

"It will take several days to cross the mountains this far west," said Rallian. "And even after we are over them, it will take at least ten or twelve more days to reach Lord Talbot's castle."

"Rest now, and an early start tomorrow would be best, then," said Alex, looking around at the pine forest.

"You are troubled by the forest?" Virgil asked, following Alex's gaze.

"Remembering troubles past," said Alex. "I think we are safe enough, at least for now."

Virgil and the other adventurers set up camp. That night as they ate, Rallian told them stories of his childhood. His father had often taken him on journeys to other kingdoms, hoping to teach him about all the lands of Nezza. Rallian always spoke of his father with great respect and pride, while also sounding sorry that his father was not here with them.

"What can you tell us about Lord Talbot?" Alex asked Rallian after the prince had finished his stories.

"A great deal," said Rallian. "I can tell you about his family history and about the land he rules. I know that he has three children, that his wife died years ago, and that he has never remarried. What is it that you would like to know?"

"I'm not sure," said Alex. "I just thought it would be good to know something about him before we reach his lands."

"You think that he might be like Lazar," said Rallian, frowning.

"No," said Alex. "I'm not sure what to think."

"I told you he is a noble lord," said Rallian. "He sent Virgil and this company to rescue me. My father trusted him, so I'm sure that I can trust him as well."

"Then I will accept your belief and hope for the best," said Alex.

"Your concerns are well-founded, but I also believe that we can trust Lord Talbot," said Virgil. "He did set up our adventure after all."

"How did he set it up?" Alex asked. "I'm sure he didn't send a geeb to Mr. Clutter's shop."

"No, not a geeb," Virgil said. "He sent some of his people to Telous, just before Lord Bray put his soldiers all around the great arch. The men Talbot sent didn't understand how adventures were arranged for, but Utmar Samuelson was able to explain things to them. I met with them when I accepted the position as leader for this adventure."

"Utmar Samuelson?" Alex asked.

"He's a traveling adventure salesman that I know," said Virgil. "Not so well-known as Clutter, and he often takes on clients that don't really understand how adventures work."

"Not the normal way things are done," said Dain, shaking his head.

"No, not exactly normal," Virgil agreed. "But they seemed

like honest men, and I could tell they needed help. It was their sincerity that convinced me to accept this adventure."

"Then I hope that Lord Talbot is as sincere as the men you met," said Skeld with a smile. "But I wonder sometimes if you are not too kindhearted, Virgil."

"I have wondered that myself," said Tom, grinning at Skeld. "After all, he chose you to join this adventure."

"And a lucky thing I did," Virgil interrupted. "If not for Skeld's friendship with Alex, this adventure would have come to a sad end weeks ago."

The talk around the fire soon died down. When the others rolled themselves in their blankets to sleep, Alex remained beside the fire. His body was tired, but his mind was busy with thoughts and ideas. Dain smiled at him from beside the fire but remained silent, a sign of his respect, and possibly fear.

Alex let his thoughts wander, not really focusing on any single idea that came into his head. After a while, he felt his mind drifting and the fire in front of him seemed dimmer, which was a little odd. He looked at his friends, sleeping in their warm blankets, and for a moment he focused on Tom's face. Tom was smiling in his sleep, remembering some happy time, or so Alex thought.

The change happened in an instant. Alex knew he was still sitting beside the fire looking at Tom's face, but now his mind was someplace else. He was standing on a pleasant gray-green hill, a warm light shining from behind him. At the bottom of the hill was a low stone wall, and beyond the wall the land was in shadows. He had been here before, but then he had a reason, now he didn't know why he was here.

Looking around, Alex saw Tom standing a short distance away. He was looking down at the wall and at the shadowlands beyond it. Alex realized he was in Tom's dream and not really near the land of shadows or the wall between life and death.

"Tom," said Alex, walking up beside his friend.

"Yes," said Tom, his eyes fixed on the wall.

"Why are you here, Tom?" Alex asked.

"The oracle said I would find my answer in my oldest dream," said Tom in a quiet voice. "This is the oldest dream I can remember, so I'm looking for my answer here."

"Why do you dream about the wall and the shadowlands beyond it?"

"I used to dream myself here so I could talk to my brother on the other side of the wall," said Tom.

"An older brother?"

"He died when I was six," said Tom. "I thought the world would end, but it didn't."

"How did your brother die?" Alex asked, his gaze turning from Tom to the wall below them.

"He was sick for a long time," said Tom, his voice choked with emotion. "A healer came, but he couldn't help. When my father asked him to call Richard back from the wall, the healer would not. It was the only time I've ever seen my father cry."

"Do you think the healer was wrong?"

"I did at first," said Tom, his eyes dropping to look at the ground. "But in my dreams, Richard told me that it was his time to cross the wall, and the healer would not have been able to call him back, even if he'd tried."

"You doubt what your brother said?"

"It was only a dream. It was what I wanted to hear, even if it wasn't true."

"And is this only a dream?"

"Yes," said Tom, looking at Alex for the first time. "You are only here because I am dreaming you here."

"You think dreams are not real, then," said Alex.

"They are not," answered Tom, looking back to the wall.

"Come," said Alex. "I have your answer, and it is not wise to stay in this place for too long, even in dreams." Alex reached out and touched Tom's shoulder. There was a moment of darkness, and then he was sitting by the fire again.

Tom's eyes opened slightly, but he did not wake up.

"Sleep," Alex said in a soft voice.

The next morning, Alex woke early, his mind clouded from his own dreams. He put his things away and sat by the fire, watching Tom. He knew what Tom had asked Tempe, and he also knew the answer to Tom's question. But how could he let Tom know that he knew?

Dain woke next and started building up the fire and preparing their breakfast. Virgil took Rallian to check on the horses, and Skeld got up slowly and went to look for water. Tom remained in his blankets, rolling over to get a little more sleep before breakfast was ready.

When Tom woke up, he sat down next to the fire but didn't look at Alex. "I dreamed of you," he said in a quiet voice. "You came into my dreams last night and asked me questions."

"Yes," said Alex. "And do you still think dreams are not real?"

"How did you know?" asked Tom, looking up in surprise.

"Because I was there, looking at the wall with you."

"But it was only a dream," Tom protested.

"Dreams are often more than they seem to be," said Alex.

"Then you know the answer to my question?" Tom asked hopefully.

"The answer, and the question. Your question was harder to find than the answer, but I know both."

"Will you tell me the answer?" Tom asked, a desperate look on his face.

"Are you sure you want to know?" Alex asked. "Answers are not always what we hope for, and having questions that are not answered is not always a bad thing."

"Tell me, please," Tom begged.

"Very well," said Alex, taking a deep breath and looking into Tom's face. "You do have some magical ability, but your magic is not what you think. You will not be a wizard. You will not follow the path of so-called greater magic."

"I had hoped," Tom began, then broke off.

"You have two gifts, Tom," said Alex. "You have the gift of healing, and you have some magic as well."

"A healer? Me? But how? I know nothing of the healing arts."

"But you know how to get to the wall," said Alex. "Not many can go there and return, even in their dreams."

"But—"

"You have a gift for healing," repeated Alex, his voice serious. "And some power as well. If you wish to use this gift, it must be trained. I know something of healing, and if you wish, I will teach you what I know while we travel together."

"Would you?" Tom asked, a hopeful tone returning to his voice. "I mean, I would like to learn. Can you teach me—" Tom started and then paused. "Can you teach me to go to the wall?"

"Yes, I can," said Alex. "But only when you are ready for that knowledge."

"Yes," Tom agreed, nodding. "If you will teach me, I will do all that you say."

"I am not a master healer, but perhaps, when this adventure is over, I can help find you a teacher who knows more than I do."

"Would you?" Tom asked, sounding both grateful and pleased.

"If Virgil agrees," Alex promised. "Now, for your first lesson. You must let Virgil and the others know that you have these gifts."

"But I'm not trained," Tom protested.

"A gift, even an untrained one, is often of value," said Alex with a smile. "And Virgil must agree before I can teach you, as he is your leader on this adventure."

"As you wish," said Tom, bowing to Alex.

"What are you two whispering about?" Dain questioned, breaking eggs into a large frying pan.

"Tom has something to say," answered Alex. "Something that the entire company should hear."

"Then it had better wait 'til after breakfast," Dain said, looking from Alex to Tom.

The others soon returned to camp, and Alex watched as Tom approached Virgil and whispered something to him.

Virgil nodded, then sat down and accepted his breakfast from Dain. While they ate, Alex could see both Tom's excitement and worry growing. Tom ate very little, and he looked almost relieved when Virgil stood up to address the company.

"A moment, before we begin our day's journey," said Virgil. "Young Tom has an announcement."

"Not tired of the adventure already?" Skeld joked, but he stopped laughing as soon as he saw the look on Alex's face.

"I must tell you all that I have a gift," Tom began, nervously looking at the ground. "Two gifts, I should say. I did not know what they were until this morning, when Master Taylor explained things to me."

"And what gifts do you have?" Virgil asked, his voice kind and encouraging.

"Master Taylor tells me I have the gift of healing," said Tom, still looking at his feet. "And that I have some magic as well."

"A great gift," said Virgil, looking at Alex for confirmation. Alex nodded but said nothing.

"Master Taylor has offered to train me as a healer, if you will agree to it," Tom added.

"It is not a little thing that you ask," said Virgil. "To be trained as a healer is to take great responsibility. If Master Taylor is willing, however, I have no objections to your being trained."

Tom looked up for the first time since he'd begun to speak, a wide smile on his face. Virgil, Skeld, and Dain were all smiling as well.

"Another moment, if you please," said Alex, getting to his

feet. "If I am to teach Tom the art of healing, I must take his oath now. I would ask you all to be witnesses."

"As you wish," Virgil answered for the group.

"Thomas Aquil," Alex began, holding Tom's gaze with his own. "You have the gift of healing and desire to be trained. I have agreed to be your first teacher, so I am your finder. As such, my honor will be linked to yours. As your honor grows, so will mine. If you ever use your gift for evil, your honor—and mine—will be diminished. If you diminish my honor, I will call you to account. Do accept this linking of our honors?"

"I accept," said Tom. "I will do as you teach me to do, and use my gift only for good."

"Then I ask all here to witness," Alex said. "Thomas Aquil has accepted the linking of our honors. Will you all witness?"

"We will witness," four voices answered. Rallian spoke slowly but firmly.

"So be it," said Alex, holding out his hand toward Tom. "Take my hand in friendship and as a brother healer."

Tom moved forward and took Alex's hand, bowing to him as he did so. Alex smiled and returned Tom's bow.

"Well then, Thomas the healer it shall be," said Virgil, slapping Tom on the back. "A fine gift for any adventurer to have."

"And a fine teacher to learn from," added Skeld, winking at Alex.

"And a lot to learn," said Tom.

Virgil, Skeld, Dain, and Rallian all took turns congratulating Tom on his newfound gift.

"Tempe said there was something special about him," Stonebill said in Alex's ear.

"Not to me she didn't," said Alex.

"She knew you would find it when the time was right."

"Did Tempe tell you things about all of us?" Alex asked, looking at the raven on his shoulder.

"A little about all and more about others," said Stonebill. "Some things she told me; others I see for myself."

"Then you can do more than spy out the land and speak to animals?"

"I see things that others do not, as you already know," said Stonebill. "Tempe would say that I am a seer, but I do not understand what she means by that."

Alex continued to ride at the back of the group and lead the extra horses behind him. As they started to climb over the mountains, Tom rode beside him but did not ask any questions. Alex was still considering the best way to start teaching Tom about being a healer. He had never thought about teaching anyone before, and the idea was something he had to get used to. He had learned a great deal about healing on a previous adventure, and he thought he might try to teach Tom the same way that he had learned.

When Virgil stopped them for their midday meal, Alex walked a short distance into the woods. He had decided to give Tom one of his own magic books so Tom could study on his own, but first he needed to make sure there was nothing too dangerous in the book. He had also decided that teaching Tom about plants and their use in healing would be a good place to start.

Alex found a familiar plant as he walked and was happy to see it was in bloom. Picking a few of the flowers, he returned to the group with them in his hand. Tom looked at him expectantly.

"Do you know what these are?" Alex asked, handing the flowers to Tom.

"I've seen them before," said Tom, studying the flowers. "In Barkia they are called sun maids, but I do not know if that is their correct name."

"Sun maids is one name for them, also day stars and midget lilies," said Alex. "Do you know what they might be good for?"

"Apart from being nice to look at, no," answered Tom.

"The flowers can be brewed into a tea," Alex explained. "The tea will relax the mind and give the drinker a feeling of well-being. The leaves and stem of the plant can be chewed to relieve headaches and small pains."

"And the roots of the plant?" Tom asked.

"The roots can be mixed with other things to make a strong sleeping potion," said Alex.

"What other things?" Tom asked quickly.

"In time," said Alex. "For now, study these flowers and the plant they came from. Tonight, I will try to find a book of herb lore for you. I think I have one in my bag that will be useful."

"You are too kind," said Tom.

Alex smiled and turned his attention to the food Dain was preparing. Tom wanted to learn, and that was good. Alex hoped there would be time to teach him. Once Virgil and his company reached Lord Talbot with Rallian, their adventure would be over. Alex knew he had to stay and help Rallian win his crown, but what would Virgil and his company do?

CHAPTER THIRTEEN
THE CASTLE OF LORD TALBOT

The days passed slowly as Alex and his friends made their way along the ancient path over the mountains. It took several days longer than Rallian had thought it would, and the need to hurry was pressing on them. The road was bad, and they were slowed because parts of the road were overgrown or covered by landslides. More than once they had to send Stonebill ahead to find the way for them.

Alex continued to teach Tom about the different plants he found in the forest, and Tom remembered everything that Alex told him. Tom was also learning from the book Alex had given him. The two of them would sit up late into the night, Alex answering Tom's many questions and explaining as much as he could. A few times Alex had to insist that Tom go to sleep because he was afraid that Tom would stay up all night if he let him.

"He learns quickly," Stonebill said to Alex as they were preparing to ride forward one morning.

"Faster than I expected," said Alex, saddling his horse.

"As his knowledge grows, so will his power."

"Do you think that will be a problem?"

"He will want to test himself at the wall," said Stonebill. "He has a great desire to know more about the shadowlands."

"I will not take him there until I'm sure he's ready," said Alex.

"He already knows the way," Stonebill warned. "He may not know that he knows, but just the same, he knows."

"I will be watchful," Alex promised.

Stonebill flew ahead, but Alex continued to think about the raven's words. Tom did know how to get to the wall. It would be dangerous if he went there alone, and chances were high he would not return. Until now, Alex had deliberately not discussed the wall or the shadowlands beyond it. Stonebill's warning, however, made Alex think that he should start talking to Tom about the most dangerous part of being a healer.

As they traveled down the north side of the mountains, the trees of the forest began to change. There were fewer pines and more aspen and birch trees now. Alex noticed the change and knew they were in Lord Talbot's lands. If Rallian was correct, they should reach Talbot's castle in ten days or perhaps two weeks.

"Lord Talbot's castle is very fine," said Rallian in an excited tone. "His kingdom has had fewer wars than most, and far less damage has been done here."

"He has an army, doesn't he?" Virgil asked.

"A large one," said Rallian. "His army is one of the reasons he's had so few wars. None of the outer kingdoms, and few of the inner kingdoms, could raise an army to match Talbot's."

"Then why has Talbot not claimed the kingdom for himself?" Tom asked.

"Talbot is a noble man and would not make such a claim for himself," said Rallian. "He knows he is not the true king of Nezza, so he is content to protect what is his and not make war on his neighbors."

"Then he is wise as well as noble," said Skeld.

The talk of Lord Talbot ended, but Alex could see Virgil still had questions and doubts. Alex also had questions, but he kept them to himself. Lord Talbot might be as noble as Rallian said he was, but would he be willing to give up his power and see someone else crowned king of Nezza? That was a question that only time could answer.

They rode more quickly once they had left the mountains, and their increased speed made Alex happy. He knew that Lazar would not have been idle during these past few weeks, and he would not be likely to surrender to Rallian no matter what happened. It was more likely that he would launch an all-out war now that Rallian had escaped. Where would he start? Would he challenge Talbot? Perhaps he would begin with some of the smaller kingdoms first, building his own strength as he went.

The most important question Alex had was, what was Magnus doing? Alex didn't know what Magnus's plans were, but he was sure they included Rallian. He had kept Rallian as a prisoner instead of killing him. The serpent in the desert had used magic to draw Rallian away but then spared him. Having Rallian alive and well seemed to be important to Magnus, but Alex couldn't guess why.

Alex was glad he had Tom's training to take his mind off his worries. Late one afternoon, when the company had camped near a small pond, Alex started teaching Tom how to focus his magic.

"Try using your magic to hold those floating sticks together, like a raft," Alex instructed.

"I'm not sure how," said Tom.

"Reach out with your thoughts, and let your mind feel the sticks and the water," said Alex. "It might help you focus if you hold out your hand like you are actually touching the sticks."

Tom did as he was told, and after several minutes, the sticks floated together on the smooth water. Tom smiled and let his hand drop. As soon as he stopped concentrating, the sticks drifted apart.

"Keep them together," said Alex. "You can't let your magic stop working like that. If you were trying to heal someone, stopping your magic like that might be fatal."

Tom raised his hand again and pulled the sticks back together. He held them in place on the water, a determined look on his face.

Alex watched for a moment and then tossed a stone into the pond next to Tom's raft of sticks. The raft came apart instantly, the sticks drifting away in different directions.

"That's not fair," Tom complained.

"No, it's not," Alex agreed. "Life is not always fair. When you can hold the raft together even when stones fall around it, you will be ready to use your magic to help others."

Tom accepted what Alex told him and continued to practice with his magic. Learning about plants and how they could be used to heal different sicknesses was easier for Tom than learning to focus his magic was.

"Has anyone ever crossed the wall and returned?" Tom asked.

It was late, and Alex was ending his lesson. Alex had explained how dangerous the wall between life and death was, but he knew that Tom would not truly understand until he stood before the wall in spirit.

"No one that I know of," Alex answered. "The call of the shadowlands is strong on this side of the wall. On the other side, I doubt that anyone could resist the desire to stay."

"How close can you get to the wall?" Tom asked, putting away the book Alex had given him.

"The closer you get to the wall, the stronger your desire to cross it becomes," said Alex. "I have been close, but I would prefer to stay as far away as possible."

Alex could see that Tom's desire to go to the wall was increasing as his understanding grew. He knew that soon, much sooner than he would have guessed, he would have to take Tom there. He would go with him the first time to make sure Tom returned, but then what? What troubled Alex most was that to be a true healer of power, Tom would have to go to the wall alone and return without help. It was a dangerous test, but one that all true healers of power had to pass.

As the days went by, the landscape continued to change, and so did the weather. It had been sunny and dry since Alex had come to Nezza, like a long and pleasant springtime. Now the sky was dark with clouds, and heavy rain fell almost every day. The muddy ground slowed their progress, but they continued north and east, counting the days until they would reach Talbot's castle.

"The rains will continue for the next month or so," said Rallian, sitting beside the fire one night. "Tomorrow we should start to see towns and villages. The roads will improve, and we will reach Lord Talbot's castle the next day."

"A village inn would be most welcome," said Skeld, shaking water from his hair.

"Do we dare stop at an inn?" Dain asked. "Even if Lazar won't send his army north, he will send his spies."

"And Rallian is well-known. It would be difficult for him not to be recognized," added Tom.

"Would Lazar dare tell his spies that they were looking for Rallian?" Alex wondered aloud. "He has let the rumors about Rallian grow. Most people think the prince is either lost on some adventure or dead."

"Which is why Lazar is ruling Karmus," Virgil said. "I don't think spies would be looking for Rallian—only for strangers."

"Which we are," said Dain, lifting his boots to the fire in an attempt to dry them. "If we ride through towns and villages, we will be seen."

"We must pass through the towns and villages to reach Lord Talbot," Rallian said firmly. "Travelers are not uncommon here in the north, and most people pay little attention to them. If we leave the roads and avoid the towns and villages, anyone who sees us will take notice."

"Then we will ride through," said Virgil in a decisive tone. "But we will not stop at any inn or tavern as we go."

The others were disappointed but said nothing, accepting

Virgil's decision. Alex thought it wise not to stop, but he wondered what the people of the towns and villages would think. It seemed obvious to him that Lord Talbot would hear about them long before they reached his castle, and there was no telling how Talbot would react.

The next day, the clouds began to break apart and the sun came out from time to time as they went along. They had not ridden far when they came to a well-traveled road. Rallian thought it was probably the road from Waymar, a city to the southwest.

"If we follow the road to the northeast, we will come to Talbas, where Lord Talbot's castle is," said Rallian.

"It follows open ground," said Skeld, glancing at Virgil.

"We will be easily seen," Dain added unhappily.

"And we'll easily see anyone approaching us," said Virgil, though Alex could see he shared the concerns of the others.

They followed the road, moving much quicker than they had in the open fields. There was little talking as they went. Alex could tell that Virgil and his company were growing more nervous, and Rallian was getting more excited as the day went on. His own thoughts turned to Lord Talbot and what kind of man he was.

"Our time grows short," Tom said to Alex, his voice lowered so the others would not hear. "The adventure we agreed to is almost at its end."

"And you are worried that your training will not be complete," said Alex, looking at Tom.

"I have learned a great deal, but there are many things I do not yet understand," said Tom.

"A few weeks is a short time to train a healer. Already you wish to test yourself at the wall," said Alex flatly—it was not a question.

"A true healer of power can go to the wall," said Tom, glancing at Alex quickly before looking away again.

"And a true healer of power knows better than to rush into danger," said Alex.

"I just thought . . ." Tom began but stopped.

Alex rode along in silence, waiting for Tom to continue, but Tom simply rode beside him, looking at the ground. After several minutes, Alex broke the silence.

"Do you think you are ready for that test?"

"I will do as you say," Tom answered.

"That does not answer my question," said Alex.

"I would like to try," said Tom, his eyes still fixed on the ground.

"Soon," said Alex.

They went on all day, riding through several small villages and one fair-sized town, but not stopping. The local people did not speak to them, but Alex could feel their eyes watching the group's every move.

Virgil finally stopped them for the night near a small stream, setting up their camp next to a grove of large oak trees. Stonebill flew off as it was getting dark, unhappy about their campsite's location and wanting to see what was around them.

Alex felt the same way Stonebill did about their campsite. The trees blocked the view to the north and east, and being so close to the stream put them in a low spot. It would be easy for a company of soldiers to sneak up on them from almost any direction. Alex wasn't too worried about Lazar's soldiers being here, but Talbot's soldiers might be just as dangerous. If they attacked without waiting to find out who Virgil and the others were, their journey might come to a sudden end.

"We can hide under the trees if we must," said Virgil, noting Alex's unhappiness.

"I will not hide," said Rallian defiantly. "Lord Talbot was a friend of my father, he is a kinsman to me, and, from what you've told me, a great friend of mine as well."

"But his soldiers may not recognize you or share his friendship," said Tom.

"And in the darkness, things could get out of hand in a hurry," Skeld added.

"I will not hide," Rallian repeated, and his words ended the discussion.

Stonebill returned just as the company was getting ready to go to sleep. He fluttered down to land on Alex's shoulder, his feathers twitching slightly.

"A large party of soldiers approaches from the north," he reported to Alex. "They are moving quietly and with purpose."

"How many are there?" Alex asked.

"At least fifty," said Stonebill. "Another group of the same size approaches from the south, but they are farther away."

"Do you think they will attack us in the night?"

"I heard them speak of encirclement," Stonebill answered. "I think they mean to capture you. They will not risk a night attack."

Alex nodded and explained to Virgil and the others what Stonebill had seen and heard.

"We cannot fight so many," said Dain. "Even with Alex on our side, it would be a difficult victory."

"We don't need to fight," said Rallian. "These must be Talbot's men, and if they mean to capture us, we should let them. We are going to Talbot's castle anyway, so why not go with them?"

"And if Talbot turns out to be another Lazar?" Skeld asked, voicing a question most of them had thought about.

"Then there is little that fighting will do," said Virgil.

"Alex, what do you think?" Skeld asked.

"We should wait for them to move first," said Alex. "I don't think they will attack us in the night. If they attempt to capture us, then we will have to decide what to do."

"Very well," said Virgil, looking around at the company. "Double watch, and keep the fire burning. We will sleep ready for battle and hope that it is not needed."

They all agreed, though Rallian seemed unhappy about it. It was obvious he trusted Talbot, but then, he had once trusted Lazar as well.

The night passed slowly, and none of them got much sleep. Alex spent most of the night listening and looking into the darkness around the camp. He knew the soldiers were there, even though they'd encircled the camp quietly. They didn't seem to be in any rush to make their presence known, however, and Alex didn't tell the others that the soldiers were waiting in the darkness.

As sunrise approached, the adventurers were all on their feet. They could easily see the soldiers in the dim predawn light, and they weren't happy about what they saw.

"Why do they not announce themselves?" Dain asked, putting on his dwarf helmet and fingering his ax. "Why all of this watching and waiting?"

"Perhaps they have been waiting for better light," said Tom. "They may be under orders to capture us all, and in the darkness some of us could slip away."

"We'll find out soon enough," said Virgil, pointing toward the soldiers. "They seem to be done waiting."

Three soldiers rode forward, each carrying a large banner. Alex looked at the banners with interest and leaned on his staff to wait.

"The banner on the right is for the house of Talbot," Rallian told them. "The banner on the left is that of the true king."

"And the middle banner?" Virgil asked.

"It is the blue-and-white banner of truce," said Rallian. "It means they want to talk to us before any hostilities break out."

"Then we talk," said Virgil, sounding grim. "I will speak for my company, but I cannot speak for you, Prince Rallian, or for you, Alex."

"Then the three of us should all go forward," said Rallian. "It is customary to meet the banner of truce on neutral ground."

Alex nodded and walked forward with Virgil and Rallian. As he walked, he wondered if he should have worn his sword. He had not yet needed it in Nezza, but he had a feeling that he would soon.

The soldiers with the banners stopped and dismounted, waiting for Virgil, Rallian, and Alex to approach before speaking. Virgil looked nervous but firm; Rallian looked happy. Alex tried to look stern, but he felt strangely happy and found it hard not to smile.

"We are the servants of Lord Talbot," the man holding the banner of truce announced. "We wish to know if you are friend or foe to our lord."

"Friends," said Virgil.

"Why do you come?" questioned the man.

"Lord Talbot sent us on a quest," answered Virgil. "We return now, our quest complete."

"You are the adventurers that Lord Talbot hired," the man said, looking past Virgil to the camp. "We were told there were six of you, but I count a dozen horses."

"We have extra horses, taken from those who would hinder us in our quest," said Virgil. "Two of our company have fallen completing our quest. Lord Talbot asked us to find Prince Rallian, and so we have."

"You found the prince?" the man said with surprise.

"I am he," said Rallian, stepping forward. "Prince of Nezza, Lord of Karmus. I have come to speak with your noble lord."

"Your Highness," said the man. All three soldiers bowed. "Lord Talbot will be pleased at your coming. Long has he hoped to see you and speak with you."

"Then we should go forward swiftly to Talbas and to Lord Talbot's castle," said Rallian. "I have much to discuss with your noble lord."

"A moment, Your Highness," said the man. He turned his attention to Alex. "Six adventurers we were told to expect, and you tell me two were lost, so you should be four. Your Highness makes it a happy five. Who is this sixth man?"

"He is my friend," said Rallian before Alex could speak. "He saved me and the adventurers from the dungeons of Karmus. I will vouch for his honor."

"Forgive me, Your Highness, but these are difficult times," said the man. "We must know something of this man, or he cannot continue."

"And what would you know?" Alex asked, taking a step toward the man. "Do you fear that I am Lazar's servant Magnus in some magical disguise? Or perhaps something worse, come from beyond the great arch to destroy all of Nezza and its people?"

"We have heard stories," said the man nervously, looking a little pale. "Word from the south says there is a demon walking in the shape of a man."

"I am no demon," Alex said with a laugh. "I am a wizard, and any word from the south is surely not to be trusted in these times."

"A wizard," the man repeated, looking even more troubled. "We know something of wizards, here in the north."

"Then ask what you will," said Alex. "You have something you would ask me to do—something that will help you to trust me."

"You see much," said the man. "Our stories say that a wizard—a true wizard—cannot lie if he swears by his staff. If you mean no harm to Lord Talbot, then swear by your staff that it is so."

"Your stories are true," said Alex, looking at his staff. "So I swear by my staff that I mean no harm to Lord Talbot or his people. I also swear by my staff that I will see the true king of

Nezza returned to his throne. If your lord will serve the true king, I am his faithful friend. If Lord Talbot fights against the true king, then I am his most deadly enemy."

"Then all is well," answered the man in a shaky voice, bowing deeply. "Come, we will escort you to Talbas and to the castle of Lord Talbot."

Alex walked back to the others with Rallian and Virgil, both of them looking shocked by Alex's comments. Alex was not concerned, because he already knew that Rallian was the true king of Nezza and that he would somehow manage to gain his throne.

"What's it to be, then?" Skeld asked, glancing from Virgil to Alex and back again.

"The soldiers will escort us to Talbas," said Virgil. "Lord Talbot wishes to speak with Rallian and the rest of us."

As quickly as they could, Alex and his friends broke camp and prepared to travel with the soldiers of Lord Talbot. The soldiers waited a short distance away and did not speak with them. Alex thought they were probably under orders not to, but he wondered if perhaps it was some sign of respect that he didn't know about.

They were soon on the road. The sun came out from behind the clouds, driving away the rain and drying the land. Rallian rode in front with Virgil, and Alex rode at the back with Tom. Most of the soldiers fell in line behind them, but about twenty rode in front, holding up the banners of Talbot and the true king for all to see. Alex tried to make out what was on the banner of the true king, but it was too far away and it fluttered in the breeze.

"What did you say to them?" Tom asked, after they had ridden a few miles.

"To the soldiers?" Alex asked.

"Yes—what did you say?"

"I told them I was a wizard and would see the true king returned to his throne," said Alex.

"Was the light around you to prove you were a wizard?" Tom asked.

"Light? What light?"

"When you spoke to them, there was a strange light around you. To me, it seemed that you grew taller, or perhaps they grew smaller."

"Did the others see this light?" Alex asked. He was concerned because he had not noticed any light, and he had not felt any magical change.

"I think they did," said Tom. "They didn't really say, but we all knew when you were talking."

Alex thought for several minutes about what Tom said. This was one more new and unexpected thing to think about, but it did not seem to be a problem. If the soldiers had seen the light, that might be a good thing, but he wasn't sure. The people of Nezza were already indifferent to or afraid of magic. Alex didn't really care about the indifference, but he didn't want to add to anyone's fear.

"Perhaps it happened when I swore by my staff," Alex said at last.

"What do you mean?" Tom asked.

"A true wizard cannot lie if he swears by his staff," Alex

explained. "They asked me to swear by my staff that I meant no harm to Lord Talbot, and so I did."

"But if Talbot fights against Rallian—" Tom began.

"Then they know I will fight against Talbot," said Alex. "I told them I would see the true king back on the throne, and if Talbot fought against the true king, then I would be his most deadly enemy."

"I bet they didn't like that," said Tom with a slight smile.

"They seemed to accept it. I am not worried; I think Lord Talbot will be on Rallian's side."

Every now and then as they traveled, Alex noticed one of his friends glance back at him. Clearly Tom was right, and they had seen some change in him when he'd sworn by his staff, and, just as clearly, they were unsure what to make of it. Alex didn't let their glances bother him because he had more important things on his mind.

"You make a great impression," Stonebill said as he settled once more on Alex's shoulder.

"I was not aware of the change that happened when I spoke to the soldiers," said Alex. "That troubles me."

"When you spoke, your feelings were strong," Stonebill said. "And the power of your feelings came out in your words."

"Then I will need to learn to guard my feelings more closely," said Alex.

"Perhaps," said Stonebill. "Yet the change was a small one, and your words will give Talbot one more reason to side with Rallian."

"I believe Talbot will side with Rallian in any event, and I don't want to make the people of Nezza more afraid of magic. They are already far too fearful."

"They have lived all their lives without knowing the truth about wizards," said Stonebill. "They have only known the evil that Magnus has done."

"Times change," said Alex.

At noon, the soldiers stopped to rest their horses and eat a meal before continuing on. Alex and his companions also ate a hurried meal, but the soldiers continued to keep their distance. Rallian seemed a little troubled by the soldiers' reluctance to approach them, but Virgil actually seemed glad for the separation.

They passed several small villages that afternoon. The people in the villages seemed happy to see the soldiers and would often wave or call out to them as they rode by. It was clear to Alex that at least some of Talbot's soldiers came from these villages and they were being greeted by friends and relatives. There were no waves or calls to Alex and his companions, however, and the villagers would seldom even look at them as they passed.

The sun was well into the western sky when they finally came to the top of a small hill overlooking the city of Talbas and the castle that stood at its center. It was an amazing sight, and not at all what Alex had imagined. A high wall of bloodred stone encircled the city, with large gates facing both north and south. There were many towers along the wall and what appeared to be several smaller gates as well.

The castle itself towered above the city and appeared to be sitting on a small hill, but it was hard to tell from a distance.

The castle looked like it was made of ice, its pure white walls shining brightly in the late-afternoon sun. Flags were flying from all the towers of the castle, and Alex thought it looked like something out of a fairy tale.

The soldier carrying Talbot's banner came riding toward them, a smile on his face.

"Welcome to Talbas," he said as he looked toward the castle. "Lord Talbot has ordered a feast in honor of Prince Rallian's arrival. He will greet you all at the castle gate."

"Our thanks to Lord Talbot," said Rallian. "We are honored by his kindness."

The soldier nodded and rode back to his own men. Alex and his friends followed the soldiers down the hill and toward the main gates of the city. The others all seemed happy with what the soldier had said, but Alex remained thoughtful, wondering just what kind of man Talbot was.

CHAPTER FOURTEEN

LORD TALBOT

lex and his friends followed the soldiers of Lord Talbot to the main gates of Talbas. The road was wide at the city gates, and many people had come out of the city to welcome Prince Rallian. It was a much warmer welcome than they'd had in any of the towns or villages they'd passed through so far, and Alex couldn't help but smile. Rallian waved and smiled at the cheering crowds, clearly happy to be there and unconcerned with what the future might hold.

Alex watched from the back of the group, more cautious than normal, even though he could see that there was little to worry about. He had only met a few of the people of Nezza, but he found it hard to believe that he would be as welcome as the rest of the company—especially when the people learned who and what he was.

"They seem happy to have you all here," said Stonebill as he sat on Alex's shoulder.

"They are happy that Rallian has come," said Alex. "Happy that the adventurers have found success in their quest."

"You think they are not happy to see a wizard," said Stonebill.

"Their tales say that all wizards are evil. Magnus has added to that belief. How can I expect them to be happy to have me here?"

Stonebill didn't reply but changed his position and looked out at the crowd. Alex also looked at the faces of the people as they rode forward. Perhaps it was just his imagination, but he thought, or rather felt, that none of the people dared to look him in the eye.

When they arrived at the gates of the castle, a tall, dark-haired man was waiting to greet them. It was obviously Lord Talbot, and behind him stood two young men who could only be his sons. Alex noticed one of the soldiers talking to Lord Talbot as they approached, and he knew that the soldier was telling his lord there was a wizard in the company.

"Lord Talbot," said Rallian, climbing off his horse and bowing slightly. "My thanks for your kindness and thoughtfulness. I have been told that you sent this fine party of adventurers to rescue me, and for that alone, I am greatly in your debt."

"Prince Rallian," Talbot answered, bowing much lower than Rallian had. "I am pleased that the adventurers did not quest in vain. We feared that you were lost to us and that their quest would be only to bring word of your end."

"Word may never have reached you, if not for my friend Master Taylor," said Rallian, motioning for Alex to come forward. "He rescued these adventurers and me from the dungeons of Karmus."

"Alone?" Talbot asked, surprised.

"He is more than he appears to be," answered Rallian. "He is a wizard of great power."

"A wizard," Talbot repeated, looking Alex in the eye. "That is a tale worth hearing, I would say. Perhaps, as we feast, you will share this tale with us, or better, by the fire after the feast."

"It will be our honor and a pleasure," said Rallian, bowing again.

"Do not bow, my lord," said Talbot. "You are a prince of the noble line, and I am but the lord of an outer kingdom."

"You are modest and kind," said Rallian. "I will remember your kindness to me and hope to reward you for it."

"Your presence is reward enough," said Talbot. "Now, let me introduce my sons to you, as they have also been hoping for your safe arrival."

Talbot motioned for his sons to come forward. As they approached Rallian, they each dropped to one knee before the prince.

"This is Colesum," said Talbot, and one of the two young men stood. "He is my oldest son and heir."

"An honor," said Rallian, bowing his head to Colesum.

"And this is Hathnor," Talbot said as his second son stood. "He is warden of the northern and western reaches."

"Again, the honor is mine," said Rallian, bowing.

"My daughter, Annalynn, should be here to greet you as well," said Talbot. "Forgive her, my prince, she is overseeing the preparations for the feast."

"The loss is mine," said Rallian.

Talbot smiled and then led Rallian and the company into the castle. Soldiers took their horses for them, bowing to each of the adventurers as they did so. Alex could see how pleased

Virgil and his company were with their reception, and once again he felt sad that he was not truly a part of the company.

Rallian and Talbot walked side by side into the castle grounds, followed closely by Colesum and Hathnor. Virgil and his companions followed next, and Alex followed behind them. Stonebill hopped nervously on Alex's shoulder as the crowds cheered for Rallian, but the bird said nothing. It was strange to feel so lonely in such a crowd, and Alex tried to shake off the feeling.

Talbot led the group into a huge hall full of long tables. Hundreds of people were already in the hall, and Alex guessed that these were the lesser lords and landowners of Talbas. Talbot escorted the company to the front of the hall where one long table stood empty. He asked them to sit where they liked, and Alex found himself between Tom and Hathnor.

"By your leave," said Hathnor, bowing to Alex as he was about to sit down.

Alex bowed to Hathnor in reply. It seemed to Alex that the young man was nervous but didn't want anyone to know. After they were all seated, only the chair to Lord Talbot's left remained empty. Alex suspected it was reserved for Annalynn, Lord Talbot's daughter, but she did not appear.

The feast began without ceremony or fanfare. Servants simply began bringing trays of food to the table almost as soon as the guests were seated. Alex saw that Rallian and Talbot were already deep in conversation, and he thought that Rallian must be asking about Lazar and what he might be doing.

"A fine-looking bird," Hathnor said to Alex. "Can he speak?"

"He can speak to me," said Alex. "Though most people cannot understand what he says."

"Most people do not listen," said Hathnor.

"If you know how to listen, perhaps he can speak to you," said Alex.

"I have . . . friends who know how to listen," said Hathnor, his voice lowered slightly. "They try to teach me, but I find it difficult."

"Friends?" Alex repeated, more to himself than Hathnor. He looked at the young man and realized that Hathnor was referring to an elf friend. "Ah, friends in the north, no doubt," Alex said. "Friends of the elder race."

"You know them?" Hathnor asked in surprise. He lowered his voice even more so no one else at the table would hear him.

"I know *of* them," said Alex. "I am an elf friend, though I have not met any of the elves of Nezza—at least not yet."

"Then you must be good, no matter what the stories say about wizards," said Hathnor, a look of joy and wonder on his face. "I only know a few elves, but I cannot believe their people would ever make a friend of an evil wizard."

"I have many friends among the elves, and perhaps I will find more here one day," said Alex.

"If you would like to go to the northern or western reaches, I would be happy to take you," said Hathnor in an excited tone.

"Perhaps, when time allows," said Alex. "Now I fear that time is short, and many things will soon change in Nezza."

"The prince," said Hathnor, looking toward Rallian. "Do you know if he will claim the kingdom?"

"Only Rallian can answer that question. It is not my place to say what he will or will not do."

Hathnor nodded his understanding and turned his attention to the food.

Lord Talbot suddenly stood up as a beautiful young woman walked up beside him. His pride was clear for all to see as he introduced his daughter to Prince Rallian.

Alex returned to his food but watched Annalynn as he ate. Her eyes kept darting from her plate to Rallian, as if drawn there by some magical power. Alex also noticed that Rallian would occasionally glance at her but was careful not to let her see him watching.

When the feast was finished, Talbot led the company to another large room filled with comfortable chairs and benches placed around a large central fire. Alex sat near the fire as several of Talbot's people filed into the room. Tom sat next to him, and Alex could see that Tom's thoughts were far away and not on the feast or the reward that he and his companions had won.

Alex listened as Rallian told his story, most of which Alex had not heard before. Rallian was a good storyteller, and though he did not say it in so many words, it was plain to Alex that Rallian believed Lazar was responsible for his father's death.

By the time Rallian reached the part in the story where Alex had rescued him and the other adventurers, Alex had made up his mind. Lord Talbot was a good man, and his people were honest and true. He could see their respect and admiration for Rallian as he told his story.

"A fine tale," said Talbot as Rallian finished. "May I ask a question or two?"

"As you wish," said Rallian.

"You have told us that Master Taylor rescued you and these fine adventurers from the dungeons of Karmus," said Talbot, glancing at Alex as if worried he might offend him. "May I ask why Master Taylor came? How did he know you were there? Was it lucky chance, or something else?"

All eyes turned to Alex, most showing great interest, some showing fear. Alex thought for a moment and then slowly got to his feet to speak.

"I came because my friend Skeld sent me a message, asking for my help," said Alex, nodding at Skeld. "It was lucky chance that I found Rallian in the tower above the dungeons because I was not looking for him. Having heard something of Magnus before I arrived in Karmus, I thought it best not to leave Rallian behind."

"Lucky for us all, then," said Talbot.

"I know what some of you are thinking," said Rallian, looking at Talbot and then around at the others in the room. "I myself had doubts and fears when I first learned that Master Taylor was a wizard. I have heard the same stories as you all have, and my only experience with magic was with the evil Magnus. But I will tell you all freely that I know Master Taylor is true and good. Twice he has saved me from evil, and I would trust him with my life at any time."

"Well spoken, my lord," said Talbot. "We can see your trust and have heard your tale. Now we should rest and consider all that we have both seen and heard."

Rallian bowed slightly to Talbot, accepting his words. Talbot smiled at the honor and then said good night and left the room.

Servants arrived to lead Alex and his companions to the rooms that had been prepared for them. Rallian and Alex each had a room to themselves, while the others were settled two to a room. Alex thanked the servant that led him to his own room, and then he closed the door and made his way to bed.

———•••———

Alex was up before sunrise the next morning, and he easily found his way to a garden that was planted on the castle's eastern side. He walked between the blooming flowers, pondering the future. Once Rallian made his claim on the kingdom, war was certain. Perhaps the war would be short, but Lazar would not give up without a fight.

"You wake early," Annalynn said, startling Alex out of his thoughts. "You walk as one who is deeply troubled, but you seem too young to know such troubles."

"I know many things," said Alex. "Including the troubles of men."

"And do you know what the people of Talbas think of you?" Annalynn asked, a slight hint of fear and perhaps a challenge in her voice.

Alex smiled, even though Annalynn's directness was surprising.

"They fear me. Magic has always been something dark to them, so they are afraid."

"It is more than fear," Annalynn said. "They think you have enchanted Rallian and will use him for your own purposes."

"And what do you think?" Alex asked.

"I do not know," Annalynn answered. "I know nothing of magic, only that the stories seem larger than reality would allow."

"Magic can be a powerful thing," said Alex. "Even in this land, where it is mostly forgotten."

"So you claim," said Annalynn, a tone of disbelief in her voice.

"You do not believe in magic, then?" Alex asked.

"I believe what I have seen, not what old women say they've heard," answered Annalynn defiantly.

"And you would see some magic before you believe in it," said Alex.

"If you are what you claim to be—if you are a true wizard—prove it," said Annalynn.

"What proof do you ask? What magic could I perform to convince you of what I am?"

"Call back my mother so I can talk with her again," said Annalynn without hesitation.

"Your mother is beyond the wall," said Alex, surprised by Annalynn's request. "No spell of magic can bring back the dead. At most I could call back a shadow of your mother, but it would be dangerous to do so."

"Dangerous to whom?" Annalynn asked.

"To you *and* to me," said Alex. "The living are in the world of light, the dead in the world of shadows. The two worlds should not be mixed."

"Real wizards would not be concerned with danger," said Annalynn, but her voice sounded unsure.

"Real wizards know better than to mix the living and the dead," said Alex. "Real wizards do not willingly harm others or take unneeded risks. Once, not long ago, I faced a wizard that was not afraid of mixing the dead with the living. I was forced to destroy him so the living and the dead could both be free."

"So you say," answered Annalynn, turning to go.

"A moment," said Alex, seeing how unhappy and troubled Annalynn was. "Perhaps a little magic would help you to believe."

As Annalynn turned around, Alex bent down and picked up a rock off the ground. He held the rock tightly in his hand, focusing on the image he could see in Annalynn's mind. For a moment there was no noise at all, no wind, no birds, nothing. The moment passed, and Alex held out his hand to Annalynn. The rock was no longer a rock but a perfect cameo of Annalynn's mother, white on a deep blue background.

Annalynn's hand trembled as she reached out to take the cameo. She looked stunned and unsure as she lifted it from Alex's hand. It seemed that she could not speak, but then she found her voice.

"How . . . how did you know? How did you know what she looked like?"

"I did not," said Alex. "I was the maker, but the image came from you."

Annalynn looked at him as if she wanted to ask another question, but her voice failed her once more.

"Go now," said Alex. "The day brings many things, and already the lords of Talbas are stirring."

Annalynn smiled weakly, and then she ran from the garden clutching the gift he had given her. It was a small thing, but Alex thought that it was needed. Annalynn would be more believing, and perhaps not so quick to judge what a true wizard would and would not do.

Stonebill swept through the garden and landed on Alex's shoulder.

"Where have you been?" Alex asked.

"Looking, listening," said Stonebill. "Rallian will make his claim today, I think, and Talbot and his sons will support his claim."

"One small kingdom among many," said Alex, walking toward the castle. "But it's a start."

Alex met Virgil and his company on their way to breakfast and happily went with them. Rallian and Talbot were not in the great hall, so Colesum sat in his father's chair, presiding over the meal. After they had eaten, Colesum told Virgil that his father had prepared payment for the company and had granted Colesum the honor of overseeing the payment in his father's place.

"You should come with us," Virgil said to Alex as they stood to leave. "Half of the payment is yours, as we all agreed."

"I have no place in this bargain," said Alex. "We will settle later. Besides, you and your company have other things to discuss. You must decide what path you will take, now that your adventure is complete."

"But—" Virgil began but stopped. "As you wish."

Alex left the castle, returning to the garden where he could think. He wandered for a time, trying to relax his mind, but his thoughts always returned to his questions. What now? What next? Who will join Rallian and who will fight against him? What will the Brotherhood do once Rallian makes his claim? Would they interfere at all, or wait and see how the other kingdoms reacted before acting themselves? It was a puzzle with too many missing pieces, and it annoyed him the more he thought about it.

At midday, a servant approached him nervously, asking him to join Talbot and Rallian in the great hall. Alex had known that this request was coming, and he tried to force his own questions out of his mind. Answers would come with time, and his worrying would not make the answers come any sooner.

The great hall was filled with all the nobles of Talbas, some of whom Alex guessed must have arrived just that morning. Rallian was sitting at the high table next to Talbot, and he looked happy but nervous. Alex found a place to stand at the back of the great hall.

"My lords," said Talbot, rising from his seat and speaking loudly. "My lords, hear me. The day that we have all hoped for has arrived."

The crowd grew silent, and all eyes turned toward Rallian.

"Prince Rallian has asked to address you," Talbot said. "He wishes to speak on a matter that is close to all of us."

Rallian rose from his seat and bowed respectfully to Talbot, then turned to face the waiting crowd. Alex could see expectant and excited looks on most of the faces, and worried looks on a few.

"My lords of the north," said Rallian, looking around the room. "After much thought and long hours of discussion with the noble Lord Talbot, I have something to tell you. As you all know, Nezza has been without a true king for many years. We have all suffered because of this, though some have suffered more than others. Many men have made claims, but none have worn the crown. Now I, Rallian of Karmus, prince of the noble line, make my claim. I offer myself to you, as your king, your protector, and your servant."

"How say you men of the north?" Talbot called out once Rallian had finished speaking.

"Hail, King Rallian!" a thousand voices answered, shaking the dust from the rafters of the great hall. "Hail the true king of Nezza!"

Alex was shocked by this vocal show of support for Rallian's claim. He had expected Talbot to support Rallian, but he'd thought that most of the nobles would need persuading of one kind or another. It appeared that all the nobles of Talbas were firmly behind Rallian, and Alex watched as each of the lords in turn swore his loyalty to Rallian as king of Nezza.

"My lord?" said a servant as Alex turned to leave the hall. "King Rallian asks that you join him in the council chamber."

"As the king wishes," said Alex.

Alex followed the servant out of the great hall and into a smaller room. Virgil and his company were already there, waiting for Rallian and the lords of Talbas. Alex nodded to them as he entered, but he did not speak. Rallian soon appeared with Talbot and several of the other nobles.

"Now to plan," said Rallian, a serious look on his face. "Lazar will not have been idle since my escape, and I fear he will attack before we are prepared to meet him."

"I've already sent messengers to Lords Caftan and Shelnor," said Talbot. "Theirs are the closest kingdoms."

"Will they join us?" Rallian asked.

"Yes," Talbot answered without hesitation. "Lords Caftan and Shelnor joined with me in hiring the adventurers who rescued you."

"Very well," said Rallian. "I will remember their kindness."

Rallian paused for a moment and then turned to Alex. "Master Taylor, you have led me from the dungeons, and your plans have always been for the best. Can you advise me on what to do now that my claim as king has been made?"

"Assemble your army," said Alex. "March south to meet Lazar's forces before they can reach these northern lands."

"Open warfare, then," said Rallian, looking pained by the idea.

"Lazar will not surrender to you," Alex pointed out. "His troops may not love him, but they know no other master. If you meet them in force and declare yourself, perhaps they will join with you. At the very least, you must not allow them to destroy the lands that are loyal to you."

"Your wisdom is sound," said Talbot. "And if we can hold Lazar's forces in place, or drive them back, other kingdoms may choose to join us."

"All of the lords of Nezza should be given the chance to join you without war," said Alex. "Some may join gladly, others reluctantly. Some may choose to join Lazar or remain uncommitted. You will do well to remember which lords do what, and reward them or punish them accordingly."

"How soon can the army be gathered and move south?" Rallian asked Talbot.

"We can leave from Talbas in two days' time," answered Talbot. "Two thousand warriors will march with us. A thousand more are already in Dunnmara. Once word goes out, the entire army will gather wherever you command. We should be at full strength in a week or ten days."

"Dunnmara holds the main roads from the south and east," said Rallian thoughtfully. "Send word for the army to gather at Dunnmara."

"Lord Talbot, how large is the army?" Alex asked.

"No fewer than ten thousand men from Talbas and the lands I control," said Talbot. "I should think we will be closer to twelve thousand before the ten days are over. Caftan and Shelnor will bring at least seven thousand men each from their kingdoms as well."

"What are you thinking, my friend?" Rallian asked.

"That Lazar will not attack Lord Talbot's lands first," said Alex. "He knows that Lord Talbot has a large army at his command, so he may seek to destroy the smaller kingdoms that support Lord Talbot, and you, King Rallian."

"That is true," said Talbot. "Lazar has never risked open war here in the north. Both Caftan's and Shelnor's kingdoms are closer and easier for him to get to. He could attack them sooner and not have to haul his supplies over the mountains."

"Yes," agreed Rallian, considering this new information. "Send word to Caftan and Shelnor to gather their armies at the gap of Luthan. It is the most likely place for Lazar to enter either of their lands. We will meet them there. If Lazar is there ahead of us, we will cross the mountains and come up behind him. If not, we will join forces and march on Karmus from there."

"A cunning plan," said Talbot. "It shall be as you command." He bowed and then left the room.

"Now, for other matters," said Rallian, looking at Virgil and his company. "My friends, what will you do now that your adventure has found success?"

"King Rallian," said Virgil, approaching Rallian and bowing. "I speak for my company, and we have decided on our course. We will serve you until your throne is secure. Only when that is done will our adventure have found its true success."

"Your offer is most kind, and I accept your service," said Rallian. "I have heard that adventurers are great warriors, and though there are but four of you, I am glad you are with us."

Virgil and the others in the company all bowed to Rallian.

"And now," Rallian said, looking at Alex, "what will you do, my friend? Twice already you have saved me. I dare not ask anything more of you."

"I will ride south with you," said Alex. "I have sworn by my staff to see you on the throne of Nezza, and I will not break that oath."

"You favor me greatly," said Rallian. "So, in two days' time we will all ride south, and may fortune smile on us all."

There was a loud cheer as Rallian finished speaking. Alex was happy both to know that Virgil and the others would remain in Nezza and that Rallian had been accepted by the lords of the north. Alex knew there were many other kingdoms to deal with, other kingdoms that might not be as happy as Talbot's to find a true king, but he held on to his hope that Rallian would become king of Nezza without a long and painful war.

Alex left the cheering lords and adventurers, wanting to spend time in the garden alone. The garden was a happy place where he could think in peace. He had a lot on his mind, particularly King Rallian's order to gather the army. As he wandered the garden, he talked with Stonebill about his thoughts.

"If you like, I can fly south," Stonebill offered. "I can spy out the land and see where Lazar's forces are and what they are up to."

"That would be useful," said Alex. "But before you go, I should put a spell of protection on you."

"Protection?" Stonebill asked. "Why would I need protection? Men going to battle do not have time to shoot at passing birds."

"I would feel better knowing you were protected both by magic and by the unseeing eyes of men," said Alex.

Stonebill submitted to Alex's request, fluttering down to a nearby stone bench so Alex could work his magic. Alex's spell took only a moment, but it would protect Stonebill from arrows and stones as well as from any evil magic Magnus might use against him.

"I will return as soon as I can," Stonebill promised.

"Take care, my friend," said Alex as the raven took flight. "Remember that spells can only do so much."

Stonebill dipped his wings in acknowledgment and then sped from the garden on his errand.

Alex watched as he flew out of sight. When he turned around, Tom was waiting for him a little farther down the path.

"Forgive my intrusion," said Tom.

"There is nothing to forgive," said Alex, walking forward to meet Tom. "I see that your desire to test yourself has grown."

"We will soon be riding south to battle," said Tom. "I thought it would be wise to test myself now, before we go."

"Tonight," said Alex after a long pause to consider things. "Meet me here at midnight, and I will lead you to the wall."

"You will lead me?" Tom asked.

"For your first journey, yes, I must lead you," said Alex, looking up at the sky. "After your first journey, you may never wish to return. Many healers will not go where you are asking me to take you."

"I do not ask lightly," said Tom, sounding troubled.

"And I do not agree lightly."

Tom bowed, then left the garden. Alex was concerned about Tom's desire to visit the wall. Tom had no idea how strong the pull of the shadowlands was or how hard the test would be.

CHAPTER FIFTEEN
A JOURNEY AND A PROMISE

Midnight came too soon for Alex. He wanted to put Tom off until another time, but he knew that Tom was determined to return to the wall between life and death. If Alex did not lead him there, he might find his own way to the shadowlands and that could be fatal. Alex remembered his own journeys to the wall, and he hoped Tom was ready for what he was about to face.

"I am ready," said Tom, his face set and his voice solemn.

Alex nodded and then looked at the sky for a moment. He focused his mind on the journey he was about to take and on the garden around him. He wanted to be anchored to life and the beauty of life before making this journey.

"Take my hand."

Tom reached out and took Alex's hand, shaking slightly with excitement and fear.

Alex looked at his friend and then softly spoke the magic words that would take them both to the shadowlands. For a few seconds Alex looked into the darkness, and then he looked at Tom, waiting to see what Tom would do.

"It's not . . . It is not like I thought it would be," Tom said. He looked stunned and pale.

"I know," said Alex.

"The call is strong," Tom went on, his voice troubled but steady. It was as if he had not heard Alex at all. "I see now why most healers do not wish to come here."

"It is a dangerous place for the living," said Alex. He continued to watch every move that Tom made.

"The lands beyond the wall are strangely beautiful," said Tom, his voice becoming dreamy. "It would be nice to go and look at them."

"If you go, you cannot return," Alex warned.

"I know," said Tom, his voice returning to normal. "It is difficult to remain focused."

"It is easier if you are looking for someone, trying to call them back," said Alex, letting his eyes return to the shadowlands.

"Yes," said Tom. "If I were looking for someone I would have a reason to be here. Now . . . now it is pointless."

"Not pointless," answered Alex, looking back at Tom. "You had to know what to expect. It is important that you remember how strong the call of the shadowlands can be and how hard it is to focus on your task while you are here."

"I understand," said Tom, calling Alex's attention away from the wall.

Tom turned to look at Alex for the first time, and his face went slack and his eyes grew wide.

Alex understood Tom's reaction. Even though he had never

seen himself in this place between life and death, he had seen his friend Calysto and her true power.

"You see my powers more clearly here than ever before," said Alex. "Are you ready to return to the land of the living?"

Tom simply nodded.

Taking Tom's hand, Alex turned and walked away from the shadows toward the light that had been behind them. After a moment of darkness, a cool breeze blew across his face. He opened his eyes and looked once again at the night sky of Nezza.

Tom was kneeling in front of him, shaken and unable to look him in the face. Alex waited for Tom to gain control of himself, but it was several minutes before Tom began to move.

"You are much more than I imagined," Tom said, his voice trembling.

"Yes," said Alex. "I am more than a healer, and what you saw was more than you expected. I am sorry, I should have warned you."

"Do not be sorry," said Tom. "I am honored that you would let me see you there."

"It was necessary for me to accompany you on your first journey," said Alex. "Now tell me, what did you see?"

"I saw a low stone wall at the bottom of a hill," Tom answered slowly. "I saw the lands of shadow beyond the wall."

"Anything else?" Alex asked.

"No, nothing else," said Tom in a tired voice. "Was there something else I should have seen?"

He's lying, Alex's O'Gash whispered. *As much to himself as to you.*

Alex considered what his O'Gash said, and then answered. "No, there was nothing else you should have seen. Now you must decide if you will make the journey again. No one will blame you if you choose not to go, as it is a dangerous journey. If you choose to go again, to take the second test, then you will go alone."

"I do not know if I can," said Tom, looking at the ground.

"You don't need to decide right now," said Alex. "In fact, it would be better if you waited for several days at least before making a decision. If you wish to take the second test, I will wait and watch as you do so. You may choose to wait for some time before testing yourself again, and then you may be the student of another. If you decide not to return, I can help you forget the path so that you won't be tempted to go to the wall alone."

"I understand," said Tom, standing up slowly. "I have much to think about and little time for thinking."

"You have all the time in the world, Tom. Your second test can be put off until you are sure you want to take it, until you are sure that you are ready," said Alex.

"I will ponder on this," said Tom, his solemn tone returning.

"We will speak again soon," said Alex, leaving Tom in the garden and returning to his own room.

Alex didn't go to sleep right away. He lay awake on his bed, wondering not only why Tom had lied about seeing something more in the shadow lands, but more importantly, why Tom would lie to himself about what he had seen.

The next morning at breakfast, Tom still looked shaken from his visit to the shadowlands. Alex watched him closely and tried to read his thoughts. He had little time to worry about Tom, however, as preparations for their move south were well underway.

"Master Taylor," Rallian called as they were finishing their meal. He waved for Alex to join him. "You carry no sword, and I would not have you go to battle with only your staff. If I can provide a weapon for you, I would be—"

"I have a sword," said Alex, cutting off Rallian's offer. "I have had no need for it yet in Nezza, but I will wear it if that will please you."

"I hope you won't need it," said Rallian. "But it would be best to be prepared for anything."

"And your lords would be happier with a wizard who is a warrior and not a schemer like Magnus," said Alex with a slight smile.

"It might make them more trusting," Rallian admitted. "Though if any of them speak against you, they will answer to me for it."

"You are most kind," said Alex. "I will wear my sword. As you've heard from the stories Skeld has told, I do know how to use one."

"And a great addition your sword will be to our army," said Rallian. "Is it really a magic sword, or was that just something Skeld made up?"

"It is a magic sword," Alex answered. "It was made long ago by the elves, and it has powers of its own."

"Can any man who uses the sword call on those powers?" Rallian asked.

"The sword chooses its own master," Alex explained. "It has chosen me. It would be dangerous for anyone else to try to use the sword as long as I am its master."

"Amazing," said Rallian. "I've heard stories of magic swords, but like most of our stories, I thought there was little truth in them."

"Perhaps, when your throne is secure and there is peace in Nezza once more, new stories will come to your land," said Alex. "If magic and adventurers are accepted in Nezza, then you and your people will learn a great deal."

"Nothing would please me more," said Rallian. "I hope that our time of learning is not far off."

Alex left Rallian and spent most of the day wandering in the castle garden alone, thinking. When he left the garden for meals or to speak with Rallian and his lords, he noticed that Annalynn was never far away. She seemed to be watching Rallian and trying hard not to be seen doing it.

Alex also noticed that Rallian would often glance toward Annalynn, though he also tried to make it appear that he did not. Neither of them seemed to be aware of the fact that Alex, at least, noticed their glances.

The day passed quickly, and everything was in motion. The part of Talbot's army that was in Talbas was making preparations to leave, and groups of soldiers and men from nearby towns and villages kept turning up all day. Alex was impressed by the number of eager and willing men who answered Talbot's call. He remembered Tempe's comment about the spell he had released when freeing the desert river, and he hoped that at least some of that magic was being turned to good here in Talbas.

Alex skipped the evening feast, preferring the quiet solitude of the garden. Tomorrow he would ride south with Rallian, hoping to find Lazar's army, though he was afraid of what would happen when they did. He was so caught up in his thoughts that he didn't hear Annalynn's approach, and he jumped when she spoke to him.

"Can you keep him from harm? Prince Rallian, I mean." She was wearing the cameo Alex had made for her, and her face was full of sorrow.

"Rallian is at the center of a great storm—a storm that may destroy all of Nezza," said Alex, his own words taking him by surprise. "I can only try to guide him through this storm."

"It is said that wizards have their price," said Annalynn, a nervous quiver in her voice. "What price would you ask to keep Rallian safe?"

"What would you offer?" Alex asked, interested in what Annalynn would offer.

"Anything," Annalynn said without hesitation.

"Anything?"

"Anything I can give or promise," said Annalynn, her tone firm and determined. "Anything and everything to keep him safe."

"Then, my lady, I will swear by my staff to do all I can to bring Rallian through this trial safely," said Alex.

"And your price?" Annalynn asked. "What will you ask for your services?"

"Nothing."

"Nothing?" Annalynn repeated, stunned. "Nothing at all?"

"You have offered everything, and the offer is enough," said Alex.

"I . . . I don't understand," said Annalynn.

"True wizards do not sell their power," said Alex. "I asked what you would offer only because I was curious, nothing more. I will do what I can to keep Rallian safe, not only because you have offered everything for this, but also because he is my friend."

"Forgive me," said Annalynn, her gaze dropping to the ground. "I have been a fool."

"You know little of wizards and even less about magic," said Alex in a kindly voice. "I cannot fault you for believing the stories you have heard all your life."

"I should have known better," Annalynn said. "After you made the cameo, I should have known the stories were not true."

"No harm has been done," said Alex, trying to cheer Annalynn. "Now you know more about wizards than you did before. You know that I will not sell my powers for any price, but I will give them away for friendship alone."

"I—" Annalynn began but stopped suddenly. "Someone is coming. I should not be here."

"Go, then," said Alex. He had heard the footsteps as well.

"I wish to speak some more with you," said Annalynn, reluctant to leave.

"Wait by the fountain," said Alex. "I will follow as soon as I can."

Annalynn hurried away as silent as a shadow, vanishing in the darkness.

Alex watched her go, and then he turned back to see Rallian walking slowly down the path toward him. He was pretending to be looking at the flowers.

"You are up late," Alex said as Rallian approached.

"Oh, I . . . I didn't know you were here," said Rallian, a nervous and slightly guilty tone in his voice. "I was just thinking that . . ."

"You were hoping to meet Annalynn in the garden," said Alex, catching Rallian's gaze.

"No, I just—" Rallian began, and then he laughed. "Yes. I see it is pointless to try hiding anything from you. Yes, I was hoping to find her here."

"Some things are plain for all to see," said Alex. "She is not far. You will find her waiting by the fountain."

"You spoke to her?" Rallian asked.

"She asked me to keep you safe," said Alex.

"And what did she offer you for this kindness?" Rallian asked, looking both happy and troubled.

"She offered everything," said Alex. "I accepted nothing," he added quickly, seeing the look on Rallian's face. "You have known me long enough to know that I do not sell my powers. I will do what I can to keep you safe because you are my friend. Annalynn's request is only one more reason for me to do what I can for you."

"Old stories are hard to forget," said Rallian after a pause.

"I do not blame her, or you, for believing them," said Alex.

"She is waiting for me by the fountain, but I think she would be happier to see you."

Rallian glanced down the pathway.

"Go and talk to her," said Alex. "We leave in the morning, so it would be wise for you to speak your heart tonight."

Rallian nodded his understanding. He smiled at Alex and moved quickly toward the fountain.

Alex stayed where he was for a long moment, considering what he had just set in motion. He looked up at the silver moon, took a deep breath, and walked back to the castle.

"Master Taylor," a voice called out as Alex was heading toward his room.

"Lord Colesum," said Alex, turning and finding Talbot's oldest son approaching him.

"Forgive me, I have not had a chance to speak with you before now," said Colesum.

"It is a busy time," said Alex. "What can I do for you?"

"It is late. Perhaps I should speak with you another time," said Colesum, looking awkward.

"Not too late," said Alex. "I am not tired, and if I can be of assistance, it would be my pleasure to help you."

"Yes, well," Colesum began, looking over his shoulder to make sure they were alone. "I was hoping you might be able to advise me."

"Walk with me," said Alex.

It was clear the young lord did not wish to be overheard or possibly even be seen talking with him. Colesum walked along the castle corridor with Alex, but he did not speak for a few moments. Finally, he seemed to collect his thoughts and find the nerve to speak.

"I've spent several hours with your friends. They have many tales of distant lands."

"They have traveled to many places," said Alex.

"Yes, exactly," Colesum agreed. "Places that my people have long ago forgotten about, or perhaps have never known about."

"And you wish to see those places for yourself," said Alex; it was not a question.

"Your friends—Virgil and the others—they seem so different from the men of Nezza."

They walked on in silence for several minutes more before Colesum spoke again.

"All my life, I have dreamed of seeing other lands, of doing great deeds. I suppose I have always wanted to be an adventurer, like yourself and the others."

"I'm sure Virgil and the others explained to you that adventurers do not choose themselves," said Alex.

"Yes, they have told me," Colesum answered. "Yet the desire burns inside of me. At times I feel that I will burst with this desire. There are times when I want to run away in search of adventure."

"Do you wish me to cool your desire with magic?" Alex asked.

"No, not that," Colesum answered quickly. "I just thought, with Rallian becoming king, perhaps Talbas will no longer need so many warriors. Perhaps I could leave my people for a time and find the adventure that I long for."

"You are likely to find a great deal of adventure in the coming weeks," said Alex.

"Yes," agreed Colesum. "Lazar will not willingly yield Karmus to Rallian, of that I am sure. I think, however, that many of the kingdoms will join Rallian willingly, so I hope the wars will not last for long."

They stopped walking, and Alex looked Colesum in the face. He could see Colesum's desire, almost need, to find adventure.

"What would you ask of me?" Alex asked.

"You are a wizard," said Colesum. "I thought you might be able to tell me if I can be an adventurer."

"I cannot," said Alex. "You must find an oracle to answer that question for you."

"The lady of the red lands?" Colesum asked.

"Tempe is a great oracle," said Alex. "The journey to her house is not as difficult as it was."

"I would ride away tonight in search of her, but I have sworn allegiance to Rallian," said Colesum, a slight look of pain on his face.

"You must keep your oaths," said Alex. "Honor is important to adventurers—more important than any treasure they may find."

"I would not break my oath," said Colesum.

"I know that you would not," said Alex. "With any luck at all, Rallian will soon sit on the throne in Karmus. Once Rallian is king, you should seek out the oracle and discover your destiny. That is, if you have not already found your destiny."

"And if I am not one of the chosen?" Colesum asked.

"Then you must learn to live with who you are," answered Alex. "Perhaps you will have enough of adventures before ever going to look for the oracle. It may take a long time to see Rallian accepted as the king of Nezza."

"You speak wisely," said Colesum, looking less troubled than he had been. "Thank you for speaking with me."

"I am honored by your trust," said Alex.

Colesum walked with Alex back to his room. They talked about the war that was coming and what Lazar might do. Alex could see that Colesum was clever and that he understood a great deal about warfare. He thought Colesum would make an excellent general for Rallian's army but would also make an excellent adventurer. He did not share his thoughts with Colesum, afraid to push him toward or away from either path.

Colesum thanked Alex once more, and Alex watched him go. He closed the door to his room and dropped onto his bed, considering each of Talbot's children in turn: Colesum, the oldest, who wanted to be an adventurer and to travel to distant lands; Hathnor, the second son, a friend of elves who wanted nothing more than to visit the far lands to the north and west; and Annalynn, the youngest child and only daughter of Lord Talbot. She was the most difficult to understand, and perhaps the most interesting of them all.

They were an impressive family, and Alex thought his trip to Nezza was worth the trouble, if only to meet Lord Talbot and his children.

CHAPTER SIXTEEN
THE GATHERING STORM

Alex woke to the sound of moving men and horses. It took a moment for him to realize what was happening, and when he did he almost jumped out of bed. Lord Talbot's army was starting south today. He was happy to be moving again but worried just the same. Being a wizard, he could see a number of possible outcomes, but he was not an oracle or a seer so he continued to worry.

Alex sat on the edge of his bed and, for the first time since he'd come to Nezza, he took his magic sword, Moon Slayer, out of his bag. He held the sword in his hands for several minutes, remembering how its power had filled him in the past. Part of him hoped he would not need to use the sword, but another part of him really wanted to use it again. Without trying to sort out his mixed feelings, Alex attached the sword to his belt and then took another item from his bag. It was the true silver mail he had made on his last adventure. He had made it to help fight off dark magic, but it would be even more useful against warriors in battle. Pulling a shirt over the chain mail, Alex left his room and made his way to the great hall.

"A day to remember," said Virgil as Alex joined him and his company for breakfast.

"I'm glad you all decided to stay in Nezza and help Rallian," said Alex.

"It seemed the best thing to do," said Virgil. "It's not like we could go home anyway. Not with Bray trying to block the great arch and doing every little thing Lazar tells him to."

"And our adventure can't be completed until we settle with you," Skeld added, slapping Alex on the back in his friendly way.

"Best not to leave kings uncrowned," said Dain, looking stern and proud in his dwarf armor.

"And it is a show of goodwill to remain," Tom added.

Alex knew that Skeld and Virgil thought of this as a game. They were both laughing and joking, which did not surprise Alex. He knew the beliefs of Norsland, which said that death in battle was the best death anyone could possibly hope for. Tom seemed nervous but happy. Only Dain seemed to be taking things as seriously as he was.

As they were finishing their meal, Rallian appeared with Lord Talbot. The king looked troubled, and Alex could see the cool determination in Rallian's eyes.

"My friends," Rallian began, "let us toast our beginning and wish for luck to follow us."

Servants appeared as he spoke, passing out mugs to all those gathered in the great hall. There was a general wish for luck, after which they all drank and cheered loudly. Alex couldn't help feeling happy with all the cheering going on around him, and he cheered with the rest of them as they marched out of the castle to find their horses.

"Lord Taylor," Colesum called. "My brother, Hathnor, and I, would be honored if you would ride with us in King Rallian's vanguard."

"It would be both my honor and my pleasure to do so," said Alex.

"You wear a sword today," Colesum said, leading Alex to his horse. "I did not know that wizards bothered with such common things."

"I could use a sword before I took my staff," said Alex. "And my sword is not as common as you might think."

"So we've heard," said Hathnor, walking up as Alex was speaking. "The king has told us the stories, and your friend Skeld has sworn that they are all true."

"I cannot say if they are true or not, as I did not hear the stories," said Alex. "But I know Skeld very well."

Colesum and Hathnor laughed at Alex's reply as they climbed onto their horses. They looked impressive in their shining armor, but only Alex knew about the true silver mail he wore under his shirt. They talked with Alex as they rode away from the castle and through the city.

"How many men has Rallian left to hold Talbas?" Alex asked as the city grew small behind them.

"Two hundred of the oldest and youngest warriors," said Colesum. "We have scouts out, so it is unlikely that Lazar's army could approach without our knowing."

"The king has ordered the people from all the nearby

towns and villages into Talbas as well," Hathnor added. "That will increase the guard to five or six hundred."

"A wise precaution," Alex said.

"Where is your raven today?" Hathnor asked.

"Stonebill flew south to scout the land," said Alex. "He will return in a day or two with news of what lies ahead of us."

"He can travel faster and farther than our scouts," said Colesum thoughtfully.

"And he sees more than most scouts as well," Alex added. "He is a wise bird, and I am glad the oracle asked me to bring him along."

"The Oracle of the Red Lands sent this bird with you?" Colesum asked in surprise.

"She asked it as a favor," said Alex.

"Then he is truly a good omen for the king," said Hathnor. "The raven is considered a royal bird here, as you may know. To have one so friendly with this company is a good sign."

Alex looked at the armored knights in front of him as they rode. There were two dozen of them in shining silver armor, each carrying a long lance with a banner attached to it. He swiveled in his saddle to look behind him, where Rallian and Lord Talbot rode along with another thirty or forty armored knights. He was glad to see that Virgil and the others were not too far behind Rallian. The sight of so many warriors gave him hope, as did the confidence of Colesum and Hathnor.

"This land looks so peaceful," Alex said. "It is hard to believe there has ever been a war here."

"It has been a long time since any army but our own has marched in these lands," said Colesum. "We have been strong for more than a hundred years, and with luck, we will remain strong."

"Luck often favors the bold," said Alex.

They rode on toward Dunnmara, talking and laughing from time to time as they went. They all knew what the future might hold, but for now they were happy to be riding together. They paused once during the day to rest their horses and eat a little. Messengers began returning as they ate, and all the news seemed to be good.

When they stopped for the night, Rallian held a meeting with his generals to discuss what was happening. Alex was invited to join the group, along with Virgil.

"There is no sign of Lazar's army," said Rallian. "If we move quickly, we can fight him on the other side of the mountains and spare this land."

"He will surely have men along the south road," Talbot said. "He will be watching for our approach."

"It would be best to keep him in the dark," said Alex. "If we could encircle the men watching the roads so no word of our movement reached Lazar or his army, we would have an advantage."

"Both wise and cunning," said Rallian. "I will send scouts to spy on Lazar's watch. Once we know where they are, and how many men there are, we can make plans to capture them."

"And the captured men may be able to tell us what Lazar is up to," Colesum added.

"There is one other matter," said Rallian, turning to look at Alex. "The weather is unusual for this time of year. The rains seem to have dried up. Do you think Magnus could be keeping the rains away so that Lazar's army can move faster?"

"No, this is not Magnus's doing," said Alex. "I doubt he even cares about the weather."

Rallian gave Alex a questioning look, but Alex didn't explain how he knew that Magnus wasn't behind the unusual weather. Tempe had told him that the weather would be dry, at least for a time. The rains would come at some point, but for the next few weeks at least, the army could move quickly.

Alex wondered how hard it would be to control the weather. Since his encounter with the stoics, Alex had been looking for a way to use more of his dragon magic and include it in his everyday life. Perhaps the power of the dragon was strong enough to change the weather, but for now, Alex would let things be.

With their plans made, Rallian sent more messengers south. Alex watched as they rode away, wondering what Stonebill had discovered. He wanted to know what Lazar was doing, or more correctly, what Magnus was telling Lazar to do. It was possible that Lazar's army would wait for them near Karmus, hoping that a battle in the place of his choosing would be to their advantage.

Magnus was another worry. The old man had to be doing something, but Alex had no idea what. He considered using the scrying orb in his bag, but unless he knew exactly what he was looking for, the orb wouldn't be much help.

After eating the evening meal, Alex wandered out of the tents to look at the stars. As he stood silently looking into the sky, he felt Tom approaching.

"May I speak with you?" Tom asked, stopping a short distance away.

"Of course," said Alex.

"I . . ." Tom began and then stopped to clear his throat. "I have been thinking about the second test. I would like to take it, but I feel I should wait until matters are settled in Nezza."

"A wise choice," said Alex. "When things are settled in Nezza, we will talk about this again."

Tom bowed and walked away, and Alex turned to watch him go. He still wondered what Tom had seen in the shadowlands, and why he had lied about seeing anything at all. Alex's O'Gash had said that Tom was lying to himself, but Alex couldn't see any reason for Tom to do that.

He has found another answer, Alex's O'Gash said softly. *One that he was not looking for.*

Alex didn't understand what that meant, but his O'Gash remained silent, so Alex let his questions drift to the back of his mind. Whatever answers Tom had found, Alex knew that he would discover them in time.

The next morning, they continued their march south and east. There was not as much laughter today, but everyone still seemed to be in good spirits. Alex watched the groups of men who were joining with the army as they went along. He was impressed by how many of these groups there were and by how happy they all seemed to be. They were much like the warriors who had marched out of Talbas—happy to serve a true king.

Rallian took the time to greet each new group that joined the army, an action that Alex thought was wise. The men had come because Lord Talbot had called, but they would be fighting for Rallian. Alex knew that the men would fight better for a leader they knew, or at least for one who took the time to get to know them.

By the time they reached Dunnmara, the sun was already dropping below the horizon. Perhaps a thousand tents were set up around the city walls, and the evening was brightened by hundreds of campfires. Men were riding and running between the tents, carrying messages back and forth between commanders.

"They will be arriving all night," Colesum said to Alex. "Some of them will have traveled farther than we have by the time they get here."

"Fortunately, we always keep a large stockpile of supplies ready," Hathnor added. "We never know when we might need them. That is one of the reasons we have remained strong for so long."

"And I believe one of the reasons we will be successful in putting Rallian on the throne," said Alex.

Just then, Stonebill arrived with a flutter, landing on Alex's shoulder. The raven looked worn out, but he was in a rush to tell Alex what he had seen.

"Lazar has sent his army east and north," said Stonebill. "They will reach the gap of Luthan in two days' time."

"Will Caftan and Shelnor be there in time to stop them?" Alex asked.

"They are gathering now, but it will be close," answered

Stonebill. "The northern lords have a fair-sized force at the gap, but it will take time to get all of their men in place."

"Then we should move more quickly and come at Lazar's army from behind," said Alex.

"There is more," Stonebill interrupted. "Magnus has bewitched the army of Lazar so they appear to be more than they really are. I would say there are no more than ten thousand men in the army, but they appear to be three or four times that number."

"Then we must let Caftan and Shelnor know, or they may withdraw from the gap," said Alex, considering what he would do faced with a force of such size.

"It will be difficult," Stonebill said. "They know nothing of geebs, so a messenger must be sent."

"And they will trust what they see more than what we tell them," Alex added. "Rest, my friend. You have done much for our cause, and we still have the advantage."

"What news?" Colesum asked as soon as Alex stopped talking to the raven. "Does Lazar march north to meet us, or does he wait in his own lands?"

"We should talk with the king," said Alex. "My friend has brought important news, and we will need to weigh our options."

Within ten minutes, Alex was telling Rallian and the lords of the north what Stonebill had discovered. Their mood became dark as they pondered what they should do. It was clear that Caftan and Shelnor needed to be told that the force attacking them was much smaller than it seemed to be, but would they believe it?

"I will go to them," said Colesum firmly. "They will believe me."

"I will go with him," Hathnor added. "Surely they will not doubt both of us."

"Colesum is needed here," said Rallian, looking at Lord Talbot as he spoke. "The journey will be difficult and dangerous. Lazar will have scouts and raiders out, trying to keep Caftan and Shelnor from sending messages to us."

"I will ride with Hathnor," said Alex, stepping forward. "I believe the two of us can reach Lords Caftan and Shelnor and convince them of the truth."

"I had hoped you would remain with me," said Rallian, his voice lowered slightly.

"We must hold the gap of Luthan. That is where I am most needed," said Alex.

"Can you break the spell of Magnus?" Talbot asked.

"I don't know. I will need to see what magic Magnus has used before I can say," said Alex. "But I think it might be best to leave his magic in place for a time."

"Why?" Rallian asked.

"The army of Lazar will want to fight as little as possible," said Alex. "If they think they can force Caftan and Shelnor to surrender, or perhaps leave the gap to their seemingly huge force, they will not attack."

"And if Caftan and Shelnor see themselves confronted by thirty or forty thousand men, they may well surrender," Rallian said.

"Hathnor and I will find some way to convince them of the truth," said Alex. "Once Caftan and Shelnor understand how things stand, we will delay Lazar's army, giving you time to come up behind them. When you are close, I will raise a fog so Lazar's army will not see your approach. When all is ready, I will let the fog melt away and then see what I can do to wipe away the deception of Magnus."

"And Lazar's army will be trapped between two larger armies," said Talbot with a nod. "A good plan, and it might work, if you can reach Caftan and Shelnor in time."

"With your permission, Hathnor and I will leave tonight," said Alex. "Near midnight, I think, would be best."

"Very well," Rallian agreed. "I will send you two, and a small group of warriors to help you."

"The smaller the group, the better," Alex said. "We need speed and secrecy."

"As you wish," said Rallian.

Alex turned to leave. He wanted to talk with Virgil and the others before he left, and it was already getting late.

"I wish I were going with you," said Colesum, following Alex out of the tent. "But, as the king said, I am needed here."

"It is for the best," said Alex. "You are the oldest, and your place is here with your people."

"And my place is to ride as messenger," said Hathnor.

"I will choose a dozen good men to accompany you," said Colesum, smiling at Hathnor. "That many should make up for my brother's lack of skill."

"Fewer would be better," said Alex. "Three or four lightly armored men on fast horses would be best. Our hope is not battle but speed."

"It will be as you wish," said Colesum.

"Now I need to talk with my adventurer friends," said Alex.

"They are camped just there," said Hathnor, pointing to a large tent.

"Very well," Alex nodded. "Be ready to ride shortly after midnight."

"All will be ready," Colesum answered.

Alex left the brothers and walked quickly to the tent where Virgil and his other friends were camped. They greeted him when he entered the tent, questioning him about what news Stonebill had brought. He relayed Stonebill's information and what plans had been made. They all listened with interest, taking in the importance of what was just beginning.

"Perhaps some of us should ride with you," said Virgil.

"I would rather you all remain close to Rallian," said Alex.

"You suspect something," said Virgil.

Alex nodded. "I know that Magnus has a plan, and Rallian is at the center of it. I can't be here to keep an eye on Rallian, so I need you all to stay alert and make sure nothing happens to him."

"As you wish," said Virgil.

"And take care of yourselves as well. I doubt you would end up in the dungeons of Karmus now, if you were taken."

"We would not be so easily taken a second time," said Dain, fingering the ax in his belt.

"Well then," said Alex, looking at his friends, "I'll wish you all luck. Stay alert, stay close to Rallian, and try not to take too many chances. If all goes well, we will meet again at the gap of Luthan."

"We would also wish you luck," said Virgil, "but as you seem to have more luck than any man should have, we will wish you good speed instead."

Alex left the adventurers with a smile and walked back toward Rallian's tent. Colesum and Hathnor were standing outside, talking in lowered voices. Four well-armed and lightly armored men stood close by, holding six horses. Alex arrived just as Rallian stepped out of his tent.

"Well then," said Rallian, "I suppose you must be off."

"It is time," said Hathnor.

Rallian nodded. "Hathnor, you are in command of these men. You have my letters to Lords Caftan and Shelnor. Ride now, and may luck ride with you."

"I hear and obey," answered Hathnor.

"Master Taylor," said Rallian, turning to Alex, "I have no power to command you, but I ask that you assist Hathnor and his men in their mission."

"As you wish," said Alex. "We will accomplish the mission you have set for us or die in the attempt."

"Then I feel certain you will accomplish it," said Rallian with a slight grin. "I doubt very much that anything in all of Nezza could kill you."

"I am as mortal as any man," said Alex, climbing into his saddle. "Though I do seem to have more luck than most."

"Then may your luck hold true," said Rallian. "And may we meet again soon."

Alex nodded and turned his horse east, galloping off through the tents with Hathnor beside him.

CHAPTER SEVENTEEN
THE FIRST BATTLE

Alex and Hathnor rode into the darkness, leaving the tents of the army behind. The road from Dunnmara was a good one and they were able to move quickly even in the darkness. Alex wanted to ask where the road led but didn't want to interrupt Hathnor's thoughts. He seemed more serious than Alex had seen him before. Alex knew the road would lead them to the gap of Luthan eventually, and that was enough for now. They rode all night, stopping only when the dim light of sunrise began to show the land around them.

"We will rest for a few hours," said Hathnor, reining in his horse and turning off the road.

"How far will this road take us?" Alex asked.

"All the way to Ossbo if we follow it," said Hathnor. "We will have to leave it when we reach the eastern edge of our lands. The road turns toward the north there, and we need to go south."

Alex looked down the road to the east. He considered everything he knew about Nezza. If Rallian got the army moving today, it would take him at least two days to cross the mountains. Once over the mountains, it would take another two days, possibly three, to reach the gap of Luthan. That was a lot of time, and Stonebill had said that Lazar's army would reach the gap in just over two days.

"We should reach Caftan and Shelnor before Lazar's army," said Hathnor, walking up beside Alex. "We will leave this road before nightfall and cross open country to the gap."

"But will Caftan and Shelnor still be there?" Alex wondered out loud. "If they know Lazar is coming, and if they believe his army to be as big as it appears to be, will they stay?"

"King Rallian sent word for them to hold the gap," said Hathnor. "They will hold the gap as long as they can, no matter the cost. I know both Caftan and Shelnor. They are brave and stubborn men; they will do all they can."

"How long before we reach the gap?" Alex asked.

"With luck, we will be there before sunset tomorrow," answered Hathnor. "Now come, eat a little and rest while there is still some time."

Alex nodded and followed Hathnor away from the road. The soldiers that rode with them already had a fire burning and were preparing to cook a hurried meal. Alex sat down beside the fire, watching the flames. He tried not to think about the battle that was coming or what might happen if Lazar's army moved faster than Stonebill predicted.

"Perhaps I should go and see how things stand," said Stonebill, standing on Alex's shoulder.

"It would be good to know," said Alex. "Tempe told me that you know some magic. Do you know enough to slow Lazar's army?"

"I cannot hold them in place," said Stonebill.

"No, but can you slow them down? Talk to the horses and ask them to move slower than they normally would. Make wheels fall off carts, things like that."

"Yes, I can do that," said Stonebill.

"Then go, my friend," said Alex. "Slow them as much as you can. We will need at least a day, if you can manage it."

"I will find you a day and maybe more," said Stonebill. "Then I will bring you word."

Stonebill took flight after he finished speaking, causing Hathnor and his men to jump. Alex explained where the raven was going and what he was going to try to do.

The sun had been up for less than two hours when they started off again. Hathnor was more willing to talk as they rode, and Alex questioned him about the lands they were riding into. Because Hathnor had traveled quite a bit, he knew the surrounding lands well.

"My father would take my brother and me with him to visit Lords Caftan and Shelnor," Hathnor explained. "Our families are related, and there has always been friendship between our three kingdoms."

"I thought all the royal houses of Nezza were related," said Alex.

"At some point they are," said Hathnor. "Though most of those relations are old, and many of the other houses choose to ignore the connections."

Alex continued to ask Hathnor questions as they traveled, learning a great deal about Nezza and its royal families. When they stopped in the afternoon to rest again, Alex asked the question that puzzled him the most.

"Why is it that your father never claimed to be king?"

"Our family line is far from King Rallian's," Hathnor explained. "The outer kingdoms were ruled by distant relatives when the true king left Nezza. None of the lords from the outer kingdoms has ever made a claim on the crown."

"I see."

Alex let the subject drop, seeing that Hathnor was reluctant to talk about it in front of his men. He focused instead on the line of mountains they had been following to the east.

"We should ride until sunset," said Hathnor as they were finishing their meal. "Then we will rest for several hours before continuing."

Alex nodded his agreement. They moved slower, leaving the road behind them and crossing open ground. The land was a mixture of rolling foothills and heavily wooded areas between the hills. Most of the woods did not have paths through them, and it took some time to work their way through. They were just coming out of a thick wooded area as the last rays of sunlight faded.

"A good spot to rest," said Hathnor, climbing off his horse. "We are well hidden, though I doubt Lazar's army has scouts this far from Luthan."

"We should keep watch," one of the guards said, his eyes scanning the horizon.

"An hour each," said Hathnor. "When each of us has watched an hour, we will ride on."

This seemed like a good plan to Alex, and he put his mark

on a stone with the others. Hathnor drew the order of the watch; Alex's stone was pulled last, so he quickly rolled himself in a blanket to rest. The long ride and his many worries had made both his mind and body tired. The rest would do him good.

Alex was up and moving before Hathnor came to wake him for his watch. He felt anxious, as if waiting for something or perhaps for someone. He stood away from the small fire that was still burning, looking into the darkness around them.

"Do you sense danger?" Hathnor asked, pulling his blanket around his shoulders as he found a spot near the fire to rest.

"I don't know," said Alex. He continued to look into the darkness, trying to feel what he could not see. For a long time he felt nothing, and that was good. There was nobody nearby, so they could travel without being troubled.

After an hour, Alex shook Hathnor awake. Hathnor then woke the soldiers that were with them. The fire was still burn-ing, and Hathnor built it up a little as two of the soldiers went to saddle the horses. Alex returned to watching the darkness.

"You do sense something, don't you?" Hathnor asked.

"No," said Alex, turning back to the fire. "Or I should say yes and no. I sense no danger close to us, but I feel as if I am waiting for something."

Hathnor didn't reply but stood for a time looking into the darkness. Before long, they were eating and preparing for a long night's ride.

They made good time across the open land, but they lost time having to pick their way through the woods in the dark. Alex's feeling of expectation increased as they continued to ride, and he began to see movement in the shadows. There was trouble ahead, Alex knew it, but he didn't know how far ahead or when it would come.

They had been riding for several hours, and the moon had risen, giving them a little light to see by. As they were approaching yet another small wooded area, the sudden twang of bowstrings filled the air. Hathnor cried out in pain, but before Alex could see if he was all right, the bowstrings sounded again.

"Quickly," yelled Alex. "Away from the woods!"

He didn't need to say it twice. Hathnor and the other four men turned and galloped back into the open grassland, Alex close behind them. He could see Hathnor was slumped in his saddle, an arrow sticking out of his shoulder.

Alex could hear the sound of horses running not far behind him, and he knew that they could not outrun their pursuers; their own horses were too tired. He glanced over his shoulder to see how far behind the enemy was and saw the glint of moonlight on steel only a few hundred yards behind.

"Lord Hathnor cannot go on," one of the men called.

"To the hill," Alex yelled back.

A small hill ahead of them stood out in the moonlight. If they could get there, they would be on high ground. It wasn't much, but it might help.

The rushing sound of wind and running horses filled the air as Alex and his companions raced for the hill. Alex saw a second group of men coming toward them from the right. He hoped they were friends, but when they called out he knew they were not.

Alex and the soldiers reached the top of the hill just as Hathnor turned and nearly fell from his horse. The four soldiers of the north all leaped from their saddles, helping Hathnor to the ground and then forming a human wall around their injured lord. The situation was impossible, and Alex knew there was only one thing for him to do.

"Stay with Hathnor," he commanded. "Guard him from the enemy. I will drive them away."

"Alone?" asked one of the soldiers.

"There is no time to explain," said Alex, wheeling his horse around. "Remember, you have nothing to fear from me."

He urged his horse forward, drawing his sword from his side as he went. The heat of the sword's power flowed into him as he raced back toward the men who were chasing them. Alex's horse began to glow like pale moonlight as the magic from his sword entered the animal as well. Alex felt the fierce and terrible joy of battle, this time mixed with the power of the dragon. It took some concentration on Alex's part not to change into a dragon on the spot. He charged forward, letting loose a battle cry as the wind whipped past him.

The pursuers reined in their horses, unsure of their pursuit. Alex didn't wait for them to decide what to do, charging straight into them. For a moment he felt their fear, but that was nothing to him. His sword flashed like blue fire, and the leader of the attackers fell from his saddle.

Alex checked his charge, turning once more to attack his enemies. The men quickly decided that this was a fight they did not want, and they scattered into the darkness as Alex approached.

They could run, but Alex knew it would do them no good. The heat of battle and the power of his sword drove him on. He followed two of the fleeing men, cutting them down as they tried to escape. He turned to pursue the others but stopped, hearing his name called in the distance.

Another group of men was attacking the hill, trying to finish off his companions while he was away. Alex let the remaining attackers ride away and charged back to his friends.

The attacking men were still on horseback. They urged their mounts up the hill, but the horses reared and turned away from the soldiers standing on the hilltop. The attackers, having trouble controlling their horses, had not seen Alex or the pale light that surrounded him and his horse. When Alex closed in on them, they screamed in terror, scattering like mice.

The combined heat of Moon Slayer and the battle filled Alex, and he did not hesitate to run down the fleeing men. Few escaped him as he turned and slashed in the darkness. His mind was filled with rage and flame, but a part of his mind remembered his wounded friend, Hathnor. He turned around, checking to see that all of his enemies were either dead or running, and then he rode back to the hill and his friends.

The soldiers looked as terrified as his enemies had been, and Alex knew how he must look to them. He had never seen himself when the power of his sword was in him, but he had seen his friend Sindar, who also carried a magic sword.

Alex dismounted before reaching the hilltop, and then he wiped the blood off his sword before putting it away. He felt the sword's power leave him, but he did not feel as drained as he had the last time he'd used Moon Slayer.

He spoke a few soft words into the horse's ear, calming the animal from the magic that had filled it just as it had filled him. The guards on the hilltop shifted their feet and formed up as if preparing for another fight.

Alex moved forward, his focus fixed on Hathnor and not on the men who were guarding him. Hearing the unexpected twang of a bowstring, his head jerked up. An arrow raced toward his chest, though it seemed to move slowly in his mind. One of Hathnor's guards had panicked and let loose an arrow in fear.

With a wave of his hand, Alex dismissed the arrow, and it vanished in a flash of flame.

"You have nothing to fear from me," Alex called.

Hathnor's men looked terrified and did not reply. Alex moved forward once more, watching the guards. The men backed away from him, their weapons ready. Alex ignored them, dropping down beside Hathnor. A black arrow was sticking out of Hathnor's shoulder, and his cloak was covered in blood.

"So, Skeld's stories were true," said Hathnor in a weak but calm voice. "I am glad I was able to see this magic for myself, before my end."

"Don't talk," said Alex, his voice firm but kind. "You've a long way to go before your end, and this little scratch won't slow you down too much."

"The wound . . ." one of soldiers began but stopped, looking nervously at Alex. "The wound is deep, and Lord Hathnor has lost a lot of blood."

"Yes," said Alex. "Gather branches to make a drag. I will tend to his wound."

The men hesitated, unsure of themselves and of Alex. Slowly, they did as Alex had instructed, mounting their horses and riding back to the woods.

Alex checked Hathnor's shoulder, considering the best way to treat the wound.

"I can ride," said Hathnor softly, his eyes unfocused.

"Rest," Alex commanded, putting a spell of restful sleep on his friend.

Alex conjured several weir lights so he could see exactly how badly Hathnor was hurt. The guard was right; the arrow was deep, and the wound was still bleeding. Without considering how many of Lazar's men might still be nearby, Alex conjured a fire and began mixing a potion. While the water heated, he pulled the arrow out of Hathnor's shoulder, whispering a spell that would slow the loss of blood.

Hathnor's guards returned to the hilltop with caution. The weir lights were still floating in the air, and it was clear that they frightened the soldiers.

"There is nothing to fear," said Alex. "The lights are here only to assist me; there is no danger."

Alex had finished his work on Hathnor. It had been a dangerous wound; if the arrow had been poisoned, Hathnor would have died. Instead, Hathnor lay sleeping under several blankets, his shoulder tightly bandaged, and his arm tied to his side to keep it from moving.

"Lord Hathnor?" one of the guards asked.

"He should rest for a few hours before we move him," said Alex.

"He will live?" the man asked.

"Yes," said Alex. "It will take some time for him to heal, but he will live."

The soldiers seemed satisfied with Alex's answer, but their eyes nervously returned again and again to the weir lights. They lashed together the branches they had brought back to the hill, making a drag for Hathnor.

Alex sat by the conjured fire, resting his body while searching the countryside with his mind. The few men who had escaped him were still running, terrified by what they had seen. He could feel no one else close by, but he cursed himself for not realizing how close the attackers had been.

"Forgive me, lord," said one of the men, stepping toward Alex. "I did not mean to let the arrow fly."

"You meant no harm by it, and none was taken," said Alex. "I do not blame you for what happened. I know how the sword changes me."

"I see now that the old stories do not come close to the truth," said the man, looking at Alex with wide eyes.

Alex motioned for the men to sit down around the fire. They did so, but they seemed reluctant and unwilling to get too close to the conjured flames or the floating weir lights.

"Magic can be a wonderful thing," said Alex. "It can do great good when used correctly."

"And great evil when not," the man who had shot the arrow added.

"Yes," said Alex. "There is always a danger that magic will

be misused. Magnus has misused his powers, but his days are numbered."

"Will you destroy Magnus?" asked the youngest looking man.

"I will face him and break his power if I can," said Alex. "If I prove to be stronger than Magnus, then I will destroy him."

"These lights," said the oldest man. "How is it they remain? How is it this fire burns without wood?"

"The lights are called weir lights," Alex explained. "They remain because I summoned them to help me see Hathnor's wound. I conjured the fire to help me heat water to treat the wound. This is only simple magic. If time had allowed, I would have used wood for the fire and sunlight to see the wound."

"And these lights obey your commands?" asked the youngest man.

"Yes," said Alex. "They go where I go, or where I tell them to go. When I no longer need them, I will put them out, like the fire."

"They are illusion, then?" asked the oldest man.

"Not exactly. The light and the heat from the fire are real," said Alex. "Some magic is illusion, some is not. Magnus is using illusion to make Lazar's army appear larger than it really is. But illusion is just a trick of the eyes. Lazar's pretend army cannot do anything but appear to be there. Still, he hopes the deception will cause Lords Caftan and Shelnor to surrender, or at least abandon the gap of Luthan."

"How can a man know what is illusion and what is real?" asked the youngest man.

"It is difficult at times," Alex answered. "Most illusions

have some flaw in them. No illusion can be touched or felt, as you feel the warmth of the fire."

"This is all strange and new to us," said the oldest man, poking a stick at the fire Alex had conjured.

"I understand," said Alex. "Once I did not believe in magic of any kind. Now I know there is magic, both good and evil. It is up to all of us to decide which is which for ourselves."

The men fell silent, and Alex watched as the oldest man took his burning stick out of the conjured flames. He examined it for a moment and then blew it out like a match.

Alex continued searching the lands around them with his mind. Hathnor would have to be carried on the drag, slowing their progress. Even if they could somehow make good time, it would be impossible for them to run away from another group of Lazar's men.

"We should go," said Alex at last. "Night is coming to its end, and we still have many miles to travel."

The men all stood up and lifted Hathnor onto the drag they had made. Alex told them to bind him down so he would not slide or be bounced off. Once this was done, Alex put out the fire and the weir lights with a wave of his hand, and they started off into the darkness.

Alex rode beside Hathnor, letting the oldest of the guards lead the company. They avoided the wooded areas they came to as much as they could. Alex continued to try to sense any danger in the land around them. It was difficult work, trying to feel out the enemy, mostly because of the high emotions of the men around him.

The sun rose in front of them, but they did not stop to rest.

They all knew that they had to hurry, but dragging Hathnor along behind his horse was slowing them down. It was nearly midday before Alex allowed them to stop.

As the soldiers busied themselves preparing some food, Alex checked on Hathnor. He was still asleep, but he looked peaceful. Alex chose to leave the sleeping spell on him, knowing that rest was more important to his healing than food.

"It will be dark before we reach the gap," said the man who had been leading them.

"It cannot be helped," said Alex.

There was no more talk, and soon they were on their way again. Alex felt the need to hurry, but he could not leave Hathnor behind. It was unlikely that Caftan or Shelnor would believe anything he said if he turned up alone. He pushed away his desire to rush forward and fixed his eyes on the mountains to his right. They were getting smaller, and Alex knew they were getting close to the gap of Luthan.

The hours passed, and the sun began to sink in the west. Alex's muscles suddenly tightened as he felt something different than what he had felt all day.

"Be ready," Alex said to the soldiers around him.

"Is someone coming?" asked the youngest man.

"They are close," said Alex. "If they are Lazar's men, I will deal with them. Stay with Hathnor and ride on to the gap."

"As you command," answered the oldest man.

Alex watched, looking for any sign of who was coming. It wasn't long before several banners appeared from a nearby wood, carried by men who rode toward them.

"They are Lord Caftan's men," said the oldest man in a relieved tone.

Alex and the soldiers stopped and waited for Lord Caftan's men to approach them. As the soldiers came forward, Alex noticed how much they looked like Talbot's men.

"Declare yourselves," the leader of this new group called, stopping a short distance away.

"Lord Hathnor of Talbas," the oldest soldier called back. "We come with a message from King Rallian."

The leader of Caftan's men came forward. He looked at each of them in turn. Alex could tell that this was a careful man, not willing to simply accept their word that they were from the king.

"Your lord is injured," said the man.

"We were attacked by Lazar's men last night," said the old soldier. "Lord Hathnor was struck by an arrow."

When the leader of Caftan's men did not reply at once, Alex became impatient.

"How far is it to the camp of your lord?" Alex asked.

The man looked at Alex. "Not far," he said after a pause.

"Lead us there, quickly," Alex commanded. "We have been too long in getting here, and Lord Hathnor has an urgent message from the king."

"And who are you to give such commands?" asked the man.

"A friend of King Rallian, and a wizard with little time for foolishness," said Alex, shifting his staff in his hand.

"The wizard," said the man, his eyes growing wide. "Yes,

we've been told of you. We will lead you to Lords Caftan and Shelnor."

The man turned to ride back to his fellows. In seconds they formed a circle around Alex and his companions. Alex thought it a bit odd, but he could feel no deception in Caftan's men. As soon as the circle was formed, the captain led the group forward once more. So it was that Alex and Hathnor came to the camp of Lords Caftan and Shelnor as honored guests and prisoners at the same time.

CHAPTER EIGHTEEN
CAFTAN AND SHELNOR

The armies of Caftan and Shelnor were well laid out, and Alex could see that the men were ready for the coming battle. Everywhere he looked, he saw men in armor, sharpening weapons and testing bows. The thought of battle made Alex sad, but part of him also felt the excitement of battle, the excitement of the dragon. He forced his emotions down, holding them back so that he would be calm when he spoke with Caftan and Shelnor.

Once they arrived, the leader of the soldiers that had escorted them dismissed his men and led Alex and Talbot's men to a large tent in the middle of the camp. He dismounted and then spoke to another guard before addressing Alex and his companions. While the man was speaking to the guard, Alex dismounted and woke Hathnor from his enchanted sleep.

Hathnor blinked a few times, a confused look on his face. "Where are we?"

"We are in the camp of Lords Caftan and Shelnor," said Alex as he untied Hathnor from the drag. "How are you feeling?"

"Alive," said Hathnor with a weak smile.

"Good," said Alex. "I hope you're strong enough to speak to Caftan and Shelnor. They will be calling for you soon."

"I am strong enough for that," answered Hathnor. He looked worn and pale, but his voice was determined.

Alex helped Hathnor to his feet and made sure he was strong enough to stand before letting go. Alex knew that his friend needed more rest, but right now there wasn't any time.

"Lord Hathnor, Lords Caftan and Shelnor bid you welcome and ask that you and your men come to them," said the man who had led them to the camp. "They also ask that your wizard friend wait here. They promise the wait will be a short one."

Alex nodded his acceptance and motioned for Hathnor's men to come forward and help their lord into the tent. Once he was alone, Alex turned his attention toward the gap of Luthan. He knew Lazar's army was out there and moving this way, but it looked as if they had not made it to the gap yet. He hoped that Stonebill had managed to slow them down, and he wondered what his friend was doing now.

As Alex waited, he noticed several of the guards around the tent of Caftan and Shelnor watching him. It seemed obvious that they knew who and what he was, and he wondered what Rallian had told Caftan and Shelnor about him. After a few moments, Caftan's guard returned and politely asked him to come and speak with Lords Caftan and Shelnor.

Alex followed the man without speaking. There were more guards inside the tent, all looking serious and worried. Alex was glad to see that Hathnor had been given a chair to sit in. He looked at the large table in the center of the tent and saw

Lords Caftan and Shelnor for the first time. He was only a little surprised by their appearance. There was a clear family resemblance between them, and to Lord Talbot as well.

"Lord Taylor, I am Caftan of Pent," said Caftan, stepping forward and bowing to Alex.

"And I am Shelnor of Ossbo," Shelnor added with a bow of his own.

"Lords," said Alex, returning their bows.

"Lord Hathnor has told us of your journey here and of the mission you are on," Caftan said. "He and his men have all sworn that you are to be trusted and that you are a true friend of King Rallian, but this is not enough."

"What more would you ask?" Alex asked.

"We would ask that you explain this illusion that you say Magnus has put on Lazar's army," said Shelnor. "Our scouts have seen the army and report that it is at least three times as large as our own. We know the scouts are truthful, so we must ask how you know that what they see is not real."

"My friend the noble raven Stonebill has seen the armies of Lazar as well," said Alex. "Stonebill is a wise bird and sees more than most."

"But the illusion," said Caftan. "Can you explain it to us? Can you show us how it works?"

"I can if you wish," said Alex.

Both Caftan and Shelnor nodded, and Alex stood for a moment, focusing his thoughts. He bowed his head as he created an illusion, and when he looked up again, seven copies of his own form were standing in the tent next to him.

"By the ancients!" said Shelnor, stepping back in surprise.

"You now see eight of me," said Alex, his voice coming from all seven copies as he spoke. "You see that each of my images can move about the tent easily enough, yet you know that there is only one of me here."

As the images of Alex walked around the tent, he kept his mind open, controlling the illusion. He could also feel what the men in the tent were thinking. He was surprised when he realized that one of the men in the tent was a traitor.

"They all look so real," Caftan said. "How can we tell which is real and which is an illusion?"

"These illusions cannot touch nor be touched," Alex explained as he moved around the tent with his illusions. "They appear to be real, but if you watch closely, you will see that the illusions all carry a flaw."

Alex continued to move his duplicates, using them to search for the traitor he knew was there. He looked into the thoughts and feelings of the men around him, and it only took a few minutes for him to find the traitor in the company.

"My lords," the traitor said slowly as Alex watched him. "This magic is meant to confuse us. This wizard can make it appear that there are eight of him, but that does not mean that Lazar's army is using the same trick."

"Yes," said Caftan nodding. "You have a point, Stephan. Tell us, Master Taylor, what is the flaw you speak of?"

"If you look, you will notice that none of the illusions leaves tracks," said Alex with a smile. All of his images smiled as well. "And I can tell you something more—something that has nothing to do with the illusions Magnus has made."

"And what is that?" Shelnor asked.

"There is a traitor here with you," said Alex. "Even now he is thinking of how he can betray you, how he can destroy me, and what he will gain once Lazar's army has its victory."

"A traitor?" said Caftan in surprise. "Name the man. We will judge if you speak truly."

"As you wish," said Alex, moving his images as he spoke.

The copies of himself formed a circle around Stephan, and Alex stepped forward to close the final gap in the circle. Stephan looked shocked but not completely surprised. Alex could see his mind clearly: he was full of anger and regret. His mind was racing, working out a way to prove his own innocence, a way to convince Caftan and Shelnor that Alex was a liar. Alex also saw what he would need to do to prove that he spoke the truth, so without hesitating he did it.

The illusions vanished like a mist, and Alex stood alone, looking Stephan in the face.

"Do what your master commanded you to do," said Alex with a taunting smile. "Do what Lazar is paying you for."

It happened in a flash. Stephan's anger took control of him. He stepped toward Alex, drawing a short dagger from inside his tunic as he moved. He aimed for Alex's heart, thrusting the dagger forward with all his strength and causing Alex to take a few steps back as the blow fell.

"Die, wizard!" screamed Stephan, a wild look in his eyes.

"Not today," said Alex, magically pushing Stephan back and binding him where he stood. "You have sold your honor, Stephan. Was it worth the price?"

Hathnor had jumped up in horror when Stephan had

attacked and was desperately trying to draw his sword with his wounded arm.

"Calm yourself, Hathnor. I am fine," Alex said.

"Lord Taylor," Caftan shouted, rushing forward to see if Alex was all right.

"Have you been injured? Should we send for help?" Shelnor added, rushing up to Alex's other side.

"No harm has been done," said Alex. "The assassin's blade did not go in."

"By the ancients," said Shelnor, picking up Stephan's dagger. "The blade is bent, as if it were struck on an anvil. What magic is this that protects you?"

"Not magic," said Alex as he fingered the hole in his shirt. "I do not rely on magic alone to protect me from the evil of men. Let me show you."

Alex unbuttoned his shirt and pulled it back, revealing the true silver mail he wore underneath. Caftan and Shelnor both looked at him in wonder. At the sight of the mail shirt, Hathnor laughed, dropping back onto his chair.

"Your pardon, Master Taylor," said Caftan. "Stephan is one of my men. I never would have thought him capable of treason."

"Such an attack should never have happened in our tent," Shelnor said at the same time.

"Lords," said Alex, holding up his hands to quiet them. "No harm has been done, and the traitor has been revealed. There are more important things to discuss, and the matter of trust to be cleared up."

"No question of trust," said Caftan. "King Rallian has sent word that he trusts you, so I will trust you as well."

"As will I," Shelnor added.

"Very well," said Alex. "Lazar's army is still on the move, and unless I miss my guess, they will not arrive until late to-morrow. The next morning, whoever is in charge of Lazar's imaginary army will want to talk with you."

"Why?" Caftan asked.

"They think you will be fooled by Magnus's illusion. They will ask for your surrender, or that you fall back and leave the gap to them," said Alex. "Naturally, they will think that you will submit to their wishes. They might even ask you to join them and fight against Lord Talbot's army."

"We would never betray Talbot," said Shelnor in a firm voice. "Better to die a hundred deaths than to betray a friend and kinsman."

"Yes, well, you will have to act like you're considering the offer," Alex continued. "Rallian and Talbot are moving across the mountains even now so they can come up behind Lazar's army. We need to delay Lazar's army long enough to give Rallian and Talbot time to move into position."

"Ah, yes, a cunning plan," said Caftan.

"Yes, we will hold them in check until the trap is ready to spring," said Shelnor, nodding his head.

"When the king is close, I will summon a fog," Alex said. "The fog will hide Rallian's army, and Lazar's army won't know they are surrounded."

"And when all is ready, you will remove the fog and break the magic of the cursed Magnus," Caftan finished.

"An excellent plan," Shelnor added. "However, if there are ten thousand men in this army, we will still need to be careful. Lazar has at least twice that number under his command, and some of the inner kingdoms may choose to join him. Lazar holds several young lords as hostage, after all."

"Seven," said Alex, remembering what he had heard.

"Yes," said Caftan, surprised. "Lazar has taken lords from the other six inner kingdoms as hostages. He also holds Rallian's cousin Jorell as a hostage. He has spread the rumor that they are all off on some quest, but we know that is a lie."

"One of the lords was Rallian's cousin?" Alex asked, troubled.

"You speak as if they were already dead," said Shelnor. "Have you heard of these young lords?"

"They will not be seen in Nezza again," said Alex. "Magnus sent them to the western desert as prisoners, and that is where they met their end."

"A sad tale," said Caftan.

"If it is true, the inner kingdoms will want their revenge," Shelnor observed. "They will not fight for Lazar if they know their lords have been killed."

"But we have no way of letting them know the truth," said Alex. "At least not right now. I think, however, that time is growing short for both Lazar and Magnus."

"Time grows short for us all," Caftan observed. "We have much that needs doing before Lazar's army arrives."

"And Lord Hathnor needs to be moved," said Shelnor, glancing toward the injured lord. "I would not want him so close to the battlefield when he cannot defend himself."

"I will not leave until the king orders me away," said Hathnor, trying to get to his feet.

"Rest," said Alex, pushing Hathnor back down with the word. "Hathnor will be safe enough. The men who traveled with us will protect him from harm."

"It seems that you did that on your journey here," said Shelnor.

"Yes," said Alex. "I did what was needed. I brought Hathnor to you so he could deliver the message of the king. Now I will do more. What work is there that needs to be done before Lazar's army arrives?"

Caftan and Shelnor were surprised by Alex's offer to help and were reluctant to put him to work. Alex insisted, and Caftan and Shelnor explained that they were building a wall to protect at least part of the gap of Luthan.

"If we can block off part of the gap with a wall, we can force Lazar's army into a smaller space," Caftan explained.

"When our scouts reported that the army was three times the size of our own, we thought it best to narrow our front as much as possible. It would not do to let Lazar's army attack us from the front and the side," said Shelnor.

"A wise plan, but hardly needed," said Alex. "Still, it would be best to make the appearance of being prepared. Can you have someone lead me to the wall you are making?"

"As you wish," said Shelnor.

"There is another matter that we must resolve first," said Caftan. "Stephan has shown himself to be a traitor and has made an attempt on your life. He has done this in the tent of his lord and brought dishonor on myself and Lord Shelnor."

"You would be within your rights to claim his life now," said Shelnor, glancing from Alex to Stephan.

"And you must name the terms for reclaiming our honor," Caftan added.

"You are honorable men," said Alex, looking both Caftan and Shelnor in the eyes. "I see you will serve King Rallian well. I have no claim on your honor and hold you both blameless for what Stephan has done."

"You are most kind, Master Taylor, but the matter of honor is an ancient custom," insisted Shelnor.

"I understand," said Alex. "Has Stephan served you long, Lord Caftan?"

"For many years," said Caftan sadly. "I would not think it possible for him to turn traitor. I would not have believed it if I had not seen it for myself."

"Stephan," said Alex, turning to face the attacker, who was still bound by his spell. "What did Lazar promise you for your betrayal? What price did you set on your honor and the honor of your lord?"

"The price was not what you think," Stephan answered as tears began to run down his face. "I would not sell my honor for silver or gold, or for the promise of lands that were not my own."

"What, then?" Caftan questioned angrily. "What price did you place on your honor and my own?"

"My family," said Stephan.

"You . . . you have no family," said Caftan, a puzzled look on his face. "You have no wife, no children—no one."

"What you say is true, my lord," answered Stephan, trying

to wipe his face but unable to move because of the binding spell Alex had put on him. "But I have a brother and a sister who both live in Lazar's kingdom. It was for their lives—and the lives of their children—that I sold myself to Lazar."

"He speaks the truth, Lord Caftan," said Alex. "I hear it in his words, and I can feel nothing but sorrow for him."

"You should have told me of your family. I would have sent for them. I would have brought them to Pent," said Caftan.

"I should have, but I did not," said Stephan. "Forgive me; I meant no disrespect. Lazar knew of my fear for my family and ordered me to speak to no one of our bargain. I did only what I had to do."

"Master Taylor, what do you wish us to do with him?" Shelnor asked.

"Hold him for now," said Alex. "I will not judge him for what he has done. King Rallian must decide his punishment."

"Yes," said Caftan. "He must face the king's justice. That is what we are really fighting for now."

"And what price will you ask of us to restore our honor?" Shelnor questioned.

"I have already said that I hold you both blameless," said Alex, holding up his hand to prevent Caftan or Shelnor from speaking. "I understand this debt of honor, and I know that I must ask a price. I will ask one silver coin for each soldier in your army. How say you, lords of the north?"

"A small price for honor," answered Caftan.

"And an honorable request in its kindness," added Shelnor.

"Then it is settled," said Alex. "Now, we have work to do.

We can discuss payment and other details after our work is done."

Caftan and Shelnor both agreed and ordered that Alex be led to the wall that was being built. Alex left Hathnor in their care, promising to return when his work was finished. The man who had led Alex and the others to the camp now led Alex back to his horse.

"The wall is hard work for the men," the captain told Alex as they rode away from the tents. "Warriors are not great builders, but we do what we can."

"How should I address you?" Alex asked in reply.

"I am Talus, captain of Lord Shelnor's guards," said the man in a proud voice.

"Well then, Talus, I must ask your forgiveness," said Alex. "Earlier today, I spoke quickly and without thought. I was worried for my friend Hathnor and troubled by the coming war. I am sorry that I spoke so sharply to you."

"I will gladly forgive you if you ask it, though I see no reason for it," said Talus.

"I ask it," said Alex. "And I thank you for your kindness."

When they reached the construction site, Alex found several hundred soldiers working by torchlight, trying to finish the wall before Lazar's army arrived. The gap of Luthan was only about a mile wide, and the wall the soldiers were building covered about half that distance. Alex watched them work for a few minutes, and then he asked Talus to have them stop their work and move away from the wall.

Talus spoke to the man in charge of building the wall, and he called the working soldiers to a halt. When the signal came down the line so that all the men had stepped back, Alex moved forward.

Focusing all of his thoughts on the partially built wall, and the wall he had pictured in his mind, Alex began the spell. A part of his mind reached out, pulling the power of the dragon into his work. He let his thoughts move along the entire length of the wall, looking at the work that had already been finished and checking it for weakness. When his thoughts reached the steep side of the mountain where the wall began, they started back again.

The wall changed as Alex's mind moved over it. The stone seemed to come alive, and the ground shook under the feet of the watching soldiers. Slowly at first, but with gathering speed, the wall grew like some strange and magical plant. What had been a simple three-foot wall of loose stone changed, becoming four, and, in some places six, feet high. What had been only a foot thick now stretched out and became three feet thick.

Stairways climbed up the wall like stone vines where the wall was highest, and places for men to stand and walk along the north side of the wall grew out of the stairways. It was more a fortress than a wall, a place where men could fight. When Alex's thoughts returned to him, he finished the spell, binding the wall together as if it were one single enormous piece of stone.

Alex stumbled forward as he finished his magic. He caught himself with his staff, breathing hard and feeling a little dizzy from the work he had just done.

"Amazing," the man who had been in charge of building the wall said, his eyes wide.

"And is this illusion?" Talus asked. "Is this like what you did in the tent of Lords Caftan and Shelnor?"

"No," said Alex, a tired smile on his face. "This is real."

Talus moved forward and pressed his hand against the newly created wall as if thinking it would vanish when he touched it. "How?" he asked.

"Magic," said Alex. "Good magic, for a good cause."

"Yes," said Talus. "I see now that there is both good and evil magic, just as there are good and evil men."

"You see much," said Alex. "Now, I need to rest. Even good magic has its price, and I am almost too tired to stand."

"Yes, of course," said Talus, a note of concern in his voice. "I will take you to Lord Hathnor's tent. I'm sure there is room there, and I am sure Hathnor—and everyone else—will want to hear about this wall."

Chapter Nineteen

Shadows and Mist

Alex slept well that night and woke late the following morning. Creating the wall had taken a lot out of him, but now he was ready for whatever the day would bring. Alex hoped that Cafton and Shelnor's soldiers would not be afraid of him and his magic when they saw the wall, but afraid or not, they had the wall and the protection it offered.

Alex looked around the tent and saw that Hathnor was not there. Getting up, he made his way out of the tent and found Talus waiting for him.

"Master Taylor," said Talus. "Lords Caftan, Shelnor, and Hathnor request that you join them for breakfast."

"As the lords wish," said Alex.

"They are all impressed by the wall you've created," said Talus as he led Alex toward the main tent. "The soldiers that were there last night have told the story, and the whole army knows what you have done for us."

"How do they feel about my building the wall?" Alex asked.

"They are pleased, of course," said Talus. "They feel more confident now that you are with us."

"Do they still believe that Lazar's army is as large as it appears to be?" Alex asked.

"There are mixed feelings about that," Talus answered honestly. "Some say that it cannot be so large, while others say that it is. It matters little, however. With the wall in place, the men all feel that we can hold the gap of Luthan until King Rallian and Lord Talbot arrive, even if Lazar's army is as large as it appears to be."

Alex was pleased to hear that the soldiers felt confident about holding the gap for Rallian. He still hoped that a battle could be avoided completely, but the wall would be helpful if Lazar's army insisted on fighting.

"Master Taylor," said Caftan as Alex entered the tent. "You've done a great work for us."

"Lazar's army will be stunned by the appearance of the wall," said Shelnor.

"It is amazing," said Hathnor. "I think we could hold the gap against almost any foe now."

"What word do we have of Lazar's army? Have they started to arrive?" said Alex.

"A few small groups of Lazar's soldiers have been seen beyond the wall," said Shelnor. "No doubt scouts sent to see what defenses we have. The main body of the army will not arrive until late this afternoon."

"And by this evening most of their army will be in place," Caftan added.

"By this evening, King Rallian and my father will be close," said Hathnor with a smile. "Once they arrive, Lazar's army will crumble before us."

"I hope their commander will not force us to attack them or foolishly order them to attack us," Alex said.

"It depends on the commander," said Caftan. "Lazar has several generals, and many of them are devoted to him."

"If Athron leads, they will yield," said Shelnor. "Athron will see how hopeless the situation is. He is not one to waste the lives of his men needlessly."

"True," agreed Caftan. "And Athron was a general for Rallian's father. He might be persuaded to fight for Rallian."

"Yes," said Shelnor. "No doubt he only serves Lazar because he believes that Rallian is lost, or dead, and his honor holds him to Karmus. If he can see Rallian alive, I believe he will join us."

"What about the men he commands?" Alex asked.

"That I do not know," said Caftan. "I know that Lazar's soldiers do not love him and that he does not treat them well. Lazar's only true followers are the members of his black guard, and I doubt he would risk them in this battle."

"Then let us hope that Athron leads the army," said Alex, taking a seat. "Rallian may be able to win the hearts of the soldiers Lazar has sent, and it would be better to win their hearts than to destroy them."

"You speak wisely," said Shelnor, ringing a small gong on the table. "Now, let us eat and prepare for the day. I doubt the army of Lazar will ask for our surrender before midday."

They all laughed, and several men entered the tent with breakfast trays. Alex was pleased to see Hathnor eating, and he hoped that his friend would not overdo things in his excitement.

After breakfast, Alex insisted that Hathnor return to his tent to rest. Alex could see that Hathnor was still weak, and he knew it would take time for the wound to heal completely. Once Hathnor had gone, Alex rode out to the wall with Caftan and Shelnor to watch Lazar's army assemble. Already there were large groups of men in the field in front of them, but Alex could tell that most of the men were only shadows created by Magnus.

"You see that Magnus's shadow army is moving faster than the real army," said Stonebill as he landed on Alex's shoulder.

"Yes," said Alex. "There are few soldiers here. How far behind is the main force?"

"They should start arriving by midday," Stonebill said.

"Master Taylor, can you speak to this noble bird?" Caftan asked in surprise.

"Yes," said Alex. "This is my friend Stonebill. He is the one who first recognized Magnus's illusion. He's been working to delay Lazar's army in order to give King Rallian and Lord Talbot time to cross the mountains."

"A most worthy bird," said Shelnor.

"How far off are Rallian and Talbot?" Alex asked Stonebill.

"They have moved faster than we thought and will begin to arrive just after dark," Stonebill answered. "Lazar's army should all be here before night falls, but most of their supplies have been left behind."

"Trouble with their carts?" Alex asked with a smile.

"The wheels keep falling off." Stonebill laughed in his croaking voice. "I think if you conjure your fog at midnight, our friends will be able to move into place without any trouble."

"Very well," said Alex, looking out across the fields in front of him. "At midnight I will hide our friends, and at dawn we will see about this illusion that Magnus has created."

Alex relayed his conversation with the raven to Caftan and Shelnor.

"So by sunrise Lazar's army will be all but defeated," said Shelnor. "I am glad that things have worked out so well."

"So far they have," said Alex. "There is still a long road to follow before Rallian sits on the throne in Karmus."

"His first battle seems well in hand," said Caftan with a satisfied nod. "Once it is won, others kingdoms may choose to support Rallian's claim."

"I believe they will," said Alex. "I have advised Rallian to give all the kingdoms of Nezza the chance to accept him before resorting to battle."

"A wise course," said Shelnor.

"With luck, there will be few battles that need to be fought," added Caftan.

"I hope that none will be needed," said Alex, his eyes fixed on the horizon. "This land has already lost too many good men in foolish wars."

Alex was finishing his midday meal with Caftan and Shelnor when Talus appeared with news. The army of Lazar had sent men forward under a flag of truce, and they wished to speak with Caftan and Shelnor. Both Caftan and Shelnor smiled, knowing this probably meant Lazar's men would ask for their surrender.

"You must act worried," Alex warned them as they prepared to ride out and meet the captains of Lazar's army. "They must think you are afraid of them and are considering surrender. They must not suspect that we know Lazar's army is made up of shadows or that Rallian will soon be here with his army."

"Do not worry, my friend," said Caftan. "I can play the part that is needed."

"And I *am* afraid," Shelnor added. "Afraid of what will happen to them tomorrow."

Standing at the end of the wall he had created, Alex watched as Caftan and Shelnor rode out into the plain. Stonebill sat silently on Alex's shoulder. The two companies met under the blue-and-white flag of truce. The meeting lasted only a few minutes, and then Caftan and Shelnor were riding back to their camp.

"Athron commands the army," Caftan called to Alex as they approached the wall.

"And he's not at all happy about this war," Shelnor added. "I could see in his face that he would rather not be here."

"The captains that were with him looked worried as well," Caftan said. "They have seen this impressive wall, and they aren't as certain of victory as they once were."

"What terms did they offer?" Alex asked.

"If we will stand aside and let them pass, they promise not to trouble either of our kingdoms," said Caftan. "It would seem they only want to fight Lord Talbot. They are saying that Rallian is dead and that Talbot is to blame."

"So, Lazar is trying to use Rallian's name to rally his troops," said Alex. "That is good for us, since Rallian is still very much alive."

"It seems obvious that he doesn't know about Rallian's rescue," said Shelnor. "If he knew Rallian was alive and free, he would not try to use him to rally his army."

"True," said Alex. "I wonder what story Magnus told him to cover up the fact that Rallian escaped?"

"We asked Athron to give us until morning to consider his offer," said Shelnor. "One day is the normal time allowed before answering the call for surrender."

"Tomorrow we will see who surrenders," said Caftan in a firm voice.

Alex stood at the end of the wall and looked south. Everything was ready, and Talbot's army would be in place before dawn. All that was left was the waiting. Still, something in the back of Alex's mind troubled him, and he was worried that he had forgotten something important.

"Things will go badly for Magnus if Lazar finds out Rallian is alive and well," Stonebill said in Alex's ear.

"Magnus deserves whatever Lazar does to him," said Alex. "Yet I don't think Lazar can do much, and Magnus is safe enough. He only pretends to serve Lazar. I think Magnus is the true power in Karmus, and Lazar is nothing more than a willing fool."

"Yes, but if Magnus lies to Lazar, and Lazar finds out . . . "

"He's been lying to Lazar for years," said Alex. "I don't think Lazar even knows what the truth is anymore."

Alex returned to camp with Caftan and Shelnor. Lazar, he knew, was just a power hungry fool and that Magnus was the real power in Karmus. Lazar might be willing to do whatever he was told, but Magnus was the root of the evil in Nezza.

And Magnus is controlled by the Brotherhood, a small voice said inside Alex's mind. *The Brotherhood, and someone using the name Gaylan.*

After the evening meal, Alex returned to the wall with Stonebill. Stonebill was nervous and excited, and he quickly flew off to see where Rallian and Talbot were. The moon was already up when Stonebill returned to Alex's shoulder, a written message tied to his leg.

"King Rallian asked that I bring this to you," Stonebill explained.

"Thank you," said Alex. He unfolded the note and read it quickly.

"What does it say?" asked Stonebill.

"It says that they are ready to move into position as soon as I conjure up the fog. Rallian asks that I have the fog move in front of Talbot's army until they are close enough to keep Lazar's army from escaping. When the fog stops moving, they will stop also. I think I can get Talbot's army close to the main road."

"They will make noise," Stonebill warned. "If they come too close to Lazar's army, someone may hear their approach."

"Not if the fog also blocks any sound," said Alex. "Rest on the wall, my friend, I will need to move both of my arms."

Stonebill fluttered away, and Alex lifted his arms above his head. The spell was something he'd read about but never actually tried, and he hoped it would be everything he needed it to be now. Slowly, as he worked the magic and concentrated on what he needed, thin wisps of mist began to form on the open plain in front of him. The wisps soon became pockets of fog, and after a few more minutes, the pockets moved together, forming cloudlike mounds. Alex continued to work his magic until the land to the south of Lazar's army had vanished, replaced by a solid wall of white.

Alex lowered his arms and leaned against his staff. As he rested, Stonebill returned to his shoulder, landing gently.

"Do you like it?" Alex asked.

"An impressive feat," said Stonebill. "Few wizards could conjure up such a fog without completely draining themselves. I can see that this took power out of you, but already that power has been replaced."

Alex knew where his renewed power came from: it was the power of the dragon. He had been looking for ways to use it with his normal magic, and summoning the fog had been the perfect opportunity to blend the two.

When morning came, Alex was still standing at the end of the wall. Caftan and Shelnor soon joined him, eager to see what was about to happen. Stonebill was circling overhead, and the men of Caftan and Shelnor's armies moved forward. They were ready for battle, but Alex still hoped a battle could be avoided. Hathnor was sitting in a chair that had been brought out for him, even though he insisted he was strong enough to stand.

"It is time," said Alex, stepping forward.

Lifting his staff, Alex concentrated on the shadow army of Lazar. He felt the magic that Magnus had used, and as he lowered his staff, the first rays of sunlight fell on the open plain. The massive force that had been Lazar's army vanished in the light, and the fog Alex had conjured drifted away in the morning breeze.

"That's cut them down to size," said Hathnor.

"It won't take long for them to see their situation," said Alex. "I think the flag of truce will appear shortly."

"Only this time it will be King Rallian who offers terms," said Shelnor.

"When the flag of truce appears, you should ride forward with us," Caftan said to Alex.

"Yes," said Alex. "I think the king will expect me to be there."

In less than half an hour, the flag of truce appeared. This time the flag did not move toward the gap of Luthan, but instead moved to a point west of Lazar's army. It was clear that Athron wanted the leaders of both sides to come forward.

"I should go as well," said Hathnor, trying to get up.

"Stay for now," said Alex. "Your wound still needs time to heal."

Hathnor bowed in acceptance of Alex's words and returned to his chair.

Alex climbed onto his horse and rode forward with Caftan, Shelnor, and their personal guards. When they reached the company sent from Lazar's army, Alex could see the fear in their faces. Lord Talbot and his company arrived soon after

Alex and the others. Alex noticed that Rallian remained hidden, his head covered by a heavy cloak.

"So, you are all in it together," said Athron. "Summoned up some demon to fight against us—that's what the men are saying. With that fog moving in, and the breaking of Magnus's spell, I can see they are right."

"It was no demon that did these things, Athron," Lord Talbot answered. "A true wizard has come to Nezza, and he fights for what is right."

"What is right," Athron repeated, his tone bitter. "How can we guess what he fights for? Lazar would have us believe that Magnus fights for what is right, though I doubt that as much as I doubt your wizard."

"What would you fight for, Athron?" Talbot asked. "Why have you come so far north? We have had peace with Karmus for many years, yet now you come looking for war."

"We know what you did, Talbot," Athron answered hotly. "By the ancients, I swear we'll have revenge on you for Rallian's death."

"So, Lazar claims that I had Rallian killed," said Talbot with a harsh laugh. "I thought you a wiser man, Athron. I never thought you would be taken in by Lazar's lies."

"Lies or truth, it matters little now," said Athron. "You've won the day—what terms do you offer? I'll not waste my men in a hopeless fight."

"Since when does a general of Karmus surrender his troops to the lord of Karmus?" Rallian asked.

"Lord of Karmus?" Athron repeated, turning to see who had spoken.

"That's right, Athron—the lord of Karmus," said Rallian, pulling off his cloak.

"Lord Rallian," Athron stuttered. The general dropped to one knee in front of his lord, almost unable to speak. "By the ancients, we thought you dead, my lord. Lazar told us you died and that Lord Talbot was responsible."

"Yet now you see I am alive and that Lord Talbot is my true and trusted friend," said Rallian. "So tell me, Athron, where do you stand now?"

"I am yours to command, my lord," answered Athron without hesitation. "If I had known you were alive, I would have done all I could to find you."

"He speaks truly and from his heart," said Alex, stepping toward Rallian.

"Yes, I believe he does," agreed Rallian. "Though he should learn not to call my friends demons."

"Forgive my words, my lord, I did not know—"

"Enough," Rallian interrupted. "I know you will do as I command, Athron, but what about your army?"

"My lord?" Athron questioned.

"Whom will they serve?" asked Rallian. "Will they fight for the king of Nezza, or will they fight for the traitor Lazar?"

"My lord, that is a difficult question," said Athron. "I believe that most will follow you gladly, though I fear some will say they follow but will instead seek to betray you to Lazar."

"I see," said Rallian.

"There is something more to consider, my lord," Athron continued. "Most of these men, true or not, have families in or near Karmus. If Lazar discovers that we have joined you, he will seek revenge on those most dear to us."

"Yes, that does seem like something my uncle would do," said Rallian.

"Then we must find a way to free their families without Lazar knowing his men have joined us," said Alex, watching Rallian.

"But how?" Rallian asked. "If we march south to Karmus, Lazar's spies will inform him of our approach."

"We can send word to Lazar that Caftan and Shelnor have stepped aside and that Athron is moving forward to fight Lord Talbot. Then we can march south and slip into Karmus without Lazar knowing," Alex said. "I will summon a storm to help hide us from Lazar's spies. Of course, we will have to travel in the rain, but that is a small price to pay for the lives of your loyal subjects."

"Yes, a very small price," Rallian agreed.

"My lord, if I might speak," said Talbot. "You should let yourself be known to all of Athron's army. Those who wish to join you will come south with us. Those who do not, we can leave here under guard."

"There is wisdom in that," said Athron. "I know those who are most likely to betray us to Lazar. I can have them remain here as guards—or prisoners."

"First, pick one of your men who Lazar will trust," said Alex, considering how best to make his plan work. "We will send him south with word of your victory and of your intended move."

"But he will know our victory is a lie," Athron pointed out.

"It would be better to send someone we know is loyal to King Rallian."

"No," said Alex. "I will speak to the man we send, and he will believe the story that he tells to Lazar."

"You can control men's minds?" Rallian asked.

"I can make them see what I wish them to see," answered Alex. "I do not do this lightly, and I only do it now because we are in great need. We must save the families of the men who will be true to you."

"Very well, assemble your men, Lord Athron," Rallian commanded. "I will speak to them. Any who are willing to swear allegiance to me will be welcome in our company."

"As you wish, my king," said Athron, bowing.

Rallian decided to stand on the wall Alex had made in order to speak to the army. He wanted as many of the soldiers as possible to see him. Alex knew it was necessary, but he worried that Rallian was making himself an easy target.

"I must let them see me," said Rallian firmly. "How else can I ask them to follow me?"

Rallian climbed the steps to the top of the wall as Athron moved his army forward. Alex was relieved to see that none of the soldiers carried their weapons. Still, he stood at the end of the wall, watching. If any kind of weapon flew toward Rallian, Alex would be able to stop it before it reached its mark.

Rallian's speech to the army was moving, and almost every soldier agreed to take an oath of allegiance. After the final tally, Rallian had added nine thousand men to his army, which meant that his entire army was well over thirty-five thousand strong.

Athron had chosen a man he knew to be one of Lazar's spies as the messenger, and the man seemed more than willing to accept the task of taking word to Lazar.

"What will you tell Lord Lazar?" Alex asked.

"I am to say that Caftan and Shelnor have moved aside," the man recited. "Lord Athron and the army are continuing toward Talbas."

"And?" Alex prodded, working his magic.

"All is well with the northern army. We will have revenge on Talbas for Rallian's death," said the man, his eyes slightly out of focus.

"Is that true?" Alex asked.

"On my life, it is true," the man answered.

"Then go swiftly," said Alex, moving toward the door of the tent. "Lazar must have word as soon as possible. Tell him that his army is true and marches to Talbas."

"I will go as quickly as possible," the man repeated. He climbed onto a horse and sped off to the south.

Alex watched the messenger leave. Lazar would believe this man. Even Magnus would be hard-pressed to detect the false story because the magic that created it would grow weaker as the messenger's own belief in the story grew stronger. That was perhaps the best part of this plan.

That night there was a grand feast, and Alex and his friends were all together in King Rallian's tent. Rallian insisted that Alex tell the story of his own first adventure, starting from the beginning, and reluctantly Alex agreed. Alex was about to begin his tale when a dust-covered messenger arrived from Ossbo.

"What word?" Shelnor questioned, his smile fading as he looked at the messenger.

"My lord, the great city of Ossbo is in need," answered the messenger in a weak voice. "The armies of Lord Bray have marched north into our lands. When I left the city they were only five days away, and it has taken me six days to get here."

"I should have remembered Bray," said Alex angrily. "He does whatever Lazar tells him to do—obviously Lazar has sent him against you."

"I must go at once," said Shelnor. He turned to Rallian. "My lord, give me leave to take my army to Ossbo. I left only five hundred men to defend the city. They cannot hold it for long."

"This will make our plans for Karmus more difficult," Talbot commented, glancing at Rallian as he spoke.

"We must send aid to Ossbo," said Rallian. "I'll not leave the lands that are loyal to me open to attack."

"King Rallian," said Alex, "Shelnor has taken an oath to go south with you. I would not have him break his oath. Leave this fight to me."

"But what can you do?" Shelnor asked. "I know you are a wizard and have great power, but what can you do against an army?"

"I will drive them back," answered Alex as flames of anger started growing inside him. "I will make them wish they never marched north."

"You will call a dragon," said Skeld. "The oracle called you a dragon lord. You will call a dragon to defeat the army of Bray."

"Yes," said Alex.

"Dragon lord?" Rallian questioned.

"A wizard who can command dragons," Alex answered without explaining.

"But how—?" Shelnor asked.

"I can do it—do not fear," said Alex.

"The prophecy," murmured Talbot.

"Prophecy? What prophecy?" Alex asked.

"The dragon will come and the true king with him," Talbot began. "When the desert river flows, and the eastern wind blows. Then the ring will come again, and the wars will find their end."

"The desert river flows," said Virgil. "We saw you break the curse on the river."

"And the eastern wind is about to start blowing," said Alex.

"I will go south with you, my king," Shelnor declared. "As I have sworn."

"And Ossbo?" asked the messenger.

"The dragon will come, and with him, the king," answered Shelnor.

"I will prepare the fastest horses," said Caftan, moving toward the tent door.

"No," Alex called out. "I can travel faster than any horse of this land."

"But how will you reach Ossbo if not on horseback?" Talbot questioned.

Alex didn't answer but headed for the door.

"Wait, Master Taylor," said Shelnor. "Take my ring. My

family will know for certain that you come from me if you have it."

"Thank you, Lord Shelnor, and do not fear. Your city will be safe." Alex left the tent, followed by Rallian and the others. Stonebill fluttered down onto his shoulder.

"I will come with you," said the bird.

"You will be hard-pressed to keep pace," said Alex. "No, I would rather you fly south with Rallian and the army. Bring me word when they are five days from Karmus."

"As you wish," said Stonebill.

"I still don't see how you're going to get to Ossbo without a horse," said Rallian.

"First things first," said Alex, remembering he needed to summon a storm to hide the armies of the north. "The storm will last until I rejoin you near Karmus. Avoid cities and towns as much as possible, and march as fast as you can in the rain."

"But there is no storm," said Caftan, looking up at the clear sky.

Alex lifted his staff and pointed it toward the east, speaking the magic words softly. Tempe had told him that the rains would come late this year, and now he understood why. Using both his wizard and his dragon magic, he reached out and summoned the rain that was already there. He poured the power of the dragon into the magic, knowing he would need that power to make the storm last. The tents of the army fluttered in the breeze, and Rallian and the others looked to the east. Alex lowered his staff, and as it touched the ground, a blast of wind came howling out of the east.

"When you see the dragon, look for me," Alex shouted over the wind.

With his final words, Alex changed himself into an eagle and rose above the camp of King Rallian. He looked down at the stunned faces of his friends, and with an angry screech, he shot like an arrow toward the city of Ossbo.

CHAPTER TWENTY
THE DRAGON OF OSSBO

The wind grew stronger as Alex flew east, but he didn't
change his shape again until he was well away from
the camp. When he did change, it was into his second
true form. As a massive true silver dragon, he moved faster
than any bird could fly. He was able to outrace the storm he
had summoned and cross the land between Luthan and Ossbo
in far less time than it had taken the messenger. The joy of
being a dragon filled him, and as he followed the road toward
Ossbo, his anger toward the armies of Bray burned hotter inside of him.

There was something more than anger in Alex's mind.
There was the feeling of connection to the land and the magic
of Nezza that he had felt before when in his dragon form. The
great dragon Salinor had told him a little about the connection, hinting that Alex would learn more in time. Now new
feelings came to Alex's mind, feelings of sorrow and of a great
hope—sorrow for the wars that had gone on for so long, and
hope that a true king would return and restore order and peace
once more. There was also hope that the magic of Nezza would

be free to help the people of this land after being held back for so long.

Alex accepted his feelings and focused his mind on what lay ahead of him. He knew that Bray's army would be terrified when he arrived, and so would the people of Ossbo. The people of Ossbo would see what he did to the army attacking them, and he hoped that would take away some of their fear.

It took Alex a little more than an hour to fly over the land that had taken the messenger six days to cross. It was raining hard by the time the city of Ossbo came into his view. He saw that part of the city was burning. Bray's army had set up catapults and was shooting huge jars of burning liquid over the city walls. Alex let out a thundering roar as he swooped down on the unsuspecting army that surrounded the city.

With his first pass, Alex let loose a jet of flame. A cloud of steam rose from the wet ground as the dragon fire spread out like water. The catapults burned, and the jars of liquid exploded, spreading the fire into the invading army's camp. He could hear terrified yells, mixed with the pained cries of those caught in the flames. Alex felt no mercy for the injured as the rage of the dragon took control of his mind.

He dove again, blasting the tents of the army with fire and ripping them away with his claws. This army would pay for their evil deeds and for the evil of their weak lord. It was time for the wars of Nezza to come to an end. If the lords of Nezza would not end the wars, then the dragon would.

Again and again, Alex dove down on the fleeing army. He tore great trenches in the earth with his tail and filled them with fire. The land glowed orange and red, and the air was

filled with smoke and steam. A few soldiers tried to shoot arrows at the dragon, but the arrows that struck him simply shattered on his true silver scales.

He dove again and was about to destroy a large collection
of carts, but he stopped himself when he saw that they con-
tained helpless prisoners. His rage flared as he realized that the
army of Bray was using the prisoners to force the people inside the city to surrender. How many people had they already
killed? How could men be so evil?

The storm kept pace with Alex's rage. Lightning shattered
the darkness, and the rain pounded the earth like a rolling
drum. The rain had put out the fires in the city. Ossbo would
not be destroyed by fire, but Bray's army would be.

The army was broken long before Alex grew tired of attacking them. A few small groups began racing back to the
south as fast as they could go. Alex let his thoughts reach out to
one group, looking for a name to go with the face he could see
so clearly. It came as he flew over the company: Bray.

The dragon's rage got the better of Alex, and without considering the consequences, he destroyed Bray and his men with
a huge ball of flame. One evil lord was gone. If another took
his place, then the dragon would make sure he met the same
fate.

Enough, a familiar voice said in Alex's mind. *You have done
enough. Return now. Help those who need you.*

"Salinor," said Alex. "How . . . How did you know?"

*The same way you would know if I were to do what you have
done,* Salinor answered, his voice kind and not accusing. *You
have saved the city and broken Bray's army, as you promised you*

would do. That is enough for now. Return, and help those who need you.

"As you wish, great one," said Alex, his anger slipping away.

Remember this, child, Salinor continued. *With all your powers of wizardry, with all your powers as a dragon, you cannot force the people of Nezza to make peace.*

"But—"

You must help the young king find peace for his people, said Salinor. *Force alone is not the path to lasting peace.*

Alex flew back toward Ossbo, changing into an eagle once more as he went. Alex knew Salinor's words were true, but he couldn't see the path Salinor was talking about. Without magic, without war and force and destruction, Alex didn't know how Rallian could win his crown and bring peace to Nezza.

The fields around the city were still burning when Alex arrived. He landed close to the city gate and changed back to his human form without being seen. Walking up to the gates, Alex could hear people yelling and running inside the city. He knew that many of the people must be hurt; he knew he needed to help them. Raising his staff, he pounded on the city gates.

"Open in the name of Rallian, king of Nezza," Alex called out.

There was no answer.

Alex raised his staff once more, but this time he magically lifted the massive iron beam that held the gates shut and moved it to one side. When Alex struck the city gate with his staff again, one side of it opened in front of him.

"What the—?" A large man near the gate started, then

stopped in surprise. "Who are you? What do you want? How did you open the gates?"

"What is your name?" Alex asked the man.

"I am Tilac," the man answered.

"I am a messenger from King Rallian and Lord Shelnor," answered Alex as he walked into the city. "I must speak with Lady Shelnor at once."

"Yes, of course, but the gate . . ." said Tilac.

"Send men to the fields," Alex ordered. "Along the south road they will find a number of people trapped in carts who need to be cared for."

Tilac hesitated, looking around for someone to help.

"Quickly!" Alex commanded.

"At once," said Tilac, and he began yelling for others to come and do what Alex had ordered.

Five minutes later, a group of men was assembled and on its way.

"Now, take me to Lady Shelnor," Alex ordered Tilac.

"As you command," said Tilac again, leading the way into the city.

The fire in the city had not been as bad as Alex had thought, but there were still many damaged buildings. There were dozens of injured people lying in the street with no one to help them. Alex was angry for a moment, but then he realized that the uninjured people in the city were busy looking through the ruins, searching for others who had been hurt.

"How long was the army of Bray here before the dragon drove them away?" asked Alex.

"Two days," answered Tilac. "If the dragon had not come, the city would have surrendered in the morning."

"Then it is well that he came," said Alex.

"Do you know this dragon?" Tilac asked, apparently shocked by the idea.

"I know him well," said Alex. "He came to protect your city, though I wish he had come sooner."

"As do I," said Tilac. "Though I never believed in dragons before this night."

"It is hard to believe in things you've never seen."

"Yes, very hard," Tilac agreed.

Alex didn't say anything else as Tilac led him into a grand palace, and finally into the private rooms of Lady Shelnor.

"My lady," said Tilac, bowing. "This man is a messenger. He has asked to see you."

"What madness is this?" said Lady Shelnor, getting up from a small bed she had been kneeling beside. "The city besieged, your lord off to fight at the gap of Luthan, and you bring a stranger into my private chambers!"

"Lady Shelnor, please," said Alex, stepping forward. "I have come from King Rallian and your noble husband."

Alex held out Lord Shelnor's ring for Lady Shelnor to see as he spoke. Lady Shelnor hesitated for a moment before taking the ring from Alex's hand.

"My husband is well?" Lady Shelnor asked after a long moment.

"He is," Alex answered. "I left him at the gap of Luthan a few hours ago. He was preparing to march south with the king."

"A few hours?" Lady Shelnor asked in disbelief.

"My name is Alex Taylor, and I am a wizard," Alex said. "I have come to aid your city and drive off Bray's army. I am here to help."

"You, alone?"

"My lady, the siege is lifted," said Tilac. "A great silver dragon came from the west and destroyed the armies of Bray."

"A dragon? Don't talk nonsense, Tilac. There are no such things as dragons."

"He speaks the truth," said Alex. "The dragon came because I called him. Bray's army is scattered and destroyed."

Lady Shelnor looked at the ring again and then back to Alex, her face full of questions. "You . . . you are a wizard?"

"I am."

"You are a healer, too?"

"Yes," said Alex.

"Can you . . ." Lady Shelnor began and then hesitated. "Can you heal my son?"

"Your son?" Alex asked.

"Young Lord Roland fell from the city walls while defending his people," Tilac said softly.

"I told him not to go, but he disobeyed me," said Lady Shelnor, a touch of pride mixed with the sorrow in her voice. "He would not let others defend his father's city while he remained safe in the palace."

"Where is he?" Alex asked.

"Here" Lady Shelnor pointed to the small bed where she had been kneeling.

Alex moved forward and knelt beside the boy. He looked

to be ten or eleven years old. He was pale, and Alex could see that he was in a great deal of pain. For a moment Alex worried that Roland was already moving toward the shadowlands, but he soon saw that Roland's spirit was still in him.

Alex took Roland's hand as he let his mind and magic move outward. As his thoughts moved to find the injuries in Roland's body, Alex slowly began to feel the pain that Roland was suffering. When he let his thoughts return, he felt drained.

Carefully, Alex moved his hands over Roland, allowing some of his own strength to flow into the boy. He shifted the broken ribs on Roland's left side, pushing them back into place with his mind, blocking the pain by allowing it to flow into his own body. When he finished his work, Alex was dripping with sweat and shaking, but he was sure that Roland would live.

"Are there any trained healers in this city?" Alex asked, dropping to the floor to rest for a moment.

"A few," said Tilac.

"Summon them," Alex ordered. "I will need their help if we are to save the injured people of Ossbo."

"And my son?" Lady Shelnor questioned.

"He has many broken bones that will take time to heal, but he will live."

"How do you know? How can you be sure?" Lady Shelnor asked, her voice shaking in fear.

"I know," said Alex.

"But—"

"He will live," Alex repeated firmly. "Now, summon the healers. There is much work to do in this city, and I will need their help."

"Go, Tilac, do as he commands," said Lady Shelnor with a wave of her hand.

"Forgive me, lady," said Alex, "but I must rest a moment before going to help your people."

A short time later, Alex left Lady Shelnor with her son and made his way back to the main entrance of the palace. He met Tilac there, with a small group of people following him. Alex could see that most of the people had at least some power in them. He felt his own strength returning as they gathered around him, waiting for him to speak.

"How many people are injured?" Alex asked.

"Most of the guards," said Tilac. "I would say a hundred of them badly, and the others only slightly."

"And the people of the city?" Alex asked.

"Many have burns and cuts," said one of the healers, stepping forward. "We know charms and simple spells to ease their pains, but we have no great store of medicines."

"What is your name?" asked Alex.

"I am Roanna."

"Go to the kitchens, Roanna, and find the largest caldron or cooking pot you can. Fill it with clean water and set it to boil. I will follow shortly."

Roanna bowed to Alex and left, running.

Alex turned back to the rest of the healers. "The people rescued from Bray's camp? How are they?"

"Weak and hungry," said Tilac. "There are few injuries among them that a meal and a good night's sleep will not heal."

"Very well," said Alex, looking at the faces around him. "Find those who are injured the worst. Bring them here to the palace as quickly as you can. I will go to the kitchens and make some healing potions for you to use. Tilac, make sure those who were rescued from the carts get something to eat, and try to find them a place to rest."

"As you command," said Tilac with a bow.

"Go now, my friends," said Alex to the healers. "We have a great deal of work to do, and the night is already growing old."

The healers left the palace, and Alex went to find the kitchens. When he finally found them, Roanna was there, boiling as much water as she possibly could in several large pots.

"I could not move the largest pots to the fire," Roanna explained, not meeting Alex's eyes. "I thought I should do as much as I could. I hope it is enough."

"It will be fine," said Alex, leaning his staff against the wall and clearing a large table in the center of the room. "Do you know anything of adventurers?"

"I have heard stories," said Roanna in a slightly confused tone.

"Very well. I don't have time to explain things now, but I'm going to disappear for a few minutes, though this bag will remain. You will not be able to move this bag while I am gone. When I return, I will try to answer any questions you might have."

Roanna nodded that she understood.

Alex lifted his magic bag and quietly spoke the password. Once inside his bag, he moved as fast as he could to collect what he would need. First, he went to his greenhouse to collect herbs and roots, flowers and leaves. Then he went to his library, where he stored his other magical items for potion making. It took him less than ten minutes to get everything, and with his arms full, he returned to the kitchen.

Alex began setting out the items he'd collected on the table, arranging them in groups so they would be ready for each potion he planned to make.

"This is dwarf's beard," said Roanna, picking up one of the plants.

"That is one of its names," said Alex.

"But it is rare here in Nezza, and it only grows in the far north," Roanna said.

"I had it in my bag," said Alex. "You said you'd heard stories of adventurers—what do those stories say?"

"They say that adventurers carry magic bags with them, bags that can hold many things in a small place," answered Roanna.

"That is true," said Alex as he moved to one of the smaller pots of water. "Magic bags make it easy for adventurers to carry everything we might need. As you can see, I have a great many things in my bag."

As the first potion began to boil, Alex started mixing a second and then a third. When the third potion was brewing, he returned to the first and removed it from the fire, checking its color to make sure it was finished.

"Take a goblet of this to Lord Roland. Make sure he drinks all of it," Alex said to Roanna. "Can you splint broken bones?"

"I have done it many times," Roanna answered with pride.

"Roland's bones are already set, but his left arm and leg will both need splints," said Alex. "You should also bind his ribs because several of them are broken."

"As you command," said Roanna, taking a goblet from one of the shelves and filling it with the potion Alex pointed to.

"When you are finished with Lord Roland, return," Alex said as Roanna moved toward the door. "There are many others who will need our help."

Alex returned to the potions he was brewing and began making one more he thought would be helpful. It wasn't long before Alex thought he heard Roanna coming toward the kitchen. He turned to ask why she was back so soon, but to his surprise, Lady Shelnor entered the kitchen. Her hair was pulled back and she wore a common work dress now, and there was a fierce and determined look in her eyes.

"Roanna told me there was much work to do," said Lady Shelnor. "How may I serve my people?"

"Great lady," said Alex with a slight bow. "I have two large cauldrons of healing potion that are ready. The healers are bringing those who are hurt the worst to the palace. Find some men to help you, and take these cauldrons to the healers. Have them give some of this potion to all who come here. I will have more potions ready soon."

"As you wish," said Lady Shelnor, turning to go.

The night seemed to go on forever. Alex continued to brew potions, and Lady Shelnor and Roanna continued to take them to those who were injured. The work seemed endless, and from time to time Alex had to call on the power of the dragon to refresh himself so he could keep going.

When he finished making potions, Alex went back up into the palace carrying a large pot full of a thick, reddish-brown mixture. The healers gathered around him when he arrived.

"This mixture is for burns," Alex explained, setting down the pot. "Spread a little of it over any burned skin. It will ease the pain and help the skin to heal."

The healers immediately did as Alex commanded.

Alex turned to Roanna. "Now, show me those who are most hurt."

Roanna led him through the palace, stopping at the makeshift cots to tell Alex what was wrong with each person. Alex did what he could for each of them, taking away their pain and their fear and setting them on a path of healing.

When Roanna fell asleep while Alex was helping a sickly old man, he motioned for one of the other healers to take her place. When he had seen all the people in the palace, he went out into the courtyard, helping those who needed him. Alex lost track of time as he worked, trying to do all he could for the injured in the city.

When he returned to the palace, it was dark. Alex didn't know how long he had been working, but he thought at least one day had gone by. Moving quietly so as not to disturb anyone, he was surprised to find Lady Shelnor and Roanna waiting for him.

"My lord, you must rest," said Roanna in a concerned voice.

"There are still many who need help," said Alex with a weak smile.

"And they will receive help, but you must rest," said Lady Shelnor.

"It has been three days since you came to our city, Master Taylor. Surely you must need food and sleep," Roanna added.

"Three days?" Alex asked.

"It has been three days since you saved our city," answered Lady Shelnor. "You have done much for my people, and now you must rest."

"Yes," said Alex, suddenly feeling tired beyond words. "A little food and sleep would be good."

"Come. A bed has been made ready for you," said Lady Shelnor.

Alex followed Lady Shelnor into the palace. He could see that many of the injured were looking better already. Most of the people in the great hall turned to look at him as he passed. He was taken to a large room where a fine-looking bed and a meal were waiting for him.

"Rest, my friend," said Lady Shelnor. "If anyone deserves a rest, it is you."

"Call me if there is need," said Alex.

He didn't eat but fell onto the bed as soon as the door to his room was closed. He couldn't remember ever feeling so tired, and the soft bed was more than he could have hoped for. He let himself sink into the softness and drift away into a happy, restful sleep.

When Alex woke, the sky was getting dark again, and he guessed that he had been asleep for twelve hours or more. He got up and changed his clothes, then hurried back to the great hall of the palace.

Lady Shelnor and Roanna were both in the main hall,

serving food to those who were well enough to eat. Alex went to them and asked if anyone needed his help. Lady Shelnor smiled and told him that all the injured were doing fine, and she insisted that Roanna take Alex back to the kitchens.

"Make sure he eats something," Lady Shelnor said to Roanna. "It will not do for an honored guest of the city to go hungry."

Roanna led Alex back to the kitchens. There were several people in the kitchens now, and the air was full of wonderful smells. The smells made Alex hungry, and he was happy to let Roanna bring him a large meal. Roanna sat down and watched him as he ate.

"You have power as a healer," said Alex.

"I am nothing compared to you," said Roanna.

"Are you so sure?"

"You did more in three days than I could ever do," said Roanna.

"I did what was needed," said Alex. "But you did a great deal as well."

"You were watching?" Roanna asked in surprise.

"I see many things," said Alex. "Tell me, who trained you in the art of healing?"

"My grandmother," said Roanna with a touch of pride. "She had great hopes for me as a healer."

"Had?" Alex asked.

"I was not able to pass the test," said Roanna quietly. "I feared the wall too much to ever even try."

"That is nothing to be ashamed of," said Alex. "There are many who do not wish to go there."

"Have you been to the wall?" Roanna questioned.

"Yes."

"I was told that I could never be a great healer unless I went there," Roanna said. "I could never find the courage to go, so I will never be a great healer."

"You may never be known as a healer of power, but you are still a great healer," said Alex. "Journeys to the shadowlands are dangerous, and only a small part of a healer's craft."

Roanna looked like she was thinking very hard.

Alex waited for a moment, then said, "Do what you can as a healer. Do not be troubled by the wall or what lies beyond it."

Roanna nodded, and Alex thought she understood what he was trying to say. When he finished his meal, Alex returned to the halls of the palace to talk with the healers about their art. He knew that he would soon need to leave this place and return to Karmus. There was still so much work to do before Rallian sat on his throne.

CHAPTER TWENTY-ONE

THE KING OF NEZZA

Alex had been in Ossbo just over two weeks when Stonebill turned up. He landed on Alex's shoulder, shaking water out of his feathers, as Alex was sitting down to dinner with Lady Shelnor and the few lords that remained in Ossbo. Alex laughed, but Lady Shelnor and the lords of Ossbo all looked shocked by the bird's arrival.

"Your storm has lasted for nearly three weeks, and I've had a hard time finding a dry place to sleep," Stonebill complained.

"Adventures are often uncomfortable," said Alex with a smile. "What news do you bring?"

"Rallian and the lords of the north were ten days away from Karmus when I left them," Stonebill answered. "That was seven days ago. I would have come sooner, but the east wind is still blowing hard."

"Do you think I've overdone the spell?" Alex asked.

"If you don't put an end to it soon, the whole land of Nezza will sink into the sea," Stonebill croaked.

"Master Taylor, can you speak to this bird?" Lady Shelnor interrupted.

"I can," Alex answered. "He is a friend, sent by the oracle Tempe to aid me in this land."

"The oracle? You have spoken to the Oracle of the Red Lands?" Lady Shelnor asked, her eyes wide.

"Yes," said Alex. "She was most kind to me and to King Rallian."

"And what does this most noble bird say to you?"

"He brings word from King Rallian and the lords of the north. They are approaching Karmus, and so my time in your fair city is coming to an end."

"It will take you weeks to reach Karmus," one of the lords of Ossbo said.

"No," said Alex. "If I leave in the early morning, I should arrive at King Rallian's camp in time for the midday meal."

"Master Taylor is a wizard of great power," Lady Shelnor said. "I am sure what he says is true."

"Do you have any message you'd like me to take to your husband?" Alex asked Lady Shelnor.

"Yes, if you would be so kind," she said.

When the meal ended, Alex wandered out into the palace garden, thinking about what was to come in the next few days. The rain was still falling hard, and Alex took shelter in a small gazebo on the edge of the garden. Stonebill sat quietly on Alex's shoulder, and after a few minutes, he broke the silence.

"How will you reach Karmus in time for the midday meal? Even in eagle form and with the east wind at your back, it will take you days to reach King Rallian."

"I will not travel as an eagle," said Alex. "If you wish to come with me, I will have to put you inside my magic bag."

"But how will you travel?" Stonebill persisted.

"Have you not guessed? You see so much, I would think you could see the answer to your question."

"You will summon the dragon once more and ride on its back to Karmus," said Stonebill after a moment of thought.

"Something like that," said Alex.

He was surprised the raven hadn't guessed correctly. Alex hadn't told anyone in Nezza about his ability to take the dragon form, not even Tempe. He suspected, however, that the oracle would guess his secret once she heard about the dragon coming to Ossbo.

"It will be a wet flight." Stonebill chuckled.

"Wet, but short."

It was well after midnight when Alex returned to his room. He was surprised to find Roanna waiting for him at the door, a troubled look on her face.

"I have a message from Lady Shelnor to her husband," said Roanna, holding out a letter for Alex.

"You also have something you wish to ask," said Alex.

"Are my thoughts so open to you?"

"You have been thinking about this since we talked in the kitchens," said Alex. "You wish to take the healer's test and travel to the land of shadows."

"You are the only healer I know who has been there," said Roanna. "You are the only one who can teach me what I need to know."

"Are you certain this is what you want?" Alex asked.

"This . . . You may be my only chance to learn this part of the healing craft," Roanna answered.

"You do not answer my question. Is this really what you want?" Alex pressed.

"I . . . I don't know," Roanna answered slowly. "I want to learn, I want to help my people, but . . ."

"But the shadowlands are a dark place, and you do not wish to go there," Alex finished for her. "I understand your fear, Roanna. Do what you can for your people, and do not let thoughts of the shadowlands trouble you."

Roanna bowed to Alex, her troubled look fading as she turned and left.

Alex entered his room, and Stonebill fluttered off his shoulder and landed on the bedpost.

"She has a great deal of power," Stonebill said.

"Yes," said Alex. "I saw it the first night I arrived here."

"I think she will be a great help to the people of Nezza, if she can stop worrying about the shadowlands," said Stonebill.

"I think you are right," said Alex, looking at the raven. "But only time will tell, and now it is time to go south and see the king. Will you travel in my bag, or will you make your own way?"

"If I made my own way, I would miss everything," answered Stonebill. "Put me in your bag, and at least I'll get some rest."

Alex spoke the necessary words and put Stonebill inside his magic bag. He would return to Karmus, and, with any luck, Rallian would be king before another week had passed.

It won't be as easy as that, Alex's O'Gash said in his head. *You may win Karmus, you may crown Rallian as king, but what about the other kingdoms? How will you make peace in Nezza?*

The spell you set loose at the river has done its work. Old angers are renewed, old hatreds remembered. A desire for revenge fills this land, and the people want someone to pay for their pain. Magnus will use this to his advantage if he can; you need to remember Magnus.

Rallian is the key, his O'Gash finished. *Rallian and . . .*

"And?" Alex questioned.

Alex waited for a long time, but his O'Gash said nothing more. It troubled him that his O'Gash did not finish what it had started to say. He ran everything through his mind again: *Rallian is the key. Rallian and . . .* and what?

Alex made his way back to the palace garden, and when he was sure he was alone, he changed into an eagle and flew into the darkness before the dawn. He would change into a dragon when he was well away from the city and then fly to Karmus before going to Rallian's camp. It would be good to see Karmus and find out what Lazar and Magnus were up to. If Rallian's army had been spotted, there would be signs of preparation in Karmus.

As he flew, Alex considered breaking the spell that kept the storm in place, but he decided against it. He didn't know what plans Rallian had made to rescue the families of his soldiers, but he thought the rain would help those plans, whatever they were.

When Alex reached the first mountains, he let his magic grow around him and changed into his second true form. The great true silver dragon rose up over the mountains, speeding off to the south and west, the storm following behind him. He let out a roar of happiness as he flew. He knew that he would reach Karmus just as it was getting light, and his appearance would come as a great shock to both Lazar and Magnus.

In the pale morning light, Alex slowed his flight and flew lower so he could get a good look at the city of Karmus. He could hear the frightened yells from the people in the streets below him. He studied the streets of the city as he circled and noticed that there were few soldiers to be seen. In fact, the only soldiers he did see were on the island prison, close to Lazar and his seat of power.

Or close to Magnus, his O'Gash whispered.

Alex let out a great roar as he flew over the city once more. He didn't see anything that looked like trouble, so he kept his eyes open as he turned north to find the army of King Rallian.

Rallian and his men were less than half a day away from Karmus, but their progress had been stopped. As Alex flew over their camp, he instantly saw what the problem was. The lords from five of the seven inner kingdoms had assembled their armies, and they now stood between Rallian and Karmus.

Circling overhead, Alex took in all the details of both armies. The armies of the inner kingdoms outnumbered Rallian by nearly two to one, which meant that fighting their way to Karmus would be impossible. He could also feel the desire for revenge that filled the armies of the inner kingdoms. They wanted someone to blame for the years of suffering, they wanted someone to pay, and Rallian and the lords of the north were the focus of their anger.

Alex flew above the clouds, hiding the dragon from the men on the ground. Once he was high enough not to be seen, he changed back into an eagle and circled down to Rallian's camp.

"At least they haven't sent word to Lazar," Alex heard Talbot say as he approached Rallian's tent.

"They haven't sent any *official* word to Lazar," said Shelnor. "Still, they seem willing to listen to reason and avoid a battle if they can."

"But we must get to Karmus soon," said Rallian, sounding frustrated. "If Lazar finds out what has happened, he could slaughter the people of Karmus before we get there."

"I doubt we could fight our way through," said Caftan. "And even if we could, it would make enemies of those you will need as friends."

Alex didn't wait to hear more. He stepped into the tent, shaking the rain from his hair.

"Alex!" Rallian exclaimed, rushing over to welcome him back. "We saw the dragon and thought you would return shortly."

"Only just in time, it seems," said Alex. "I have news, but perhaps you should tell me what is happening here first."

"Lazar is forcing the inner kingdoms to take his side," said Talbot. "They recognize Rallian and his right to claim the crown, but Lazar holds the young lords of the inner kingdoms in Karmus. If the lords of the inner kingdoms want to save their young lords, they have to do what Lazar says."

Alex shook his head. "The seven young lords Lazar held are dead. They were sent to the western desert some time ago. I'm sure Rallian can guess their fate."

"The serpent," said Rallian, going pale. "The serpent killed them all."

"Yes," said Alex.

"When did you find this out, Alex? How long have you known that they were dead?" Rallian questioned.

"I found out when we faced the serpent in the desert," said Alex. "At the time I didn't know that your cousin was among them. I am sorry for your loss, my friend."

"Lazar and Magnus will pay for this evil," said Rallian, his fists clenched in anger.

"If their lords are dead, it means that Lazar has no true power over the inner kingdoms," said Shelnor.

"But will they believe us?" Talbot asked. "Will they believe that Magnus and Lazar have already killed their lords?"

"I doubt they will believe anything we say," said Caftan. "They will want to believe Lazar, as his story offers them hope that their loved ones are still alive."

"They are gone," said Alex. "The serpent knew that the seven were lords of Nezza. He admitted it to me."

"Then all is lost," said Shelnor. "We cannot advance to Karmus, and we cannot prove to the lords of the inner kingdoms that their lords were killed by Lazar and Magnus. We must withdraw and prepare to defend our own lands."

"No," said Rallian firmly. "There must be some way to convince them. There must be something we can do to prove that what we know is true."

Rallian is the key. Rallian and . . . Alex's O'Gash whispered once more.

"Tell me," said Alex, his mind catching on an idea. "Is

there something we can say—an oath or some item we can swear on—that all the lords of Nezza would believe?"

"Only the ring of the kings would hold that power," said Talbot. "But it was lost when the last king of Nezza rode north."

"And found again when I rode on my first adventure," said Alex.

"Found?" Rallian asked in disbelief.

"You've heard the story of my first adventure," said Alex as he reached for his magic bag.

"Yes, but you never mentioned the ring of the kings," Rallian said.

"When I fought the three-legged troll, I won a ring," said Alex. "I did not know what it was until I spoke to the oracle Tempe. She told me that it was the great ring of the kings of Nezza."

"You have this ring—now?" Shelnor asked in amazement.

"Tempe said that I should hold on to it until the time was right," Alex said. "She didn't want me to give it to Rallian while we were still in the desert. She didn't want to force him into making a claim on the crown."

"A kind thought," said Rallian.

Alex spoke softly into his magic bag, telling Stonebill where the ring was and asking him to bring it out and give it to Rallian. With a rush of feathers, Stonebill appeared in the tent, fluttering gently onto Rallian's shoulder, the golden ring held in his beak. He bent down and let the ring fall into Rallian's open hand, and then flew back to his normal place on Alex's shoulder.

"The great ring of the kings," said Rallian as he looked at the golden circle in his hand.

The gold seemed to shine more brightly in Rallian's hand than it ever had before, and the black stone reflected the light like water at midnight. Rallian slowly put the ring on his right hand, and Alex felt a sudden rush of magic. All the lords of Nezza dropped to one knee in front of Rallian, and Alex bowed to his friend.

The magic was ancient, perhaps as old as Nezza itself. At first Alex couldn't see what the magic was, but as it continued to grow around Rallian, Alex realized what was happening. The ring was a magical link between the true king and the land; it was a source of power that had once helped to hold the kingdom of Nezza together. This ancient magic was like a spring, and the water that flowed out of it was hope for better times.

"With this ring, you could have claimed all of Nezza as your own," Rallian said to Alex.

"But I am not the king of Nezza," said Alex. "You are."

Rallian nodded, and for a moment it looked as if he would cry with joy, but he stepped back and asked his lords to rise.

"We must ride forward under the flag of truce," said Rallian. "The lords of the inner kingdoms must be made to see the truth."

"As you wish, my king," said Talbot.

"With your permission," said Alex, bowing, "I would like to ride forward with you. I would like to see the lords of the inner kingdoms for myself."

"I would be honored to have your company," said Rallian.

As Rallian turned to speak with the rest of the lords, Alex

stepped away from the group. He was pleased to see Rallian so much in command and the lords of the north so willing to follow. His own hopes for peace in Nezza had been renewed, and now he felt certain that the wars would at last come to an end.

Rallian wanted to ride forward as soon as possible. As the details about who would ride forward with him were worked out, Alex delivered Lady Shelnor's message to Lord Shelnor.

"Forgive me, Lord Shelnor," said Rallian, noticing Alex handing the message over. "Before we ride, we should find out how things stand in Ossbo."

"You are most kind, my king," said Shelnor with a bow. "Perhaps Master Taylor will tell us what has happened there."

"Of course," said Alex, bowing slightly to Shelnor. "When I arrived at Ossbo, Bray's army had already surrounded the city," Alex began. "Part of the city was burning, and Bray's men were working hard, sending barrels of flaming liquid into the city; no doubt they hoped to destroy as much of Ossbo as they could. Unfortunately for them, the dragon arrived and destroyed their catapults, and most of Bray's army as well. Bray was destroyed in a blast of dragon fire as he fled to the south."

"And the city?" Shelnor asked. "How many of my people were lost in the attack?"

"Few were lost," answered Alex. "The rain helped to put out the fires, and the people of the city worked hard to rescue the trapped and injured. The healers of your city and I were able to help the injured as well, and I believe that most, if not all of them, will recover."

"I am in forever in your debt," said Shelnor, bowing to

Alex. "I will try to find some small way to repay the great kindness you have done for my family and my people."

"As will I," Rallian added. "It seems that all of Nezza will be in your debt before I sit on my throne."

"I am happy to have been of service," said Alex, bowing to both Shelnor and Rallian. "Now, if you will excuse me, I should like to check on my adventurer friends and see how Hathnor is doing."

Colesum led Alex to his friends, and Alex was not surprised that they were telling stories and that Hathnor was with them. They were all excited and happy to see Alex and quick to ask about his journey to Ossbo and what had happened there. Alex told them what he could as he checked to make sure Hathnor was recovering from his wound.

"So, will we have to fight the army in front of us to reach Karmus?" asked Virgil. "We've done little enough on this adventure after all."

"I don't think we will have to fight yet," said Alex. "Rallian wants to talk to the lords of the inner kingdoms first. I think they will believe what he says, and I think they will join him against Lazar and Magnus."

"A hardheaded lot, these men from Nezza," Dain commented. "Rallian is king; they should follow him without explanations."

"Rallian is not yet crowned as king," Alex pointed out. "There has not been a true king in Nezza for a long time. I doubt even the dwarves would be quick to accept anyone claiming to be king in this situation."

"The dwarves would take a hundred years to decide,"

Skeld teased. "Then they'd take another hundred just to make sure they'd done everything right."

"Enough," said Virgil. "When will King Rallian ride forward?"

"They are preparing the horses now," said Colesum.

"Then I should speak to him," said Virgil. "I believe I should ride with him, just in case."

The rain was still falling as they moved forward, the blue-and-white flag of truce leading them. Alex hoped that the lords of the inner kingdoms would believe what he and Rallian would tell them, and that there would be no need for a battle now that they were so close to their goal.

It wasn't long before the lords of the inner kingdoms rode out to meet them. Alex suspected that the appearance of the dragon over their camps might have had something to do with their quick response.

"Hail, lords of the north, Prince Rallian," one of the lords said as they rode up. "A day of strange happening, and stranger news."

"You will address Rallian as king," Talbot said hotly.

"That is a claim not yet proven," the lord answered, bowing slightly. "There are other matters we should discuss, however. We have asked you to return to the north as we do not wish to fight you, yet you show no sign of moving."

"We will return north when King Rallian orders us to do so," Talbot answered, his anger getting the better of him.

"It is poor weather to fight in, Talbot. Be careful what you say," said the lord.

"My lords, hear what I say," said Rallian, stepping forward.

"I have news of the captives—those that Lazar claims to hold in Karmus."

"What news?" asked the man.

"The young lords of your lands, my friends and my cousin, have already died at Lazar's command," said Rallian. "I have seen the creature—a desert serpent—that Magnus used to destroy them. Were it not for Master Taylor, who rides with me this day, I would also have been destroyed by that creature."

"Ah, the wizard," said one of the lords, turning toward Alex. "We have been told that a wizard has come to Nezza and that we should be careful of him. Lazar told us he would spread lies and bring war to all the land."

"You would believe Lazar?" said Rallian, his own anger growing. "Be careful, my lords; the dragon you saw this morning is not that far away."

"You claim that your wizard controls it?" asked the lord.

"I know that he does," said Rallian in a confident tone. "His dragon has already destroyed Bray and scattered his army to the winds. Take warning, or the same may happen to you."

"Idle words," said another of the lords, but there was a nervous tone to his voice.

"No," said Alex, moving forward. "If you will not accept Rallian as the king, and if you continue to stand in our way and prevent us from reaching Karmus, then I will summon the dragon and destroy you all."

"Enough of this," said Rallian. He lifted his right arm, plainly showing the great ring of the kings to the lords in front of him. At that moment, Alex magically shifted the clouds above them. A single beam of sunlight broke free of the clouds, falling on Rallian. The ring looked like a circle of flame on Rallian's finger, the black stone a dark mirror, reflecting the magical light.

"I swear by this ring—the great ring of the kings of Nezza—that all I have told you is true," said Rallian in a loud voice. "Your lords, those you loved—they are lost to us. I beg you—do not make that loss worse by serving the one who destroyed them."

"My lord . . . my . . . my king," the first man stuttered. "Forgive my doubts. I cannot speak for the others, but I and my house stand ready to serve you."

"As do I," called another of the lords, moving forward. "Only the true king of Nezza could hold the ring."

"And I," called another. "I will do as you command, my king, and hope that you command the destruction of Lazar and the evil Magnus."

It happened in an instant. Alex was both surprised and relieved as all five of the lords of the inner kingdoms came forward, dropped to one knee, and bowed to Rallian. Each of them swore his allegiance and then waited for Rallian to command them.

Something else happened, something only Alex noticed. The magic of Nezza, the magic that had waited for more than five hundred years for a true king to appear, was waking up.

"Rise, my noble lords," Rallian said, overcome by the show of support. "Rise and join with me. We must reach Karmus before Lazar knows what has happened. We must not allow him to destroy more of our people."

"We hear and obey," the five lords of the inner kingdoms answered.

"We need a plan," said Rallian. "Lazar still has an army in Karmus, and it will not be easy to take that city, even with this host."

"King Rallian," said Alex, "this very morning I saw the city, and there are few guards or soldiers anywhere but on the island at its center."

"A careful man, Lazar," Talbot commented. "The island will be difficult to take, and the bridges are easy to defend."

"We must find a way," said Rallian. "I know that my uncle will never accept me as king, and he must know by now that his life is forfeit. If he holds only the island, things will be easier. I would not risk this army without good reason, and I fear that storming the island will cost many lives."

"My lord, if you will permit me," said Colesum. "If Master Taylor is correct, and there are only a few soldiers in the city, then we can capture the city and lay siege to the island fortress. Why risk storming the island when time and hunger will deliver it to us?"

"Yes, that might work," Rallian said in a thoughtful tone. "My uncle still has a sizeable army at his command, though it seems that the army is not in Karmus. We should send out scouts to try to discover where his army is. While our scouts look for answers, the rest of the army will move into Karmus."

"I will have men out searching within the hour," said Colesum. "If what remains of the army of Karmus is near, we will find it."

"Very well. How soon can all the lords of Nezza be ready to march?" Rallian asked.

There was some discussion about how soon the combined armies could start moving toward Karmus. Supplies were the main concern, as nobody believed there would be much to eat inside Karmus. Though the lords all wanted to move as soon as possible, they agreed that most of the army could move forward at first light, while a part of the army would remain behind to protect the supply wagons that would follow as quickly as possible.

"Now, my lords, prepare your men to move," Rallian commanded. "Tonight I ask you all join me for our evening meal. At first light, we will free Nezza from the evil that has lived in Karmus for too long."

There was a great cheer from all those present. Alex thought that if their luck held, Nezza would have a new king by morning. Lazar and his army would be trapped and unable to cause any more trouble. But what about Magnus? Alex knew that Magnus still had at least one plan, even if it was only a plan to escape.

The lords of the inner kingdoms rode back to their camps, and Rallian led the lords of the north back to theirs. Alex rode beside Rallian. The news that they would move forward was greeted with many more cheers from the men in Rallian's camp, but Alex did not join in with the cheers. Thoughts about Magnus filled his mind, and he racked his brain, trying to think about what Magnus would do now.

CHAPTER TWENTY-TWO

THE BLACK GUARD

T he armies of Nezza spent the rest of the day preparing
to move and preparing for a grand feast. A massive
tent was set up in front of Rallian's tent so that all
the lords of Nezza could sit down and eat with the king that
night. Alex didn't think a grand feast was a good idea, but with
Rallian being accepted as the king, a customary feast was expected.

As the sun was setting, Alex made his way to the giant tent.
It was large enough for seventy or eighty people to sit in com-
fortably, and there would still be room for the people serving
the food to move without trouble. To help, Alex conjured up a
few dozen weir lights and placed them inside the tent to keep
things well lit.

The feast began with Rallian welcoming his new lords.
Alex sat near Rallian, but his mind wasn't on the food. The
lords of the inner kingdoms were all talking about how things
would change now that Rallian was king. They talked about
trade and the division of lands that had been fought over
for years. They all seemed to think that Rallian was already

crowned and sitting on the throne in Karmus, and their talk troubled Alex.

Lazar still had an army, and Alex didn't know where that army was. If Lazar's army was already moving, they could cause a lot of trouble before Rallian's army could track them down. Lazar's army, however, was not Alex's biggest worry. Magnus was still out there, somewhere. Alex knew that Magnus was more dangerous than any army Lazar might command, and not knowing where the old man was or what he was doing troubled him.

"Magnus," Alex said to himself, staring at the food in front of him.

He thought about what he would do if he were in Magnus's place. There should have been some kind of attack, or some magical barrier to slow Rallian down. Magnus had worked for years to keep the kingdoms of Nezza divided and fighting, and yet he had done nothing to stop Rallian from becoming king of Nezza. It didn't make any sense, and Alex was worried.

As the feast went on, Alex slipped out of the tent un-noticed. There was too much talking and noise for him to think. As he prowled around the camp, Stonebill landed on his shoulder, but the raven had nothing to say. Alex checked everything he could think of. He made sure the guards were in place and alert, not off celebrating Rallian's acceptance as king. Everything was as it should have been. Finding noth-ing wrong and unable to come up with any ideas about what Magnus might be up to, Alex went to the tent he shared with his adventurer friends.

"Well done," Virgil said as Alex entered the tent.

Alex looked to see what Virgil was talking about and smiled when he saw Tom next to a large tub of water, practicing his magic.

"Your student is learning quickly," Virgil said, looking up at Alex. "I have a hard time breaking his rafts apart, unless I manage to hit them directly."

"Even then the rafts don't break apart as they once did," said Tom with a touch of pride. "They move a bit and then come back together."

"You are doing well," said Alex. "Don't let me interrupt your practice. I just need a quiet place to think."

"You'll have a hard time finding anything like a quiet place in this camp," said Virgil. "There are too many happy soldiers and too much work to finish before we move in the morning."

"At least it is quieter here than outside," said Alex, sitting down. "Please, continue what you were doing. I wouldn't want to keep Tom from practicing."

"We were almost finished. Perhaps we should get some sleep," said Tom, glancing at Virgil.

"Yes, we should," Virgil agreed. "We need to relieve Dain and Skeld later tonight, so sleep would be a good idea."

"Relieve Dain and Skeld?" Alex asked.

"They are keeping an eye on Rallian," said Virgil. "With so many new faces in the camp, and now that we are so close to Karmus, I thought it best for two of us to remain close to the king at all times."

"Yes, that is a good idea," said Alex. "Thank you."

"It is what you asked us to do," said Virgil.

Alex smiled. "I'm glad you all stayed in Nezza to help Rallian, and to help me."

"It is an honor to be of service," said Virgil. "But now it will be an honor to get some sleep."

Tom and Alex both laughed. The two adventurers moved to one side of the tent, and Alex put out the lights so they could sleep. Alex left only one candle burning and sat looking into the flame. His mind was filled with questions, and they all came back to why.

"Why?" Alex whispered to himself.

Why had Magnus done nothing? Why had he not killed Rallian when he had the chance? Why had the serpent let Rallian live? What was Magnus's plan for Nezza? The questions kept coming, but Alex couldn't find any answers. He took a deep breath and remembered what the retired adventurer Savage had said.

He will have at least three plans, Savage's voice echoed in Alex's mind. *One to defeat you, a second one for his own escape, and a third one that you never thought about.*

Leaning back in his chair, Alex closed his eyes. His head hurt and that made it hard to think. Magnus might have three plans—he might have even more—but knowing that didn't help. Alex desperately wanted to discover just one plan, the one that Magnus was working on now.

The pain in Alex's head continued to grow, and then, all at once, he felt peaceful. He looked around, realizing he had slipped into a dream. A warm light shined from behind him. Ahead of him was the gentle slope of a hill and a low stone wall. He was at the edge of the shadowlands, at least in his dream.

He stood looking down at the wall, trying to find some meaning to his dream. For a moment he thought he saw someone just beyond the wall, and then he realized there were two people, but Alex couldn't make out who they were. As the figures moved deeper into the shadowlands, Alex felt a mix of sadness and joy, but he didn't know why.

The dream shifted, and Alex found himself in a dimly lit corridor. Torches burned along the stone walls, but there was nothing to see. He moved forward, but the stone walls went on and on, unbroken and unchanging. There was something he needed to find, something he desperately wanted. He started to run, but running didn't bring him closer to his goal.

Finally, when he could run no more, Alex stopped and reached forward. An invisible barrier stopped his hand. He pushed against the barrier, and it seemed to bend, just as the barrier around the great arch had done. He leaned forward, pushing as hard as he could, and slowly the barrier moved.

Alex continued to push, and, inch by inch, he moved forward. He knew the thing he wanted most was just beyond the barrier. If he could only bend it far enough, he would find what he was looking for. He struggled for what felt like hours, never reaching his goal. He thought one more step would be enough, one more step and he would have his answers. He pushed with all his might and then fell forward into darkness.

Alex woke with a start. His candle was still burning, but there wasn't much of it left. He rubbed his eyes and listened. He could hear Virgil snoring softly on the other side of the tent, and he let his own eyes close. Almost immediately his eyes snapped open again, and he knew something was very wrong.

"What is it?" Stonebill questioned.

Alex held up his hand to silence the bird and then placed it over Virgil's mouth before shaking him awake. Virgil looked lost for a moment but regained his senses quickly. Alex woke Tom as well, muffling Tom's yelp of surprise when he woke.

"What is it?" Virgil whispered.

"Listen," said Alex.

"I don't hear anything," said Tom.

"When was the last time you didn't hear anything at night?" Alex asked.

"Before we started traveling with the army," Virgil answered, understanding what Alex was telling them. "It is too quiet. Something is wrong."

"We need to get to Rallian's tent as fast as we can without making any noise," said Alex.

"What do you want me to do?" Stonebill questioned.

"Search the camp and the land around us," Alex answered. "Look for anyone or anything that is out of place. If we are about to be attacked, it would be good to know from which direction the attack is coming."

Stonebill flew out of the tent as soon as Alex finished speaking. Alex put out the candle and led Virgil and Tom into the darkness. Torches and campfires were still burning, filling the spaces between tents with strange shadows. The silence pressed in on them, and every move they made sounded far too loud. Alex looked at the places where he knew guards had been, but there was no one to be seen.

It only took a minute or two to reach Rallian's tent, and they all froze in the shadows a few yards from the entrance. Someone else was moving toward the tent, coming from the opposite direction and moving almost as quietly as they were. Alex put his hand on his sword, ready to fight if he needed to.

In the dim light, Alex could make out the figure of a man in armor, and as the man moved toward the tent, Alex recognized him. It was Colesum, Talbot's oldest son, and he wasn't alone.

Moving forward into the torchlight, Alex found a spot where Colesum could see him. He held up his hand to keep Colesum from calling out, and then pointed at his eyes and waved his hand at the tents around them. It took a moment before Colesum understood what Alex was asking: Had he seen anyone in the surrounding tents? Colesum shook his head and pointed at Rallian's tent. Alex nodded and moved forward, Virgil and Tom right behind him.

A low moan came from inside Rallian's tent as Alex and Colesum reached to pull back the flaps that covered the entrance. They both rushed forward at the sound, and what they found made Alex's heart stop. Bodies covered the floor of the tent.

"Father!" Colesum cried out, rushing forward.

"Skeld!" Virgil yelled at the same moment, pushing past Alex.

Alex's head spun, his brain unable to take in what he was seeing. He caught hold of a tent pole to keep himself from falling and closed his eyes to block everything out.

Control yourself, Alex thought. *There's work to be done, and you need to control your emotions.*

Pushing away from the tent pole, Alex went to Lord Talbot. Talbot had been lying across one of the tables as if he were dead, but he let out a groan of pain as his son moved him to a chair.

"The others," Talbot mumbled in a weak voice. "They need your help."

There was a rough-looking wound on one side of Talbot's head, but no other obvious injuries so Alex moved to Skeld. Virgil had propped up his cousin and pulled open his shirt to reveal a wide gash in Skeld's side. Blood was still gushing out of the wound, and Alex knew he only had seconds to act.

Alex put his hand over Skeld's wound and set his magic to work. His hand seemed to glow for a moment, and Skeld let out a gasp of pain. For a few seconds, Alex kept his hand in place, and when he took it away, the gash in Skeld's side was only a dark red line.

"They were only shadows," Skeld mumbled. "We couldn't see them until they came in here, into the light."

"Where is Dain?" Alex asked.

"Here," Tom answered from the opposite side of the tent. "He . . . I don't . . . I can't . . ."

Tom's halting words were clear to Alex. He knew before he saw his friend that there was nothing he could do. Tom was sitting on the floor, holding up the dwarf and staring into his vacant face. Alex reached down and closed Dain's eyes, careful to avoid the arrows buried in his chest.

"He's gone," Alex said, putting his hand on Tom's shoulder. "There is nothing we can do for him now."

"My father is badly hurt," Colesum said, looking at Alex. "You must help him."

"I'm not important," Talbot said in a weak voice. "They've taken Rallian. You must go after them. You must save the king."

"We will," said Alex, moving back to Talbot.

Alex ran his fingers across Talbot's head wound, and slowly the blood stopped flowing. He let his magic do its work, and then he added more magic to help clear Talbot's mind. He needed to know what had happened, and Talbot was the only one who could tell him.

"Check the other lords," Alex said to Colesum, though his eyes never left Talbot's face. "Make sure they are not hurt."

"They would all be dead—and myself as well—if not for these two adventurers," Talbot said.

"Tell me what happened," Alex said. "I need to know everything you saw."

"I . . . I was in the back of the tent, resting," Talbot started. "My head was pounding, and I was lying down to ease the pain. I heard a crash, as if a table had been overturned, and I came to see what had happened."

"The others appear unhurt," Colesum interrupted when his father paused. "Drugged, I would guess. They appear to sleep, but they won't wake up."

"Yes, drugged," Talbot said. He coughed a little, and then went on with his story. "I heard the sounds of battle before I entered this part of the tent. I drew my sword and hurried forward. I found the tent filled with black guards. The two ad-venturers were fighting madly for their lives and trying to keep them from taking Rallian at the same time. I . . . I joined the fight, but I was unable to turn the tide of battle. There were too many of them, and they took the king as they retreated."

"Was Rallian alive?" Alex asked urgently. "Do you know if he was alive when they took him?"

"He seemed to be unconscious, but they had tied his hands behind him," Talbot answered. "You do not take time to tie up a dead man."

"We must go at once," said Alex.

"Go? Go where?" Colesum questioned.

"After Rallian," Alex answered. "How many men do you have with you, Colesum?"

"Twenty," Colesum answered. "We were scouting the road to Karmus, and finding no guards on duty when we returned, we hurried here."

"Have your men saddle fresh horses," Alex ordered. "We need to move as fast as we can."

"But how will we find them in the darkness?" Colesum questioned. "They could be taking him anywhere. We need to consider our camp. It appears that all our men have been drugged. If Lazar's army attacks us now, they could slaughter us all."

"Do as the wizard commands," Talbot said, putting his hand on Colesum's arm. "Go, and save our king, whatever the cost."

"I hear and obey," Colesum answered with tears in his eyes.

Alex doubted Lazar's army would attack their camp, but he still didn't want to leave Talbot injured and alone.

"Of your twenty men, how many are married?" Alex asked.

"About half," Colesum answered.

"Leave the married men here to help your father," said Alex. "Have them splash fresh water on the faces of everyone who's been drugged. If that doesn't work, force the sleeping men to drink."

"That will only leave twelve of us to go after Rallian," Colesum said in a concerned tone.

"Thirteen," Virgil corrected.

"You mean fourteen," said Tom.

"I can ride," Skeld mumbled from the floor.

"Lie still and rest," Alex said to Skeld. "If you break open that wound, I'll let you bleed to death."

Stonebill swooped into the tent and landed on the table next to Alex.

"Only part of the army has been drugged," Stonebill reported. "And only those soldiers camped closest to Rallian's tent. The rest of the army is resting, the guards alert. Lazar's army isn't anywhere close, but I did see a group of men who looked more like shadows then men. Rallian was with them, and they are riding hard toward Karmus."

"Then we will follow them," said Alex. "Can you catch them along the road?"

"It will take some time, but I believe I can," Stonebill answered.

"Then go after them, follow them, and bring me word about where they take Rallian," said Alex.

"As you command," Stonebill replied and flew out of the tent.

"What news?" Colesum questioned.

Alex shared the information Stonebill had brought. The others were relieved to hear that most of the army had not been drugged and that there was no sign of Lazar's army.

"I will get the army moving as soon as I can," said Talbot. "With luck, we should be able to get at least part of the army to Karmus before midday."

"Good," said Alex. "You must save the people of Karmus, as Rallian wished."

Alex wondered if he was doing the right thing. He didn't know why Magnus had arranged for Rallian to be taken. He had no idea what he was about to ride into. He was certain, however, that it would be dangerous. Magnus would guess that he would come looking for Rallian; Magnus would be ready and waiting.

"What did Skeld mean when he said the black guards were only shadows?" Virgil asked as they hurried out of the tent. "Was it because they couldn't see them until they were in the light?"

"I would guess that Magnus put some spell on them," Alex answered. "Something to hide his men in the shadows so they could sneak up on the guards without being seen."

"His men?" Colesum questioned.

"The black guards may claim to serve Lazar, but they really serve Magnus," said Alex.

"There are still a lot of shadows," said Virgil, looking into the darkness around them. "If they are hidden by magic, there could be more of them, anywhere."

"The men who took Rallian are riding south, to Karmus," said Alex. "Whatever Magnus has planned, it will happen in Karmus."

"What do you think he has planned?" Colesum asked as he climbed onto his horse.

"I don't know," Alex answered, climbing into his own saddle. "But whatever his plans are, we are the only ones who can stop him."

"Men," Colesum shouted, wheeling his horse around to face the company. "Our king is in peril, and we few are his only hope. I call upon you to ride now with me, to save the king or to die in the attempt. For the king!"

"For the king!" came the reply.

Without waiting for Alex, Colesum spurred his horse forward, galloping away from the camp. Alex caught up to him and fell in beside him. They rode for several minutes before Colesum spoke.

"Magnus could have two or three hundred of his black guards waiting for us. Do you have a plan to deal with them?"

Alex didn't answer. Only two thoughts filled his mind: save Rallian, and destroy Magnus. Nothing else in all of Nezza mattered.

CHAPTER TWENTY-THREE

MAGNUS AND RALLIAN

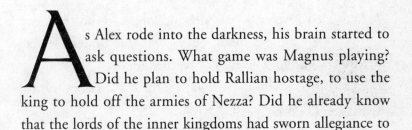

As Alex rode into the darkness, his brain started to ask questions. What game was Magnus playing? Did he plan to hold Rallian hostage, to use the king to hold off the armies of Nezza? Did he already know that the lords of the inner kingdoms had sworn allegiance to Rallian? Where was Lazar, and where was his army? Answers did not come, but a different idea came into his mind.

I will take my other form, Alex thought. *I will become the dragon. I can catch the men who have taken Rallian before they reach Karmus. I can free Rallian and then fly to Karmus and destroy Magnus.*

No, his O'Gash answered. *Your dragon form cannot help you now.*

Why? Alex questioned.

Nezza needs heroes—heroes who are from this land. The men you ride with will become those heroes, and Nezza will be a better place because of them, his O'Gash answered.

Alex didn't like it, but he knew his O'Gash was right. Nezza needed heroes. If he did everything, if he saved the king and destroyed Magnus, what would Nezza have? They would have a king, and they might have peace, but the king would only rule because a wizard had put him on the throne. The peace would not last once Alex left Nezza. He had to let others do their part. He had to help them become heroes, even if that meant Rallian would not live long enough to be crowned as king.

Being a wizard is never easy, his O'Gash whispered, and said no more.

The ride to Karmus was both too long and too short for Alex. He wanted more speed, but at the same time he feared what they would find when they reached the city. The coming day seemed to echo his dark thoughts: the eastern skies turned bloodred as the sun started to rise.

"The city gates are open and unguarded," Colesum commented as the company slowed their horses.

"That can only mean Lazar's army is not guarding the city," Virgil said from behind Colesum.

Stonebill came flying through the open gate, landing on Alex's shoulder. "They have taken Rallian to a massive building on the south end of the island fortress. There are no guards between you and the building, and I have seen no sign of Lazar's army," the raven reported.

"A massive building on the south end of the island?" Alex questioned, looking at Colesum.

"He must mean the halls of the dead," said Colesum. "It is the burial place of the ancient kings of Nezza. Why would Magnus take Rallian there?"

"I don't know," Alex answered. "Not for anything good, I'm sure."

"What more can I do?" Stonebill questioned.

"See if you can discover where Lazar's army has gone," said Alex. "Search the lands near Rallian's army first. If you find anything, take word to Hathnor. He is an elf friend; make him understand you if the army is in danger."

"It won't be easy, but if there is danger I will make him understand," Stonebill said and took flight once more.

"There are no guards between us and the halls of the dead," said Alex. "But I have no idea what we'll find inside the ancient building."

"Then we'd better go and look," said Colesum, starting his horse forward.

The city appeared to be empty. There were no people to be seen, no smell of smoke in the air, and no sounds but the echoes from their horse's hooves. Alex knew that the city was not empty. He could feel the emotions of the people who were hidden in their homes. Fear and despair had driven all hope from Karmus, and Alex struggled to keep his own hopes up.

The company made their way onto the island fortress without any trouble. They rode up the hill at the center of the island before turning south and riding back down. Alex discovered that the entire south end of the island was a grave-yard, filled with house-sized crypts and giant gravestones. One building, however, stood out. It was, as Stonebill had said, massive.

"The tomb of the ancient kings," said Colesum as they approached the building. "It holds the remains of more than a hundred true kings of Nezza. It has not been opened for nearly five hundred years."

"It's open now," said Alex, pointing to two giant doors that were only just hanging in place. It looked as if some great force had hit them, crushing them into the building and then roughly pulling them out again.

Colesum's face flushed red at the sight, and he hurried forward and dismounted. "Magnus holds nothing sacred," he said. "For this act alone, he should be put to death."

Alex moved toward the doors and looked inside. There were no torches or lamps in the entrance hall, but the high windows in the walls allowed light in. The light reflected off a polished marble floor, and everything seemed to glow as red as the sunrise.

Alex moved into the building with the others, and they soon found a path they could follow. Torches had been lit along one of the walls, and following the torches was the only guide they had. They moved forward with caution, expecting an attack at any moment. No attack came, though, and they continued deeper into the building. Soon they were beyond the reflected sunlight, and only the flickering torches showed them the way. They were led to a wide set of stairs leading down, and Alex gave Colesum a questioning look.

"There are many levels under this building," Colesum whispered. "I don't know how many there are or where they lead. It is said that the ancient kings are buried in separate chambers under the island. The tunnels might even go under the river and the rest of the city as well."

Alex nodded and started down the steps. He felt sure this was a trap, but there was nothing he could do about it. They had to find Rallian, whatever the cost. He shifted his staff to his left hand and stretched the fingers of his right. He thought about drawing his sword but decided to wait.

They went down two sets of stairs, and then the torches led them down a wide hallway. The air was cold, and a slight breeze blew into their faces. After about fifty yards, the hallway seemed to vanish from sight as it dropped down a steep ramp. The bottom of the ramp was completely dark.

"Be ready," Alex whispered as he moved toward the darkness.

The ramped ended in what appeared to be a chamber with a single torch on the far side. Alex was about halfway across the dark chamber when he felt something move. Without hesitating, he ignited the end of his staff and at the same time conjured a dozen weir lights.

His magical lights spread out around the chamber, revealing the chamber to be a giant circle with several passageways leading out of it. Shadows suddenly appeared, some in the middle of the hall, others moving out of the side passages.

"Into the passage!" Colesum yelled.

Alex ran forward with Colesum, stopping when he was several yards into the passageway. He turned and looked back, checking to see who was still with him. Five of Colesum's men were fighting black guards at the edge of the round chamber, slowly backing into the passage. Colesum was standing behind them, but there was no sign of the others.

"Virgil! Tom!" Alex shouted, moving back toward the main chamber.

"I think they are in the hallway we came down," said Colesum, catching Alex before he could go too far.

"Then we go back," said Alex, reaching for his sword.

"No," said Colesum, grabbing Alex's arm. "We must get to Rallian."

"But . . ." Alex started and stopped.

Colesum was right and Alex knew it. He couldn't fight his way back to the others and save Rallian at the same time. There were too many black guards in the chamber, and probably many more in the other passageways.

"You are the only one who has a chance to defeat Magnus," Colesum said to Alex. "Go, and save the king. We will hold them here as long as we can. We will guard your back."

Alex nodded his acceptance of what had to be and turned away from the chamber. He would go on alone, hoping against all hope that his friends would be able to hold back the guards. He would do whatever he had to do to save the king of Nezza.

Alex moved down the dim hallway, feeling like he was trapped in a terrible dream. He couldn't help his friends, and he didn't know what new danger awaited him. The torches continued to lead him, and after what felt like a long time, the floor dropped away once more. He moved forward but stopped a few feet away from the edge where the floor dropped.

A strange cobweb-like magic hung in the air in front of Alex. He focused his mind on this new magic, and after a moment, he understood what it was. It was a spell of suggestion and control. The magic would give Magnus some control over anyone who walked through it, and it would also make anything he said sound more reasonable than it normally would.

If I let this spell take me, if I can make Magnus believe he has the upper hand, I might be able to discover more about the Brotherhood he works for, Alex thought.

A risk, Alex's O'Gash warned. *You don't know how strong Magnus's magic is.*

Some risks are worth taking. If I can discover more about the Brotherhood, if I can learn who is part of it or who is controlling it, I might be able to stop them. I can save other lands from what Nezza is going through now, Alex reasoned.

Would you gamble with the lives of your friends—with your own life? his O'Gash questioned.

If the Brotherhood isn't stopped, none of the known lands will ever be safe, Alex pointed out.

Then protect yourself as much as you can before walking into this trap, his O'Gash answered.

In the dim passageway, Alex worked his magic. He pulled all the wizardly magic he could inward, wrapping it up inside his mind to protect his thoughts from Magnus. With his first barrier in place, Alex did something more. He remembered the fear he had felt in the dungeons of Karmus, the magic Magnus had used that had almost destroyed him. Calling on the power of the dragon, he created a second barrier around his emotions and his heart. He put his emotions in the care of the dragon, and then he stepped into Magnus's trap.

Alex hardly noticed Magnus's magic as he moved forward. He walked down the slope, all his senses alert, and found himself at the edge of another round chamber. This chamber was much larger than the last. The ceiling was a high dome, and there were no passageways leading out of the room except the one he had just come down. Torches were lit all along the walls of the chamber, and there were candles burning everywhere, filling the room with light.

Alex saw Rallian as soon as he entered the chamber. Rallian was tied up and gagged, lying on the floor near the wall to Alex's left. He wasn't quite halfway across the room, and it looked like he was still drugged. There was a pale green light around Rallian, like the light that had been around the lockbox in Magnus's rooms. Alex took a few steps toward Rallian and stopped, his staff up, ready for battle.

"You'll not need that, at least not yet," said Magnus, appearing from the other side of the room.

"I'll decide what I need and when," Alex answered, shifting his position to put himself between Magnus and Rallian.

"Yes, of course you will," said Magnus with a smile. "I thought we might talk a little before things get out of hand, that's all."

"Talk?" said Alex. "I have little to say to you, Magnus. I am here to call you to account for your evils, and to save the true king of Nezza from whatever fate you have planned for him."

"Save him?" Magnus laughed. "What terrible fate do you think I have planned for the young king?"

"I don't know, but I know you need him alive," Alex answered. "I won't allow you to make him your puppet, Magnus."

"My puppet?" Magnus repeated. "Oh, no, nothing like that would do for the true king of Nezza."

"You said you wanted to talk, so talk," said Alex, shifting closer to Rallian.

"Put down your staff, young wizard. Put down your staff,

and I will enlighten you," said Magnus, his voice calm and soothing.

Alex felt his left arm drop to his side. He didn't try to fight Magnus's magic; he let it work while at the same time putting his own magic to work. His magic touched the edges of Magnus's mind, slowly, gently asking questions, looking for the answers that only Magnus could give him.

"Relax," Magnus's voice said. "The knowledge I'm about to give you will change the way you see the world."

Who belongs to the Brotherhood? Alex thought. *Who is Gaylan, and what part does he play?*

Alex's staff clattered to the floor. He felt like he was falling asleep, but this wasn't sleep, it was better than sleep. Slowly he dropped to one knee, his head lowered and his eyes closed.

"I don't know what the council of wizards has told you about us, but I'm sure they have lied," Magnus went on. "They don't agree with what we are trying to do. They don't want things to change in the known lands."

"The council doesn't know who or what the Brotherhood is," said Alex. "They don't know what you are doing, or why you are doing it."

Who belongs to your group? Who does Gaylan work for? Alex's thoughts pressed into Magnus's mind.

"Don't be a fool. Of course they know what we are doing and why," said Magnus. "They love to be thought of as wise. They love the praise of men and dwarves and even elves—but what do they do to deserve that praise? When trouble comes, they say, 'Yes, we thought this would happen,' but what did they do to stop it from happening?"

"They do what they can," said Alex, his voice a whisper. "They try to protect the known lands from evil."

"Ha!" Magnus laughed. "They protect themselves and do as little as they can. They hide their power and allow lesser, weaker men to lead. That is what we are fighting against. We are tired of watching the destruction and waste that weak leaders bring to the known lands. We can put an end to this foolishness. We are working for a greater good, if only you could see that."

"I . . . I don't understand," said Alex.

Who is Gaylan? What does he look like? Who does he serve?

An image flashed in Alex's mind of a face that had once been handsome but now the left eye was half closed by a scar that ran from his eyebrow halfway down his cheek and then turned sharply back toward his ear. The image's right eye was dark and cunning, but the left eye was milky white and cold.

"We, and I include you in this, have been given power," said Magnus. "It is our duty to use that power, not to gain the praise of men and dwarves, but to use it for the greater good. We must use it to take control, to create order in the known lands. What good is power if it is not used? What good comes from replacing foolish kings with new kings who are just as foolish as those who came before them?"

A new vision flooded into Alex's mind, a vision of the future that Magnus had planned for Nezza. The kingdoms of men were united and there was peace, but preparations for war continued. Everything in this new, united kingdom was done with war in mind. The army would grow larger and stronger, and in time, it would march to the east.

In the far east of Nezza were the dwarf realms. Magnus's armies would enslave the dwarves, and they would serve in the war machine he was planning to build. Individuals did not matter, only the greater good mattered—and the greater good was centered in war. When Nezza was fully under the control of the Brotherhood, the armies would march to other lands, spreading like a cancer.

"The greater good," said Alex, his voice slightly stronger than it had been.

Alex had heard things like this before. "The greater good" was just a twisting of words, something to make evil sound good and noble. The real meaning was simple. Those with power should rule; those with power should force the people to obey. It was the Brotherhood's plan to rule the known lands, not for some greater good as they claimed, but simply for the sake of power.

"Tom, no!" a distant voice called.

Alex's eyes snapped open, and his left hand closed around his staff. His head slowly turned to the left, and he saw Tom trying to use his own magic to free Rallian from the ball of green light that surrounded him. Alex couldn't find the strength to move, and he couldn't look away. The green light shifted like a living thing, pulling back from Tom's magic and then slamming forward into Tom's chest.

"Fool," Magnus said to Tom. "You should not interfere with things that are beyond you."

Alex's right hand curled into a fist. His mind cleared as Magnus's magic slipped away, and then the rage of the dragon filled him. In one quick movement, Alex stood up, his right arm coming up so sharply that his fist slammed into Magnus's chin. The old man stumbled backward a few steps and then fell down hard. Magnus's eyes were glassy, and it looked like he was about to pass out. The stunned look on Magnus's face told Alex that being punched was one thing he had never expected to happen.

Alex turned to his left, looking for Tom. Virgil was there as well, holding Tom up and looking almost as surprised as Magnus did. Colesum was standing just inside the room, his sword in his hand.

"Get Rallian and Tom out of here," Alex ordered. "Get all of the men out of this crypt."

Alex didn't wait to see if Virgil and Colesum obeyed. He turned his full attention to Magnus. The magic he had used to pry into Magnus's thoughts was still there, and now Alex put all of his power into that magic, squeezing Magnus's mind like an orange.

"What was your plan for Rallian?" Alex demanded. "What evil magic were you going to work?"

"We . . . we were going to take his body," Magnus answered with a shudder. "It was a spell of great power, some ancient dark magic I don't understand. It would rip his soul from his body and allow us to replace it with mine. I would become the king of Nezza, and our plans could move forward."

"'We'?" Alex questioned. "Who are you working for?"

"Gaylan was going to assist me," said Magnus. "I don't know the magic, but he does."

"When is Gaylan coming, and how?"

"He should be here now. The portal, I—"

"Portal? What portal?"

Alex's eyes scanned the chamber, but there was no magic to be seen. The dark magic Magnus was talking about would need to be done in a place of death, a cemetery, which explained why Magnus had brought Rallian here.

Magnus shook his head and tried to fight off Alex's magic. He sent a weak lightning bolt toward Alex. Alex deflected it with his staff, but the magic had done its job. Magnus had distracted Alex long enough for the magical portal to start opening.

Alex had never created a magical portal, but he did know something about them. They connected two places together, creating a passageway that could be used to move from one distant place to another. If Gaylan used this portal, then Alex was about to be outnumbered. He couldn't let that happen, not if he wanted to stay alive. Gaylan, Alex was sure, would be a much more dangerous foe than Magnus was.

As the portal opened, Alex sent a wave of dragon fire into it. He hoped the magic would stop Gaylan from entering Nezza, and he also hoped the magic that held the portal open would be weakened by his spell. If he could throw enough power into it, the portal would fall apart and close.

"Yah!" Magnus screamed, charging toward Alex with an ancient spear in his hands.

Alex knocked the spear away with his staff, then sidestepped Magnus. He managed to kick out and trip the old man as he rushed by. Magnus tumbled across the floor, and Alex turned back to the portal to let loose another wave of dragon fire.

This time, the fire stopped at the edge of the portal and then bounced back into the room. Alex managed to turn the flames back toward the portal, blocking this side of the passageway, at least for now.

Hot wax splattered across Alex's hand as something flew past his head. He turned to see Magnus snatching up candles to throw at him. The old man's face was almost purple with rage, and it seemed he'd forgotten how to use his magic.

Alex pushed out his right hand, and his magic sent Magnus crashing into the wall.

He turned back to the portal just as a ball of blue light came flying out of it. The ball hit him squarely in the chest, forcing him to take a few steps back. The true silver chain mail he wore kept magic from doing any real harm to him, but Alex still felt like every hair on his head was standing straight up.

The spell spun around his body for a moment, then bolts of blue lightning suddenly flew off the chain mail in every direction.

Alex dropped to the floor as the lightning struck the walls and ceiling. Deadly bits of shattered stone filled the air and bounced wildly around the room. Alex jumped up and sent a freezing spell into the portal, then a ball of fire, and then a lightning bolt. He sent more power into the dragon fire that still burned in front of the portal. Then he turned to look for Magnus.

The old wizard was not on the floor where Alex thought he would be. Instead Magnus was crouched like a cat close to the flames and the portal. His face was twisted with rage and hate, but his eyes were fixed on the portal. The magic of the portal was falling apart; the opening was starting to close.

"You may have won today, wizard, but I swear that one day I'll have my revenge," Magnus yelled.

Before Alex could stop him, Magnus leaped forward, diving headfirst into the shrinking portal. Unwilling to let Magnus escape, Alex threw his right hand out as if he held a whip. A rope of flame wrapped around Magnus's left leg, stopping him halfway through the portal. Alex pulled on the flaming rope with all his strength, trying to drag Magnus back into Nezza.

Suddenly, a different power took hold of Magnus from the other side of the portal. Alex could feel a power trying to pull the old wizard away. The strange magical tug-of-war lasted for only a few seconds, Magnus's body moving in and out of the portal as each side pulled hard. Then a surge of power pulled Magnus almost all the way through the magic passageway. Alex's rope of flame was snuffed out. A strangely muffled, echoing scream of pain filled the room but stopped as the portal snapped shut.

Alex stared at where the portal had been. There was no trace of magic now, and no way for Alex to know where Magnus had gone. Magnus's lower left leg and foot remained in Nezza, sticking out of the wall at an odd angle. Alex lifted his staff and tapped the boot that had been left behind. The leg and boot turned to dust, crumbling and leaving no trace of the old man they had belonged to.

Dropping to the floor, Alex wiped his face on his sleeve. He was tired and sore, and nothing sounded better than lying down and going to sleep.

What about the others? Alex's O'Gash questioned.

Alex jumped up, his desire to sleep vanishing as his mind filled with new worries. Tom had been hit by Magnus's spell, and Alex had no idea what that spell had done. How had Virgil and Tom found him? Had they fought through all of the black guards in the first chamber? Was Rallian all right? Was Nezza in danger of losing its new king?

Alex started to run, but running wasn't fast enough. He changed midstep into a raven and flew down the passageway that would lead him out of the crypt. The torches still burned to show the way, but now the floor was littered with the bodies of dead men. Most of the dead looked like black guards, but Alex didn't take the time to check. He flew though the tunnels, looking for the living, looking for his friends. He found them just outside the doors to the crypt.

"We have to go back," Rallian said hotly.

"He said to get everyone out," Colesum answered.

"We can't just leave him there alone," said Rallian. "There might still be black guards lurking in the passages. Magnus may have some deadly trap that Alex doesn't know anything about."

"Or Magnus may no longer be in Nezza," said Alex, taking his own shape in front of Rallian.

"Alex!" Rallian shouted in surprise. "Thank goodness, I thought, well, I . . ."

"I'm fine, and Magnus is no longer in this land. You appear to have recovered as well, but where are Virgil and Tom?"

"Here," called Virgil from behind Colesum. "Quickly, Alex. It's Tom—he's . . . I think he's dying."

Alex almost knocked down Colesum in his rush to get to Tom. Virgil was kneeling next to Tom, holding his hand and trying to get him to talk. Tom didn't move, his eyes closed and his face calm. Alex put his hand on Tom's forehead and a groan escaped him. Tom's skin was already growing cold. Alex didn't know how much he could do for his friend.

"The spell seemed only to stun him at first," said Virgil. "He could almost walk, and he could talk, but . . ."

"It's draining his life away," said Alex. "I must go to him."

"Go?" Rallian questioned from behind Alex.

Alex didn't answer. He took Tom's hand in his own, quietly working the magic that would take him to the shadowlands. Almost before he'd finished saying the words, Alex found himself standing on the shaded hill looking down into the land of shadows. Tom was only a few feet away, a confused, lost look on his face.

"Tom," said Alex, moving closer.

"I . . . I don't understand," said Tom.

"What don't you understand?"

"When I was here before, when you brought me here the first time, I saw him," Tom answered. "I'm sorry I lied to you, but he was so close. He was just beyond the wall, waiting for me. Now the land is empty. He isn't there anymore."

"Who isn't there?" Alex asked, knowing already who Tom was looking for.

"Richard," said Tom. "I . . . I thought that . . . I don't know what I thought."

"You thought your time to cross the wall was close and that

your brother would come to lead you into the shadowlands," said Alex.

"Yes."

"Now you feel betrayed, lost, because your brother is not there," Alex went on.

Tears ran down Tom's face, and he had lost the ability to say anything.

"It is not your time, Tom," said Alex. "Come back to the world of light. There are things you still need to learn and work that only you can do."

Tom let Alex turn him around and lead him up the hill toward the light.

After a few minutes, Alex found himself kneeling beside Tom. He could feel the warmth returning to Tom's hand, and he gently laid that hand on Tom's chest.

"Is he gone?" Virgil asked in a troubled voice.

"He is not," said Alex. "He will sleep for now, and he will recover in time."

"Then you have done myself and my company another great service," said Virgil.

"It was not his time," Alex answered as he stood up. "Now, what else remains to be done?"

"Nothing remains to be done," Colesum answered. "We are victorious."

"How did you defeat the black guards?" Alex questioned. For the first time, he looked around to see how many of Colesum's men had survived, and he was surprised to see hundreds of soldiers in the street. "Where did all these men come from?"

"My father," said Colesum. "He understood the trouble we were riding into and was quick to send help."

"And a good thing he did," said Virgil. "When we were divided in the first chamber, things looked bad. The group I was with was pushed back almost to the doors of this building."

"These men are from the armies of the inner kingdoms," said Rallian. "They answered Lord Talbot's call and arrived just in time."

"Very well," said Alex, leaning on his staff. "If we are all safe, and if the city is under the king's control, then there is something I really need to do."

"What is that?" Rallian questioned.

"Rest," Alex answered with a weak smile. "I am tired beyond words."

"If anyone deserves to rest, it is you," said Rallian. "But I have to ask—what happened to Magnus? You said he was no longer in this land, but what did you mean? Have you destroyed him? Did he escape?"

"I was not able to destroy him as I had planned to do— well, not all of him anyway," Alex answered with a slight laugh. His friends looked confused, and it took Alex some time to explain exactly what had happened to Magnus.

"So he is free to return to Nezza if he wishes," said Rallian when Alex had finished.

"I don't believe he will return to this land," said Alex. "In fact, I think he is facing a far harsher punishment than anything I had planned."

"How so?" Colesum questioned.

"He was working with people outside of Nezza," said Alex.

"If I'm right, those people will not be pleased when they learn of Magnus's failure here. I think they will make him suffer a worse fate than simply being destroyed."

"He deserves whatever they do to him," said Rallian.

"Perhaps he does," said Alex. "And now, if there are no other questions that can't wait, I would really like to rest."

CHAPTER TWENTY-FOUR

HOME AGAIN

Alex felt a great deal better when he woke up. He was alone in a tent, and after a bit of painful stretching, he'd managed to pull on his boots. He stepped out of the tent into the morning sunlight and found Talus, the captain of Shelnor's guards, waiting for him.

"My lord, I trust that you are well rested," said Talus, bowing deeply.

"I am," said Alex, returning the bow. "How do things stand in Karmus?"

"Very well, and very busy," said Talus. "The king has been sending messengers in all directions since last night. He has also sent out scouts, hoping to discover where Lazar and the rest of his army have gone."

"The king is wise," said Alex. "Do you think he has time to talk with me?"

"I believe he would make time for you even if the city was burning around him," said Talus with a smile. "In fact, he asked me to see if you were awake and invite you to join him for breakfast."

"Then lead me to the king, most noble Talus, as I am very much awake and also very hungry," said Alex.

Talus laughed and led Alex through the massive camp to Rallian's tent. Alex was happy to find Virgil and most of the lords of Nezza already there, waiting for Rallian to appear. Talus led him to the chair to the left of Rallian's, then bowed and hurried away.

"Alex," Rallian almost shouted as he entered the tent. "I mean, Master Taylor. I wasn't sure you would be up and about so quickly after your battle with Magnus."

"I am rested and restored to full health," said Alex, bowing to the king.

"I know some of what happened in the tombs," said Rallian, taking his seat. "It appears that all of Nezza is deeply in your debt. I know that my own debt to you may never be repaid."

"I am happy to have served," said Alex. "I am also glad I was near in your hour of need."

"My hour of need," Rallian repeated with a laugh. "You make it sound like a story, a great legend of heroes and dark villains fighting to save the world."

"Was it not so?" Alex questioned with a smile. "Did not all the heroes of Nezza, and even some heroes from distant lands, come to the aid of the true king in his time of need?"

"Yes, yes, I suppose they did," said Rallian, his smile fading. "And sadly, many of those heroes fell and are no longer with us."

"Yes, that is so," Alex agreed. "That is the one part of the legends I wish was not true."

"The fallen heroes will be remembered," said Rallian in a serious tone. "But now the living need something to eat."

"Your wisdom is great," said Alex, bowing.

Rallian smiled and clapped his hands. Trays of food were brought into the tent, and without ceremony, they all started to eat. Alex could see that everyone in the tent was happy, but their mood was not overly cheerful. There was still the question of Lazar's army, and it appeared that everyone knew it.

The camp was busy that day. More soldiers were arriving, more scouts were sent out to search for Lazar, and there were many things about the city of Karmus that needed to be discussed. Personally, Alex didn't have much to do, so he spent most of the day with Skeld, Tom, and Virgil.

Skeld was still sore from his wound, and both he and Tom were weak. The two seemed to take turns dozing off while Alex and Virgil talked. Colesum and Hathnor joined them that afternoon, but they said there was no news of Lazar's army and that it would be several weeks before Rallian's messages to distant kingdoms could be answered.

"I think most of the kingdoms will accept Rallian as king," Colesum said in a hopeful tone.

"With all that has happened, I can't see any of them denying his claim as king," said Hathnor.

"Lazar will," said Alex. "He will never surrender to Rallian. I wish we knew where he is and what he is up to."

"Lazar will turn up soon enough," said Colesum. "Our scouts will discover him, and the royal army will deal with him and whatever is left of his army."

"Royal army?" Virgil questioned.

"As all the lords have sworn allegiance to Rallian," said

Hathnor, "all the armies have been combined into one royal army."

"With Rallian as king, the lords have no need to keep private armies," said Colesum. "I thought it would take longer for them to all agree, but King Rallian has convinced them. The lords will have some power to command the men posted in their lands, but only Rallian can command all of the army."

The four of them left Tom and Skeld to rest and made their way back to King Rallian's tent for the evening meal. They had only just sat down when Stonebill flew into the tent, landing on the table in front of Alex.

"I have discovered Lazar's army," Stonebill said. "They are miles away, and unless I am much mistaken, they are in great danger of being destroyed."

"Destroyed?" Alex questioned.

"Lazar has taken his army east to invade the lands of Lord Bray," said Stonebill. "He knows that Bray's army was destroyed in the north, and he thinks to claim Bray's lands while his kingdom is in disarray."

"And?" Alex asked.

"And it appears that the people of Bray's kingdom are not as confused as Lazar might hope," said Stonebill. "They have grown tired of their weak lord and were planning to replace him. He did, after all, do everything Lazar command him to do, and the people are sick of it. They have raised their own army, and their lords are all working together. Lazar is marching into a trap. I don't think he is strong enough to take even the smallest city in what was Bray's kingdom."

"Lord Taylor, what news?" Rallian questioned.

"Good news," said Alex.

Alex relayed what Stonebill had told him, and Rallian was quick to take action. The evening meal was delayed as Rallian arranged for part of his army to travel east. He sent riders with messages to all the lords of Bray's kingdom, and he ordered his own army to try to capture Lazar and his army without battle, if possible.

"We cannot blame the men who follow my uncle," said Rallian. "They have been blinded by his lies and do only what their honor demands of them."

"And your uncle?" Lord Talbot questioned.

"I want him alive," Rallian answered, his tone growing cold. "I want him to answer for all the evil he has done in this land. He will face the king's justice, and he will answer for his crimes."

A great cheer rose in answer to Rallian's statement, and it made Alex happy. Rallian would rule by law, and Alex knew that would make him even more popular with the people of Nezza.

Days went by, and all the news that reached Karmus was good. Lazar's army had turned against him and put him in chains. The same army then surrendered without battle to the royal army, and each man swore his allegiance to King Rallian. The lords and people of Bray's kingdom were also quick to accept Rallian as the king of Nezza.

There was other good news as well.

Messengers started to arrive in Karmus a week after Rallian had taken control of the city. The more distant kingdoms of Nezza had heard rumors of Rallian making his claim on the crown and had decided to accept him as the true king. The messengers had been sent to find Rallian, wherever he was, and let him know that they supported him and were ready to do whatever he commanded. Celebrations were held everywhere, as long-forgotten happiness spread like wildfire across the land of Nezza.

Alex, Virgil, Tom, and Skeld decided to remain in Nezza until Rallian was officially crowned king. The ceremony was only three weeks away, so it didn't seem like a great delay. Besides, Skeld was still healing from his wound, and Tom was still a little weak. Their plans changed, however, when Rallian asked Alex and Virgil to stand up for him at his wedding to Lady Annalynn of Talbas. The wedding was set for two weeks after Rallian was crowned, and Alex and Virgil were happy to accept.

"I would ask Skeld and Tom to stand up for me as well," Rallian told Alex. "But I'm not sure they can stand up long enough for the ceremony to finish."

"I think if you asked them, they would stand up for you no matter how long the ceremony," said Alex.

Alex was sitting in the garden of Rallian's restored palace a few days later. It was still early in the morning, and he was watching some small fish dart around the weeds in a pond. He was relaxed and happy but a little sad as well.

"It seems you have done your work well, wizard," said Annalynn.

Alex looked up and saw Annalynn standing on the opposite side of the pond, watching him. He smiled and bowed to her, remembering the first time they had met. She had arrived the day before, but Alex had not had a chance to talk with her until now.

"I will ask you once again, now that you have found success, what price do you ask for your services?" said Annalynn, moving around the pond.

"What would you offer?" Alex asked in reply.

"Anything and everything for the happiness you have brought me," said Annalynn. "But not just the happiness you have brought me, but also for the peace and happiness you have brought to all of Nezza. Name your price, and I will gladly pay it."

"I will ask for only one thing," said Alex.

"And what is that, master wizard?" Annalynn questioned.

"Your friendship," Alex answered, bowing once more.

"If anyone can claim to be a true friend, it is certainly you," Annalynn answered, returning Alex's bow.

The time came for the wedding of Rallian and Annalynn. Alex, Virgil, Tom, and Skeld all stood as guards of honor for the king on his wedding day, while Colesum and Hathnor stood as the guards of honor for their sister. The wedding was one of the grandest events Alex had ever seen, but the celebrations that followed were almost beyond belief. People sang and danced in the streets, and free food and drinks were handed out to everyone. The celebrations went on for days, and every night the story was told of how Rallian had won his crown and brought peace to the kingdom of Nezza. It was said that parties to celebrate the wedding were held in every city and town of Nezza, and that wherever two or more people met, toasts were made to the new king and queen.

Finally it was time for Alex and his friends to leave, though they were all sad to go. Rallian gave them all titles in his kingdom and rewarded them for their service to him. Alex was reluctant to accept any reward, but he let Rallian have his way and kept his complaints to himself.

"Farewell, my friends," Rallian said as they mounted their horses. "May your paths lead to good fortune, and may you return often to my kingdom."

Alex and company bowed to Rallian, and then the four of them rode out of Karmus with crowds cheering for them all along the way.

Stonebill landed on Alex's shoulder as they passed through the city gates. The raven didn't say anything until they had ridden for a few miles, and Alex didn't ask any questions.

"You'll be off on new adventures, I suppose," Stonebill said, breaking the silence.

"I'm sure I will be," said Alex. "What of you, my friend? What will you do now that our adventure is over?"

"I'm not sure," the raven answered. "I have enjoyed our time together, and I would like to travel with you to new lands, but . . ."

"But?" Alex asked.

"But I miss the red lands of Nezza, and I miss Tempe," Stonebill answered.

"Then I think you should go home, at least for a time," said Alex.

"And I think that you are right," said Stonebill. "I will miss you, dragon lord. I will hope to see you again, someday."

"May your feathers never fall," said Alex, bowing his head

slightly. "I hope we will meet again, my friend, and have another adventure together."

Stonebill took flight, letting out a single loud caw as he caught the breeze and flew into the west.

"I'm going to miss that bird," Skeld said. "I think I was starting to understand what he said."

"Are you sure he didn't get hit in the head when he was wounded?" Alex asked, looking at Virgil.

"I'm afraid he's always been this way," Virgil answered. "A blow to the head might do him some good."

They all laughed and rode on, happy to be together and on their way home.

When they were getting close to the great arch, Alex noticed a change in Virgil. It seemed like some shadow covered him, a great weight that pressed down on him. Alex thought he knew what the problem was, but he didn't say anything until they had made camp for the night.

"You are wondering if you can call this adventure a success," Alex said as they sat beside the campfire.

"Hard to call it a success when so many of our company were lost," said Skeld.

"But we won in the end," said Tom. "Nezza has a king, and there is peace in the land."

"I know we have won a great victory, and we have done more in this land than we set out to do," said Virgil. "So, yes, the adventure is a success. The price for our success, however, has been a high one. Much higher than I ever thought to pay."

"The others knew the risks," said Skeld. "We all knew and accepted the risks when we accepted the adventure."

"Knowing the risks and paying for them are two different things," Virgil answered.

"I understand your feelings," said Alex, his tone thoughtful. "I never met the dwarf Thorson, and I only knew Cam for a few days. Dain, I truly miss. I wish they could all be here with us. Still, I think they would be proud of what has happened and proud to have given their lives to make it so."

"A kind thought, but . . ." Virgil started and stopped.

"There are no buts," said Alex. "I believe that all of them would have still come on this adventure, even if they knew beforehand that they would die. They were true adventurers. They were heroes from distant lands, just as I told Rallian they were. They will always be remembered in Nezza, and their families, wherever they are, will be proud of them for what they have done."

"Alex is right," said Tom.

"Yes, I know," said Virgil. "But that does not make their loss any less painful for those they've left behind."

"Perhaps, but it does give meaning to the loss," said Alex. "It is the meaning, the reason why, and the knowledge of what was gained that will bring comfort to those who are left behind. If there was no reason, if nothing was gained, then I think the loss would be far more painful for us all."

They sat in silence for a long time, looking into the flames of the fire. Alex wasn't sure he had expressed himself as well as he might, but he couldn't think of any other words to say.

They left the land of Nezza late the next day. They had reached the great arch near midday but had stopped to remember and pay tribute to the fallen adventurers before riding on.

The shadow seemed to lift from Virgil, and Alex was glad that it did. They made their camp on the Telous side of the great arch, and Skeld was just starting to cook their dinner when a loud ding interrupted them.

The geeb that appeared had a message for Alex. He retrieved the message and paid the geeb, noticing that the handwriting on the envelope was Whalen's. He sat down on his blankets and tore open the envelope, wondering what his teacher had to say.

> *Dear Alex,*
>
> *I have no idea how far along you are with your current adventure, and I don't want to worry you, but I need your help. I think I have discovered something important in our hunt for the Gezbeth. I don't need you just yet, as there are things I need to check into before I'll be ready to move.*
>
> *Please try to finish your work in Nezza as soon as you can. If your adventure has concluded, start for home at once. I will be arriving at your home in Alusia tonight, and I will leave a message for you there. I would like to talk to you in person, but I cannot wait.*
>
> *Let me know how things stand in Nezza and how soon you think you will be available to assist me.*
>
> *Yours in fellowship,*
> *Whalen*

"I need to go," said Alex as he finished reading the letter. "I'm needed at home."

"Of course," said Virgil. "We understand. Is it something we might help you with?"

"No, I'm afraid not," said Alex, gathering his blankets and putting them back into his magic bag. "I'm not sure what it is, only that I'm needed. I suppose you can all find your way home from here, can't you?"

"I'm sure we can," Virgil answered with a smile.

"Alex," Skeld said as Alex was turning toward the great arch. "I just . . . We are greatly, well . . ."

"I know," said Alex, smiling at his friend. "You don't need to say it."

"I may not need to, but I will," said Skeld. "Thank you. Thank you for everything."

"Yes," Tom and Virgil both added. "Thank you for everything you have done."

"You are very welcome," said Alex, bowing slightly. "Take care of yourselves, my friends, and may we meet again soon."

Alex didn't wait for his friends to answer. He turned to the great arch, worked the magic that would allow him to pass through it and return to Alusia, and was gone.

Alex instantly changed into an eagle and flew away from the great arch. If Whalen needed him to come quickly, that could only mean trouble. Whalen was a great wizard—perhaps the greatest of all the living wizards—so if there was something he couldn't handle by himself . . . well, Alex didn't like to think about what that might mean.

Whalen had mentioned the Gezbeth in his letter, and Alex wondered what his friend could have discovered and how he had discovered it.

The sun was setting in the west as he climbed into the skies of Alusia, only a few hours away from his home and Whalen.

The miles could not pass quickly enough for Alex as his worries continued to grow. There were no answers to be found in the night sky, and Alex feared he would get few answers from Whalen when he found him. He had his own news to share as well, though it wouldn't be much help in their search. Magnus had known only one member of the Brotherhood— Gaylan—but at least Alex now knew what Gaylan looked like.

Dropping slowly out of the night sky, Alex could see Whalen sitting on the porch of his own house. The old wizard was smoking his pipe, deep in thought. For a split second, a wild idea entered Alex's mind. He wanted to fly away, leave Whalen on the porch, and never return. It was a mad idea, and it seemed out of place. Pushing the thought away, he dropped to the ground and changed back to his human form.

Whalen looked up with a half smile on his face, but he did not speak for a moment.

"Did you feel it just now?" Whalen finally asked. "A thought, a wild idea that was not your own, entering your mind?"

"Yes," said Alex, shaken by the question.

"That is one of the reasons I wanted to talk to you, face-to-face. I didn't think I would get the chance to see you so soon, but I'm glad you're here," said Whalen, getting to his feet and moving toward his horse. "I've had many such thoughts in the past weeks, and I am troubled by them."

"Where are the thoughts coming from?" Alex questioned.

"I do not know," answered Whalen. "I thought there was only one place such thoughts could come from, but now . . ."

"What place? What power could possibly put strange thoughts into our minds?" Alex asked.

"To be honest, I originally believed these thoughts were coming from you," said Whalen. "I thought perhaps the part of you that is a dragon was doing this, but now I see that is not the case."

"But how could I put thoughts into your mind?"

"The link between wizards, and especially the link between student and teacher, is a strong one," Whalen explained. "The only explanation I could find was that link. Now that I'm sure it is not you, it can only mean . . ."

"Yes?"

Whalen shook his head. "I won't trouble you with my guesses or suspicions. For now it is enough to know that these thoughts are not coming from you. Now, about the reason I wanted you to come as soon as you could."

"Whatever you need, I am ready," said Alex.

"Yes, I'm sure you are, my friend. And what I need you to do right now is wait."

"Wait? Wait for what?"

"Wait for me to send word or to come for you," said Whalen. "If I send word, be ready to move. I need to find some answers to my questions, but when I am sure, we will need to move quickly."

"Questions about the Brotherhood?" Alex asked.

"Possibly, possibly," Whalen answered.

"How long do you wish me to wait?"

"A month, perhaps less," said Whalen. "Be ready to move and stay alert. If you have more of these strange thoughts, keep track of them when they come. I wish I could say more, but until I find a few things out it is pointless."

"I will wait until you call or until you come," said Alex, bowing. "You are my master, and I will do whatever you ask."

"Ah, of course. You say you are my student and I am your master, yet I have no doubt which of us is the greater wizard," said Whalen, climbing into his saddle.

"Neither do I," said Alex.

"Oh, no doubt?" Whalen questioned.

"You are known as the greatest living wizard. You are both feared and respected in all the known lands. Clearly you are much greater than I am," said Alex confidently.

"So many would say," replied Whalen. "I, however, know that you are greater than I, and in time you will know it as well."

"But, how can I be?"

"In time," said Whalen, turning his horse away. "I will send word when I can. If you haven't heard from me within a month, come and find me."

"As you wish," said Alex.

Whalen galloped away from the house, and Alex was alone.

Whalen hadn't answered any of Alex's questions, and now he had new worries to think about. Alex didn't know what Whalen was trying to find out, but it clearly had something to do with the strange thought that had entered Alex's mind.

Alex stood for several minutes, watching the darkness. Slowly his mind emptied, and then a memory returned to him, and it troubled him more than anything Whalen had left un-said. It was a memory of Whalen talking about how many wiz-ards he had trained. In all the long years, Whalen had only ever asked two people to take a staff, and Alex was one of those two.

Could it be? Was it possible that the thoughts that were coming into Whalen's mind were from the other wizard he had trained? Alex wondered who the other student was and why Whalen had seemed so concerned.

It was pointless to worry, and in the end Alex let his thoughts drift away. Whalen would send word when he was ready, and until then, Alex would have to wait.

DISCUSSION QUESTIONS

1. At the beginning of the story, Skeld sends Alex a letter asking for help. Alex immediately starts on a quest to help his friend. Why do you think Alex does this? What would you do if one of your friends needed your help?

2. When Alex is fighting the water stoic, he tries to use the power of the dragon, but it isn't there when he needs it. Later his O'Gash tells him that it's because he hadn't practiced using it. Do you have talents that you don't practice using? What happens when you don't use your talents for a long time?

3. While making his escape from the dungeons of Karmus, Alex is overcome by fear. Have you ever been afraid of something? How can you overcome your fear?

4. When Alex talks to Rallian about visiting Tempe, he says that it would be good to know what the possibilities are. Would it be helpful to you to know what the possibilities of the future are? Are there ways to find out the possibilities without talking to an oracle?

5. Alex agrees to teach Thomas about healing, and they have a ceremony that links their honors together. What do you think it means to have their honors linked? Have you ever

had your honor linked to someone else's? Have you ever been judged based on the actions of your friends?

6. Salinor tells Alex that even with all his magic and his dragon form, he can't force the people of Nezza to make peace. Have you ever been forced to do something by someone else? How did that make you feel? Do you think forcing people to make peace really works?

7. After Rallian makes his claim as king, Alex tells him to give all the other kingdoms a chance to join him without fighting. Why do you think Alex tells him to do that?

8. Whalen Vankin once told Alex that a wizard should do his work and then be gone. What do you think Whalen meant by that? Why is it not a good idea for wizards to hang around after their work is done?

Take the Adventure
with You on Audio

978-1-60641-059-2
$39.95

978-1-60641-255-8
$39.99

978-1-60908-918-4
$39.99

978-1-60907-696-2
$39.99

Available at bookstores nationwide
and online at Audible.com

Visit AdventurersWanted.com

SHADOW
MOUNTAIN

ABOUT THE AUTHOR

M. L. Forman was born and raised in Utah and now resides in the foothills of the western Rockies. He tries to write as much as possible while still attending to his many other hobbies, such as fishing, camping, hiking, and almost anything that will allow him to enjoy the magic of nature. He is also the author of *Slathbog's Gold, The Horn of Moran,* and *Albrek's Tomb,* the first three books in the Adventurers Wanted series.